Your Mouth Is Lovely

YOUR
MOUTH
IS
LOVELY

YOUR MOUTH IS LOVELY

NANCY RICHLER

HARPER
PERENNIAL

Published by Harper Perennial, an imprint of HarperCollins Publishers Ltd

Originally published in Canada in a hardcover edition
by HarperCollins Publishers Ltd: 2002
First trade paperback edition published by Harper Perennial Canada: 2003
This Harper Perennial trade paperback edition: 2013

"City of Slaughter" by Hayyim Nahman Bialik, translated by A. M. Klein. Reprinted by
permission of University of Toronto Press. "The Angel's Punishment" from *Jewish
Folktales* by Pinhas Sadeh. Reprinted by permission of Doubleday, a division of Random
House, Inc. *The Road to Bloody Sunday* by Walter Sablinsky. Copyright © 1976 by
Princeton University Press. Reprinted by permission of Princeton University Press.

HarperCollins books may be purchased for educational, business, or sales promotional
use through our Special Markets Department.

HarperCollins Publishers Ltd.
2 Bloor Street East, 20th Floor
Toronto, Ontario, Canada
M4W 1A8

www.harpercollins.ca

Library and Archives Canada Cataloguing in Publication
information is available upon request

ISBN 978-1-44342-387-8

Printed and bound in the United States
RRD 9 8 7 6 5 4 3 2 1

For my parents, Dianne and Myer Richler,

and for Jason Richler, in memory

This book takes place between the years 1887 and 1912. At that time Belarus and Ukraine were part of the Russian Empire. The official language was Russian, and for that reason I have used Russian rather than Belorussian or Ukrainian for place-names: Gomel instead of Homel, for example.

The narrator of this book would have been speaking Yiddish, the language used by most of Russia's Jews at that time. Hebrew, the language of the Torah, is the language of most Jewish liturgy and ritual. Pronunciation of Hebrew would have been Ashkenazic: bayis instead of bayit.

The YIVO Institute has established a standard transliteration from Yiddish to English. I have chosen instead to spell the words as they most often appear in nonscholarly contexts: heder instead of kheder, to give one example.

— NANCY RICHLER

Most devious is the heart;

It is perverse—who can fathom it?

JEREMIAH 17:9

Siberia, April 1911

Spring has come, even here. We smell it first in the mold that spreads along the floor, hear it in the slow dripping away of the ice that has coated our walls all winter. Soon will come the rush of water down the mountains that surround us, the drifts of smoke as peasants from distant villages burn off last summer's grass, then the fragrant grass itself, sweetness and life wafting through the bars of our open windows. For now, though, we content ourselves with the slow softening of the ice cave we've inhabited since autumn, the smells of mold and decay released at last from the grip of winter, our plans for our tiny garden in the courtyard. Maria turns the compost, encouraging the rot that will nourish our vegetables and flowers. "Surrender yourself," she whispers in all earnestness to her pile of stinking parings. I glance up but she is intent on her task.

Surrender yourself, we began to hear in those years leading up to the failed revolution. From the intellectuals like Maria who roamed the countryside alight with their vision of a new future, from our own lips as their fever spread, from the natural world around us where a single drop of rain suddenly became significant for its willingness to subsume its own form in the gathering torrent of a river in flood. *Surrender yourself,* your father once implored me. Destruction births creation.

IT'S MY FIFTH SPRING AT MALTZEV PRISON. EACH WINTER I'm sure will be my last. *Dust to dust,* I find myself saying as my frozen fingers struggle to hold the pen with which I write these words to you. *Ashes to ashes,* I mutter, and nothing but suffering and joy in between. I've had my share. Hot and sharp—I taste it still in the blood that fills my mouth when I cough.

They've put me with the politicals. A mistake. My act was criminal—this I know—but well-dressed in beautiful words: the higher good, the loosening of humanity's shackles. So instead of languishing in the filth and squalor of the criminals' section, I am here among the exalted, the political prisoners of Maltzev.

"Your mother was a heroine," you'll be told. "She sacrificed her own life for the betterment of others." It's a lie, but not entirely. No person can be so neatly understood. Hence these words I write to you, my meager offering, my attempt to clear a path to your own beginning.

WE ARE STRICT WITH OURSELVES. ALWAYS, BUT PARTIC-ularly in winter, when the frosty silence threatens to obliterate us as thoroughly as it has the world outside our four walls. In the mornings we study. Anatomy, antiquity, mathematics, philosophy. Any book that isn't forbidden is devoured and regurgitated, its contents shared and discussed. "The socialization of intellectual property." This is what my comrades call this most ordinary of human endeavors, this discussion and sharing of ideas. They're a high-thinking bunch. They don't simply discuss ideas as humans have done since receiving the gift of speech. They "make common property of the learning that, in freedom, was unequally divided."

Lunch is quick—it affords us no pleasure. A slice of black bread, a bowl of thin soup, then a return to our studies. We heat ourselves with tea—our stove is inadequate—then run around the courtyard swinging our arms and clapping our hands. Supper is quick too—buckwheat turned blue from the iron of our frying pan. In the long evenings we huddle together, sharing a candle, a blanket, the heat of our bodies. My coughing never stops.

We try, but by late winter our resolve wavers. We're beyond tired, beyond cold. The blood that fills my mouth is sticky, souring even as I still draw breath. Job floats unbidden into mind. *Naked came I into the world and naked will I leave it thither.* The cold drags on even as the light returns. I write to you, but my hand falters. *To everything its season,* and mine was this: twenty-three years in the bowels of the turning century. I feel my end coming. *The Lord giveth and He taketh away.* Then I cough again and it's the taste of my own blood that spurs me on. Is it not still thick and pungent and rich as the heart that pumps it? I pick up the pen once again and move it across the page.

And then one morning I awaken to the drip of water and inhale the stirrings of early spring.

IT'S BEEN ALMOST SIX YEARS SINCE YOU WERE BORN, six years less a day since you were taken from me. Taken from me, do you understand? I would never have let you go. I was still in Kiev, awaiting execution. I would hang as soon as you were born; that was my sentence: death, postponed until your birth. I sent a note out to Bayla, begging her forgiveness for what I was about to ask of her, begging her to find you, to save you from death. Then I waited to hang. A week I waited, two weeks. In the third week after your birth my sentence was commuted to "life." Mercy, they called it. I had no illusions about what lay ahead. But still, I was happy. That was one of the happiest days of my life. That was the day Bayla's note reached me.

"She's beautiful," Bayla wrote to me. You, she meant. She had claimed you from the foundling home where they had taken you. "Beautiful, but skinny like her mother."

Skinny like your mother, but hardy like me too. This I knew from your first moments of life. I felt your mouth on my breast before they took you from me. I felt the power of your hunger, the beauty of it. Hayya, I named you. For Life.

"I've booked passage to Montreal on the third of next month," Bayla wrote. "Shendel has kindly offered me a bed under her roof. Generous as always—I expect I'll be her maid. But it's a start, isn't it? Just when I thought it was the end of days, the end of my days, anyway, it turns out you're still alive, your daughter is safe, and I'm booked to begin my life again."

As for forgiveness, Bayla said, if there was any to be begged, it was she who had to beg it of me. She would spend her life atoning for what she had taken from me.

"Your daughter is safe," Bayla reassured me again. "Whatever else you must contend with, rest at least with the knowledge that your daughter is safe and well loved. I'll raise her as I would my own until you come to claim her from me. And you will come to claim her, Miriam. This I believe."

CHAPTER ONE

M I N S K   G U B E R N I A ,   1 8 8 7

IN THE SEVENTH MONTH OF HER PREGNANCY HENYE
dreamed of thirst. It was the month of Tammuz, but not like Tammuz.
Nowhere was the high blue sky of previous summers, the afternoon
breeze sweet with blossoming rye. The air was so thick with heat that
the wheat in the field bent under the weight of it, and the sky hung yellow and low over the town, portending nothing good. Night after night,
Henye lay on her bed dreaming of thirst. Such thirst as she had never
experienced in her waking life. Unslakable thirst. Unearthly.

The pregnancy was her second. The first had ended in shocking
misfortune. Shocking, because the signs—until the birth itself—had all
seemed so favorable. Seven months into that pregnancy the kicking inside her had been so vigorous that she could place a crust of bread on
her swollen belly just to have the pleasure of watching it fly across the
room. It was a boy, she knew, and one endowed with such power and
obvious strength of purpose that surely he could only be destined for
greatness.

Her first mistake: second-guessing Divine intention.

Compounded by a second: she told the other women in the town.
That was reckless. Foolhardy. The evil eye couldn't help but be
tempted. Not to mention Lilith, who delighted in nothing so much as
stealing other women's babies.

Still, the kicking persisted. And on the new moon of the month of Av, the first pangs of labor began. The midwife was called; pangs turned to pain. All seemed as it should: the crown appearing soon enough, followed by the torso, long and perfect, and finally the legs, kicking in movements by now so familiar to the mother.

"A boy," the midwife pronounced, but when he opened his mouth to howl, he couldn't take a breath.

He tried again. And again. Mouth open like a fish, he gulped and gasped, but to no avail. Used to the rarefied air of the other world, he found ours too thick. Too cluttered, maybe, with mortal desires and disappointments. It collected like mud in his lungs. He began to strain and thrash, his small back arching, his skin turning blue. His legs still moved, but in more of a twitch than a kick, like the dance of a chicken whose head is already rolling in the dirt. The midwife slapped him, shook him, breathed whatever she could spare of her own breath into his gasping mouth, but his lungs weren't like ours. More like wings than lungs, they flapped inside his chest, transporting him back to the world in which he belonged.

They named him just before he died. A final attempt, perhaps, to ensnare his fleeing soul. Yaakov, they named him, for his grandfather who had loved life.

The third mistake. They should have named him Yaakov Simcha. That was our grandfather's full name. Yaakov, who fought with the angel, and Simcha, who is joyful. A balanced name, full of luck—that's what should have been my brother's. Instead, they returned him to the earth eternally fighting with his angel.

And fight he did. From the moment he crossed back into the other world his strength returned, but it was coupled now with a cruelty he hadn't exhibited before. His kicking resumed. Timid at first, daring only to interrupt her dreams. Then bolder, brasher, it began distracting her at all times of the day and the night. Those same kicks that had so delighted her once with their promise became taunts now, torments, a rain of blows and mockery under which she soon began to falter.

She conceived again quickly enough—she was young and healthy in body—but her spirit was changed. She could barely eat, would no longer meet anyone's eye, and as her pregnancy progressed she took on stranger and ever more disturbing behavior. She could be in the middle of a task, a conversation—it didn't matter what—when all of a sudden she would stop still, face frozen, as if listening to something far away. The daily tasks that root us to this world became odious to her. The elements left to women's care—water and fire—she neglected. Her stove remained unlit, her cisterns collected dust. The call from the other world was relentless.

All through those months of pregnancy with me, she drifted further and further from this life—and me, all the while, trying to draw my nourishment from her.

Nights were the worst. The thirst. Tormented by it in her dreams, Henye tossed and cried out in her sleep. Night after night she cried—rasping cries, half-strangled gasps. My father, Aaron Lev, upon hearing such sounds, feared for her life, for her soul, for the soul of the unborn child—*my* soul. But no sooner than he had decided to consult the rabbi, relief came. Relief in the form of a stranger, a boy carrying a jug of water. The boy poured some water into his hand, water so cool and refreshing that as Henye drank from his cupped hand, she moaned in pleasure. My father, hearing such a moan, mistook it for another kind of pleasure and woke her immediately. He was a pious man, you understand. He woke her so that she wouldn't have to carry the burden of sin along with the weight of the child growing inside of her.

But was Henye grateful toward her husband for saving her from sin? How could she be? Her thirst had reduced her to a single longing, a perfect arch that strained toward its one point of desire. She was angry to have come so close only to be snatched away, enraged to be pulled back from the union she had been about to enter.

The boy returned. His jug of water now empty, he took her by the hand and led her to the source: a pool smooth as glass and deep with water so pure and clear that she could see the speckled stones that formed its floor twenty feet below its surface. She had just lain across the sun-warmed slate that bordered the pool, her lips touching the cool surface, when her husband's shaking pulled her back once again. Back to the airless heat of her home, the prickliness of her straw bed, the heavy burden of the new life growing inside her.

The meaning of the dream was immediately obvious to my father, to the other women of the town, to anyone who heard it. The boy was none other than Yaakov come to take his mother back. Had Aaron Lev not awakened her when he had, had her lips actually dipped below the surface of that pool, that deceptive, seductive pool . . .

The next evening, only seven months into her pregnancy, Henye went into labor. A bad beginning, I won't deny it, but what choice did I have? Does a child choose such an entrance if she's thriving in the paradise of her mother's womb? I was starving in there, parched, already exhausted. I made my escape and was delivered alive and named, at first, Nechama. For Comfort.

Some comfort.

Born just eleven months after the loss of her firstborn, some women might have considered their new baby a miracle, a gift, a second chance, at the very least. But not my mother. Not Henye. Named for Hannah, a woman so sorrowed by her own barrenness that the fervor of her prayers for a child became the model of piety toward which we all strive, this Henye wouldn't even look at her own child. Not that I was much to look at—no bigger than a rat, and black-and-blue from all his kicking—but still her own, no?

The midwife placed me on my mother's breast, but she was dry as stone. This was no surprise. Not at that point. Milk from her I didn't expect, but a look? One look?

I was dispatched to a wet nurse, and the following day, without so much as a glance at the new life she'd brought forth, Henye walked into the river and slaked her unearthly thirst.

I SHOULDN'T HAVE LIVED, OF COURSE. A MORE RE-spectful child would have died. Or at least kept quiet, in deference to the grief that surrounded her birth. But I've never known respect of that sort and would not still be here if I had. My mouth was as wide and grasping as my poor brother's had been, except that the air of this world was sweet to me. Nourishing, after the deprivations I had suffered in the womb. I filled my lungs over and over, my mouth never closing, waiting for life to fly into it.

No one expected me to live—a child born under such circumstances, untouched by a mother's hand or eye. I was ugly, bad luck, more like a crow than a child, with cries like caws and a dark down that covered my body. They handed me over to my wet nurse with every expectation that I would be returned to the earth before the next moon. But my wet nurse took pity on me. She looked me in the face. No human had looked me in the face until then. No human eyes had met mine. How could I know what I was? Lipsa looked me in the face, and only then did she put me on her breast.

Too late, perhaps. Note my beaked nose, my sharp eyes, my spare, bony body built more for flight than for land. Even the way I occupy this chair—don't occupy it, actually; I occupy nothing—perched on its edge as if its wood frame is the low-hanging branch of a tree I've been missing all of my life. Imagine the moment of my birth: the wooden hut baking in the summer heat, the moaning woman on the bed by the window, open to catch whatever hint of wind is passing through. And just outside that open window, the lone crow perched on her low-hanging branch, looking in. Longing.

Still, Lipsa tried. She sang to me, sweet, human songs. Night after night she sang, and when I had survived the first month of my life, she tied me to a tree and laid a picnic beside me. Under the yellow sky of that summer, she tied me to a tree while a few feet away she laid a feast of honey, dates, and small cakes she had baked. To tempt my luck, you understand. To induce it to leave me. As if luck as rotten and clever as mine could be fooled by such a pathetic scheme. As if the delicacies Lipsa scrounged up were sweeter than the soul of a baby girl. But Lipsa was hopeful. She had tricked luck before, and sometimes with happy results. Honey, dates, and small cakes she offered up in my stead, then she retreated behind a tree to watch what would happen.

I whimpered at first, then howled, while just a few feet away the honey glowed and the dates released their fragrant scents. The air was humid, alive with insects; I wiggled like a grub against the tree. But Lipsa waited. Ants began to gather at the picnic, a few bees, some wasps. Crows, of course. The air thickened in the afternoon heat, shimmering as the unseen made their passages through it. And still, Lipsa waited. In due time—I don't know how long—my wiggling lessened, my cries turned to hiccups, and finally, at the very moment that my eyes shut and I dropped into sleep, Lipsa untied me and stole me away.

She renamed me that evening. Miriam. Just to be on the safe side. So that if my luck, tired of sweets, should come back, looking for Nechama, it would find only Miriam. Bitter Sea. A better name for me anyway.

CHAPTER TWO

1894

SIX YEARS I STAYED WITH LIPSA AND SIX YEARS I FOR-
got I wasn't hers. I don't blame Lipsa. She was a busy woman. There
were seven children in her house—six of her own and me. Her husband
was a peddler and was gone for days, sometimes weeks at a time. Lipsa
plucked chickens, sold eggs, took in other women's babies and washing. One winter she packed matches for the factory in Mozyr. Another
she made pickles to sell in the market. She had no time to remind me of
my misfortune.

We worked, all of us, packing matches, pushing carts of laundry to
and from the river, but we had our pleasures too. I took mine from the
eggs I cleaned for market. Delicate and fragile, each one was heavy with
the secret of life. I removed dirt and feathers with three-year-old fingers
without ever breaking a shell.

In my seventh year, my father remarried. It was unusual for a widower to have waited so long, unusual for a man to have lived alone for
so many years—a young man, at that. There had been talk, of course.
None of it good. My mother was thought to be behind his unnatural
behavior. Her body had never been recovered, after all, had never
been properly laid to rest. There was no saying where her restless spirit
hovered.

A woman in my father's position would have been forbidden to marry. *Agunah,* we would have called her, an abandoned wife. Our town had two. Sima, whose husband was surely dead—his blood-spattered coat had been found in the forest shortly after his disappearance—and Fruma, whose husband had left for America ten years earlier and forgotten to send for her. Those women were unfortunates. They remained bound to an absence for the rest of their lives. Abandoned men, however, could more easily obtain dispensation from their marriages. And in the seventh year of my life, my father obtained his.

Tsila was the name of his bride. Avram the Hero's eldest daughter. He was called the Hero because ten years earlier when his house had caught fire in the middle of the night, he had run outside alone and sat on the snow, head in his hands, rocking and weeping, while his wife ushered their five children to safety.

Tsila was twenty when my father married her. A tall girl, she was slender as a reed and had long, velvet hair the color of honey. Hardworking and practical, with clever hands and a strong back, all things being equal, she could have married much younger and found a far better match than a shoemaker whose first wife's spirit had never been properly put to rest. But all things are never equal: Tsila's face was marked by Divine anger. Across her left cheek and extending down to her chin was the unmistakable red handprint of the angel that had slapped her before birth.

In a sweet-natured girl, such a birthmark might have been talked away as a mistake, a momentary lapse in Divine judgment. "Look at her hair," a clever matchmaker might have pointed out. "Her eyes like emeralds. Her voice like a flute. And her disposition . . ." But Tsila wasn't sweet. Sour as spoiled milk, there were those who said that when the angel marked her face, he also placed a slice of lemon under her tongue, prohibiting her from sampling any of the more pleasant seasonings life might offer.

Their wedding took place two days after Purim, and he sent for me soon after. Spring was early that year; the roads were rivers of mud. Lipsa walked with me along the planks of wood that had been lain across the mud to prevent us from drowning in it. "You'll be a good girl," Lipsa said as we walked. I stared at the dark sludge that oozed through the spaces between the planks. "You'll be helpful and you'll do as she says."

The day was mild, the air thick with the smells it had held frozen all winter. "She's your mother now," Lipsa said. I inhaled unfurling greens, thawing excrement, softening earth. "You had no mother, but now you do."

Past the butcher's we walked, the smells of fresh blood, chicken's feet. Past Reizel's stand of rotting fruit. It was Thursday. Lipsa's husband would be home tomorrow. Sometimes, if he'd been away a long time, he brought us small gifts. Once he had brought us candies. Hard yellow balls so sour, they raised sweat from my forehead. "I was never your mother," Lipsa said.

We turned down the narrow passage where Malka the Apostate had lived. I wasn't usually allowed in that passage. Malka's mother had long since died of shame, but her wails could still be heard on certain nights of the year. A fat drop of water fell on my face. I looked up at Lipsa. Her eyes were black stones. More drops fell. Lipsa clutched my hand tighter and hurried us along. We were close to the outskirts of town now—the planks of wood didn't extend this far. With each step we sank ankle-deep into mud. A lark sang but I couldn't see it. The mud was alive, sucking hungrily at our feet.

I hadn't been to my father's house since my birth, hadn't seen him except in passing, had never heard his voice. We started up the hill. I knew that when we reached the top we would be there. The rain was falling more steadily now. Lipsa adjusted her kerchief, gave her chin a quick pat. She had a tuft of coarse black hair that grew out of her chin like the beard of a goat. Saturday evenings, when the men were at *shul* and we waited at home for the three stars that would end Shabbes and start the week, she would take me onto her lap. The hair on her chin tickled my cheek when she laughed.

We reached the top of the hill and stopped in front of a one-story house. It looked like any other house. The walls were logs, the roof steep, the windows on either side of the door were squares of yellow light in the darkening afternoon. Chickens scratched in the mud of the yard. Smoke piled straight up out of the chimney as if it weren't sure where to blow. Lipsa released my hand and thrust a small cloth bundle in my arms. "You're a lucky girl," she said. "I couldn't have kept you forever."

Tsila was tending her stove when I pushed open the door. Down on her knees, her back turned to me. Her hair, which had once draped her back like a thick, golden curtain, was gone. In its place, a matron's wig perched on her head, its color indeterminate in the late afternoon light. *Pretension,* I had heard women say. *Immodesty.* Since when did an artisan's wife wear a matron's wig? Who was she, a sour lemon of a thing, that a plain kerchief—silk on Shabbes—wasn't good enough? I stood in her doorway, waiting. I knew enough not to approach a creature that wasn't prepared to face me, not to enter a new life that greeted me with its back.

"Don't just stand there dripping rain," she said without turning around.

I had known she wouldn't want me. Lipsa's oldest had warned me. "Why would she want you?" Rohel had asked. "A new bride like her just starting out and you, a misfortune from her husband's first marriage?"

"In or out," Tsila said. "Don't you know it's bad luck to tarry on a threshold?"

Against my own judgment, I entered.

"Do you know how to tend a fire?" she asked, still bent over her stove.

I determined it was better to hold my tongue.

"Are you mute?" she asked, and turned half around.

The side of her face that she presented to me was unmarked, and although I had not seen beauty in my life until then, I recognized it immediately in the profile I beheld.

"Well, sit down, then," she said, and gestured vaguely toward the window.

I followed her gesture and saw a small table beside the sewing machine by the window. Alongside the table were two chairs. I stood between them, uncertain which to choose.

"Sit," Tsila said, pointing to the one closer to the stove and settling herself on the other. "Here," she said, and pushed a plate of cookies my way.

It was Thursday and the cookies looked fresh. Who had fresh cookies at the end of a week unless there was a special occasion, a special guest, something to celebrate? I reached over and took one. They were almond bars, dipped in sugar, then baked until they formed a sweet crust. Holiday cookies. At Lipsa's we would have dipped them in tea.

Tsila watched me eat, then took one for herself. "I suppose your father will have to make another chair now," she allowed.

AT LIPSA'S THERE HAD NEVER BEEN A MOMENT IN THE day or the night when the sounds of human life unfolding could not be heard. Her home was one of several grouped around a small courtyard, each one filled to bursting with its noisy generations. Reb Sender's nightly tantrums, his mother's snores, the whooping laughter of the Halpern old maid, the low moans of the fishmonger's wife—all that and more had filled the two rooms of Lipsa's house and passed freely through the walls that barely separated us from our neighbors. "There's time enough for quiet in the world to come," Lipsa said once to a neighbor who complained. "We don't have to invite it before its time."

But in the house where Lipsa had just left me, the house where I had had the misfortune to be born, quiet had already descended. I strained my ears, but nowhere was the hum of human conversation, the shrieks of children playing, voices raised in anger or lowered in fear or in love. Even Tsila's intake and output of breath was unaccompanied by sigh or cough. I knew I had not yet crossed into the world to come, but I couldn't feel certain. I listened for human sound, but all I could hear was my own blood racing through my head.

We sat for a long while, Tsila mending, me clutching my bundle of belongings in case Lipsa should come back to return me to the noisy world of the living. I was still wearing my coat and was both too hot and shivering at the same time.

"It's good you don't look like her," Tsila finally uttered. It was late in the afternoon by then and already dark. I started at the sound of her voice but felt a relief so great that I immediately began to weep. "Don't be silly," she said harshly. A harshness sweet and reassuring in its earthly tones. I wept harder. She looked at me without expression, then laid her cool hand on mine. "Don't be silly," she said again. "A man doesn't like to be reminded of past misfortune every time he looks at his daughter's face."

She didn't speak again. She continued her mending, I clutched my bundle of belongings, the rain fell on the roof and windows. I cleared my throat once to check if my voice had taken flight. For some time I had felt it flutter in my throat as if it longed to break free, return to Lipsa, and abandon me to the silence, but it had not, as yet. Tsila looked at me. *Eyes of a cat,* one of Lipsa's daughters had said about her. "What are you staring at?" she asked, then turned back to her mending.

I risked a look at what she was working on. She was a gifted seamstress, renowned not just in neighboring villages but in towns as large as Mozyr and David Gorodok. And not merely for the lines of her creations—though they were elegant and flattering—but for the way she drew color and light out of the fabrics and threads available to her. Other seamstresses made do with the reds, browns, and blues that came to them out of the textile factories, but not Tsila. No, Tsila made her own dyes, searching forests and marshes for the roots, flowers, and barks that would yield the exact color she was seeking. She could catch the ruby flash of a hummingbird and stitch it into a sleeve, October forests flamed at her necklines, and the silver of birch trees glimmered in the satin ribbons of her blouses.

Such colors lured women, of course. Like the scarlet flicker of a blackbird, Tsila's colors drew females from miles around. Rich and poor, Jew and gentile, women came to her with kopecks and rubles in their hands. Kopecks and rubles that some said would be better spent on less frivolous purchases.

"Beauty is not frivolous," Tsila was heard to respond, which, of course, immediately raised more than eyebrows.

"An attitude such as hers . . . ," voices whispered. "To what could it possibly lead?"

To frippery, some said, even as they squirreled away their kopecks for a sample.

"To a proper living," Lipsa responded. No small thing in those times, and certainly a feat my father, a shoemaker, could never have hoped to accomplish. "A living for an entire Jewish family, may they prosper and be healthy," Lipsa pronounced, attempting to put the matter to rest.

But the matter didn't rest. Questions persisted, as they do wherever the unusual dares to show itself. Where did she get the inclination to create such finery, women asked one another. Did her creations not lead to immodesty and the flaunting of the female form? Was it not possible that the Evil One was her guide?

I peeked at Tsila's lap where her hands were working, but a simple rust skirt was all that she held. We sat in silence as she finished her mending, then silence again as she took up a white slip.

Eventually I heard footsteps approaching. My father, I knew, though I had never heard his footfall before. I looked up as the door opened and met his eyes for the first time. *A man of the earth,* people said about him, and I recognized immediately the clay of the riverbank in the hues of his face and beard. His eyes were the color of mud.

He looked away and began to shake the rain off his clothes. He stamped his feet a few times, took off his cap to shake it, then shook his clothes yet again.

"*Nu?*" Tsila said after a while. "Are you going to stand there all night shaking like a dog?"

My father took off his coat and hung it on the peg by the door.

"Maybe you can take your daughter's coat too . . . unless she prefers to sit wrapped up like an old woman as if I'm denying her heat."

I stood up, walked over to my father, and handed him my coat. His hands were large, his nails darkly stained from the blacking of the threads he used for his work. I didn't dare raise my eyes to his face.

"A glass of tea?" Tsila offered, getting up from her chair as I returned to mine.

My father said "please"--I had never heard a man say please to a woman before—and sat down in the chair Tsila had just vacated. I jumped up and joined Tsila at the stove.

"Sit," she said to me. Then, to my father, "She hops around like a wounded bird, but she doesn't talk too much."

My father nodded again and risked a look at my face.

MY FATHER, AARON LEV, WAS STILL A YOUNG MAN AT that time—no more than twenty-six or twenty-seven—but already he had the bearing of one well advanced in years. His life had long become a wound from which he knew he would never recover, and he bore it uneasily, in the stoop of his back—a slight hunch that swelled between the blades of his shoulders and pushed him inexorably downward.

He was a strong man but not well built. Out of balance, as if the Creator had assembled him hastily at the end of too long a day, throwing in handfuls of this quality or that without considering necessary counters and complements. Intelligence he had been given, but not the tongue to express it; a large appetite, but the stomach of an invalid. His heart was too delicate for a man of his circumstances, his feet too small for a man of his size. Walking up the hill to his home, his large hulk stooped over his tiny feet, he gave the appearance, more obviously than most, of one perpetually teetering on the edge of his own destiny.

The Stutterer, he was called in our village, though he had long learned to hold his tongue. He had been born at the start of the typhus and was just learning to speak as the worst of the fever swept the village. Was it grief that strangled his tongue? Perhaps, though Henye had also lost her parents to the fever and her tongue—by all accounts—was smooth and unfettered.

He was raised by his mother's cousin, a kind enough man but one prone to bouts of melancholia so severe that only ceaseless recitation of the Psalms enabled him to endure each new day that rose up against him. The cousin's wife was more able—she supported the family by selling the bread she baked—but her meager stores of kindness had long been expended on her own children. Hungry but not starving, literate but not educated, Aaron Lev was apprenticed at nine and betrothed at seventeen to Henye, also seventeen—her dowry provided by the Society for Widows and Orphans.

The wedding took place a year later, as planned, but it was well known that between betrothal and marriage canopy, Henye had requested a release. Her stated reasons were vague: premonitions, it seemed, cold feet—nothing to justify her reluctance, which was peculiar, because an orphan like her, with no other prospects or family, should have felt only relief that a bridegroom had been found and a dowry provided.

Aaron Lev hadn't wanted to force her, so a meeting had been arranged. Then another. And another. He didn't try to persuade—his tongue seemed to twist even more than usual in her presence—but to show her by his patience that he wasn't a bad man and that he meant her no harm. And she did, at last, acquiesce, so by eighteen, Aaron Lev was a bridegroom, and by twenty, a widower and a father. A widower whose wife's body was never found and a father whose child brought him no joy.

MY FATHER DRANK HIS TEA IN SMALL, EVEN GULPS. THE tea was hot—I could see steam rise off it—but he didn't pour it into his saucer or slurp it up with cooling sucks of air. He drank precisely, quietly, as if heat didn't burn his mouth.

Tsila placed a plate of potatoes and onions on the table and a pitcher of sour milk between us. I waited for my father to recite the blessing for fruits that have been pulled from the earth, but he thanked Tsila first. Before God. "Thank you, Tsila," he said, and I looked up in confusion.

I remembered the disquiet of the women by the river when the news of his match reached their ears. It was early winter then, the week before Chanukah. Snow had not yet fallen, but the first skin of ice had formed upon the river. The air was clear and cold—free of snow, moisture, and other obstructions.

"Aaron Lev and Tsila?" the women muttered among themselves. They were unsettled, disturbed. They had great sympathy for my father, a quiet man with sad eyes, and only suspicion for Tsila, who was too arrogant and too sharp. The match offended any proper sense of balance.

"Impossible," one of the women, Freyde, said. Freyde the Sinus. Her voice was so nasal that words seemed to bypass her throat altogether and flow directly through her nostrils. "After what he went through with the other . . ." She glanced quickly my way. "What would he want with a pickle like Tsila? What would any man want with such a pickle? It must be Bayla he's marrying."

Bayla was the second of the Hero's daughters. A pretty girl but very pale.

"Aaron Lev and Bayla," Freyde repeated, beginning to tap at the ice with her long pole to break an opening in its surface.

"Aaron Lev and Bayla," the other women agreed, their murmurs already more peaceful as they drew together in one breath the names of those two gentle souls.

"And why not?" Freyde asked. "Bayla's a pleasant girl, kind . . ."

"Very kind," all the women agreed. So kind, Rivka reminded them, that for a while there had been talk she might be simple. "Better simple than sour," Freyde pronounced.

"Maybe so," Rivka conceded. "But it's sour he's marrying. I have it from the mother of the bride herself. Aaron Lev and Tsila. The *chupah* will be right after Purim."

Freyde shrugged but didn't argue further. The other women were silent as they considered the news.

"Maybe the parents didn't want to marry off the second before the eldest," Lipsa ventured.

"Maybe," the others agreed, unconvinced.

"Maybe it was *parnassah*," another suggested. A few heads nodded. Tsila's value as an earner couldn't be discounted.

"Or maybe Tsila bewitched him," Freyde droned.

WAS MY FATHER BEWITCHED? I WONDERED AS I WATCHED his eyes meet Tsila's. What passed between them was strange, certainly. There was a look on my father's face—a softness—that could have been part of a spell. But there was boldness as well, a boldness that didn't speak of bewitching. And wasn't it Tsila who looked away first? *Her* cheeks that filled with blood? I watched them look at each other and understood that the dangers in that household were many.

I tried to eat the meal she had laid before me, but her potatoes and onions seared the inside of my mouth. I took a sip of cooling milk, then turned the whole mess back onto my plate.

"My food's not good enough for your daughter," she said.

I pushed my plate to the edge of the table. I didn't know why. My father watched me push my plate. Tsila watched me too. I pushed it over the edge and heard it land with a dull thud. Potatoes and onions splattered the floor and I waited for the blow to the back of my head that might have exploded what was building within me.

"No one's taught her anything," Tsila said, her voice dull with resentment. "She's been living like an animal, and now I'm to raise her."

I opened my mouth to protest, but no words came and I couldn't fill my lungs. My father averted his eyes as if I were obscene.

"Well, come on, then," Tsila said to me. "Clean up your mess."

My father pushed away his plate of half-eaten food and closed his eyes to recite the grace after meals. He took a long time, although only the short grace was required, and when he finished, he remained with his eyes closed, his head nodding, as if reluctant to break off his communication with God and return to the scene before him.

There were those who said it was my mother herself who inhabited the air of that house. *He'd do well to find new quarters before bringing home a new bride,* they whispered, and maybe they were right. Was it my mother I was feeling tightening my chest, smothering conversation and laughter?

My father pushed himself back from the table. I heard his chair scrape against the boards of the floor, then felt him standing over me.

He was a giant of a man, very close now. I smelled the leather of his workday, saw the patterns of dried mud splattered up the legs of his pants. His hands hung at his sides. One hand—it was open and very large—began to swing toward me. A careful swing, deliberate and slow, a swing that might have turned into a slap or a caress. It stopped an inch from the skin of my cheek—I felt the heat of him, my own burning skin radiating out to meet his—then it swung back to hang again, clumsy and useless as an oversized paw. His step was heavy as he retreated to the door.

"Will you be late?" Tsila asked him.

The wind was up and from the north. I heard it against the rear wall of the house.

"Don't wait up," my father said.

I stared at them, uncomprehending. The wind was high—surely they must hear it—and coming from the swamps.

"The wind," I said, but Tsila was already on her feet, approaching my father in the doorway. She stood close to him, her face turned up toward his. Something glinted in the mud of his eyes. He stroked her cheek once, easily, then stepped out into the night.

OUR VILLAGE SAT IN THE MIDST OF THE POLYSEH SWAMP. To our south were pine forests where the air was sweet and trees grew straight and thick, but to our north stretched an endless tract of roadless swamp. The Pripet River meandered through the Polyseh, flooding freely over most of its flat course and turning here and there to avoid any obstacle that might disturb its lazy flow. Our town occupied one such obstacle—a slight rise in the land that the river curved around rather than cutting a path through. We sat in the crook of the river's curve—a few streets, a crowd of wooden houses, some cultivated fields that flooded every spring, a market, two synagogues, and two churches, Orthodox and Catholic, that served the Russian officials, the local gentry, and the peasants from neighboring villages.

Why our town existed, no one knew; how it had started, no one remembered. The train station was in Kalinkovich, the match factory in Mozyr. All we had were trees. In the local forests were thick pines that men could cut and float down the river, in the swamp a profusion of aspens, easily transported to the match factory in Mozyr. From such endeavors others grew—so that by the time of my birth in 1887, we had our own mill and more than a hundred Jewish families eking out their lives in that rise on the edge of the swamp.

The swamp was an unhealthy place—a wilderness where snakes lurked in black waters, vapors and mists befouled the air, and the earth opened itself like water to swallow the foot that dared to walk upon it. There were lights in its vapors, lights anyone could see. They moved about in strange, weaving patterns and sometimes they moaned. Those lights were the souls that had departed our world but not yet entered the next, souls without peace that were detained between worlds for reasons only He could know. Lonely and comfortless, they waited for north winds so they could ride into town and look for solace among the living. It was on such a wind that my brother, Yaakov, for example, had drifted in to lay his claim on our mother. Rohel had told me. And on such a wind that my mother would come for me. You could smell them coming, damp and musty as they wafted in from the swamp. We closed our windows against them.

"The wind," I said to Tsila when she shut the door behind my father. I had never known anyone to venture out when the wind from the north was blowing so strong, but Tsila seemed unconcerned. She looked at me for a long time, impatience growing all the while.

"Your head is filled with *bubbe meises*," she said. "What *wind*? The wind is wind. That's all it is."

I didn't answer, but her impatience grew. "I'm not interested in the foolishness Lipsa taught you."

It wasn't just Lipsa, and Tsila knew that. The streets of our town were all but deserted on nights such as this, for who could say with perfect confidence that the souls of their loved ones had found their final place of rest? But Tsila, born and raised in our town, wasn't really of it.

"Do you think your mother is waiting to snatch your father? Is that what you think? That she'll rush in to snatch him now when she never wanted him in life? Idiocy," she said, but she did rub her fingers on the amulet she wore around her neck, whether from habit or to ward off the evil her scornful words might have invited, I couldn't know for certain. "Your mother wasn't one to tarry," she said.

She led me then to a corner of the room—behind the stove, against the back wall of the house. There was a wooden bench there, small and narrow as I was, and upon it a straw mattress, a quilt, and a pillow. The quilt was the color of young leaves and stitched with blue. The pillow was white and unstained. I had not seen such brightness in the objects of Lipsa's home.

"You'll sleep here," Tsila said, and I closed my eyes. "Now what?" she asked, but how could I explain?

Until then I had slept in the middle furrow of a tamped-down mattress, wedged between Lipsa's two middle girls. Our blanket was rough but warm, leached of all color and ripe with the smells of our accumulated nights. There I had drifted easily into sleep, the warmth of living flesh keeping me from drifting too far, the breath of other lungs leading my own breath into morning. What Tsila led me to was my bed, I knew, but how could it offer me rest when I was expected to enter it alone?

Tsila watched me undress, then ran her hand across my naked back, my neck, and through my loosened hair. Her touch, unburdened by affection, was lighter than Lipsa's. She probed at my temples and between the partings of my hair but found neither louse nor flea.

"I'll bathe you tomorrow," she said.

I turned away from her to recite my *Shema,* the same prayer that I had recited every night from the first moment my lips could form the words. "Sleep is a perilous journey," Lipsa had instructed. If death should overtake us before morning, we should enter its embrace with praise of His Name on our lips.

"Are you finished?" Tsila asked. I hadn't even shut my eyes yet, had not begun to summon the necessary concentration. Out the corner of my eye I saw the brightness of the bed. I shut my eyes to clear my mind of distractions that were leading me away from Him.

"Nu?" Tsila said.

"Hear O Israel," I began, but as I did my mind exploded with colors. The pale green of the quilt, the blue of its stitching, the honey of her hair, the crimson of her birthmark—new life, eternity, sweetness, anger—each color had a meaning, and more beyond. I fell silent before it.

"Even this she didn't teach you?"

"She taught me," I said.

"Hear O Israel," Tsila prodded.

"The Lord is our God," I continued, then stopped. White now, as brilliant as the new pillow on which I was to rest my head, refracting to the emerald of her eyes, the unyielded copper that had glinted in his. Longing—but for what?—swept through me like wind. Then fear—of what, I didn't know.

I felt Tsila's hands on my shoulders. She turned me—a half turn—to face her. My eyes were still closed, but upon them I soon felt a presence, a pressure, cool and calming. Tsila's hand. My eyelids fluttered against it, the colors exploding beneath.

"Hear O Israel," she began, and I listened, word by word, my mind ablaze. "Blessed is the Holy Name," she continued, praise of His Name calming the colors, each in its turn until they rested, still vivid but quiet beneath her hand.

She removed her hand and met my eyes with her own. She shook her head slightly as if dismayed by what stood before her. "We'll begin tomorrow," she said, and extinguished the lamp by my bed.

BUT WHEN I AWOKE THE NEXT MORNING HARM HAD COME to me. The storm had passed with the night, and sunlight flooded the room. My skin felt hot, as if the air of the room had scorched it, but my core had grown cold in the night and I shivered underneath the bright quilt. I felt a pain in my throat but did not yet understand its meaning. Tsila was tending the oven. Her hair, unbound, fell golden across her back.

"*Nu?*" she said when she saw my opened eyes.

I pushed back the quilt and swung my legs over the side of the bed.

The floor was smooth and solid on the soles of my feet, but the room spun around me.

"*Modeh Ani,*" Tsila prodded. The prayer upon waking. This too Lipsa had taught me, but when I attempted to utter the words, I could not. The prayer was there, lodged in my heart, but the instrument for its delivery had been taken from me.

"I stand before Thee," I rasped. The theft had been incomplete. A ragged shard of my voice still remained, but it hurt to use it, so raw and sore was the place from which the rest had been torn.

I waited in terror. Afraid of Tsila's anger, yes, but more of the damage that had been done to me.

"King of the Universe," Tsila went on, "who has mercifully returned my soul to me . . ."

"My mother," I whispered to Tsila without thinking, understanding at once who had swept through me the night before.

Tsila looked up from her oven. I saw her as from a great distance away. She was kneeling as she had knelt the day before, but her face was turned to me now. She put down the poker she had been using, arose, and walked over to me. Her hand was rough on my forehead.

"You have a fever," she said. "Get back into bed."

I obeyed her, as Lipsa had told me I must, drinking the tea that she gave me and allowing her to wrap a warm towel around my neck, but she was misguided to think that tea and a towel might bring back what had been taken.

"Sleep now," she told me, and I did. Through that day, and the following.

I awoke at one point to the sound of whispers. It was night then, the lamps extinguished and darkness pressing against the windows. I lay in the darkness confused, a stream of whispers drifting toward me from the alcove where my father and Tsila lay.

At Lipsa's no one had whispered except in prayer. What needed to be said among people was to be spoken aloud, Lipsa had taught us, claimed by clear, unashamed voices, or not to be spoken at all. But now as I lay in my bed in the place that Lipsa had brought me to, I was engulfed by the forbidden: a stream of unclaimed words, a flood of the unutterable, interrupted only by Tsila's light laugh.

I began to shake and pulled my quilt closer around me. The same quilt that had dazzled me—when? Was it the night before, the week before? Simple cotton under my fingertips, that's all that quilt was. Simple cotton and useless against the chill that now gripped me.

Tsila's laughter rose from the whispers and I heard his laughter too now, a low rumble. And yet more whispers. My body shook under the quilt, but my cheeks burned. Shame, perhaps, in the presence of the unutterable.

I curled myself into a ball—only my hot forehead exposed. I lay like that, burning and shivering all at once until I felt a breath on my skin. That breath was balm, soothing as a cool hand, and though I had not felt her touch until then, I knew at once whose it was.

I must have called out—but how? and with what?—because when I opened my eyes both Tsila and my father stood by my bed, Tsila's hand on my brow now.

"My mother," I whispered. Come for me, at last.

"It's the fever," Tsila said.

"Should we not call Lipsa?" I heard my father suggest as I fell back into sleep.

LIPSA'S LIPS WERE PINCHED TIGHT, HER EYES UNNATUrally bright—two dark stars glittering out of a milky face.

"How long has this been?" she asked, then without awaiting an answer told Tsila to boil water with the lemons and honey she had brought.

"My mother," I whispered to her, but she placed her finger on my lips to silence me.

"*My mother, my mother,*" Tsila mimicked. She was suddenly by my bed, waving her wooden spoon around. "What kind of curse have you brought into my house?"

Lipsa rested her hand on Tsila's waving arm. "Go stir the lemon. It shouldn't boil too hard." She removed her hand from Tsila and lay her fingers on the point of violation. My throat fluttered beneath her touch. I waited for her to appeal to my mother. I had heard her make such appeals before. Just the week before my father's wedding I had accompanied her to the cemetery, where she had begged Hanna-Gitl to loosen her hold on her daughter's heart. Two years after Hanna-Gitl's death, the daughter was still so stricken with grief that she was barren and unfit as a wife. *Have mercy on your poor daughter,* Lipsa cried out to Hanna-Gitl. *Release her from her mourning. Free her for the life that is still hers to bring forth.* I closed my eyes now and waited for a similar appeal to my mother.

"Your mother wouldn't do this," Lipsa said quietly. She removed her fingers from my throat and I felt a damp warmth. A towel. She was laying a towel at my throat, no different from the towels Tsila had been laying throughout the week. "Your mother doesn't need your voice," Lipsa said to me. "What would she need with your voice?" But Lipsa's own voice trembled and there was fear in her face. "It's your father who needs to hear your sweet voice."

"What, sweet?" Tsila muttered. "She has the voice of a crow."

"And Tsila, Tsila needs it too," Lipsa said.

"What do I need with her voice?" Tsila asked. "She wants to be mute all her life? Excellent." She handed the concoction she had boiled to Lipsa. "Let her be mute. Deaf too if she wants."

In Tsila's voice too, though, there was the tremble of fear, and it was from her that I understood just how close the Angel of Death hovered. *Leave her be now,* Tsila was imploring. *She is ugly, unloved, not worth your trouble. Go and find yourself a sweeter child.*

Lipsa brought a spoonful of syrup to my lips and I swallowed it. Hot, sour, and sweet, it stung my throat as it passed through.

"Your father and Tsila need to hear your voice," Lipsa said as she continued spooning syrup down my throat. "What's a household without the voices of children?"

She pushed a lock of damp hair off my forehead.

"The next time I see Tsila, I want to hear you've been singing for her. Do you understand me?" I nodded miserably, hot tears sliding down my cheeks. "Tsila's your mother now," Lipsa said.

MUD FILLED MY THROAT, A THICK AND STICKY LAYER OF it. It gurgled and thickened with each breath I tried to take. I strained for breath, gulping air in huge and useless swallows, but the mucus only spread across my throat, blocking the passage to my lungs.

Tsila forced steam through my nose and mouth with towels so hot that they burned the skin of my face. But though the steam filled my nostrils and mouth, it couldn't penetrate the mud. I strained harder, clawing at the air, then at my throat, which wouldn't admit it. With each failed breath my legs kicked up from the bed, then fell back. Tsila gripped my head against her lap, pressing harder with her hot, rough towels.

I heard Lipsa's voice again, then felt her hands upon my head, and though her touch was gentle, the very hairs on my head ached beneath her fingers.

"Master of the universe," I heard her say.

"Save this child . . ." The prayer continued, but in Tsila's voice now.

I opened my eyes. It was daytime and nighttime at once. Candles burned in the room, yet light poured through the window. Moonlight or sunlight, I didn't know, but in that one beam of light I saw the suspended dust of the room begin to dance in a slow and swirling pattern. It circled my ankles once, twice, then again and again, gently tugging and lifting my now weightless legs from the bed. And though I did not see my mother among the particles of dust, I knew she was there, lifting and pulling me toward her. In the shadow behind me, though, Tsila clutched me against her hard and bony lap, holding me to the roughness of life.

Around the edges of my eyes a darkness began to gather. The dust still swirled, but it moved within a shrinking circle of light. Faster and wilder as the darkness pressed in around it—I watched, entranced, until the cool smoothness of Tsila's hand shut my burning eyelids. "Lord of my fathers, I beseech you," I heard from the shadow behind me. "Guide my hand in the act I am about to perform." My head was pulled back, my throat bared like that of a calf prepared for slaughter. "Hear O Israel . . . ," Tsila whispered in my ear, preparing me to die. My mind followed the path of her words.

In peace will I both lay me down and sleep. For thou, Lord, makest me dwell alone in safety.

My father sat by my bed when he thought me asleep, softly reciting the Psalms. Time had passed. I didn't know how long. A cold wind still blew through the chinking of the walls, but Tsila had begun her Pesach cleaning.

The fever had left me, and with it my strength. I awoke each morning and placed my feet on the floor, and each morning the air of that place pushed me backward into my bed. The wound in my throat where Tsila had cut through the mud still hurt me, but air moved freely through my throat to my lungs. Every few hours Tsila boiled a new towel in water and laid it upon the wound.

The Lord is nigh unto them that are of a broken heart . . . None of them that take refuge in him shall be desolate.

My father recited in darkness. His workdays were long—except on the Sabbath he was never in the house in daylight. I would hear him early in the morning, before the sun rose, and at night again, after the first calling of the nightingale: *I am come into deep waters and the flood overwhelms me. I am weary with crying; my throat has dried.*

I had not spoken since my illness. It was not from stubbornness, though Tsila accused me of that. Where my voice had once been, there was now only pain. I showed Tsila without words the ache that I felt there.

"Pain is no excuse for your stubbornness," she scolded me, as she brought me cup after cup of honeyed tea. Her face was pale and strained, her eyes rimmed with red as vivid as her birthmark. "Life is painful, but you don't see people lying down dead in the streets because of it."

"Should we not call Lipsa?" my father suggested.

"Has that woman not caused enough damage already?" Tsila asked.

My father's eyebrows arched with surprise, but he didn't answer right away. He took a swallow of tea, then another as he considered the question put before him. "What damage?" he asked finally.

"What damage?" Tsila's eyes, flat with exhaustion all the weeks of my illness and convalescence, lit now with anger. "What would you call cutting us off from a living? Doing us a good turn, perhaps?"

All the weeks of my illness no one had come to our house to be fitted for a dress or to pick up an order. No one had crossed our threshold at all, except Lipsa. My father still left for work before dawn each morning, but Tsila sat idle save for keeping house and nursing me.

"People were afraid, Tsila," my father said.

"Afraid of what? And by whose tale bearing?"

My father closed his eyes, as he often did when faced with an argument with Tsila. He pinched the bridge of his nose between his thumb and forefinger, as if that might somehow give him the strength for the harsh words that loomed.

"It was safe for Lipsa to cross our threshold all those weeks but not my customers? What, Lipsa can't infect other children, but my customers can?"

"Lipsa is a healer. She can't heal the sick without going to them."

"It wasn't Lipsa who healed your daughter, Aaron Lev. And I didn't see her fear mongering when Freyde's Itche burned with fever last summer."

"Itche didn't have diphtheria."

"*Diphtheria.*" Tsila spat the word. "Don't give me diphtheria. She thinks I've stolen the child from her, so now she tries to starve us."

"Tsila, Tsila," my father chided. "She's not trying to starve us. Why would Lipsa try to starve us? She's a good woman, and besides, she knows the child is ours."

"Yours. She has always known the child is yours, but when six years passed and still you didn't call for her . . ."

"I always meant to."

"Still, you didn't until you married me."

"I don't think—"

"You never think," Tsila spat back. "Just what business do you think Lipsa still has here? In my home?"

My father didn't answer.

"You don't answer because you don't know anything. I am the one who knows. I am the one who watches her scuttling up the hill, hunched and oily as a cockroach rushing to do her evil sorceries. I am the one who knows what she wants. She wants the child back in her clutches, Aaron Lev—on my own good health I swear this to you . . ."

"Don't," my father said.

"Her potions are nothing. Do you understand me, Aaron Lev? You think she has a potion that will return your daughter's voice, but I am the one who can return your daughter's voice. I am the one who saved your daughter from death."

"Only the Eternal One—"

"You know nothing," Tsila snapped and my father fell silent.

"The child will speak again. Trust me, Arele. Have I not loosened your own tongue and freed it from its fetters?"

My father did not answer.

"Your daughter will speak, Aaron Lev. I will lead her to words."

"WATER," I CALLED OUT THAT NIGHT IN MY SLEEP. THE first word I had uttered since falling ill. When I opened my eyes, Tsila was standing by my bed. "Water," I said again, and she handed me a glass of the cool water I had called for. I drank it empty and handed it back to her.

"What do you say?" she whispered.

"Thank you," I said.

"Again?"

"Thank you," I repeated, and she dropped to her knees beside my bed.

"Your mouth is lovely," she whispered to me, the same words I had heard Lipsa say to her two youngest boys when they uttered their first words.

Help us guard his little mouth from obscenities, Lipsa had said. *May he never curse or lie, but speak only words of Torah and wisdom, pleasing to God and men. Amen.*

Tsila said none of that. She stayed half kneeling, half leaning against my bed, her face close to mine, her long, soft hair falling around my head. "Your lips are a crimson thread," she whispered, softly tracing the outline of my mouth with her finger.

WE STARTED THEN, THE VERY NEXT DAY, WITH BES, THE second letter of the alphabet.

"*Aleph* was chosen to be first, it's true, but what came of it?" Tsila asked.

She looked at me, awaiting my response, but I had no response. I didn't know about the letters.

"*Bes* came second. A disadvantage, no?" I nodded and that seemed to satisfy her.

"But look," she said, pulling an egg from the basket beside her.

"*Baytzah,*" she pronounced, teaching me the Hebrew word as well as the letter. She placed the egg in my hand. It was warm and heavy with promise, but as my fingers closed around the perfect curve of its shell, pleasure and sadness filled me in equal measure. The promise that swelled against my palm was not to be fulfilled. Its fate had guided Tsila's fingers to pluck it from the dirt of the yard so that it could be poured out of its shell and scrambled with potatoes and onion for our supper. "*Baytzah,*" I said as I handed it back to her.

"*Bayis,*" Tsila said next, using Hebrew again instead of Yiddish and sweeping her hand to indicate the house that encased us. Like the shell of an egg were the walls of our house, protecting the life within.

"*Bimah,*" Tsila said. "Are you listening?"

"*Bimah,*" I repeated. The podium at the front of a *shul*. But now

Tsila wasn't satisfied. "We've hardly even started and already you're daydreaming."

"I'm not daydreaming," I protested.

"You can't afford to daydream," she said. "Other girls, yes, they can daydream all they want, but you—you cannot afford to daydream when I am trying to teach you the *aleph-bes*. Do you understand me?"

I did not understand her but nodded my head anyway.

"Do you want to end up like Simple Sorel?"

It was said that something had scared Sorel in her infancy and that was why she walked around with her hands covering her ears and eyes, humming lullabies to herself all day.

"I'm not like Sorel," I said.

"Sorel wasn't like Sorel either until she started daydreaming and scaring herself half to death. Now you pay attention."

"I am paying attention."

"So then what else starts with the letter *bes*?"

I thought about it, making the sound *B* over and over again. Tsila tapped her long fingers on the table.

"Bayla," I said finally. Tsila's younger sister whom my father should have married.

"Bayla," Tsila repeated. "And what else?"

"*Bagel*," I said. "*Bracha, Binyamin, bubbie . . .*"

"Good," she said, with obvious surprise. "*Bagel, bracha, Binyamin, bubbie*—a lot of words, no?"

I nodded, but she wasn't looking at me.

"But most of all," she said, "most important of all the words *bes* leads into the world . . . Can you think what it is?" She looked at me with hope. I wanted to satisfy her, but couldn't. She opened the *Humash* on the table before us, opened it to the first page of the first book. Genesis. The beginning.

"*Breshis*," I said before she could.

She looked at me. Her eyes were flashing emerald light. Her color was high, obscuring the mark of anger in her cheek. "*Breshis*," she repeated. "The beginning. Do you see?" she asked, excitement swelling her voice. "Second in line after the letter *aleph,* yes, but chosen by God to begin the Torah, to begin all creation. Do you understand?"

I was only a child, and an ignorant one at that, but I sensed a blasphemy in the charged atmosphere of our lesson.

"And where's the *aleph*?" she asked. "The great first letter?" Her eyes were lit as if by fever.

"*Nu?*" she prodded.

"I don't know," I said.

"Exactly." She took my finger, the second finger of my right hand, and pointed to the third letter in the word *breshis.*

"*Aleph,*" she said. "First in line, but silent now after *bes.*"

She sat back in satisfaction and I waited for her to bring out the sweets she would now lay before me, the drop of honey she would now place on my tongue. Lipsa's boys had been carried to *heder* their first day; Lipsa herself had baked the sweets and provided the honey. A light golden honey she had chosen. "Knowledge is sweetness," she whispered to her boys, as the letters of the *aleph-bes* paraded before them for the first time.

"I'm not your mother," Tsila said, her face still flushed, her eyes flashing sparks of light. "I mean no cruelty, but I am not your mother. You and I have an understanding on that, no?"

I nodded my head, though uncertain as to the nature of the understanding I was entering.

"I will raise you and teach you to be a human being among human beings." She paused as if to digest the significance of such a promise. "But as for your mother . . . this is your mother now." She indicated the letters before us, a long line of unnamed letters, their mysteries still unrevealed.

"Your first mother was unfaithful to you."

I wouldn't nod my head to that. I knew the commandments even if I could not read them.

"But you mustn't blame her," Tsila went on. "All mothers are unfaithful to their daughters."

Another blasphemy. I felt it in the knotting of my stomach and the flutter in my throat.

Tsila looked at my face and laughed. "You mustn't close your ears when I tell you the truth." Her laugh was light, almost kind. "I'm going to tell you many truths. And what I'm going to give you will be faithful. Far more faithful than your mother could be."

Knowledge, she meant—I understood that. But mine would not be sweet. I had expected honey, but my mouth tasted of bile. Fear and dread, but also excitement mingled on my tongue.

"Knowledge will be your mother," she said. She took my finger then and pointed to the third letter of the alphabet. *"Gimel,"* she named it. "For *gevurah.*" Strength.

CHAPTER THREE

1897

"I CAN'T POSSIBLY MAKE YOUR HAVA A DRESS FROM this material," I heard Tsila tell the mother of a bride who was to be married on Lag b'Omer, the thirty-third day after Pesach.

Three years had passed, and in that time Tsila hadn't failed to take time out of her busy days to teach me as she'd promised she would. "Your daughter has a clever head," Tsila often told my father, pride, if not love, evident in her voice. "But as for her fingers . . ."

My fingers were clumsy, there was no denying it, and it was hard to know who suffered more during the hours I spent, needle in hand, trying to improve my impossibly sloppy sewing. Tsila, I suspect, for on most days she cut my sewing sessions short, grabbing the fabric from me as if trying to save something precious from butchery and sending me out, in the warmer months, to tend our kitchen garden.

"This material is already spoken for," Tsila said to Hava's mother. "And besides, this shade of rose . . . with Hava's coloring . . ." Tsila hesitated, but just barely. "She'll look like a turnip."

An unnecessary cruelty. Hava Leibowitz already looked like a turnip—bulbous and yellow, with rings of purple around her eyes. No color she wore, rose or otherwise, could ever affect that.

"What about this?" Tsila offered, unrolling a length of cobalt brocade.

"She's not a sofa," Hava's mother responded. "For whom, may I ask, are you saving the rose?" Her hand, bent with arthritis, reached out to stroke the blushing fabric.

"It doesn't matter," Tsila said.

"For Shendel," Hava's mother guessed, the other Lag b'Omer bride. Shendel's match wasn't as well-off as Hava's, but neither was he as old. And no one could deny Shendel's loveliness.

"Hush," Tsila said. "The rose is too flimsy for the wife of an established businessman." Hava was marrying a merchant from Pinsk. It was said he smelled strongly of fish.

"So she has to swelter in brocade?" the mother asked.

"A married woman has to get used to discomfort. But look . . ." Tsila stroked the fabric she was offering. It was a deep blue, dark but luminescent, like a dark sky rent by lightning.

Hava's mother touched the fabric. "I wonder," she said. "I suppose, in the company she'll be keeping in Pinsk . . ."

"Flimsy won't do in such company. This is much better," Tsila assured her.

"And you'll have enough for a little hat as well?"

"What, little? In Pinsk she can even get away with a feather or two."

Tea was poured, a glance cast my way. "How's the child?" Hava's mother asked.

Tsila shrugged. She was not a superstitious woman. In fact, she made no secret of her disdain for the backward notions other women subscribed to. Still, it would have been imprudent to invite the evil eye by saying anything positive about me.

"You're not sending her to Hodel's with the other girls?" Mrs. Leibowitz prodded.

Hodel Gittleman was a young widow whose husband had been caught on the wrong side of a falling pine in a woodcutting operation, leaving her with four children to raise. In desperation she had started a *heder* for girls—a first in our town—where she taught the *aleph-bes* as well as the prayers and blessings and *mitzvahs* that were incumbent upon women to perform. Girls of all ages attended.

"It might do her some good to get out among the other girls," Hava's mother persisted.

"Miriam is sickly," Tsila said. "She caught enough colds this past winter without sending her to town for more."

"Still, it might do her good. Nobody sees her anymore, living up here as she does. Weeks go by, a few months—people start to wonder: is there something to hide?"

"I'm not hiding her, as you can plainly see."

"Still, people love to talk. I don't have to tell you that. It doesn't take much."

"Their talk doesn't interest me."

"I've heard questions about just what it is you're teaching the child."

"And I've heard talk that your daughter threatened to kill herself if you forced this match on her."

They drank their tea in silence. Tsila didn't offer fruit or sweets. Hava's mother drained her cup but another wasn't offered.

"Have Hava come for her fitting," Tsila said, rising to show Mrs. Leibowitz the door. "The dress can be ready in two weeks."

Mrs. Leibowitz rose to leave. Another glance was cast my way. I averted my eyes but felt her gaze like a stain upon me. "Her mother was such a beauty," she sighed. "But so long as she's healthy . . ." She turned her eyes away. "Maybe it's better this way," she intoned in parting. "A beautiful woman is a double curse."

"That woman gives me a headache," Tsila said as soon as she shut the door. "*A double curse*," she said angrily. She put away the brocade and took up preparations for our supper.

"Was my mother beautiful?" I asked.

Tsila thought for a while before answering.

"Your mother was an illiterate orphan with no dowry of her own," she said at length. "That was her curse. Not her beauty."

"So she *was* beautiful?" I persisted.

"Her face was lovely enough," Tsila allowed. "*A double curse*," she muttered again under her breath. "That woman should only wish her own daughter could be so cursed."

"Will Hava be happy in her new dress?" I asked.

"Don't bother me with nonsense."

"But will she?" I persisted.

Tsila handed me a head of cabbage and a knife. "It is not everyone's fate to be happy," she said.

A FEW WEEKS LATER—IT WAS THE NEW MOON AFTER Pesach—early in the morning, when we were still cleaning up from breakfast, there was a knock on the door. This was not unusual—women came at all hours of the day to place their orders or pick up their dresses and blouses. On this particular morning the door opened before Tsila called "come in," and Tsila's sister Bayla slipped into the room like a ghost. Her face was pale as always, though the tip of her nose and the rims of her eyes were pink. Everywhere about her face were wisps of red, wavy hair that had escaped the long braid hanging down her back.

Bayla was nineteen then, an age when most girls were getting married, becoming mothers, or working at their trades. Bayla was doing none of this. Her father, Avram, a cabinetmaker, was one of the rare artisans in town whose skill and artistry—like his daughter Tsila's—assured him of a proper living, so Bayla didn't have to go out to work yet, and her nature didn't incline her toward any particular trade or study.

She was the sort of girl who should have married young and well—kindness and compassion were her salient qualities and there was a prettiness to her despite her pallor—but the matches that had been proposed to her parents had not yet led to a betrothal. Although nineteen was by no means considered old, she was already developing an air of languor, as if she sensed that a state of suspension was to be her fate, that she was doomed to perpetually wait for her life to ignite even as she went about the daily business of living out her time.

"*Nu?*" Tsila greeted her as she slid into the empty chair at the table.

Just the night before, the latest proposition had made the long trip from Minsk to meet Bayla.

Bayla didn't answer her sister's query right away. She toyed with a spoon left on the table from breakfast. Her hands looked like Tsila's—long-fingered and well shaped—but they possessed none of the skill and knowledge of her sister's.

"There was nothing really *wrong* with him, I guess," Bayla said at last. "And Taube certainly liked him." Taube was the third of the Hero's daughters. A robust seventeen-year-old, she was already bothering her parents for a match. "She was falling all over herself offering him more tea and pushing cakes at him. Not that he needed more cakes. His vest was already so tight over his paunch that he could hardly breathe."

A slight smile played at Tsila's thin lips. "He's fat, then?"

Bayla smiled too. "Full."

"Too much grain, most likely," Tsila said. The proposed groom was a grain dealer in Minsk. A very prosperous grain dealer, which was why Chippa, their mother's cousin in Minsk, had been so confident about proposing him. "No wonder Taube liked him," Tsila added. Taube dreamed of being a society wife in a city. Odessa was her first choice, but any city away from the Pripet swamp would do.

"And breathing seemed to present a challenge for him," Bayla continued, her eyes starting to come to life now. "When he had to draw a breath, he puffed a few times and turned pink."

"The tight vest," Tsila said. "There's probably no woman around to take proper care of his clothes. Didn't Chippa say his mother was ill?" The mother, a widow with whom he still lived, was said to be close to death—not a terrible quality in a mother-in-law, Chippa was quick to point out. "Still, you'd think he could afford a decent tailor," Tsila said. "I hope he's not stingy. Did he have any hair?"

The last match Chippa had proposed had been bald, which would have made no difference at all, Bayla insisted, had it not been discovered that he had a deserted wife and three children in a village near Karlin.

"Oh, yes," Bayla said. "No shortage of hair. Or sweat either."

"He was sweating?"

"Just little beads at first, and only along his nose and brow . . ."

Tsila brought both hands to her face and shook her head. "There was nothing really *wrong* with him," Bayla started to say again, but her sister waved her quiet.

"Did Mamma bring out her lace tablecloth again?" Tsila wanted to know.

"And Bubbie's bone china."

Rosa, their mother, was the youngest daughter of a once well-off family from Minsk whose fortune had already begun to reverse by the time she was born. She retained none of the glory of her background beyond the tablecloth, the china, a slightly haughty bearing, and some attitudes that she and her daughters considered enlightened but that others in the town thought impious.

"He's supposed to be a kind man," Bayla said.

"Kindness flees an unhappy marriage," Tsila pointed out.

"I suppose," Bayla conceded, then she sat up straight, suddenly reminded of another, livelier topic of conversation. "Have you heard about Hava?" she asked.

"More than I can stand," Tsila said. "Her mother doesn't leave me alone. You'd think I'd never dressed a bride before. Now she wants lilac organdy for the wedding dress."

"She's disappeared," Bayla announced.

This, Tsila had not heard. "Hava?" she asked. She sucked in her breath sharply and said nothing. Then a strange smile curved her lips. "Alone?"

"Of course alone. What kind of question . . . ?"

Tsila picked up her mending and asked me to get Bayla some tea.

"Just last night, apparently. Her mother is wailing like I've never heard her," Bayla said. "I'm surprised you can't hear her from here." I handed her a glass of tea and she rewarded me with a smile as if she had just noticed me for the first time that morning. "Every time I see you you've grown sweeter looking," she said to me. It was a lie, but from her mouth I almost believed it.

Tsila measured out her length of thread and bit it cleanly with her teeth. "I knew I should have taken a down payment for that dress. And now I've already gone and cut the material for it."

"They're searching for her now. I saw a group heading down to the swamp just as I was coming over here."

"Hava Leibowitz," Tsila said, shaking her head in amazement.

"She could well still come back, mind you," Bayla said.

"True enough," Tsila agreed. "She never could resist a disaster, that one. Remember when that wagon went through the ice?"

Of course Bayla would remember. *I* remembered, even though it happened years before I was born. It was in the spring, just before the breakup. There had been a thaw, then a freeze, a hard freeze—but still, the coachman shouldn't have tried to cross. He should have gone the long way, back through town to the bridge. They were no more than a third of the way across when it happened. The carriage went through first, dragging the horses back. The horses squealed and pawed at the air, but the carriage sank quickly. Like a stone, people said.

There had been a group of children playing by the river when it happened. They all ran to get help. All but Hava, who had remained at the site of the accident, as if rooted to the spot.

"If her father hadn't carried her home she might still be there to this day," said Bayla, who had been one of the children who ran away. "Like Lot's wife . . ."

"What happened to Lot's wife?" Tsila turned on me suddenly.

"She turned to salt," I answered automatically. Three years in Tsila's house had taught me to be prepared, always.

"And why?"

"Because she disobeyed God."

"She turned to salt because she couldn't resist a disaster," Tsila said. "She was given an opportunity to escape. Was commanded to escape. 'Flee for your life,' the angel commanded. 'Do not look behind you, nor stop anywhere in the plain; flee to the hills, lest you be swept away.' But she couldn't resist looking. Some people are like that."

"Maybe she just couldn't turn her back on her home and her people," Bayla said. "Maybe she turned just for one last look at all that had been beloved to her, and in that hesitation . . ."

"You're saying hesitation is a sin?"

Bayla thought for a minute. "A danger more than a sin." She

thought for another minute. "Yes, in some instances . . . the looking backward instead of forward . . . but we're confusing the poor child." Bayla smiled at me affectionately. "You're right that Lot's wife disobeyed God," she said to me. "She witnessed His work without His permission. She witnessed the suffering of others without pity. For all those reasons . . ."

"Now you sound like Lipsa," Tsila said.

Bayla laughed. "Then it's time for me to go. I've already kept you long enough from your work for one day, anyway. If I hear anything else I'll let you know."

"No doubt." Tsila put away her mending and took up her position at her sewing machine.

"Come," Tsila said to me after Bayla left. She had her market basket in hand with some fruit in it and a loaf of bread she had baked the day before. I thought she was taking me to market, but we turned away from town and began to descend in the direction of the swamp. I hesitated, faltered, but Tsila already held my small hand firmly in her large one. "Don't be a donkey," she said, pulling me along.

It was a warm day, the sun was hot on my back and shoulders. The mud of the road had already dried to the caked surface of summer, but dust did not yet rise around us as we walked, and the sprigs of grass along the way were still the fresh, bright green of spring. Down we walked to the flat bank of the river.

The river was smooth and placid as it cut its wide, lazy curve around our village. We crossed it by way of the old wooden footbridge. The path on the other side followed the bank of the river for a long while, sometimes diverging slightly around a thicket of nettles or an expansive willow, then returning to the low bank. Only gradually did it lead us away, into the thicker air of the swamp.

I had heard much about the dangers of the swamp—the snakes that lurked in its waters, the quicksand that waited to swallow the unsuspecting foot, but the path we followed was firm underfoot and the sun still warmed my back. All around us were channels and pools of water out of which tall grasses grew. Tsila picked one of these reedlike grasses, pulled a white strip out of the center, and ate it.

"What is it?" I asked. She placed a piece in my mouth. It tasted like fresh-baked bread.

"If you eat enough it will give you a baby," she explained, then she looked at my face and laughed. "Don't worry, you need a husband too for that to happen."

Over three years had passed since her wedding to my father and still there was no baby and no sign that one was coming. The talk in town, according to Bayla, was that my mother might be part of the problem. And why wouldn't she be, the women were saying—Bayla had told Tsila just the week before. Why would she allow her own child to be supplanted by Tsila's natural children?

"Idiots," Tsila had muttered. "As if Henye wouldn't have better things to do than meddle in my life."

"It's not that they think she's trying to meddle," Bayla pointed out. "It's more a matter of her looking out for her own."

At that, Tsila laughed outright. "Yes, so much concern for her own that she left her for another to raise."

Tsila pulled off another white strip from the reed and popped it into her mouth.

"Is it manna?" I asked.

She stopped eating and looked me squarely in the face. "You're a peculiar child," she said. "Does life seem so easy to you that you think the Almighty Himself is personally providing food for us now? This is no Sinai," she said.

I looked at the marshy landscape all around us, the channels of black water, the flat expanses of tall swamp grasses, the stunted pine trees. Tsila followed my gaze.

"I'll never be delivered from here," she said. She ate another bit of reed. "Other people, yes. My sister Taube. You watch. She'll get to America yet, that one. Hava Leibowitz, it would seem—although who knows with her." She looked at me. "Maybe you."

Delivered from what, I wondered. And to where?

"Where am I going?" I asked.

"I don't know," she said. "Away. Somewhere where you can live as a human being among human beings."

"Our town is nice," I offered uneasily. I had never heard Tsila sound wistful before. It made me more uneasy than her sourness.

"Our town isn't nice," she said. "Our town is backward and poor and full of fear. Nice is somewhere else. But come now," she said, suddenly brisk again.

The path was sandy underfoot, then spongy with moss, then sandy again. And all around us, heavy heat and the buzzing, croaking sounds of the swamp. A heaviness had settled on me as well. My home wasn't nice, Tsila had said. It was poor and full of fear.

I remembered with a chill what had befallen Yasha the water carrier not more than two weeks earlier. Early one morning two peasant girls driving their cows along a path had been drawn to the riverbank by a strange low moaning. They followed the sound until, in a small clearing in the brush, they found the source: Yasha, lying on his back, his face a mess of blood and pulp, his mouth working like a fish, and in his outstretched hand, his two eyes staring sightlessly at the sky.

The culprits had been caught—two peasant boys from a neighboring village—but our village still vibrated with fear. What was the meaning of such an event, people asked one another. Why would two boys commit such an act? The hoodlums themselves said they hadn't liked the way Yasha had looked at them, but there were many in our town who thought that there had to be more to it than that. A warning, perhaps, of rising resentments among our gentile neighbors. A message from the Almighty that as Yasha was now blind, so were we willfully blinding ourselves to something important. But to what? Everyone had their theory. The Bundists gathered in the woods to speak of the injustice of our times, the Hasids bemoaned the impiety, the Zionists the futility of setting roots in soil that would always be foreign and hostile. And Yasha, meanwhile, lay on a cot in his hut as a collection was taken up on his behalf.

"Aren't there hoodlums and bandits in the swamp?" I asked Tsila as we pressed onward.

"No more than in town," Tsila said.

The air was warmer and thicker with each step we took, and here and there mosquitos rose up in thick clouds. We passed, single file, through an area of thick brush from which red berries hung. I picked one, but Tsila slapped it out of my hand. "That's poison," she said.

We came finally to a channel that was wider than the others and filled with swift-flowing clear water. The bank was thick with nettle but we picked our way through it so I could have a drink. I cupped my hands but the cold, sweet liquid dripped through them, so Tsila cupped her hands over and over until I had drunk my fill. Then she hitched her skirt up as high as her waist.

"Wait here," she said, and began to wade across the channel.

I stayed where I was, half buried in brush, and watched the water rise around Tsila's legs. Her calves disappeared, then her knees. It was a shallow channel, but water swirled around the middle of her thighs before beginning to recede. She emerged on the other side, let her skirt down, and picked her way along the bank to a pile of old boards. The pile was haphazard, a weather-beaten old cabin so exhausted by the struggle to remain upright that it had simply collapsed on the spot. Tsila placed her fruit and bread among the boards, then hitched up her skirt again and waded back to me.

When she reemerged on my side, she quickly ran her hands up and down her wet white legs, then turned around and asked me to check if there were leeches on the backs of her legs. There were none. Nor were there any on the bottoms of her feet or between her toes.

"Hurry," she said, taking my hand. "We've come a long way."

"Who did you leave the fruit and bread for?" I asked.

"What is the highest form of charity?" she responded.

I didn't know.

"That in which the giver does not know who receives and the receiver does not know who gives."

"Was it for Hava?"

"You're impertinent," she said, and quickened her pace, even though my legs were already stumbling trying to keep up. She grabbed my hand tighter and pulled me along the path.

"Do you think I have nothing better to do than give up half a day's work and drag myself through the swamp for a girl who can't face her own bridegroom?"

"What if bandits take the bread?"

"What's with all the questions about bandits? Do you think we're not surrounded by bandits in the village? Is Shlomo the Righteous not a bandit?"

Shlomo was the shoemaker my father worked for. Only Tsila referred to him as the Righteous, and that was only since he had started cheating my father out of his wages.

"Who is a bandit in times such as these?" Tsila asked. She had been asking that more and more as it became obvious to her, if not to my father, that Shlomo was not only going to cheat my father out of his wages but out of his job as well. "Everything is upside down," Tsila said. "Honest people have to beg while scoundrels rule the villages and towns."

The air was still and hot when we finally reemerged onto the bank of the river. The river itself was like glass. We walked slowly alongside it, the heat of the day pressing heavily upon us. A group of peasant women were laying out their linen to bleach in the sun. Tsila exchanged greetings with them, her eyes assessing the quality of their linen. I longed to dip my feet in the coolness of the water but I knew we were hurrying. Tsila reached down, cupped water in her hand, and cooled first my face and then her own.

MY FATHER WAS ANGRY. TSILA DIDN'T EVEN BOTHER TO ask how he knew where we'd been. We lived on the furthest outskirts of the town, it's true, but the eyes of the town were farsighted as well as nearsighted and could see in darkness as clearly as in the full light of day.

"She barely survives one illness, so you decide you have to drag her somewhere where she is sure to catch another?" my father shouted.

I had never seen him truly angry before. He and Tsila quarreled every day, but always over trifles, and with obvious pleasure about the cleverness of their insults.

"It's three years since she survived her illness, Aaron Lev."

"Just look at her," he shouted again. Tsila didn't comply. She stood at the stove with her back to him, frying eggs for his supper.

"Already she has a rash," he yelled.

"Everyone gets a rash when they go into the swamp at this time of year," Tsila said evenly. She stirred the eggs.

"That's supposed to be an answer? *Everyone gets a rash?* What, *everyone?* What other child gets dragged into the swamp? Do you know there are reports of cholera in Kalinkovich?"

"If cholera is looking for her, it will find her wherever she's hiding."

"But you have to make it easier? God forbid the cholera should tire itself out looking for her—do you have to bring her to it?"

Tsila had spoken the truth when she told my father she had unfettered his tongue. Anger unleashed the eloquence that grief had strangled.

"And the hoodlums that congregate there," he continued. "Do you realize that they still haven't found the Leibowitz girl?"

"Good for her," Tsila answered.

"Good for her? Good for her, you dare to answer? What, *good for her?* Good for her that she lies slaughtered somewhere? Or worse, captured by God knows who for God knows what?"

"Calm yourself, Arele. You know how your stomach reacts when you upset yourself."

"It is not I who have upset myself. You, my wife, have upset me."

"Shush now," Tsila said. She transferred the eggs to a plate and placed it on the table. "Come wash."

My father washed his hands and made the blessing over bread. He ate in silence, hunched over his plate, looking at neither Tsila nor me, only at the food he shoveled mechanically into his mouth.

"We went to do a *mitzvah*," I explained. "We gave *tzedakah*."

"*Tzedakah* you could have given in town," he said.

That was true. There was a *tzedakah* box right on the shelf by the door, and the poorhouse would have happily taken our fruit and bread.

"These are difficult times," I explained. "Everything is upside down."

"Shush now, Miriam," Tsila said. She cleared the table and brought tea.

"What possessed you?" my father asked in a calm and quiet voice. She didn't answer.

"Do you know what people are saying?"

"I've long learned to ignore the wagging tongues, Aaron Lev, and thought you had too."

"They're saying you went to make an offering. To open your womb. That's what they're saying."

"I can't help their stupidity," Tsila said.

"Did you?" he asked.

"You surprise me," she answered.

"It is I who am surprised, my wife."

Tsila's color rose instantly, like a flash fire, her cheeks bursting into flame. Her mouth exploded too.

"Their stupidity I can't help. I'm forced to live among it my entire life. For what sin I committed, I don't know, but such is my sentence, to live among this ignorance. But your stupidity, Aaron Lev, yours on this matter—that I won't abide."

"You made an offering, did you not?"

Tsila stared at him as if he were a stranger.

"You begin to sound like Lipsa," Tsila said. "I married a man only to wake up to a fool."

"I won't think the worse of you, Tsila. It's been over three years now; you're worried. It's only natural for you to worry. I won't think the worse—just tell me the truth."

"Are you such an old woman that you believe the departed can find nothing better to do than hover around this world once they're finally free of it?"

"For whom?" my father asked, without expression.

And now Tsila's eyes looked away. "For whom, what?" she asked.

"For whom did you leave your offering?"

"For the child," she said. "To show her there is nothing to fear in the swamp, to clear her head of these whisperings . . ."

"Why fruit and bread, then?"

Tsila didn't answer.

"Could you not have taken her to the swamp without that?"

"These are hard times," Tsila said vaguely. "You never know who is hungry."

TSILA AROSE BEFORE DAYBREAK, LIT THE STOVE IN DARK-ness, and reached for the delicate rose of Shendel's dress just as the first light of dawn brushed the surface of her table.

"A dress like this must be made in the freshness of morning," she said, as I stood silently beside her. She pulled the fabric together at the waist, then folded, pleated, and stitched until the dress itself resembled a rose.

The cobalt brocade, meanwhile, lay in a dark pile in the corner.

"Did Hava die?" I asked. I'd heard reports from Tsila's customers that a pack of wolves had eaten Hava, that she had been seen on the road to Kalinkovich just a few steps ahead of the cholera.

"Brides run off from time to time," Tsila answered. "They don't usually die of it." She held Shendel's new dress up to the morning light. "It's pretty, no?"

I nodded happily and reached over to stroke the soft fabric. "Like Shendel," I said.

"Not like Shendel," Tsila said sharply, then she sighed a deep un-happy sigh, as if the dress had suddenly filled her with sorrow.

"Shendel's pretty," I reminded her.

"Yes, but this . . ." She gestured toward the dress. "This is intricate, delicate . . ."

There was tenderness in Tsila's face as she looked at the dress, the sort of soft, radiant tenderness I had seen on women's faces when they carried a new baby or beheld the Torah scrolls in their Holy Ark. But this was a dress, I knew, not a living child or a holy object. I watched Tsila gaze radiantly at the object of her own creation and I felt blas-phemy sweep the room like a chill wind.

"A dress like this is wasted on the likes of Shendel Entelman," she said.

"Won't Shendel be happy with it?" I asked.

"Shendel will be happy," Tsila said. "But Shendel would be happy with one of the rags Blema could piece together for her." Blema was another seamstress in town, able at her trade but not excessively so. "Shendel's a good girl, don't get me wrong," Tsila continued. "But this dress . . ." She reached out to stroke it. "It would take a far finer woman than Shendel to appreciate such a dress."

"Who could be finer than Shendel?" I asked, a girl whose inner goodness was said to match the loveliness of her face, whose voice was so charming when she raised it in song that she voluntarily refrained from singing, even in the privacy of her parents' home, lest a man passing by overhear her sweetness and be overcome by the evil inclination.

"Who could be finer than Shendel? No one around here, I can assure you."

Around where, then? Although Tsila's tone was tart, there was longing in it also—I heard it—a soft aching that pulsed behind her sourness. What was this place my stepmother longed for, I wondered, and where might it lie? I couldn't imagine its shape or form, or what kinds of strangeness it might hold, but my mind was suddenly bright with it. Bright and bathed in a warm, pink light that could only be *fineness*—fineness that outshone even the loveliness of our Shendel.

I looked at Tsila, but whatever world she had hinted at had already receded from view, the longing that I had sensed in her had now vanished. Her expression was sour as she folded the dress to deliver to Shendel.

"Shall we go deliver this to the bride?" she asked.

SHENDEL'S FAMILY LIVED ON THE OPPOSITE SIDE OF town from us, past the narrow maze of streets where Lipsa lived, past the market, past the new synagogue where the wealthier merchants prayed, and up a slight incline. The neighborhood was as far from the swamp as you could get and still be in our town. Beyond it was a sweet pine forest.

Shendel's father, Lazer Entelman, dealt in lumber. His house had ornate gables and was said to have floors of polished wood and rooms filled with feather sofas and colorful tapestries. Shendel received us in the kitchen, but even the kitchen was grander than any I had seen before. The floors gleamed as if someone had finished polishing them just moments before, and the light that shone through the windows of that kitchen seemed of a different nature from the dust-filled element that filtered into ours. "Sit, please," Shendel said, gesturing generously to the bench along the table. She was, if possible, even prettier than I had ever seen her. Her skin was as rich as the deep-hued wood from which her father had made his fortune, her dark eyes flashed humor and light, and her hair, which would soon be shorn for her wedding, was pulled for now into two shining black braids that she charmingly tossed over her shoulders, as if their lustrous beauty had become a distraction she was now impatient to be rid of.

I watched closely as she unwrapped her dress--I was fully confident once again in the absolute fineness of Shendel. She lifted the dress from its wrapping with careful hands and sighed with pleasure. She held it to her body, then out at arm's length so that she could look at it, then to her body again. "It's so beautiful," she said to Tsila, happiness lighting her already lovely face. "It's so delicate. It's . . ."

"It's like a rose," I said.

"Like a rose," Shendel agreed, and holding the dress to her body, she danced a little around the room. Just a little, she danced, and not in any immodest way; she was a pious girl. Then she turned her gaze to me. "And how are you, my little chicken?" she asked me. "I haven't had so much as a glimpse of you since you left Lipsa's. I miss seeing your sweet face around town."

Now here was a bit of strangeness. Since when was I Shendel's little chicken? While Shendel had always been kind to me, only rarely whispering something when I walked past her and her group of friends, I had never until this moment been her little chicken. Nor had she ever found my face sweet before. But such was Shendel's happiness: it infused everything she gazed upon with goodness.

Possibly Tsila had been right, then. As happy as Shendel was with her dress, she might have been just as happy with something Blema had made. She might even have danced the same little dance.

"It's very intricate," I said, and received a blank stare in response.

"What is?" she asked.

"The dress."

"Of course it's intricate. Does Tsila ever make anything that isn't intricate?" Even Tsila, the village lemon, was bathed in the soft light of Shendel's happiness.

"Will you be happy in it?" I asked.

"Stop with that question already," Tsila said, and boxed my ear lightly.

"Such a serious little chicken," Shendel said gaily. "Will you have tea?"

"Please," I said.

"Please don't bother," Tsila said, and boxed my ear again, not quite as lightly as before. "Shendel has better things to do than serve us tea," she warned.

"How can you say that, Tsila?" Shendel protested, but she did not insist.

"I know how busy you are," Tsila said. "I too was a bride. You can serve us tea when you're a properly married lady in your own house."

"Yes," Shendel said, her face glowing. Construction on Shendel's new house had already begun. During the break between the services at the new synagogue, her father could be heard bragging about the cost of materials he had imported. Shendel clapped her hands together once, then held them clasped in front of her. "You'll be my very first guests," she said.

"If not your first, then among the first," Tsila said, beginning to usher me out the door.

"WHAT IS WRONG WITH YOU?" TSILA ASKED ANGRILY, almost as soon as we were out the door. "Do you not know how to behave anywhere?"

My silence served only to encourage Tsila's anger.

"When you went with Lipsa to drop off laundry, did you sit like ladies and drink tea?"

"No one asked us to."

"Of course no one asked you to. Why would anyone invite the likes of you to tea?"

"Shendel did," I pointed out.

"*Shendel did,*" Tsila mimicked. "Since when does Shendel Entelman have the likes of us in for tea?"

"She wouldn't have asked us if she didn't mean it."

Tsila didn't argue with this immediately. She stomped on ahead, leaving me to trot after her. As soon as I reached her, though, she turned on me.

"You are not like Shendel," she said. Never had I imagined that I was. "You do not have Shendel's face, you do not have Shendel's parents, you do not, thank God, have Shendel's brains. Shendel is a simple girl who prefers not to see the way things are. And the way things are, *my little chicken,* is that girls like you do not sit around sipping tea with the Shendels of the world. Do you understand me?"

I didn't answer.

"Shendel can afford to pretend differently. She can afford to close her eyes to whatever she doesn't want to see. But you, my little one, cannot. You cannot afford to close your eyes to the way things are. Do you understand me? Your eyes must be open at all times, your ears attentive, your head alert and working, all the time working. And even so, even with all that . . ."

"She invited me," I pointed out again.

With this, Tsila turned back around and stomped home.

"SO YOU'LL HAVE YOUR TEA HERE," LIPSA TOLD ME. I had gone straight to her house after Tsila had left me on the street.

Lipsa's house seemed darker than when I had lived there—the light from the small window didn't reach into much of the room—but it still smelled of Lipsa and her family.

"Anyway, the way things appear is not always the way they are," she said, putting aside the matches she had been packing to pour me some tea. "Have you forgotten so quickly the three ways in which you and Shendel are alike?"

I wasn't sure I had ever known them to forget them.

"You were both created from one tiny drop of liquid, as we all are. You are both destined for the grave, a place of dirt and worms and maggots. And you must both give an account before the King of Kings. As we all must. Have you eaten?" she asked, and placed some bread and a chopped onion in front of me.

I ate and drank my tea while Lipsa went back to her task. We were the only ones home. The younger children were playing in the courtyard. The older girls were probably delivering laundry.

"When a girl like Shendel invites you for tea, she is not simply making noise with her tongue," Lipsa said after a while. "That's not the type of girl Shendel is. Have another slice of bread." I took the bread she offered. "I've known Shendel longer than your stepmother has," Lipsa continued. "Who do you think nursed Shendel?"

"You?" I asked.

Lipsa nodded. "Her mother had no milk. I know this girl from her first moments in this world—as I know you, my little bird—and I can tell you that if Shendel Entelman invited you to tea it's because she meant to have you."

A warmth filled me so completely at that moment that I no longer even wanted my second slice of bread. "When will she have me?" I asked. "After she's married? In her new house?"

But Lipsa simply shrugged her shoulders and said, "When the time is right, she'll have you."

"AH, THE HONORED GUEST HAS ARRIVED AT LAST," Tsila said as I walked through the door. There was a bowl of *schav* sitting on the table. I sat down.

"Have you washed?"

I got up, washed, then sat down again.

"And did the lady of leisure enjoy herself in town?"

I tried to eat the *schav,* fresh with sorrel I had picked that morning, but was full from the bread I had eaten at Lipsa's.

"Perhaps the food I've prepared is no longer good enough for one who has been invited to tea by Shendel Entelman."

"I had tea with Lipsa," I said.

Tsila's face flamed red and for a moment I thought she might hit me with her spoon, but when she spoke her voice was calm and no longer cut with the sarcasm with which she had greeted me.

"Will you forever run to Lipsa when I try to teach you something that is unpleasant to learn?"

"I don't know," I said.

"At least you're not lying to me. Tell me what Lipsa fed you this time."

"Just tea and bread and onion."

"I meant what old wives' tales did she tell you?"

"She told me that Shendel meant it when she invited me to tea."

"I see," Tsila said. "Because you and Shendel have so much in common, so much to discuss."

I began to tell Tsila the three ways in which Shendel and I were alike. "We were both created from—"

"Believing that will never put food on your table."

I dipped my spoon into the *schav* but had even less appetite than a moment before.

"Freyde said hello to you," I told Tsila. What Freyde had actually said, when Lipsa and I had stopped in there, was that I should ask my stepmother if she thought she was too good to visit old friends now that she was a married lady. For Freyde, though, that was like saying hello.

"How did you come to see Freyde?" Tsila asked with a scowl so deep I wished I had kept my mouth shut.

"Lipsa took me by there on my way home."

"Did she?"

I nodded, though Tsila's tone had put me on guard.

"And why do you suppose Lipsa took you by Freyde's? It wasn't exactly along your way, was it?"

It wasn't. Freyde lived down a little side alley, not far out of the way, but certainly not along it.

"Did Lipsa have something to drop off? To pick up?"

No, she hadn't.

"So why do you suppose, then . . . ?"

Now that Tsila asked me, I could see that there was a bit of oddness here. It's not as if Freyde was fond of me. *The urchin,* she called me. Even today, after she had looked me over, she had droned in her deep nasal tones: "I see the urchin is still among us."

"Clear the table and I'll tell you something," Tsila said.

WHEN THEY WERE FIRST MARRIED, AARON LEV FOUND Henye a house in the village. A cheerful house, with whitewashed walls and nice wood shutters and room out back for a little garden.

"You know the house," Tsila said. "You were just there. Freyde and her family occupy it. It's not so nice now, of course—she lives like a pig, Freyde does—but at that time there were only two other families in it and they always kept it freshly whitewashed."

The walls were gray and weather-beaten now, the shutters half rotted, but the garden grew wild with flowers and herbs, and children and chickens filled the yard.

"You could see it was nice once, no?" Tsila asked.

I nodded.

"But Henye wouldn't have such a house. Do you know why?"

I shook my head.

"It was too noisy for one such as Henye. Quiet, your mother suddenly wanted. She who had refused Aaron Lev at first on account of his silence."

"She had?"

"Yes, of course. His tongue wasn't smooth enough for a girl like Henye. She preferred her tongues clamorous and well oiled, but that's another story. She refused Aaron Lev as if she weren't an orphan and all alone in the world, as if she could afford to be choosy about a man who would have her. She refused him as if she were suddenly Queen Esther. I'm not saying your mother was above herself—God forbid I should speak in such a way about one who can no longer answer on her own behalf . . ."

She looked at me to make sure I understood that one could never be too careful in speaking about the departed. I nodded understanding.

"But she did refuse a perfectly good match—she wouldn't deny that, I'm certain—and with no parents around to force her hand, what could your father do?"

"What did he do?"

"He followed her around. For a year he followed her around. A silent shadow of a man, that's what Aaron Lev became until finally . . ." Tsila paused again.

"Do you know when silence grows on a person?" she asked me.

In the world to come, I thought, bleakness replacing any curiosity I had been feeling about my own origins. But Tsila wasn't leading me to my mother's death.

"When a person wants to hear her own heartbeat—that's when she begins to seek silence," she said.

I remembered the terrible silence that first afternoon Lipsa had brought me to my father's and left me with Tsila, the sound of my own blood rushing through my veins. The sound of my own life. Terrible.

" 'Quiet you'll have,' your father said when he saw the house your mother had chosen. Sender the tanner lived here for years—you wouldn't remember, of course. How could you? Not that there was much to remember. He worked winters, drank summers, and smelled all the while of the rot that would eventually kill him. He died right here in this house, did you know that? Just a year before your brother's birth. His death was an agony—his whole body black from the rot. That's the house your mother chose for her married life."

"Why?" I asked.

"*Why,* I'm not telling you right now. There are theories aplenty, I can assure you. But I'm telling you *what* now.

" 'And what about the times you're alone?' your father asked her. Because a shoemaker has to travel for his work, no? Winter months he could be gone the whole week, weeks at a time, even, making his rounds of the neighboring villages, and Henye, all the while, on the edge of the swamp with no one but her thoughts for company. Is such a life right for a young bride? This is what Aaron Lev wondered when he saw the fine house Henye had chosen. This is what everyone wondered. And do you know what your mother answered?" Tsila asked.

I concentrated but could not think what my mother might have answered.

" 'I am never alone.' That's what your mother answered. *I am never alone.* Can you imagine such an answer?"

I had no response.

Tsila shrugged. "Who knows what a person hears in her own heart when she finds the silence to listen. Some say it's dangerous to listen—to what good can it lead? That's why we don't live alone like wild animals. We live together, in a community, like human beings."

"So we won't listen to our own hearts?"

She looked sharply to see if I was being cheeky, then continued.

"They say your father shouldn't have let her have her way, that he should have put his foot down as a man properly does and insist she live in the house he had found for her. In a cheerful house, in town, among people. Some even go so far as to suggest that her end is on his shoulders, hence his stoop. I don't know if Lipsa is among those, but she does blame him. Yes she does," Tsila said emphatically, waving an impatient hand to silence my protest.

"Why else would she have shown you the house today? What else would she be doing taking you to Freyde's?"

I didn't know.

"*This is where you should have been born.* That's what Lipsa was telling you. I know how she thinks, that one. *Remember this house when you return to the dangerous silence of your father's.* That's what she fed you today, along with your tea and bread and onions. You washed and said the proper blessings?"

I nodded. "Lipsa didn't say anything . . ."

"She didn't have to. She thinks I'm a fool, but she's the fool, with all her tricks and sorcery that are useless in the face of fate. Changing your name . . ." Tsila shook her head as if what Lipsa had done was unusual in some way and worthy of scorn. "A person's fate is inscribed in her heart," Tsila said. She took my hand and laid it flat against my chest. "Do you feel your fate?" she asked me. I felt only the strong, steady beat of my heart. "Do you think sorcery and tricks can change what is beating beneath your hand?" she asked me.

Siberia, May 1911

I t was my mother I thought of when I first glimpsed Maltzev, her words that rose to save me, filling my mind, guarding its furthest edges, barring the entry of any other thoughts.

I am never alone.

We came to Maltzev from Akatue, the receiving prison of the Siberian katorga, and though I had thought my life was ending when I arrived at Akatue after two difficult months of transport away from all I knew and held dear, Akatue, in retrospect, was like a country inn compared to what awaited us at Maltzev. It was summer, first of all, when we arrived at Akatue, and the valley in which the prison sat was green. And when we passed through the outer gates of the prison itself, the courtyard was filled with young people, men and women like ourselves—and children too, I noted with a pang—all calling out their welcome to us. "Welcome, dear comrades," they called in greeting. "Glory for the fallen and freedom for the living!"

Maltzev, in contrast, we approached in winter. The order came in January, when the frost was most bitter.

Akatue was too crowded in the summer of 1906 for proper discipline to be maintained. All that's changed now, of course, but in that first summer after the failed revolution, the walls of Akatue and the will of its guards were no match for the spirit of the youth pouring into it in ever increasing numbers. Within Akatue's walls, prisoners moved freely, tongues as unshackled as their limbs, exciting themselves with ideas and plans, organizing themselves into communes devoted to the overthrow of tyranny. And then, just before my arrival, Grigor Gershuni managed to escape. Gershuni, the leader of the Socialist Revolutionary Party's Combat Battalion, who had authored so many "daring blows" against the oppressive regime.

Gershuni escaped by hiding in a barrel of sauerkraut that was being carried out of the prison. Prisoners regularly prepared their own sauerkraut for the winter, cleaning and cutting the cabbage and packing it into large barrels for storage. At the bottom of one of those barrels, Gershuni crouched, rubber tubes in his mouth leading to two airholes cut out of the side of the barrel, a metal plate on his head to stop the thrust of the sentry's bayonet, fermenting cabbage filling the space around him. His comrades carried him to the gate, but it was the guards and soldiers themselves who lowered him into the cellar from which his tunnel to freedom had already been dug.

Reaction was swift: joy and hope among the prisoners, retribution from the jailers. Fifty male prisoners were transferred immediately to Gorni Serentui—the harshness of which was recently made public through the suicide of Yegor Sazonov, a man many once called irrepressible. And then, in winter, the transfer of the women to Maltzev.

Seven days we had to travel to reach Maltzev. We traveled by sleigh—there was no other way—wrapped in skins that kept us alive but not warm. Seven days we traveled across a lifeless landscape where swirling ice and snow were the only movements besides our own. Nights we spent locked in the Siberian étapes—holes so disgusting with vermin and excrement that to breathe their foulness into our lungs was a form of torture as severe as the cold. On the eighth day, Maltzev came into view: a lone gray structure barely rising out of the desolation around it.

"God save us," Lydia muttered. Lydia the atheist, who was serving ten years for her preachings against God and the Tsar.

"It looks like a lizard," another whispered. Maria. She was so ill she had to be carried to and from the sleigh at the start and end of every day. Perhaps in her delirium the prison did look like a lizard. Perhaps she mistook the snow all around for the sun-warmed sand where a lizard might survive. Delirium it must have been, for what stood before us was no lizard. Low to the ground, yes, but gray as the face of death. It was no living thing that lay in wait for our arrival that day, but a coffin, a coffin built to entomb us until we could be properly turned into the ground.

"I will not survive this," I heard myself utter. "With God as my witness, I will not survive this."

The sleigh had stopped—a momentary break so we could stand up and try to move our freezing limbs. I raised my eyes to my situation. We were surrounded by barrenness, gray and white for as far as the eye could see and beyond. We were three hundred versts from the nearest railroad station, seven days by sleigh from our comrades at Akatue. When I moved out of range of the sound of my companions' breathing, the silence was so powerful that I felt it as pain. An unendurable pressure in my ears—that's what I felt, a band tightening around my head, a weight crushing my chest, my lungs, squeezing me from all sides. I raised my hands instinctively to protect myself, but there was no protection.

I stamped my feet, clapped my mittened hands, but as soon as I stood still, silence moved back in around me. It was twilight by then. If I stayed where I was standing I would be dead by nightfall. By morning the moving snow would cover any trace of my physical existence. Already the sweeping snow and darkness had obscured me from my companions. I was utterly alone.

And that's when I heard her. *I am never alone.* In a clear, strong

voice, those words rose from my core as lava might, filling my chest with
heat, spilling inside my head until there was room for nothing else. *I am
never alone. I am never alone. I am never alone.* I couldn't ponder the
meaning of the words, could only grab hold of them as a drowning person might grab blindly for anything within his reach, allowing them to
carry me to their source. Down the comforting slopes of their tones I
slid, deeper and deeper inside myself. There I found Tsila's voice, my
mother's words, my own noisy heart—at that moment, sufficient.

about my daughter," Rosa said. "A good question, I think, and unexpected. He had been prepared, it was obvious, to assure us of Leib's capacity to support Bayla, to impress us with his learning. But now, to have to explain what it was about Bayla that had captured his cousin? And do you know what he said?"

"How would I know?"

"He said, 'There was a moment at the wedding when she laughed, an instant just before her hand flew up to cover her mouth . . .' As if the unguarded laughter of a young woman is suddenly the proper basis for a marriage." Rosa paused at this to meet her daughter's eyes. "And it was at that moment that your father took out the shot glasses."

"What?! What was he thinking? Is he so desperate to marry her off that . . ." But here Tsila stopped. Something in her mother's expression, perhaps. "It wasn't just Papa, was it?"

"I wasn't smiling like your father was, but neither did I restrain his arm from pouring the brandy."

"But why, Mamma? Are you also so desperate . . . ?"

"It has nothing to do with desperation," Rosa said.

"What, then?"

"She is not without spirit, my Bayla," Rosa said quietly. "I'm glad she found someone who can see it."

TWICE A WEEK THAT SPRING, TSILA SENT ME DOWN TO the swamp. On Mondays and Thursdays, the very days of the workweek when the Torah was read as part of the morning service, she filled my apron pocket with samples of the roots and barks that she needed for her dyes, filled my head with warnings, and sent me on my way.

"And you won't forget the reeds?" she would call after me, as if an afterthought, though that was the real reason for the excursions: the white-centered reed that put babies in married women's wombs. Six years had now passed since Tsila's wedding day and still she had no baby to show for it. She didn't complain about her plight or utter special prayers, nor did she consult with Breina, who specialized in removing curses and dispensing advice about the evil eye; but the spring of Bayla's engagement, Tsila began eating those white-centered reeds with a devotion she had previously reserved only for her dressmaking. All day long, while she cleaned, while she cooked, while she taught me my lessons, while she sewed her dresses—no matter how busy her hands were, she was always able to steal an instant from her work to pop a bit of the breadlike substance into her mouth. Only when she heard my father's returning footsteps at the end of the day did her mouth stop working and the reeds return to the darkness of the pantry.

I was not afraid of the swamp. In this I was different from the others of the town. It was not that I was not aware of the swamp's snakes and bandits and prowling gray mists, but those perils paled, somehow, next to the shame I had begun to feel on my trips into town. It was the whispers of other girls that I feared, the murmurs and turned heads that my appearance prompted.

Just look at her, I heard them whisper. Me, they meant, as if the separateness of my life was engraved on my face for all to see. I held my head high as Tsila had instructed me, looking neither right nor left, but that seemed only to sharpen the tongues. *Proud, like her stepmother—and of what?* It isn't pride, I wanted to cry out. Didn't I know more deeply than they my shameful beginnings, the unloveliness of my face? *The marriage is barren, no surprise there,* a young housewife would contribute. *Barren as a rock, but still she finds cause to act proud. And the emptier her womb, the higher she holds herself,* another would comment. *That poor Aaron Lev—the luck that man has had with wives. The higher she rises in her own mind, the lower he stoops under the weight of her. Just yesterday my David saw him crawling home and mistook him for a worm.*

Such were the greetings I received in town. They shouldn't have bothered me, perhaps. They didn't bother Tsila—ignorant boors, she called the town gossips—but I had been shaped from different forces than had Tsila. The cold indifference that had greeted my birth, the averted eye of my mother as I hung naked in the midwife's grasp had chilled me so deeply that I craved warmth, sought it from every gaze that came my way, warmth and reassurance that were rarely forthcoming.

Have you seen her neck? one of the girls would whisper. *It's marked by death,* she would add, referring to the scar on my neck, the point at which—according to the town's *yentas*—death had been forced to retreat from me and would, at some point, reenter to claim me. More whispers would follow, a gauntlet of whispers through which I had to pass to reach the center of town.

For this reason, the swamp seemed kinder to me at that time than the town. If it was true that it harbored the spirits of the dead in its mists, then those spirits did not seem to mean me any harm. If anything, I felt they were welcoming me, rising to greet me, wrapping themselves around me to escort me safely into the swamp.

I quickly learned the paths of the place, the sandy tracks that wound past thickets of nettles and hemlock, and the spongier trails that led to the bog. I found the firm footholds, the dry hillocks carpeted in moss, the groves of aspen that fed the match factories of the towns. I knew the pools of black water from which skeletal hands might rise to pull an onlooker in, and the clear channels where fresh water flowed. In the channels were snakes, and giant water bugs floated on the top, but the water, when I scooped a handful into my mouth, was clearer and sweeter than any in the village.

The swamp was not a quiet place, but the sounds that filled the air were the buzzings of insects, the croakings of frogs, the calls of wild ducks in flight overhead. Only rarely did I hear human voices. Sometimes it was the voices of boys from neighboring villages laughing and calling to each other as they fished and played in the channels. Other times it was the deeper voices of men on their way to lumbering operations or the makeshift camps of vagrants and beggars that were sprinkled throughout the region. I didn't want to meet the embodiments of these voices, but neither was I afraid. When they seemed too loud, too close, or too drunken in tone it was easy enough to duck into a shrub off the path and avoid being seen.

Only once that spring did someone actually surprise me on the trail. It was a boy, not much older than I. He was alone and so light in his step that I didn't hear him until he was almost upon me.

"Aaiee," I exhaled, surprise and fear filling me until I realized he was just a lone boy, and a sickly one at that.

"I'm sorry," he murmured. "I didn't mean to scare you."

His voice was gentler than any I had ever heard, beautiful to my ears, but his face was unpleasant to behold: clammy skin, gray in tone, eyes yellow where the whites should be, teeth already blackening in his mouth. "Are you ill?" I asked him, just to hear his voice again, but forcing myself to look at his face as well, knowing the pain an averted gaze could cause.

"Not very," he said. He looked me in the face for a long time, as if trying to find something there. I smiled, and color rose to his cheeks. He glanced then at the small bundle of reeds I had gathered and took one. Before I could stop him he had split it open, the precious white center discarded on the path. He brought the reed to his mouth and blew into the hole he had made, and through that absence came a single note, a tone of pure sorrow. Then he lowered the reed and slipped past me.

"Wait," I called out to him, but he was already quickly moving away from me and soon dropped out of sight.

"IT WAS PROBABLY YOUR IMAGINATION," TSILA SAID when I told her about it later, but her face darkened and the next time I went to gather her reeds, she came with me.

"Do you think it was my brother?" I asked her. He was the age Yaakov would have been by now and he had the look of someone who had died years before.

"Don't be silly," Tsila said sharply.

"I'm not silly," I said. "His face was gray, his eyes were yellow—"

"Were his teeth not black?" she interrupted.

"Exactly," I said.

"Exactly," she mimicked me. "Don't you know the teeth of the dead don't rot? It's only the travails of this life that rot the teeth out of our

heads. The teeth of the dead are always strong," she said. The boy was nothing to be afraid of.

"I wasn't afraid," I answered. My meeting with the boy had consoled me. Though I'd felt a shock when I first looked at his face, that first shock had soon given way to recognition. Here, finally, was another being like myself, it seemed, someone more at home in the swamp than among his people. And there was that gentleness in his voice when he apologized for scaring me—when had I ever felt the caress of such gentleness before?—as if he immediately recognized a fineness in me that no one else had ever noticed. And the sorrow I had heard when he raised the reed to his lips, my own life, it seemed, distilled to a single thread of sound.

"Where was it you met this unfortunate?" Tsila asked.

I led her to the place where he had overtaken me.

"You shouldn't be here anyway," she said, though the place I had taken her to was not different from other areas of the swamp. "Look how stunted the reeds are," she pointed out, and I could see that they were, though all around them other vegetation grew lush and thick. "The soil must be sour here."

I pointed out the willows flourishing nearby.

"What nourishes one species sometimes chokes another," she said. "I wouldn't want to put into my mouth anything choked by such soil." Then she hurried to remove us from that place.

I asked her what it was about the reed that would help her have a baby, and she revealed to me, as we walked home, the mystery of conception as related in the Talmud. The mother provided the red parts of the body, she explained. Blood, muscle, hair, the dark of the eye—all that came from the woman's monthly blood, the same blood that would soon start flowing out from my own body and would one day flow into a new being forming within me. The father provided the white parts: bones, teeth, the white of the eye, the tissue of the brain. This came from a liquid that only men could produce.

"But all that is simply matter," Tsila hastened to add. "Lifeless sinew and flesh. It's the Creator Himself who breathes life and spirit into every new being, He who puts sight in our eyes, intelligence in our brains, expression in our faces, and motion into our muscles and limbs. The soul," Tsila said. "Without which there is no life. The soul is the salt of the body, the preserver of flesh. The moment it departs, the flesh rots away."

My mind filled now with red and white: flesh and bones and teeth and blood, all woven together, in my case, by one thin thread of sorrow. Was that all my soul was, one thin thread? How would such a flimsy soul be strong enough to sustain my body? We walked farther and farther from where I had met the boy, and I felt the lengthening and shortening of my muscles, the beat of my heart, the flow of my blood, red and warm, coursing to the farthest reaches of my limbs. Was not the strength of my body and warmth of my blood also part of my soul? *The movement in the muscles and limbs,* Tsila had said. *And the intelligence of the brain.* Which meant my thoughts and ideas, the questions that formed so continually in my mind as we walked that it was only when we reached the bridge back to town that I remembered my original question: the reed that I gathered for Tsila, the white-centered reed. I asked how that would help her have a baby. Tsila stopped walking and leaned on the railing of the bridge. I leaned with her, staring into the placid waters of the Pripet. A fish jumped, flashing silver and light.

"An injury to the soul affects the flesh, just as injury to the flesh can crush the soul," she explained. "In the matter of conception . . ." Here she hesitated. "Sometimes when a man has sustained an injury of a certain sort, there's a shortage of white matter he can contribute."

I didn't ask what sort of injury my father had sustained. It was the reeds I turned my mind to. Would the reeds I provided be sufficient to remedy my father's problem? I had been careless about where I had gathered them, not understanding the role they had to play. How many had I gathered that were withered or stunted or otherwise lacking in white matter? I knew I would have to make another trip to the swamp as soon as possible to replace any of Tsila's store that seemed inferior.

TWO DAYS LATER, ON SHABBES AFTERNOON, I WAS WALKing along a path in the swamp that connected Mozyr to Kalinkovich. It wasn't an easy route—you had to know how to follow its bends and when to emerge onto the main road to avoid an expanse of bog. It was used mostly by vagrants or others who had some reason to stay off the main road, and I had chosen it precisely because it was so little used. I did not want to be seen on Shabbes carrying an armful of reeds; what I was doing was a violation of the day.

I expected total solitude, or at most a vagrant as anxious to remain invisible and anonymous as I was, so it surprised me to see a young couple taking their Shabbes afternoon stroll there. The girl was small and nicely groomed, except for her hair, which she had cut short like the young radicals who had been coming more frequently through town. It was she who was talking as they walked toward me, her hands gesticulating as if she couldn't trust her mouth alone to make her point. The man was tall and well built, with strong limbs and wide shoulders and masses of thick black hair. He was bent toward his companion as if to better hear what she was saying, but he wasn't as attentive as he was making out to be. His dark eyes were flitting nervously at the wilderness around him, which is how they lit on me, crouching behind a shrub, pulling at a reed.

"Excuse me, little sister," he addressed me. "Is this the right way to Mozyr?"

"Have I not told you this is the way?" his companion scolded him. "Don't you trust me anymore?"

He didn't answer her, did not even acknowledge that she had spoken. He kept his dark eyes locked on mine, so I could not look away had I tried. "This is the way," I told him, and pointed in the direction that his companion had been taking him. Released by his gaze now, I glanced at the young woman. Her complexion had the sallowness of a match-factory worker, but her eyes had a brightness that animated her face. "Thank you," she said to me as they continued on their way.

"So, my little Golda, am I to trust you now?" I heard him ask in a teasing tone as they walked on. The rest of their words were muffled by the growing distance between us.

Siberia, July 1911

In the evenings we are silent, a self-imposed silence so as not to disturb the sleep of our companions who have retired early to their cots. We sit around the table at the center of which burns our petrol lamp. In the winter we are wrapped in blankets—a dozen well-wrapped figures huddled over their books and papers. On a summer evening like tonight, though, we sit uncovered, our bodies a little straighter for the reprieve from the gnawing cold.

We begin our silence after the evening inspection, when the door to our cell is locked for the night. This is a difficult time: the moment when the key turns, completing our isolation from the living world, the plunge into silence that follows. In that moment I see the panic that rises in the eyes around me. We are young, were once hopeful. We expected fire, revolution, perhaps a martyr's death. Never this monotony, this slow rot, this silence in which they have entombed us. I feel the tightening of my own skull as

I struggle to regain the composure necessary to survive. This is the moment that madness seeks its entry.

Madness, hunger, and cold. Each is our mortal foe, but it is madness we fear most. It hovers in the room, always, like the deadliest of vapors. By day we keep it at bay. Our tightly honed discipline, the intensity of our focus—with these we push it into the corners of the room. But in the transitional moments—the descent into quiet at night, the waking from dreams in the morning—it surges full-strength from the margins to which we've banished it, brushing up against each of us in turn to find a weakness it can penetrate.

I feel its touch on the back of my neck, its weight on my chest. My heart beats rapidly, my thoughts begin to race. Fragments of memory fly through my head: Tsila's face, my father's eyes, your tiny hand closing around my finger. Faster and faster these images assault me until I know my head will burst from them. I will not survive this, I tell myself. With God as my witness, I will not survive this. But my head does not burst despite what it knows, and my heart, despite what it feels, does not break apart in my chest. I force myself to the table. There, eleven sets of eyes meet my own. Natasha's eyes are wide and dark with fear. Lydia pulls a chair up close beside her and tries to draw her attention to a book of mathematics, a subject that never used to fail to harness her thoughts. I pull out this notebook, dip my pen in the ink. Out the window behind Natasha's bent head the half-moon of Tammuz rises over the prison wall.

CHAPTER FIVE

*I*T WAS IN THE SPRING OF 1902 THAT I MADE MY first friend. I was in the market, standing at the edge of the small crowd that had gathered to watch a dancing bear. The performance was hardly inspired—the creature was so thin and ragged that his movements seemed more a pitiful attempt to escape future beatings than the humorous spectacle it was meant to be. Still, it had been a whole winter since we'd seen our last dancing bear, and when this one finally managed to rear up on his hind legs and wave his paws about, a murmur of appreciation passed through the crowd and coins began to clatter on the cobblestone.

"Pathetic," I heard a voice mutter beside me, and I turned to see Sara Gittleman, the oldest daughter of Hodel the widow. A lively girl two years older than I, Sara had never directed a word toward me before.

"The poor thing's half starved," I ventured.

"I was referring to the audience, not the bear," Sara said. "Why are they laughing and clapping? Are they so ignorant that they don't even realize they're watching themselves?" She turned to walk away from the crowd.

"What do you mean?" I asked, falling into step beside her.

"I mean that the common people everywhere are no less in chains than that bear is, their children are as skinny and full of worms, and their lives are spent dancing whatever tune their masters demand of them."

I looked at Sara in surprise. "You're comparing us to that . . . that beast?"

Sara's eyes flashed as they met mine and a flush of blood rushed just beneath her skin. "Tell me how we differ," she demanded. "Tell me one way that we differ." Her nostrils flared as she warmed to her outrage.

The comparison she was making was so absurd that had I dared to utter it to Tsila she'd have boxed my ears before demolishing my words with her own. "The bear can't choose between good and evil," I said without even having to think. "Nor does he know what it is to sanctify the Sabbath."

Sara's eyes narrowed as I spoke, and her nostrils flared even more dramatically. Normally such a look from a girl in town would have silenced me, but the subject we were discussing was so removed from my usual concerns, and Sara's statement was so silly and easy to refute, that I felt liberated from my own awkwardness. "And furthermore," I continued, "the master whose tune we dance to is the Almighty."

She stared at me an instant longer, then asked me if I'd like to go for a walk with her.

I had often observed Sara as she talked and laughed with her group of friends, admiring her long chestnut hair and cheeks that dimpled when she smiled. It was beyond my fondest imaginings that she would ever take an interest in me. I was fourteen years old and no girl besides Lipsa's daughters had ever asked me to join her on a walk before. I agreed immediately.

"I've been watching you for some time, you know," Sara admitted as we left the market.

"You have?"

"Oh, yes. I've seen how you stand off by yourself, always alone."

My cheeks flushed with shame, but there was no pity in Sara's voice. She'd been drawn to me without knowing why, she was saying. But now, of course, she understood.

I nodded, not daring to ask what it was she understood.

"Serious girls are so rare in this town," she sighed.

I nodded again, not sure what she meant by serious, and afraid, already, of disappointing and losing her interest.

"You're stronger than I am, I can tell," Sara said. "Younger, but already stronger. I'm drawn to such strength, you see."

"I don't know," I muttered, and dared to glance at her. Her dark hair gleamed in the afternoon sun.

"Oh, yes," she assured me. "You have the strength to stand by yourself, refusing to join the giggling silliness of the others, while I . . . I just can't seem to help myself." She sighed deeply. "I know I should be studying more, improving myself." She brushed a lock of hair from her eyes, then turned a serious gaze to me. "Look at how you just bested me in our argument. Even though I know in my heart that my comparison is correct, it's you who silenced me. And why? Because you obviously condition your mind by applying yourself to serious study, while I . . . I continue to fritter away precious time promenading with my friends."

Had Sara only known how envious I was of girls like her, how often I watched her and her friends, how longingly I imagined one of them approaching me, taking my hand, leading me into their happy, giggling circle.

"The other girls . . . Sima, Mirel, Lena . . ." Sara uttered each name with a disdain bordering on contempt. "Their heads are filled with nothing but air."

I knew that wasn't true. Lena, for one, had a talent with a needle. Just a few weeks earlier, her mother had come to consult with Tsila about a possible apprenticeship, and Tsila, looking at samples of her work, hadn't pursed her lips in disdain. And Mirel, Lipsa's second-oldest daughter, might giggle, but it was she, I knew, who helped her mother compute the household income and expenses. I didn't contradict Sara, though, and was rewarded with the sensation of her warm hand reaching for mine.

We walked up the incline through the wealthier part of town, past the Entelmans' house and into the sweet pine forest that started at that edge of town. Sara told me about the job she had recently taken as an assistant in Mrs. Gold's shop. Mrs. Gold had started out selling candles in the market from a tray that hung off her neck like an apron, but had expanded to soap, buttons, pencils, and other goods and now had a shop on the street that ran behind the market. The shop was so tiny and crammed so tight with goods that no more than two customers could squeeze in at one time. It was hard to imagine how she'd made room for an employee. "It's dull," Sara said of her work. "But she pays me on time and doesn't yell at me. Nothing like that seamstress in Mozyr."

Sara had been apprenticed to a seamstress, she told me, but had quit after two years. "The first year she paid me nothing," she said. "None of them do. The second year, twenty-five rubles, and for that I had to take care of her squealing brats and run her errands in addition to the sewing. And the air in that room . . ."

We followed a wide, well-traveled path through the tall, sturdy pines, past stands of walnut and birch. "Still, it was good to be in Mozyr. When I ran her errands I took my time. There were intelligent people to talk to, unlike here—present company excluded, of course." She flashed a deeply dimpled smile at me. "There's a bookseller by the river there . . ."

"Horowitz's?" I asked, to which Sara responded with a derisive laugh.

"Horowitz only sells religious books, you goose. I mean a real bookseller, with current thinkers and poets and novelists." She began then to talk about the course of study she followed after leaving her mother's *heder*, a stream of authors' names that meant nothing to me. I stopped to admire a particularly huge old oak, enjoying the sound of Sara's voice, the fragrant air of early spring, the feel of her hand in mine.

"What do you study with Tsila?" she asked me.

"Torah," I said. "The prophets, Pirkei Avos . . . my Hebrew is as fluent as my Yiddish."

The wrong answer, I could see from the scowl on my new friend's face.

"At a time when thinking people are putting forward solutions for the great problem of universal happiness, our great Jewish thinkers are making a deep study of ancient tomes whose ideas are as dry and withered as leaves that have fallen from the tree."

It took me a moment to understand that it was the Torah and Talmud she was referring to as dry and withered.

"Lilienblum said that. Have you read him?" I shook my head no. "How about Ansky?" I had to shake my head again. "Bialik? Darwin? Karl Marx?"

No, no, and no again, I admitted, my heart sinking as I revealed each new layer of ignorance. "But I do read and write Russian fluently," I offered.

"That's a start," she conceded, and she told me about a novel she had just read that I might enjoy. "By Semyon Yushkevish. Have you read much of his work?"

"Not much," I mumbled.

We passed a pond, a small pond that seemed particularly inviting, surrounded as it was by willows, its waters smooth and peaceful in the late afternoon calm. "Would you like to sit for a while?" I asked Sara, and she nodded.

TWO YEARS HAD PASSED BY THEN SINCE THE ANNOUNCE-ment of Bayla's engagement, and still she wasn't married. A date for the wedding had been set, then postponed several times, already, and while there were always good reasons for the postponement—sickness in Leib's family, a prolonged strike at the factory—there were those who were beginning to feel the presence of an omen.

"Will Bayla and Leib move to Bialystok?" I asked Tsila one evening after supper.

"Why would they move to Bialystok?" Tsila asked. "They both have work in Mozyr. It's we who should move to Bialystok."

It was just after Pesach, and my father had been laid off. Fewer people needed shoes in the warm months, so he was helping Noam the teamster load and unload coaches bound for the train station in Kalinkovich. The pay wasn't good—three rubles a week—and as much as Tsila had hated Shlomo the Righteous for cheating Aaron Lev, she seemed to resent Noam even more.

"To think that you would be reduced to working for such a man," she would say every night when Aaron Lev came home from work, and every night Aaron Lev would shrug that he had no other choice.

"We could move," she would argue.

"To where?"

"To a proper city where people know enough to wear shoes through the warmer months."

This would bring a smile to Aaron Lev. "Tsila, Tsila," he would say, "do you think if we move to Minsk there will suddenly be an endless supply of customers lining up to buy my shoes?"

"More feet, more shoes," she'd respond.

"More shoemakers," Aaron Lev would mumble. He was not of the opinion that cities offered opportunity to Jews. Not the cities of the Russian pale. Montreal, maybe, where Yehuda seemed to be making a fortune in buttons. New York, of course. And wasn't Hershel, Elke Leah's son, making a nice way for himself in Liverpool? He had changed his name to Henry and had managed to learn a thing or two about scrap metal.

"So we'll move to Liverpool, then," Tsila would say, to which Aaron Lev would shake his head. Great leaps such as those might offer opportunity, but they were for men more agile than Aaron Lev, who, at thirty-four, already felt old and tired. His own ambition, he would tell Bayla, was to get out of shoemaking altogether and become a dealer in fruit. Not for any increase in riches—he was resigned to a life of limited means—but for the pleasure such a change might bring to his working days.

Tsila would sigh.

He was tired of feet, he would tell her. He was tired of leather too, a substance that filled him, more and more, with visions of death. As he stretched and nailed his strips of rawhide, he caught himself longing for the soft curve of a peach in his hand, the fragrance of apricots, the hard, shining flesh of ripe cherries.

"Who said anything about them moving to Bialystok?" Tsila asked me sharply now. "What have you heard?"

It was Rivka who had suggested that maybe Bayla and Leib would depart for Bialystok after the wedding. We were standing together in line to buy bagels from Freyde at the market.

"What wedding?" Freyde asked from behind her basket of bagels. "I'll believe it when I hear the glass shatter."

"He's from Bialystok, after all," Rivka went on, ignoring Freyde's comment. "Why would they settle here, a young couple like that? I've heard he has a degree in pedagogy."

"Never mind where he's from or his fancy degrees," Freyde droned. "So-called teachers like him have no homes. They move around like wild seeds, sowing discontent."

"What, *so called?*" another customer asked. "A cousin of mine attends his classes after work and says he's a good teacher. A good man."

Freyde shrugged. "I heard the mother's cousin managed to find her some nice men. Fine men. Was there not a scholar among them?"

All eyes turned to me. "She didn't like him," I told them. Chippa had unearthed a disciple of a great rabbi in Lithuania for Bayla—a *gaon,* Chippa had intimated, but widowed twice already by the age of twenty-five. Bayla had shaken her head in refusal and walked out of the room.

"The Hero should have put his foot down then and there," Freyde said to much nodding among her female customers. "Merchants and scholars he allowed her to turn away, but an agitator—that he decided to give his blessing to."

"How was the Hero to know?" someone asked. "The cousin said he was a teacher."

"He *is* a teacher," said the cousin of Leib's student. "Since when is teaching the alphabet and a bit of history agitation?"

"A man who knows he's going to land himself in jail shouldn't take himself a wife," someone said.

"I don't see him rushing to marry her," Freyde pointed out.

"A man never knows where his life will land him," Rivka said. "Should they all therefore stop marrying?"

"And anyway," someone pointed out, "these days a man is arrested for the way his nose sits on his face."

"Only if he displays it," Freyde droned.

"WHAT DID YOU HEAR IN TOWN?" TSILA PRODDED ME.

"Nothing, really. I just thought that since Leib's from Bialystok . . ." But Tsila's eyes were too hot upon me. "Freyde said Leib's an agitator."

"She said what?"

I repeated what I had heard, incurring more of Tsila's anger.

"And did you say nothing in his defense?" she asked.

"I don't know Leib."

"Who said you had to know him? Didn't you tell them he's a teacher?"

"Someone else did."

"And you said nothing? You just stood there like a lump of a girl while those *yentas* were discussing your own family . . . ?"

"Calm yourself, Tsila," my father said. "What difference is it to us or to Leib what the likes of Freyde think?"

"What *difference*?" Tsila asked, but there was something else in my father's tone that caught her attention. "It's not just Freyde who says it, is it?" she asked my father.

"There's talk," he acknowledged.

"Talk like that in the wrong set of ears can ruin a life," Tsila said, then turning to me: "He's a teacher," she said. "A man with high values. That's what you tell those *yentas,* do you hear me? A teacher." She shook her head in annoyance. "The man teaches people to read. That makes him an agitator?" She looked at me and my father in turn, but neither of us dared answer. "If Leib is an agitator, then Aaron Lev is the Messiah himself. That's what you tell those chattering mouths. Do you understand me?"

My father smiled at that, then Tsila smiled too. "God forbid it should turn out that you are what our people have been waiting for all these years," Tsila said.

"From your mouth to God's ears," my father agreed.

WITH BAYLA, HOWEVER, TSILA TOOK A DIFFERENT AP-
proach. "Do you know what people are starting to say about this Leib
of yours?" she asked when Bayla came for her fitting a few days later.

Bayla didn't answer.

"They're saying he's an agitator. That he's going to land himself
in jail."

Bayla still didn't answer but shrugged her shoulders as if such an
eventuality was of little concern to her. "Since when have you started to
bother yourself with gossip?" she asked.

"Since the consequences of it became a threat to my sister's life."

"My life is not in danger," Bayla answered.

"Your happiness is."

"My happiness?" Bayla asked. "What do you know of my
happiness?"

"Nothing," Tsila admitted. "Absolutely nothing. And do you know
why? Because you no longer speak to me. Since you've taken up with
this beloved Leib of yours, you've cut me out of your life entirely."

"I haven't," Bayla started to protest, but Tsila interrupted.

"Oh, yes. All your life it was me you talked to. Every little problem,
every little heartache, I listened, I helped you. I was happy to do it. I'm
your older sister. But then you meet this man, this mysterious man
whom I haven't even met yet—do you realize it's two years since your
supposed engagement and you haven't once brought him to meet
me?—and all of a sudden a wall comes down. Your wall, not mine."

"It's not that . . ." Bayla tried to explain but Tsila waved her
quiet.

"Still, you're my sister," Tsila continued. "I dare to think I may still
know a little bit about you. I dare to think I'm not being overly pre-
sumptuous in assuming that if this Leib of yours is arrested and exiled
to God knows where, that might interfere in some small way with your
happiness."

Bayla waited to see if Tsila was finished, and when it was clear that she was, Bayla nodded her head. "He's a teacher, Tsila," she said slowly. "He teaches people to read and to think. Might he land himself in jail? That I don't know. These days a man is arrested for the way his nose sits on his face."

It was the same statement I had heard from the customer at Freyde's stall.

"Only if he displays it," I said.

"Hush, Miriam," Tsila chided me, but Bayla turned to me and asked if I would have my father trim his beard or uncover his head or not display his *tsitsis*. "To be a Jew and display it is dangerous too, you know," she said.

Tsila bit the piece of thread she'd been pulling through the brocade. "I have a bad feeling," she said.

"Now you sound like all the other *bubbies* with their omens and premonitions," Bayla said. The two sisters locked eyes for a moment, neither speaking, then Tsila looked away.

"Come," Tsila said with a sigh. She held up the half-finished dress. "Let's see how it looks."

The material Tsila held up was so substantial in form, and Bayla such a stick of a girl, it was hard to imagine how she wouldn't break under the weight of it. Bayla took the brocade from Tsila and turned to the wall to remove her blouse and skirt.

"Sometimes I feel I should be sewing a shroud out of this brocade for all the joy this marriage is going to bring."

"What?" Bayla wheeled around to face her sister. "How could you say that? Don't even think that!"

"Two years you've been engaged and I've never even met the man. So in love you're supposed to be that not a word about him has passed your lips, and I have to wait for Miriam to come running home from the market to learn anything about him. I have a bad feeling . . . ," Tsila said again.

"I've had enough of your bad feelings for one day," Bayla said firmly, but she too looked pale and a little shaken. She turned around for Tsila to pin up the back of the dress. Tsila, however, made no move toward her sister.

"Take off the dress," Tsila said. "It's not for you."

"Stop it," Bayla said, remaining where she was with the back of the dress open, revealing a V-shaped expanse of her back. "If I took every unpleasant feeling I experienced to be an omen of sorts . . ."

I had not known until then that a back could be as expressive as a face. I saw a resolve in Bayla's slight, straight back that her milky face had only recently begun to reveal.

"Turn now," Tsila said, her voice still weaker than usual. Bayla's pale skin glowed against the dark fabric like fresh fallen snow that glows against the night. Her narrow shoulders and upright spine were not only able to carry the fabric but seemed to subdue it so it followed her form like the softest silk.

Tsila smiled in satisfaction, despite herself. "It suits you," she said, the highest compliment I had heard her pay anyone. "I wouldn't have known beforehand."

Bayla smiled weakly in return. "I can only hope there's much you don't know."

IT WAS THE FOLLOWING WEEK THAT SARA GRABBED MY arm just as I was leaving the market to head back up the hill to my home. "There's something going to happen soon that we can't miss," she said. It was May Day and there was to be a demonstration by the main bridge in town, right before sundown.

My heart stopped in my chest. A demonstration? Right in town? I couldn't go to a demonstration. The police were known to ride into the crowds at such events, beating and arresting those present. "I can't," I said. "Tsila will kill me."

"She won't even know. Tell her we're taking a walk."

"I can't."

"If you can't, you can't. Far be it from me to get you into trouble at home." We walked a few steps in silence. "It's too bad, though," she said after a while. "I've heard Golda will be there to address the crowd."

"Golda from the strike?"

"Who else?" Sara answered, a smile widening on her face. Golda was the girl leader of the strike at the match factory in Mozyr the previous winter. Unlike Palefsky, the male leader who had been found hiding in the slaughterhouse and arrested, she still remained at large.

"How do you know?" I asked.

"I've heard," Sara answered.

Golda was from Kalinkovich. Her mother was a hatmaker, her father a cantor who didn't speak to his family so as to save his voice for holiness. It was said that without Golda the women at the factory would not have agreed to the strike that previous winter. It was said too that she always carried a pistol. My fears about Tsila's anger fell away at the prospect of laying eyes on such a girl.

The sun was setting as we reached the bridge. A crowd had already gathered. I recognized a few faces, but many were strangers. Access to the bridge itself was barred by a chain of young men with linked arms. They wore black shirts with red woven belts and carried rods made of iron.

"Who are they?" I whispered to Sara.

"Workers," she whispered back. "Bundists."

I recognized one of them, a tall, well-built man with masses of thick black hair. It was the man I had encountered in the swamp two summers previous when I returned there on Shabbes to gather reeds for Tsila.

"Look," Sara said, pointing to the very man I recognized. "That's Leib Zalman, whose cousin Yehuda married the daughter of our very own capitalist, Lazer Entelman."

"That's Leib?" I repeated. "Leib who's engaged to Bayla?"

"The very one," Sara answered. Then she bent to whisper in my ear. "He's in love with Golda," she whispered.

I barely had time to react to what Sara had told me when the crowd started murmuring and pointing. At the outside edge of the crowd appeared four young men. Like their comrades they wore black shirts and red belts, but instead of iron rods they carried two barrels of the sort that were usually filled with pickles or herring. The crowd parted to allow their passage, and the chain of workers momentarily opened to admit them to the bridge. Once there they set down the two barrels and laid a plank of wood upon them.

They were followed by a young woman, a religious housewife in a long skirt, her head modestly covered with a kerchief. Before I had time to wonder who she was, two of the men had lifted her onto the board of wood. I recognized her then, even before she tore off the kerchief to address the crowd. It was the woman whom I'd seen in the swamp. *My little Golda,* her companion—Leib—had affectionately called her. She was small and wiry, standing alone on her platform with her short-cropped hair and sallow complexion, but she vibrated with energy, and her eyes animated not only her own face but the faces in the crowd that they lit upon.

What she said, I barely remember, so taken was I with my own excitement. The speech was in Yiddish with Russian words thrown in here and there.

"What's an exploiter?" someone beside me asked.

"A capitalist," Sara answered.

"A deceiver," someone else said.

Golda continued speaking, but what she said didn't matter. It was her eyes that captured me, eyes so brilliant that each time they lit on me I felt a new shiver of excitement rush through my body.

"Down with the autocracy!" she shouted finally, her right arm punching the air.

"Down with Tsar Nicholas!" the crowd shouted. "Long live the revolution! Long live the Bund of Poland, Russia, and Lithuania!" the workers shouted, their chain unlinked now as they too raised their right arms to punch the evening air. When I looked back at the bridge, Golda and her makeshift platform had disappeared. The crowd began to sing the *Shevuo*—the Oath—but the minute the song ended, the workers in their black shirts and red sashes disappeared. The crowd too began to disperse.

"We have to clear out quickly," Sara warned, hurrying me along. "We don't want to be here when the police arrive."

Siberia, August 1911

Last night we were supposed to discuss our political awakenings. That was the planned topic for the discussion we have as part of every evening meal: the moment each of us awakened to social injustice and the events that led us to devote ourselves to revolution. But like so much else in our lives, it didn't proceed as planned.

It had been a difficult day. The previous evening Lydia had returned from her regular visit to the criminal cells—she was a medical student before her arrest and has been granted permission to attend to the criminal women. "There's illness there," she reported. A new illness on top of the usual fevers, gastric problems and ailments of the nerves that strike us all with such regularity. A child had died two days earlier and two more were gravely ill. Diphtheria, Lydia feared, and with so many children living in such crowded conditions . . . "The filth in there is indescribable," she said. "I'm afraid of what may be coming."

Around our cell noses rose from their books, and eyes weakened by years of dim lighting squinted in concentration.

"A doctor must be called," Vera said, a comment that hung stupidly in the silence that followed. Even getting permission for Lydia to continue her ministrations has taken enormous will and effort. But there is a streak of optimism in Vera, a seemingly ineradicable faith in inherent goodness waiting to surface, which is alternately a source of great comfort and great irritation to the rest of us.

"And who, exactly, are you expecting to call a doctor?" Lydia finally asked, making no effort to hide her irritation.

It was decided after further discussion that in the absence of a doctor a group of us could at least go with Lydia the next day and offer our assistance. This also is forbidden—contact between criminal and political prisoners is severely restricted—but enforcement of the rules is left entirely to the discretion of the guards, and as we made our way across the prison this morning no one tried to stop us.

There are six cells of prisoners at Maltzev—three for politicals and three for criminals—and while the political cells are simply overcrowded, the conditions in the criminal cells might better be described as infested with humanity. I don't know how many women there are exactly, but when Vera was still permitted to hold classes for the children of these women, she always had about one hundred pupils.

The filth is not, as Lydia had maintained, indescribable. I can describe it to you easily. The light is dim and the walls—blackened with soot—add to the impression of gloom. The children are pale and unwashed. They stare out of the dimness, their eyes too wide and, in many cases, streaming with pus. There is vermin everywhere—in the bedding, along the floor and walls, on the heads and bodies of the women and children, at the edges of their eyes. The smell is that of excrement, since five latrines would be insufficient to meet the needs of the crowd and there is, of course, only one per room. To save the floor, buckets—brimming with it—are scattered throughout the room.

And yet this, one woman confided to Lydia—a roof over her head, a bed to sleep in, food of some description every day—is heaven compared to what her life had been on the streets of St. Petersburg.

We intended to spend the day cleaning, in an attempt to improve the sanitation, but the women would not allow it. We are honored ladies to them. *Baryni,* they insist on calling us, to the consternation of my more radical companions. For *baryni* like us to clean their filth would be more shameful than helpful. "Please," they implored us, indicating the table in the center of the room where they wanted us to sit. They served us tea but did allow us to mind the children while they attended to the cleaning.

Meanwhile, one more child had died in the night, and another had fallen ill. But Lydia was less concerned about the possibility of diphtheria. "It's looking more like a throat cold," she decided. A simple cold that, in these conditions, is proving itself deadly.

Quiet and order greeted us when we returned to our own cells: our clean whitewashed walls lined with bookshelves and adorned with postcards, our neatly made beds lined up against the wall, our table in the center of the room where we share companionship, if not wholesome food. Our quarters seemed palatial compared to where we had been, but this afforded us no happiness.

"What was our real motivation for going over there today?" Lydia asked as we gathered around the table for our evening ration of blue grits and bread. "Was it for their sakes, really, or for our own?"

"Don't start," Vera warned. With the questions, she meant. *What is our motivation for this? What is our motivation for that? Were our acts ever truly impelled by the needs of those on whose behalf we claim to have acted? Or were we motivated by some baser need of our own, including the need to believe ourselves selfless?* These are the questions Lydia asks endlessly.

A deep gloom descended on us as Lydia's unanswered question hung in the air. We ate our grits in silence, waiting for Lydia to go on, as she has in the past, about the boredom of the life she had been living on her father's estate—*Was that my motivation, then, boredom?*—the dullness of spirit that she had felt as she stood among her peers at dance after endless dance, waiting for young men to tie the velvet ribbons around her wrists that claimed her for each waltz, mazurka, and reel; the thrill she felt when she first heard her voice addressing a crowd; the excitement as she held a Browning in her hand for the first time. But she said nothing more, just stared dully ahead until, at length, she left the table to retrieve a book of anatomy.

CHAPTER SIX

ON THE EVE OF SHAVUOS OF 1903, I MET UP WITH
Bayla as I was leaving town after running an errand. "I was just on my
way over to see if Tsila needed any help," she said. Tsila was pregnant
at last, a condition she had revealed with great happiness just three
months before. "How is she?" Bayla asked now.

"Fine, I guess." It had been several weeks since I had last seen
Bayla. She almost never came to town anymore. Her work kept her in
Mozyr, she claimed. More likely her shame, Tsila thought. Three years
had now passed since her engagement to Leib and still she was unmarried. "Actually, she's very tired."

I had felt uncomfortable around Bayla ever since Sara's revelation
about Leib's love for Golda. I felt I knew something about her that I
shouldn't and that I was lying, somehow, by not revealing it. Yet I knew
also that revealing it would be even worse than lying. I found it difficult
to look her in the eye. Bayla, though, didn't seem to notice. So preoc-
cupied was she with her own thoughts—thoughts she never revealed—
that she barely looked at me anymore either and didn't ask me anything
about myself. We climbed the hill to my home in silence.

The house was warm and smelled of holiday baking. On the table
was a plate of cookies, the sugar on them melted to burnt caramel by the

heat of the oven. The same cookies Tsila had made the first day I came into her home.

"I just have to finish the *challahs*," Tsila said.

"You sit," Bayla said, taking the goose feather from Tsila's hand. She spread a mix of oil and egg yolk across the braided loaves and put them in the oven. Then she heated chicory and milk and placed three steaming cups on the table.

"You don't have to treat me as if I'm an invalid," Tsila said, but she wrapped her hands happily enough around the warm mug her sister offered and settled in her chair. Bayla sat on the bench by the sewing machine.

"Miriam tells me you're tired."

"A little," Tsila conceded. She was so exhausted she could barely drag herself through her days. "And you?"

"I'm fine," Bayla answered. She started to drink her chicory. "You don't look so well, to be honest."

"Neither do you. To be honest."

"I'm fine," Bayla assured her.

"So am I," Tsila said. Neither of them uttered another word as they sipped their drinks. Several times Bayla sat up straight as if about to say something, but then she sank back in silence.

"Some Shavuos," Tsila finally commented as she peered out the window at the heavy gray sky.

"I don't remember a Shavuos so cold," Bayla agreed.

"There's a rabbi from Slutsk visiting for the holiday," I said. "His son is going to lead the learning tonight."

The son of the Slutsk rabbi had created a stir that morning as he hurried across the market square. He was tall, pale, and still unmarried, and the news quickly circulated that a match was being considered between him and Hadassah, the daughter of the new *shul*'s rabbi. There was an elegance to the young man as he slipped through the narrow passages of our town—his beard was blond and curled softly around his face, his caftan clung to his body, revealing a slender form—and his mind was said to be fierce. The girls of the town fell silent under the weight of their envy of Hadassah. The young man's teaching tonight would be a final test of his mettle before his prospective father-in-law, and all the town waited to hear if an engagement would be announced at the close of the holiday.

All the town but Tsila and Bayla. Neither of them displayed the slightest interest in the news I had brought to them. Tsila had finished her chicory and was staring out the window. Bayla kept sitting up as if to speak, then retreating.

Unable to withstand the tension, I announced finally that I was going to the riverbank to collect the greenery that would decorate our house for the holiday.

"I'll come with you," Bayla said quickly.

Other women were already at the riverbank: Lipsa with five of her children; Freyde with her simple Itche and the two boys she had managed to produce after him; Rivke, the fishmonger's wife—they all wanted to know how Tsila was. Tsila's pregnancy, like her engagement, had caught them by surprise, but they had quickly recovered and seemed to have forgotten that just a few months earlier they had all agreed no seed could possibly sprout in such sour soil as Tsila.

"Tsila's fine," we both answered, but to Lipsa Bayla confided that her sister seemed exhausted and was swelling everywhere but her belly. Though Tsila herself seemed unconcerned, Bayla wondered why Tsila's fingers would swell like sausages while her belly remained flat. And the exhaustion, it seemed to Bayla, was excessive.

"I'll go see her," Lipsa promised, a promise I knew would make Tsila angry.

Bayla smiled and thanked Lipsa, seemingly innocent of her sister's ongoing feud with the woman, and began filling my arms with reeds.

"Do you know why we decorate the house with greenery on Shavuos?" she asked me.

The question surprised me. Since her engagement to Leib, Bayla had become staunchly secular, uninterested in anything to do with religion.

"It's the harvest for the barley and wheat in the Holy Land," I answered.

"And do you know why we stay up all night studying?"

Now I was annoyed as well as surprised. Did she think I was an ignoramus? That her sister taught me nothing? Just a few feet away Lipsa had begun pointing out to her daughters which plants could cure different ailments and which could make barren women fertile. I wanted to listen to that. I wanted to discuss the reeds that Tsila had eaten so much of in previous summers, and my concerns about the questionable quality of some that I had gathered and how that might be affecting the baby, but Bayla was repeating her tedious question about Shavuos.

"We stay up all night learning because we fell asleep at Sinai, so now we want to show God our eagerness to receive the Torah," I said.

Bayla nodded and smiled. Her face was white except for the two red spots burning through her cheeks. "Only, we never really woke up, did we?" she asked. "I mean, any people that stretches its neck out to be slaughtered over and over again is obviously still asleep, no?"

Bayla's words had a startling effect. No sooner were they out of her mouth than a strange stillness overtook the assembled women. They seemed to have frozen in their places, even their tongues momentarily stilled, as if Bayla's words were like a powder she'd concocted at the pharmacy that in falling upon women's ears had the power to induce paralysis.

Rivka was the first to find her voice. "Do you think such talk is fit for the ears of children?" she asked.

The children present had all heard such talk before, of course. News of the Kishenev pogrom had reached our town just after Pesach, and although we had not seen trouble like that in many years and relations with our gentile neighbors were friendly enough, there was fear in the town and talk of starting a defense group.

"Since when have any of you ever hesitated to speak the truth to children?" Bayla asked. No one present would admit to such a failing, but Freyde thought to answer that the only truth she spoke to her children was Torah.

Bayla nodded and turned a serious face to Freyde. "And is there anywhere in the Torah that speaks against defending one's own life and the lives of one's children?"

It was an unfair question. The assembled women, though pious, were not well versed in the specifics of Torah. They lived Torah, of course, but they didn't learn it. So common sense had to prevail, and what Bayla said did make sense. Wasn't the saving of life the highest value? Were there not tales recounted in the Torah of our people having to defend themselves against invaders and attackers? Were there not imprecations against the dreaded Amalek and calls to battle against the likes of Haman? The women began to nod and talk amongst themselves. What Bayla had said was not so outrageous, they agreed, though God willing, it should not come to pass that such a defense group would be needed in our town.

By the time we had finished gathering our reeds, a peaceful holiday feeling prevailed again. "Good Yonteff," they wished us as we prepared to leave. "And to Tsila too," they added as we began to climb back up the hill.

A cold drizzle had begun to fall. Bayla looked at me worriedly, then removed her coat and placed it on my shoulders.

"You'll get wet," I protested.

"Hush now."

I didn't argue further. She looked so tall and straight that it seemed nothing, let alone rain, could harm her, and I, on the other hand, was already feeling chilled. I pulled the coat closer around me but only felt colder and colder.

"I'm leaving," she told me. "That's why I came over today. To tell Tsila."

"Leaving?" I asked.

"With Leib."

"For Bialystok?"

"Bialystok? Why would we be going to Bialystok?"

"Leib's from there."

"Where a person is from is less important than where he's going," she told me.

"Where's Leib going?" I asked.

Bayla smiled. "I'm not speaking in a literal sense. I mean that the future is more important than the past. As a people we've tended to dwell on the past and ignore the future. For centuries we've done that, and where has it gotten us?" Bayla swept her hand dramatically to encompass the scene around us. It was a particularly bleak day. "Leib and I are moving forward," she said firmly.

"When?" I asked.

"Tomorrow."

"On Shavuos? You're going to travel on Shavuos?"

Bayla smiled. "On the evening train."

We walked in silence while I digested her news.

"I've never been on a train," I said after a while.

"I've only been once."

"What's it like?"

"Fast," she said. "So fast you can hardly see what flies by your window. Entire villages sweep into view, then fall away before you have time to blink an eye."

I thought, in contrast, of the huge, slow oxen that lumbered along our muddy rows and lanes, our horse-drawn carts, and I felt a restless curiosity quicken within me. "If you wait until after the holiday, I'll come to the station to see you off," I told her.

Bayla tousled my hair affectionately. "I'm afraid my sister is not so fond of the course I've chosen that she'd come to the station to bid me farewell."

"Then I'll go with my father."

"Your father?" Her laughter stung me. Why not my father? He was working for Noam the teamster again, departing every morning for the Kalinkovich station in a wagon made of oak, with thick iron wheels. "You think an exploiter like Noam would allow your father to carry you back and forth to Kalinkovich?" Bayla asked.

That I couldn't answer. I was a little afraid of Noam for reasons I couldn't explain. He was not an overly large man, but our house always seemed uncomfortably crowded when he stepped inside it. One time he'd stood in the doorway looking me over. It was mud season—there were splatters of it up and down his high boots and leather leggings. Even his whip was splattered. He hadn't come in or gone out; he had just stood there for the longest time looking at me. "Not much like her mother, is she?" he'd commented finally. My father hadn't answered but had instinctively shifted his posture in such a way that his body blocked me from Noam's sight.

"Your father's not one to stand up to the likes of Noam," Bayla said.

"LEAVING?" TSILA ASKED. "WHAT DO YOU MEAN, LEAVing?"

Bayla colored slightly.

"Oh, I see now. Where's he dragging you to?"

"He's not dragging me."

"Where's he going?"

"That I can't tell you."

"Of course not. You can't tell me anything anymore. Not what you think, not what you do, not what you feel about this great fiancé of yours who continues to humiliate you. But maybe you can tell me this: does he even want you to follow?"

"Of course he does."

Tsila snorted. "I'll believe that when I've danced at your wedding."

"Then I'll have to make do without your belief, since I'm leaving tomorrow."

Tsila, for once, was stunned to silence. "Tomorrow?" she finally managed to utter. "Unmarried?"

Bayla didn't answer.

"You're leaving with him, unmarried?"

"It's just for a short while," Bayla said gently, but Tsila's tongue had already recovered its sharpness.

"You prefer to be abandoned in a strange city where no one cares whether you live or starve?"

"He won't abandon me," Bayla answered.

Tsila nodded without seeming to agree.

"Try not to worry so much," said Bayla in a tone suddenly soft with affection. She reached over to stroke her sister's cheek. Tsila waved her away.

"Will you want your wedding dress?" I asked. It still lay in a pile of fabrics by Tsila's chair. Bayla turned to me. "I don't think I'll need it," she said softly. "Maybe Tsila can save it for you."

I looked at Tsila but her expression was blank. Sorrow, I know now. I've seen enough faces mirroring an emptiness inside to recognize that vacant expression on Tsila's face, but I hadn't then. Tsila's gaze floated without focus and her hands, usually so busy, did something I had never seen them do: they pressed idly at the tabletop. Ten fingers, swollen as sausages, pressed uselessly against the wood grain of the table.

MOST WOMEN WOULD HAVE DISCARDED THE BROCADE after Bayla left. There was no longer any question as to the luck it carried. At *shul* the next Shabbes Freyde said it should be burned and its ashes buried outside of town. Rivka reminded her that rare was the dressmaker who could afford to burn such a fine material. It was true, Rivka conceded, that maybe it shouldn't be kept as a dress, particularly for a bride, but there were other purposes to which it could be put. An armchair, perhaps, window shades. Freyde said she wouldn't have such bad luck hanging as shades in any home of hers.

"I'll wear it to *my* wedding," I said.

"You'll wear something luckier," Lipsa said to me, and gave my arm a reassuring pat. "Where's your stepmother?" she asked. She had come by to see Tsila a few days earlier but Tsila hadn't let her in.

"She's not feeling well," I explained. "She's at her mother's."

"And your friend Sara?"

"Also not well," I said, reluctant to divulge Sara's decision, since Kishenev, that she was an atheist.

"So you'll sit with me," Lipsa said as she shifted a little to make a tiny space next to her on the bench. I wedged myself in.

"My father is worried about Tsila," I confided to Lipsa in a whisper. "The swelling."

The swelling in Tsila's fingers had spread to her legs, her neck . . . everywhere, it seemed, except her belly. The local midwife, Dvoire, had come and gone, having done nothing but purse her lips and dispense a few herbs that had not helped.

Our Dvoire was a kind enough woman but neither intuitive nor skilled at the business of bringing babies into the world, which was why Lipsa's Rohel and other young women went to other towns for their midwife apprenticeships. No one said anything aloud, but there were murmurings about how many births went wrong in our town, and more than one woman in childbirth had seen the Angel of Death peering out through Dvoire's eyes as she ministered to them. It was for this reason that my father took me aside as I was drawing water from our storage barrel to ask if maybe Lipsa shouldn't be called again to look in on Tsila. His tone, confiding and worried, was no longer one of an adult addressing a child.

I didn't answer right away. We both knew how Tsila had reacted to Lipsa's first visit and neither of us cared to face her anger. Rosa too seemed to resent Lipsa's presence, as if it implied that her own ministrations were insufficient. But there was no question that something was going wrong with Tsila's pregnancy, and Lipsa, though untrained, was the one person we knew who could coax life from the embrace of death. "I'll speak to her in *shul,*" I promised my father.

"YOU'RE EATING?" LIPSA ASKED TSILA WHEN SHE ARrived the next morning. Tsila had been surprised to see Lipsa at her door again, but not angry. Her fingers were so swollen that she could not hold a needle. This worried her enough that she entreated Lipsa to come in.

"Of course I'm eating," Tsila said. "Do you think I would try to starve him?"

Lipsa pulled on Tsila's eyelids until she could see the red underneath. "Eggs and milk are important. You're eating eggs and milk?"

Tsila assured her that she was.

"And sleeping?"

"Sleeping is more difficult," Tsila said. "He presses on me so."

Lipsa felt the hard flatness of Tsila's abdomen and pursed her lips as Dvoire had done. "Do you dream?" she asked.

"How can I dream when I hardly sleep?"

"What do you see in your dreams?" Lipsa asked.

"Fish," Tsila said.

"Fish?" Lipsa pursed her lips again. "What sort of fish?"

"All sorts. Carp, herring, whitefish . . ."

A sharp intake of breath from Lipsa. "On a platter?" she asked.

"No, swimming."

"Ah . . . swimming," Lipsa exhaled, her face relaxing for the first time since she'd begun her examination. "Good," she said. "Very good."

Lipsa pressed her fingers behind Tsila's ears and along the glands in her neck, then she took Tsila's hand in hers and pressed on the swollen knuckles and fingers. "This is why you're dreaming of fish. All this water . . . he probably thinks he's in a river. You're drinking dandelion tea for the swelling?"

"A little," Tsila said.

"Forget a little. You have to drink a lot. Whenever you can manage a swallow, you should be drinking. And aside from that you need to rest more." Lipsa began rummaging in her bag for the herbs she had brought with her.

"Rest more? How can I rest more? Who will put food on our table?"

"Does Noam no longer pay Aaron Lev a wage?"

"Not enough of one," Tsila snapped.

Lipsa looked up from her herbs. "And you must try to turn your thoughts from unpleasantness. Otherwise the river your baby swims in will become a sea of bitterness."

But as Lipsa said that her eyes shifted—as if they were pulled without her accord—to an unpleasantness that could not be avoided or pushed from one's mind: the cobalt brocade that lay in an unfinished heap in the pile by Tsila's chair. She forced her eyes back to Tsila without asking if we'd had any word from Bayla. We had not, and the entire town knew it.

"Miriam should be helping out now," Lipsa said.

"She helps," Tsila answered, and then: "Despite what others might think about me, I'm not about to sacrifice my stepdaughter's education for the sake of my own baby."

"Who's talking about sacrifice?" Lipsa asked. "She can read, can she not?"

The widow Ida had received a letter two days ago, Lipsa said, an official letter that might well reveal the whereabouts of her son, Moishe.

"No child I've raised is taking money from a poor widow," Tsila said.

"Better the poor widow should sit alone day after day with a letter she can't read?"

"Miriam will read it for her. She'll go over right now and read it to Ida, but for no payment."

"And deny Ida her pride?"

Tsila didn't answer.

"Deny an old woman the one thing she has left in the world, a bit of pride?"

A few kopecks, then, Tsila agreed, but just a very few, and only to save Ida's pride.

And Mrs. Entelman was said to be rising less and less often from her bed, Lipsa said, so crushed was she by Shendel's departure to Montreal. Wouldn't she benefit from some company a few hours a week?

Tsila stared at Lipsa open-mouthed, her cheeks coloring with anger. "No child of mine is taking money to sit with the lonely."

"Who said she'll sit?" Lipsa asked. "Do you think a woman of that standing would accept the company of a poor girl like Miriam without pretending there are chores that need doing?"

"I didn't raise her to be a maid," Tsila responded, and that might have been the end of it were it not for what came of my assistance to Ida. The widow Ida's was the last hut in town before the rise up to our home. Hers was a particularly poor dwelling, with cardboard in the windows instead of glass, an earthen floor, and a thatched roof that was black with rot. Inside it was dark, even on a summer afternoon, so it took a few moments for me to make out the lay of the room. Ida was seated by the stove, in the one chair in the room. Other than her chair and stove there was a table and a curtain, behind which, I knew, was the bed. There was no place for me to sit, so I stood, only a weak lamp to read by, so I held the letter in the open doorway.

Moishe, Ida's beloved son, had been arrested ten years earlier. His crime centered on the silver candlesticks that had always occupied a place of honor in his mother's home. A gift from Ida's own mother, they were the one possession of value that Ida had managed to retain through the hard years of raising her children following her husband's death. They sat in the center of her table, their brightness comforting the eye in that dark room. She polished them every Thursday in honor of the Sabbath's approach, and it was a point of pride for her that even in her reduced circumstances she could usher in the Sabbath with the style and beauty befitting the visit of a bride. It was therefore a point of particular humiliation for Moishe when he heard that the tax collector, seeking his arrears, had forced his way into his mother's home, scanned the room for something of value, then swept the candlesticks into his bag.

Moishe was not known as a hothead. He was a steady youth who had worked at one of Entelman's lumbering operations since he was old enough to handle an axe. But when he heard what had just happened at his mother's, he threw his axe down and strode purposefully into town.

Ida tried to calm him, she later told the women at the market. She feared the look in his eye. "What are a pair of candlesticks?" she asked. Material objects. What was the material in life compared to the spiritual? Was it not the feeling in one's heart that mattered most when welcoming the Sabbath bride? Still, as she spoke, she was surprised how broken her heart felt by the loss of those candlesticks, a gift from her mother when she was a bride herself and full of hope for her future. And when Moishe saw the pain in his mother's eyes, he marched out of her home toward Markowitz's tavern, where the tax collector was enjoying a meal before departing our town for the next. The candlesticks were in the man's satchel—easy to remove—and for this crime against the government, Moishe received a sentence of ten years hard labor, ten years that were now coming to an end.

Moishe would be twenty-nine now, no longer a youth but not too old to start his life again, a family. The letter that Ida thrust into my hands the moment I appeared at her door contained the possibility of good news she had waited ten long years to hear. I opened it with a flourish, warm with the importance of the moment and my own role in escorting in the happiness of another. It was obvious from my first glance at the letter, however, that the news it contained was not good, and that rather than performing an act of kindness by reading its contents, I was about to remove the last shred of hope from a woman's life. The sentence was served. That much the letter acknowledged. But to read those words aloud, fleetingly raising hopes, when the very next line informed the reader of the death of the prisoner—a number, followed by the name, Moishe's name—this I couldn't do. I stood silently for a moment, and in that silence the content of the letter revealed itself to Ida without my reading a word.

"Tell me," she said. "I want to know how and when."

But that too was denied her. The letter didn't say.

She nodded her comprehension. "Go now," she said, and maybe I would have had it not been for the next sound to rise out of her throat, a cry so like a tearing, a rending of muscle and flesh, that I instinctively encircled her with my arms to hold her together. The cries continued, accompanied soon by a shuddering, a terrible vibrating from within, as if the grief inside her was lashing itself against the walls of her body. I held her tighter, fearing the fragility of her body's frame—the brittle cage of her ribs, the soft aging flesh. How could it withstand the violence of her grief? We stayed like that, I don't know how long, my smaller body absorbing her vibrating shudders, until a pressure on my shoulder, Lipsa's firm touch, released my arms and she took Ida into her own.

Ida's cries had reached beyond the walls of her home and comforters were coming now, singly and in pairs. I did not want to be seen—the messenger of grief and death—and started up the hill to my home.

It was night by then, a humid night, filled with the buzzes and saws of insects. There was no moon, the road was utterly dark. I walked slowly, exhausted by the day's events. My arms ached, a dull heaviness that spread to my shoulders and seeped into the cavity of my chest. My legs felt heavy too, each step an effort, as if walking through water or a dream. I smelled cigarette smoke, a curl of it wafting through that thick darkness. I knew then that I wasn't alone, but, strangely, I was unafraid. I walked slowly, quietly, aware of another's presence, a silent presence, unwilling to identify itself with sound or movement, just that thin curl of smoke snaking through the heavy air.

Then he was beside me. I smelled his clamminess, the rot of him. I stopped in my tracks but saw nothing, heard nothing. He was still there, I could smell him, but when I reached my hand out I felt only air. Go! I knew I should say in a firm, strong voice. That was the way Lipsa spoke to the dead. They must always be aware of your strength, she had told me. But at that moment I felt no strength, only the heaviness of my limbs, the exhaustion of that day and all the days that had preceded it. Now I heard his voice, a soft, urgent whisper, but I couldn't make out his words. Go! I knew I should tell him, but my tongue was too heavy in my mouth, my head too heavy on my neck. The air thickened around me and I couldn't take another step, so I lay down in the soft, moist earth by the side of the road.

In utter darkness I lay, overcome but not unaware. I heard noises—soft, even breathing above me, the fall of footsteps on the road, the calling of my name. I might have answered, but the air around me was thick as water and closed around me like a seal. I was alone then, utterly alone; even my thoughts had flown from my head.

How long I lay there I don't know, but eventually there was a light. A harsh light more blinding than illuminating, yet as I clenched my eyes against it, it returned my other senses to me. I became aware of a noise, a clatter different and apart from the far-off noises I'd been hearing. It was my own teeth clattering against each other. Bile filled my mouth. I spat and at once felt the dampness of the earth against my back, the stiffness of my neck, my own hands lying inert beside me. I raised one hand from the dirt to cover my eyes, to shield them from the light that pried so painfully beneath their lids. A strong hand grabbed mine then, a warm hand, my father's. It pulled me to my feet, then his two arms enclosed me, drawing me to the warmth of his body.

I could not explain what had happened. I sat wrapped in the blanket Tsila threw around me after removing my wet, soiled dress. "No one hurt me," I said, and my body, under Tsila's careful inspection, revealed no wounds. I drank the cherry brandy my father gave me and told them about Ida. They watched me as I spoke, Tsila's eyes sharp, my father's soft as mud. I told them about Ida's cries of grief, the convulsive shudders that had risen out of her and threatened to break her apart, the darkness of the road, the exhaustion that overtook me, the sudden clamminess of the air. "Did Moishe smoke?" I asked.

"Hush now," Tsila said.

"Was it Moishe I met on the road?"

"Shush," Tsila said, placing her hand on my mouth to halt any further flow of words. It was my imagination I had encountered on the road, Tsila said, not Moishe. The dead didn't go for strolls down the road. I'd smelled the smoke of a cigarette, had I not? Since when did the dead smoke? The dead didn't smoke. The living did. The broad-shouldered men who stood in clusters in the market, along the road, outside Markowitz's tavern—that's who smoked. Young men like the one Moishe had been, lumberers and carpenters with their caps at jaunty angles and a cigarette always dangling from their lips—that's who I had encountered on the road. My own imagination. My own vision of who Moishe had once been. But Tsila shuddered despite herself, afraid perhaps that it might indeed have been death I'd encountered on the road to our house when the birth of her own child was so near.

My father, meanwhile, had not removed his eyes from my face. He watched me without blinking, without glancing away, as if in raising me from the earth in which I had lain he had noticed something that had escaped him until then. "Imagination in itself is no sin," he said, "but it has to be turned toward good."

"Do you choose to turn your heart toward death?" Tsila asked, her voice rising in frustration. "Do you choose to squander your life in this world yearning for the next? There are people like that, you know. The graveyard is full of them. Shall I take you tomorrow to see them?"

She read an answer from my face.

"Then enough with your fainting fits," she said. "Enough with your nonsense." She took my chin in her hand and brought her face close to mine. I smelled the clean health of her, felt the bracing sharpness of her gaze. "Lift yourself now," she commanded me. "You're a big girl, almost a woman. It's time you lift yourself from the grave of your own morbidity."

CHAPTER SEVEN

MY EXPERIENCE HAD FRIGHTENED TSILA. WHERE once she would have shaken it off, refusing to submit to superstitious fears and premonitions, the presence of another life within her had made her more vulnerable to those fears. Swollen with a pregnancy that was not going as it should, she felt painfully aware of all that she didn't understand in the universe and the many harms she was powerless to prevent. It was not just to raise me from my own morbidity that she decided to send me out to work, but to free her own house of it for a few hours a day.

I knew this as I left the house the following Sunday, and I half expected Mrs. Entelman to turn me out as well, preferring her own loneliness to the morbidity that Tsila had accused me of, a morbidity that both she and my father had likened to a kernel of evil that I carried within myself. Mrs. Entelman, though, seemed delighted to see me. Would I be a dear and bring her the valerian drops from the bureau, she asked as soon as Ghitel, the maid who had escorted me upstairs, left us alone. "I would get them myself, of course . . . ," and she immediately began talking.

It wasn't merely Shendel's departure that had felled her, despite what I had heard. Certainly she missed the girl. Who wouldn't miss such a daughter, she asked. Of course she'd wept bitterly—would I be a dear and change the cloth on her forehead? No, never mind; this would do for now.

"Of course I long for my daughter, but take a look at me lying here . . ."

Her face was pinched, though her color was good.

"Does mere longing reduce a woman to this?"

That I couldn't answer. I had only begun to guess at the feats longing could accomplish.

"No, it doesn't," Mrs. Entelman said. "Longing, when it's pure, drains tears from the eyes and joy from the heart, but it's only when it's twisted by anger and regret . . ." She paused now. "And to think we rejoiced at the match. Mr. Entelman as well, and he's no fool, my husband, as anyone in town can attest."

So it was Yehuda, then, I thought, something in the marriage.

"And to hear now that Bayla is also in the clutches of that family . . . oh, that sweet girl," Mrs. Entelman moaned. "I hear Rosa and Avram blame us for the match," she said, glancing at me only long enough to confirm her fears. "If they would only talk to me—do you know they've stopped talking to me now?"

I nodded. How could I not? The whole town knew that Rosa and Avram turned their backs when anyone related to the Entelmans walked past them.

"They blame us as if we knew something about the Zalmans and didn't let on, but if they would only come talk to me . . . has the family heard anything from Bayla?"

"Nothing," I said.

"Not even if he's married her yet?"

Even that information had not reached our ears.

"If they would only come see me, they would know I'm every bit as heartsick as they are. More heartsick. Look at my condition compared to theirs. Do they even know the condition I'm in?" She glanced at me to confirm that I would tell them. "They blame me for the loss of their daughter, but have they forgotten they have four other daughters? Four beautiful, healthy daughters, and a grandchild on the way." She spit three times to distract the evil eye's attention from the pregnancy she had just mentioned. "Not to take away from their pain—but compared to mine, a sickly woman like me losing the only flesh that could warm her old age . . ."

"You're not old," I rushed to assure her. Her face, beneath her sick-room bonnet, was unlined, and her hands were as smooth and un-marked as her daughter's.

"*Feh!*" she responded. "I'm a dried-up old woman doomed to spend the rest of my days lying alone in the dark, rotting like a dog."

It was hard to follow everything Mrs. Entelman said. The lying alone part, for one thing. The house seemed to have an inexhaustible supply of servants who appeared at regular intervals to see if there was anything Mrs. Entelman might need. And the darkness she spoke of— the house was as light-filled as I remembered it, even without Shendel to enhance it. And as for the comment about her rotting like a dog—but there was no time to ponder whether dogs rotted more readily than hu-mans, as Mrs. Entelman was now explaining the curse that Yehuda had laid on her when he returned to drag Shendel away.

"Shendel was sobbing," Mrs. Entelman explained. "She did not want to go—I don't need to tell you that. She was clinging to me, both arms like this . . ." Mrs. Entelman demonstrated by flinging her own arms around my neck, drenching me with the scent of lilac. "Yehuda, meanwhile, looked puzzled, feigning confusion as to the source of the tears. 'What?' he kept asking in that unctuous voice of his. You've heard his voice? 'Tell me, Shendel, please,' he begged. And to think it was that voice that charmed us just a few years earlier, and Bayla's parents too. 'You'll have a new home,' he promised her. 'And built of solid stone. That's how they build houses in Canada. Out of stone and brick. None of this wood that goes up in flames at every whim of nature.' Did you ever hear of such a thing? Nature he ascribes whim to, that unbeliever, as if the Almighty is a mere handservant of the very forces that He Himself created. 'With a wrought-iron gate,' he continued, 'and electric lights that go on with a flick of the finger, and indoor toilets, and water you can drink from a tap without dying of typhus.' As if anyone has died of typhus around here in recent years—not to take away from your loss. I knew your grandparents, may they rest in peace. Lovely people, all of them.

"Shendel wasn't much comforted by his promises. Why would she be? 'My mother,' she wept, throwing herself on me again. 'I'll give you children,' he answered, as if the future erased the need for a past.

" 'But Shendel's roots are here,' I said to him. 'Will you tear her out and then wonder why she withers?' To which he fixed a cold eye on me, the same eye that just three short years ago was all obsequiousness and twinkling. 'Shendel is not one of your husband's trees,' he said to me, as if I could not differentiate my daughter from a sapling. 'Trees have roots, Jews have legs.' That's what he said to me, the *khokhem.* "

Why such a statement—hardly an original or shocking observation—should have *felled her,* as she put it, was a mystery much discussed in the lower part of town. No one knew the answer, but it was then, as those words passed his lips, that the strength passed from her legs. "One moment I'm standing by my daughter trying to provide what comfort a mother can in such a situation. The next, I'm on the floor like a worm. Yes, a worm that crawls on its belly, that's what that man reduced me to. But come closer, dear, I haven't had a good look at your face."

I obeyed her, felt the light touch of her fingers on my cheeks, lips, the lids of my eyes. She examined my face as a blind person might. "You look nothing like a crow," she pronounced at last, and my cheeks heated with shame. It hadn't been that long since the boys and young men along the sides of the roads had stopped making cawing sounds as I passed. "The hair may be black, the skin dark, the eyes small, the nose prominent, but to me you're a beauty, and do you know why?"

I shook my head miserably. Just a few weeks earlier Lipsa's daughter Mirel had looked at me long and hard and said I was coming along, that if I could just learn to sew a straight hem and let my face catch up to my nose, my father might make a decent match for me yet.

"You have a good heart," Mrs. Entelman said. "I felt it through my fingertips. I felt the heat of your heart. I'm never wrong about such things. Now go get me that water. Down in the kitchen. Ghitel will show you. But mind you, be careful on the way up and don't spill. Your mother used to spill."

"My mother?" I asked.

"Yes, your mother. She worked for me; didn't you know that? In the year before her own marriage. She was a good girl—don't mind what they say—but unsteady. She couldn't carry a tray from here to there without slopping and spilling. Go now, quick. My head's killing me."

And so I went, my own head spinning now, to get Mrs. Entelman's water, and when I returned, full of questions about my mother, she was already onto another topic. That's how it was at Mrs. Entelman's. She talked, flitting from one topic to another as a bird might hop from branch to branch, while I flitted from task to task as her whim dictated, pressing compresses to her forehead, fetching her water, dusting the already glistening surfaces of her bedroom, often switching from one task to another before the first was completed. "Be a dear and do *this* . . . ," she would say. "No, on second thought, do *that* instead." Until I understood that in this house there was nothing, really, that needed doing. I might do *this* as she suggested, or *that,* or nothing at all except listen to Mrs. Entelman's melodic voice skim the surfaces of conversation.

"You're a good girl," she said to me at some point in the afternoon. Had I just rearranged the flowers Ghitel had brought in from the garden? Or was it after I smoothed the coverlet over her legs, which were cold, she insisted, even in the summer heat. "Your mother was a good girl too," she told me again as she sipped the chamomile tea I brought her in the late afternoon. "And such a daughter she was. We should all be blessed with such a daughter. Do you know that not a day of your mother's life passed without her visiting her parents' graves?"

I shook my head no.

"Oh, yes. I can tell you. No matter what the weather, what the demands upon her—and there were many, an orphan like that with no relatives to raise her—she always found the time to spend a few moments with her parents." A pause. "It's true that in time she found other company at the cemetery to spend a few moments with, but was that such a sin? Two lonely souls spending their youth with the dead . . ." Mrs. Entelman's eyes misted over now. "Two lonely orphans." Another pause. "Of course, Noam wasn't really an orphan. It was just his mother he had lost. *Just*. Listen to me. *Just his mother,* as if such a loss was the less wounding for the father being spared. And such a lovely woman his mother was. Who can understand the ways of the Almighty that such a woman would be taken—an angel among women—leaving a husband and young son, while the wicked are spared to unleash their evil among us."

"Noam?" I asked. The same Noam that my father now worked for? The teamster Noam whom Bayla had called an exploiter and against whose gaze my father had once shielded me with his own body?

But Mrs. Entelman didn't approve of the distaste for Noam that she caught in my voice and face. It was unbecoming, she said, for anyone to set herself as a judge of another's character. Such judgments soured the face, to say nothing of the spirit. And me, with such a long and skinny face to begin with—I didn't want to turn into a pickle, did I?

I shook my head no.

And did I imagine, Mrs. Entelman continued, young and well cared for as I was, that I had ever tasted so much as a sample of the bitterness life offers to some? "Have you not been to the swamp?" she asked me.

I had, I assured her.

"Then you have seen for yourself the twisted shapes living beings assume when they must suck their nourishment from bitter offerings."

I nodded, a sickening tug in my gut reminding me of the bitter reeds I had provided for Tsila's baby.

"He scares you?" Mrs. Entelman asked about Noam, her tone less chiding now, and I saw Noam in full gallop, his eyes narrowed, his face hard as he spurred and whipped his horses ever faster.

I nodded. "There's talk that he's cruel. Hard," I amended, afraid to say anything that could be construed as *loshon hora.* "To his horses."

"I wouldn't know about that. I don't know from horses. But tell me this, would a cruel heart care for an old man as he cares for his father?"

Noam's father, Chaim, also a teamster as a young man, had fallen under the wheels of his coach some years back, and though his mind and breath had survived the ordeal, his body had never repaired itself. He lay paralyzed on a cot in Noam's house. Every morning Noam rose early to wash and feed his father's broken body, and every evening he returned home to spoon another meal into his waiting mouth. It was said in town that the only luck the old man had ever had in this life was the failure of Noam to marry, for what daughter-in-law would bring such gentleness and love to the tending of her useless father-in-law?

"My mother and Noam?" I asked.

"Oh, yes," Mrs. Entelman said, wiping her brow where the hot tea had raised beads of sweat. "Most assuredly yes. After the visits to their parents' graves he and Henye would walk for hours along the river, Noam talking and Henye laughing, a laugh so light and silvery that those who heard it never forgot it." There was another pause now as Mrs. Entelman lay back on her pillow and seemed to listen for that faraway silvery laugh.

I heard it then. Unbidden, it came to me—a laugh sweeter and lighter than any I had ever heard. And with it, a girl took form in my mind. I had not, until then, ever had a clear image of my mother. She had appeared to me always as a shadow, a glimpse of downcast eyes and sunken cheeks, a dark blur that passed through my mind as a cloud scuttles across a summer sky. But as I sat in the afternoon sun of Mrs. Entelman's room, a light breeze ruffling the curtains by the window, Mrs. Entelman's spoon tinkling against the fine china of her teacup, I heard my mother's laughter and with it a girl took form, a slender girl, not much older than myself, with long hair, black as my own, and a narrow face lit by sunlight as she raised it in laughter toward her companion. I closed my eyes and saw him too, a young man, well built and tall, without a hint of a stoop. He was in the high boots of a teamster, riding crop attached but idle at his waist. I watched them walk along the banks of the river, the last rays of the day's sun filtering through the flickering leaves of the poplars.

Mrs. Entelman sighed heavily. "Your mother understood the commandment to honor one's parents, a commandment that doesn't end with their death."

The river scene faded, but I saw her still, crouched now by the side of a gravestone, her hand lightly brushing its surface to clear it of dirt, her hair falling like a dark veil around her.

"A person's roots lie where her parents are buried," Mrs. Entelman said. "We draw our nourishment from the earth they have returned to. Your mother knew that, even if others seem to have forgotten." Mrs. Entelman paused and her eyes misted over as her thoughts turned, perhaps, toward her own daughter, so far away, or toward her own future grave, unvisited and unkept, the earth she would return to nourishing the children of strangers. She shook her head clear and continued. "No, a girl like your mother was not one to walk away from her parents."

But what about her infant child, still living, I wondered. And the unloved husband? And the man she did love, if a word of what Mrs. Entelman spoke was true. But Mrs. Entelman made no mention of the living left behind, just the dead, and the laughing girl in my mind was pushed aside by another with lank hair, dull eyes, and a narrow face pale with longing for the dead.

"Was she morbid, then?" I asked Mrs. Entelman.

"Morbid?" The question seemed to make Mrs. Entelman cross. "Is it morbidity now to tend to the graves of your parents?" she asked. "Is this what the enlightened members of our community teach their children?"

I pretended not to have noticed the dig at Tsila, lowering my eyes as I busied myself with Mrs. Entelman's compress.

WHEN I LEFT MRS. ENTELMAN'S MY HEAD ECHOED WITH her voice and all she had told me, and my body churned with a restlessness that her words had ignited in me, a restless energy bereft of any focus or purpose. I went over to Mrs. Gold's shop, though I knew it would be hours before Sara was free. The air in the tiny space was close and still, and I had to blink several times to accustom my eyes to the dimness after the brilliant sunlight of the afternoon. Sara was on a stepladder, arranging coils of rope on the highest shelf.

"Can I help you?" Mrs. Gold asked me, her sharp gaze more subduing than a lashing tongue.

"I was hoping to talk to Sara for just a minute," I explained.

"Sara's working, as you can see."

I nodded and began backing out of the store.

"Your stepmother is well?" Mrs. Gold asked.

"Yes," I lied.

"We never see her anymore. Send her my best."

I ambled then toward the river, trying to conjure up the image of my mother that had flown so easily into my mind earlier that day, but the memory of her was not my own, and without Mrs. Entelman's voice to paint it for me I was left only with the unfocused churning of my body. The air remained warm as afternoon gave way to evening. The light that filtered through the trees lining the river was soft and thick, the heat heavy against my skin. I stood and watched the sluggish Pripet, so lazy in its summer flow, the *berlinkes* with their loads of lumber drifting south to Kiev, then I turned away from the river toward town.

The last vendors in the market were closing up shop for the day. Young men stood in clusters around the edges of the market, spitting out the shells of sunflower seeds as they talked amongst themselves. Pairs of girls paraded hand in hand, their heads inclined toward each other, their free hands shielding their mouths as they whispered secrets to each other. I watched them, feeling my separateness in a way I hadn't since Sara and I had become friends.

I was just about to turn toward home when Sara came rushing through the lane that led from the street behind the market. "I thought she'd never let me go," she said. "We had no customers after you left, so she decided we should do inventory."

"I thought you did inventory last week."

"We did. And two weeks before that. The less she sells, the more she counts. And it was so hot in there today I thought I'd faint." Sara projected her lower lip and exhaled sharply to blow away a lock of hair from her eyes, but the hair was plastered by sweat to her forehead. "So how did it go for you? Is she as crazy as they say? I see she let you out early, at least."

I had wanted to tell Sara everything Mrs. Entelman had said to me, but as I stood before her it was impossible to put any of it into words. "She talks a lot," I said of Mrs. Entelman.

"That's what I've heard. Too much time on her hands." Sara took my hand and we began walking away from the market. "I could stand a swim, could you?" she asked as we headed toward the river. There was a spot just outside town where some of the women cooled themselves on especially hot days.

"I have to get home. It's late already."

Sara looked at me. "There's something happening tonight," she said. "It's a secret, though."

"What?" I asked, and Sara explained that a girl she had known in Mozyr was starting a study circle, a new cell of the Bund.

"Right here. In this mudhole," Sara said, grinning. "I can't tell you where, but if you meet me at—"

"I can't," I said.

"You *can't*?" she repeated, more astounded than angry.

"I'm sorry, but Tsila's been alone all day. It's hard for her to get things done in her condition, with her swelling. And today was so hot . . ."

"You don't even *want* to attend," Sara said, angry now. "And here I thought you'd be as excited as I am, honored to even be invited."

"Of course I want to," I protested, more out of concern about disappointing Sara than from an honest desire to spend the evening studying after my day at Mrs. Entelman's. "What are you going to study?" I asked.

"Matters of relevance," Sara said curtly.

"If I can get away I will," I promised.

"You won't get away," Sara said.

NOAM'S PATH CROSSED MINE AS I WALKED UP THE HILL toward my home. Usually at his approach I would lower my eyes and stand to the side of the road until he had passed, but Mrs. Entelman's tales that afternoon had infected me with curiosity about the man. I dared to raise my eyes as he passed, hoping to catch a glimpse of the young man by the river who had raised my mother's silvery laugh.

He was leaning forward on his horse, flicking the animal with his whip but not spurring it to any great speed. He looked at me as he passed, and though I met his gaze with my own, it was not Noam who was revealed to me. I looked him in the face but was aware only of the weight of my own dark hair on my shoulders and back, the slenderness of my limbs, the darkness of my eyes, the narrowness of my face. I was not the beauty my mother had been, that I had always known, but I wondered now if there was not one part of me at least—a feature of my face, a particular gesture—that might remind him of her.

I nodded my head once, the slightest of movements, a greeting, barely perceptible, the first I had ever accorded to him. Though not one muscle in his face flickered in response, he returned my gesture with a slight nod of his own, briefly bringing his two fingers to touch the peak of his cap.

I walked quickly the rest of the way up the hill. It was almost dark; I should have been home hours ago. Only a band of light remained at the edge of the sky. It seemed particularly luminous, smoldering under the encroaching cover of the night sky. *Blessed art thou, Lord our God, King of the universe who has such as this in thy world,* I uttered, pausing to admire it.

With the night had come a cooling of the air, a slight breeze from the marshes that now played against my damp skin and ruffled through my thin cotton dress. I closed my eyes to better enjoy its coolness on my forehead, my arms. I knew I would receive a scolding when I got home on account of my lateness, a scolding sure to worsen with each moment I delayed, but for one moment longer I stood alone on the crest of the hill, my arms outstretched, allowing the evening breeze to gently lift my hair from my neck and brush the surfaces of my skin.

A tale from the Hasidim relates the dilemma of a man trying to enter heaven. Standing before the Heavenly Judge, he recounts all his good deeds but concedes that there was one time when he did, in fact, commit a sin. "I succumbed to the temptation of a woman," he explains, to which one angel laughs scornfully, asking, "Are you so weak that a woman is enough to make you sin?"

The man is denied entrance to heaven, but the angel too is punished: sentenced to a lifetime on earth as a woman.

"I am that angel," Henye told Aaron Lev the day they were introduced. "My life on this earth is a punishment."

"This is how your mother began her life with your father," Tsila told me as we sat in the heavy darkness of our home. It was late at night and neither of us could sleep. The heat. Our own thoughts. My father was out at a meeting of the self-defense group that the town's artisans had formed in the wake of the Kishenev massacre, and Tsila and I had lain separately in our hot beds, listening to each other toss and turn until Tsila finally rose to get herself some water.

"Shall I read to you?" I had asked, joining her at the table. She liked me to read the Psalms to her when she couldn't sleep, but on this night she just fanned herself listlessly and asked what Mrs. Entelman had had to say for herself. I told her and she nodded, as if neither disturbed nor surprised to hear talk of my mother and Noam.

"Did she tell you what happened then?" Tsila asked. "The great charity she and her sister Zelda performed for the orphan Henye?"

I shook my head no and leaned against the warm wall of the house as Tsila began to speak.

"The introduction between Henye and Aaron Lev was arranged by Zelda Chayvitz," Tsila told me.

I knew Zelda, of course. She was the wife of Feivel the butcher and younger sister to Yitta Entelman, my new employer. Less high-strung than her older sister, and not as lucky in marriage, Zelda's reputation in the town rested on the work she did for those less fortunate than herself. It was said that as a young girl she had felt an ache in her shoulders, a heaviness that she had come to recognize early on as the pain of others, and that her own good fortune held no pleasure for her if she could not share it with others. "A saint," some said about her, and certainly the matchmaker did when Zelda reached marriageable age. And had there been a supply of saints looking for brides at the time, who knows what kind of match she might have made? As it happens, only ordinary young men were available, and so she married Feivel from down the street.

"Zelda was a great friend of Perla Zuptnik's. Did you know that?" Tsila asked me.

I shook my head no, uncertain who Perla Zuptnik even was.

"Oh, yes," Tsila said. "A great friend. It was a childhood friendship—they were the same age and lived across the lane from each other. My father lived in the same laneway and says you never saw one without the other.

"Zelda was the stronger. She was taller than Perla—a full head taller—but it wasn't just her height. She had an urge to arrange people's lives, Zelda did. Even then. And Perla, I suppose, had an urge to be arranged. Some people do. Zelda could be heard all day long giving Perla directions about all manner of things—how to sit so as to be more modest, how to stand. Once—they couldn't have been more than nine or ten at the time—my father even overheard Zelda choosing names for all of Perla's future children."

Tsila met my eye and shrugged at the thought.

"The bonds forged between them endured into adulthood, and although they no longer lived across the lane from each other as they had as girls, they didn't live far and one could usually be found in the kitchen of the other, their laughter rising up as it always had. The difference being that now the babies they dangled on their knees were their own firstborn rather than their little brothers and sisters.

"When Perla fell ill, just three years into her married life, Zelda was in constant attendance, and on Perla's deathbed Zelda made a vow to watch over Perla's only child, Noam, as if he were her own, and to do whatever she could to ease his way through this life."

"Noam the teamster?" I asked.

"That's right. But listen now. The vow took just a moment to pass Zelda's lips, but the honoring of it was to tax her for many years to come, since Noam, who was just a little toddler at the time of his mother's death, grew into exactly the sort of ruffian Zelda preferred her own children to avoid. A lesson to always be careful what you promise."

I nodded.

"Poor Zelda," Tsila sighed. "She tried to be understanding. 'A boy without a mother is bound to be a little wild,' she would say in the first years after Perla's death. Especially with a father like that. Zelda had never liked Chaim, you see. She had never understood how her sweet Perla could lie with such roughness. She shuddered every time she saw Chaim's coach go flying by with Noam on the bench beside his father, a whip in his innocent hand instead of a tractate of Talmud, and she made sure to buy holy books for Noam whenever the bookseller came through town. Also, never did she allow a Friday to pass when she didn't stop by the child's home with a couple of *challahs* and some of her own gefilte fish so that Noam and his father could at least have a proper Shabbes.

"In such a way did Zelda try to honor her vow to Perla, and at first, Chaim didn't stand in her way. He accepted Zelda's offerings, even asking her in for a glass of tea on occasion. After his accident, however, Chaim didn't want to be seen by anyone who had known him in his strength—he could hardly be blamed—and Noam stood in the doorway when Zelda called, blocking her entrance. He had become a large young man. There was none of Perla in his build. And Zelda's heart sank to see the beginning of a hardening in his eyes."

Tsila paused here to drink a little before continuing.

"In the summer of 1884, fifteen years after Perla's death, the sound of laughter reached Zelda's ears as she walked by the river. It was light laughter, pleasant; it lifted one's spirits just to hear it. Zelda found herself lingering by the riverside to enjoy the warm fragrance of the summer evening that just moments before she hadn't even noticed. As darkness fell, she saw a young couple emerge from the wooded path that followed the river.

" 'Good evening, Mrs. Chayvitz,' they greeted her.

" 'Good evening,' Zelda answered. She noted the glow that lit Noam's face, the answering shine of Henye's eyes.

"Now, Zelda is not a hard woman, but neither is she impractical. Henye was a poor orphan with nothing to bring to a marriage but her shining eyes, and Noam was the son of her great friend to whom she had made a binding vow. It was not cruelty that impelled Zelda. So she would claim. It was loyalty. Loyalty to her dead friend and to her own vow.

" 'Maybe you should just let things be,' her husband, Feivel, suggested. 'She's supposed to be a good girl, this Henye, a nice girl. And so pretty. And Noam's had such heartache, why shouldn't he have a pretty wife?'

" 'Would you have her for our own sons?' Zelda asked.

" 'Our circumstances are different,' Feivel pointed out.

" 'I promised Perla I'd look out for him as for one of my own.'

" 'But he's not your own,' Fcivel said. 'Do you think parents are lining up to marry off their precious daughters to him? Do you think he's such a great catch, with no education, a crippled father, and a mother with such weak lungs that she died of a cold?'

" 'It wasn't a cold,' Zelda argued. 'It was pneumonia.'

" 'Who's to say that this Henye isn't the best he'll find? Who are you to judge such things?' This is what her husband asked.

"Zelda didn't answer, but Feivel's arguments had swayed her a little. She decided she would speak to the girl, just speak to her. If Henye clung to Noam after that, then that would be God's will. Of course, if she desisted, then that too was God's will.

"Zelda approached her in the early evening, at the hour when she knew Henye would be making her way to the graveyard for her nightly visit with her parents. Zelda placed herself on the same path at the same time. 'Good evening,' she said.

" 'Good evening, Mrs. Chayvitz,' Henye responded. She was a pretty girl, your mother was, there's no denying that, and her manners were good.

" 'A lovely evening,' Zelda said.

"Henye smiled pleasantly, and Zelda felt her resolve waver. Who knew what was best, she asked herself. It's well known that a person's husband or wife is determined forty days before their birth. Could she really be certain that Henye wasn't the one who had been chosen for Noam? Who was she, Zelda Chayvitz, to tamper with fate? This is what she asked herself. Or so she later claimed. She was about to bid the girl good evening again and be on her way when a vision of Perla filled her mind: Perla as a young mother, her round face glowing with pleasure as she bent over her baby boy and tickled his belly, 'You'll be my little scholar,' Perla cooed as she tickled him. 'You'll marry a rabbi's daughter.' She kissed his belly. 'You'll have ten healthy sons, each of them a scholar.' The baby shrieked with delight.

" 'Henye, forgive me,' Zelda said to the girl before her. 'I know you're a fine girl, and I mean you no insult.'

"She did nothing underhanded, employed no forceful measures. She simply explained her dilemma, describing the scene with Perla and Noam that had just replayed in her mind, the hopes that Perla had harbored for her only son, Noam. Would Henye have Zelda betray her vow to her dying friend, she wondered aloud. Would Henye deny a dead woman's wishes for her son's future?

"Of course she wouldn't. Not Henye. She was unswervingly faithful to the dead."

"Morbid?" I interrupted.

"It could be said," Tsila answered.

"Orphaned at three, her ensuing years had been dismal, her life a torment of loneliness until, at the age of seven, her parents had come to her to reveal that her purpose on this earth was to remember them. She had not been asleep when her parents came but fully awake, breaking the spines of feathers at Elke's—Elke the Feather Plucker, who took her in and put her to work when no other living relative came forth to claim her. She felt her parents before she saw them: a flush of warmth despite the damp of Elke's basement apartment, a feeling of peace that quieted even the rumbling of her empty stomach. Their faces, when they did reveal themselves, were peaceful, unperturbed despite the misery of their daughter's conditions. They saw the cramped, cold house in which she lived and worked, her hunger, the monotony of her days, but they did not weep for her or stretch out their arms to reclaim her at last. "Remember us," they pleaded, and she understood why she had been left behind to suffer this life.

"And suffer she did until one evening when she was fifteen years old her eyes met Noam's across the rows of gravestones. She felt a jolt then unlike anything she had experienced before. A current, not unpleasant, filled her body. It was life, of course, and despite her allegiance to the dead, she welcomed it. She did not forget her parents, but alongside their memory something new flared within her: hope that there might be a place for her in this life after all. Had she betrayed her parents with this hope, she wondered now as Zelda stood before her. How else could she understand this strange intrusion of Zelda's into her life?"

" 'An alternative bridegroom will be found for you,' Zelda assured her. 'A dowry arranged.' "

Tsila took another sip of water, then continued.

"Aaron Lev and Henye were not strangers to each other. They had not spoken but their eyes had met, more than once. Aaron Lev had to pass Elke's house twice a day, don't forget, on his way to and from his work. Still, Henye seemed hesitant. Zelda found herself inquiring about conditions at Elke's. She was a difficult employer, was she not? Then Zelda wondered aloud whether a position in her sister's house—Mrs. Entelman's house—might not interest Henye. Just that day her sister, Yitta, had been talking to her about needing a new maid.

"Henye was afraid now. From Elke's to Mrs. Entelman's? From a feather plucker to a maid in the finest house in town, all for giving up Noam and marrying another? Surely such a turn of events could only come from beyond the grave. She had obviously offended her parents, betrayed them with her love for Noam. They had interceded, sent this woman . . .

" 'For light work,' Zelda was saying. 'Nothing too heavy . . .'

" 'I'm used to hard work,' Henye murmured. She was sixteen years old and had spent her life amidst the carcasses of chickens. She had heard Mrs. Entelman's rooms were filled with lilacs even in winter."

"She gave Noam up for a job as a maid?"

"You ask that with the disdain of one who has never known a moment of material hardship," Tsila said. I flushed deeply as she continued.

"That Henye saw her life on this earth as punishment did not disturb Aaron Lev. Was his own life such a reward? Had he not lost his own parents to the same epidemic that had taken Henye's? He felt a kinship with the girl. He thought he could protect her, ease her sojourn on this earth."

"He loved her?"

"He felt a kinship. And Henye too felt a kinship when she met Aaron Lev, but it was, unfortunately, one she instinctively shrank from. She recognized the yearning in his eyes, the sadness, and she quickly looked away. Eyes like quicksand, she told her friends. Were she to stare too long she would drown in the mire of his melancholy."

"She didn't love him."

"But she would have him for her husband; he was her parents' choice. He was sent to her through their chosen messenger, Zelda Chayvitz—that Henye entirely believed."

"She never loved him?"

"She tried. She talked softly to him at their first meeting. She talked, but Aaron Lev didn't answer. He couldn't. He saw something in her eyes. Something hard glittering deep within her eyes. She looked away, but he had already seen it. He tried to speak, to answer her questions— he knew she was waiting—but as he met the eyes of his prospective bride, words fled from his mind.

" 'He doesn't speak,' Henye said to Mrs. Entelman when asked how she had found Aaron Lev.

" 'He who curbs his tongue shows sense,' Mrs. Entelman said, quoting from the Book of Proverbs, but your mother didn't know from Proverbs. She asked for a release from the betrothal. It was granted and she ran away, to Mozyr, only to come crawling back a few months later. They were married before Chanukah. Your poor brother was born the following summer."

I imagined the wedding, Henye looking into the muddy eyes of her bridegroom and Noam's eyes rising up in her mind, hard as diamonds and full of light. Aaron Lev meeting her gaze and seeing it again: that glitter in her that strangled his tongue with doubt. And Henye looking away, losing the path through this life that Noam might have cut for her with his hard, glittering eyes.

Siberia, September 1911

At first the letters from Bayla were frequent and full of complaints. "Not that Shendel is an unkind employer," she would say. "She's actually more generous than I expected her to be. Perhaps because she's happy. They say happiness brings out the best in a person, though my own life hasn't provided the occasion to test that particular hypothesis."

Yes, Bayla reported, Shendel Entelman Zalman was happy in her new life in Montreal. While her home was not quite the mansion Yehuda had promised—not *yet*, Yehuda would admonish—there were other compensations. Yehuda, for one. Shendel had known before her marriage that her husband-to-be was a handsome man. That anyone could see. And she had assumed he would provide well—her father, Lazer, could sniff out business acumen in another man with the accuracy of a village dog sniffing out a breeding female. But it was his softness toward her, she had told Bayla, that had been her happiest surprise when she finally joined him in Montreal, the gentleness of his voice when he wished her good morning, the tenderness in his face when he opened his arms to her at the end of the day.

That and her own newly discovered strength. She had set up house in her new country quickly, and with an ease she would never have suspected of herself. She had learned a new language, new ways, had borne two children, then a third—and all the while showing no hint of the nervous weakness that she had assumed would plague her all her life.

"She would never admit it, of course," Bayla wrote. "She would claim until she's blue in the face, in fact, that the pain she suffers about missing her mother is like a knife through her heart every day of her life, but the truth is, with each added day she puts between herself and her mother she seems stronger and more assured than before. Or could it be the distance from her father? I wonder. In any event, she's a different Shendel from the one we once knew. Do you know she sings out loud now? Men or no men. Her voice rings out so clear and loud when she's puttering in the kitchen that you'd think she's forgotten that the voice of woman is a temptation to sin. And she's stopped covering her hair. Can you believe it? Our Shendel, the most pious of the pious. The minute she realized that that's what the smart women do here and that no one was going to talk too badly about her, she pulled off her wig and grew her own hair out. And guess what? The sky didn't fall. This she told me. Which I could have told her years ago. Which, in fact, we tried to tell women like her years ago, and what were we rewarded with? Fear, scorn, and insults."

As for Bayla, though, the picture wasn't so rosy. She didn't mean to complain, of course, but the tasks she was expected to perform, the maid's uniform that she had to wear, she, Bayla Rubin Zalman, an educated woman. "The only comfort I take is that I'm keeping your Hayya safe for you. I have to keep up the pretense that she's mine, of course. Even to her. It pains me to do it—and especially when I see hints of you in her features and manner—but what choice do I have? Shendel is kind, but I'm in no position to test the limits of her kindness. What if in a moment of forgetfulness little Hayya were to give herself away? Maids are not so scarce here that Shendel needs to keep one who comes equipped with someone else's illegitimate daughter. Not that I believe Hayya is illegitimate, of course. All children, no matter what their origins, are legitimate. This I believe. But does Shendel? Even in her newly expansive state of mind? Our material security—mine and Hayya's—is still too precarious to risk finding out that she doesn't."

Then Bayla would apologize for using the word *precarious* in reference to her material situation when my own was so much worse. "Yet as unpleasant as your situation is in a material sense, spiritually you are so much more elevated than I am," she went on. "Not that I for one minute romanticize your situation—I think the events of the last years have stripped me of the last of my romantic notions—but when I dress in the morning, when I put on the black dress and white apron of the serving classes, I am more demeaned than I would be in any prison uniform. This I believe."

We don't wear uniforms here at Maltzev except when we are expecting outside officials for a prison inspection. But I haven't told Bayla this.

"To think that after all we dreamed and put ourselves through, I should end up a maid in a wealthy household, no better off than an impoverished orphan like your mother—not that I am in any way a *better* or more *worthy* person than one such as your mother. But still, when I look at my situation, the larger situation . . ." (This she leaves for me to fill in to avoid censor by the prison officials.) "I have to ask myself what it was all about. I know I shouldn't think that way. It does me no good. It's important to look forward in life, never back—you know how strongly I believe that—but I can't seem to help it. I lie awake in the stifling heat—it's a hot summer, and our attic bedroom has not so much as a hint of cool air. I toss and I turn and I think of all we went through and for what? This is what I ask.

CHAPTER EIGHT

1903

I WAS HAPPY WORKING FOR MRS. ENTELMAN, HAPPY TO rise with the sun each day and walk alone down the hill into town in the fresh morning air, to have a glass of tea in the light-filled kitchen with Ghitel, then spend the day dusting and cleaning and attending to Mrs. Entelman. I was happy, also, to feel the weight of the coins Mrs. Entelman paid me heavy in my pocket as I lingered in town waiting for my evening walk with Sara before returning home.

On one such evening Freyde called out to me from her stall, offering me a special price for her last dozen bagels of the day.

"A special price for the high-class wage earner," she called, and a flush of embarrassment swept over me. It was a source of amusement to Freyde and other women in town that Tsila's educated stepdaughter was working as a maid for Yitta Entelman.

"A special price for staleness, you mean," I responded.

"Impudent girl," Freyde said, but when I bought one of her bagels she told me to sit and keep her company while I ate it.

I hesitated—since when did Freyde seek the pleasure of my company?—but my legs were tired, and I hadn't eaten anything since breakfast.

"So?" Freyde asked the moment I sat down. "How do you find her?"

Mrs. Entelman, she meant, whose unhappiness despite her husband's great wealth was always a popular topic for discussion. Who would squander such good luck by drowning herself in unhappiness, people wondered. If ever such good fortune should land in one of their lives, even a fraction of such good fortune, you wouldn't find them lying in bed moaning. But then, who could say? Wasn't wealth known to weaken the character? I should be so cursed, someone would comment. Never mind the wealth, it's that husband, Freyde would drone, her words producing a round of knowing nods, because Mr. Entelman, while not unkind to his wife, was not unkind to other women either. There were few in the town who had not felt the heat of Lazer Entelman's appraising gaze, and though no one would admit it, there was something in his gaze that compelled one to return it, a concentrated energy in his face that drew one's own. Freyde's sigh was always the deepest as she compared the gray blur of features that comprised her own husband, Sender, a seller of pots, with the darting black eyes of Mr. Entelman, the white teeth that glittered beneath his curled mustache. "That poor woman," she would sigh. "Poor woman," the others would agree, their spines tingling all the while at the memory of their most recent glimpse of Mr. Entelman.

"Are her bedclothes made of satin?" Freyde wanted to know. And did I find her as soft in the head as they said? And her attitude . . . it was said she was haughty to those she considered beneath her. Freyde's hands were already on her hips in indignation at my possible mistreatment.

I chewed my bagel slowly, offering whatever bit of gossip might prolong Freyde's newfound interest in my well-being. No, Mrs. Entelman didn't treat me badly, I answered, and yes, her head was perhaps a bit soft, I said, describing the odd way Mrs. Entelman had of staring at me as I arranged flowers or dusted, as if she had forgotten for a moment who I was or why I was there. But her head didn't seem nearly as soft as her hands, which looked like they had never done anything more strenuous than wring each other in anguish.

"Soft hands, hard heart," Freyde commented, as if callouses had suddenly created an epidemic of kindheartedness among our town's working people. I said I'd not found Mrs. Entelman's heart to be particularly hard.

"Just wait," Freyde warned me, but enough of Mrs. Entelman. Had I heard that Mrs. Leibowitz, Hava's mother, had been seen returning from one of the neighboring peasant villages late that afternoon?

"From whom would I have heard?" I asked.

"It was your own father who found her. On the most deserted of roads. He picked her up immediately, of course, and brought her safely home, but I'm sure he could scarcely believe his eyes when he first saw her. Imagine a Jewish woman alone on such a road. Did you ever?"

I had never, I agreed, and happily accepted the second bagel Freyde offered me.

"She'd been to the Gypsies," Freyde informed me, lowering her voice to an appropriately confiding tone. Gypsies often came through the region in the summer months, camping outside town or the neighboring villages, bringing news from far away. Often it was through them that we heard of mishaps or happier occurrences: a pogrom in another town, a wedding, a sighting of someone long thought dead. "She didn't want to admit it, of course. At first she told your father she'd been to the village on business. *Business*. Did you ever? What possible business might she have in such a village? It's barely a village, just a line of huts, each more squalid than the next. Even my Sender has never found business there, though God knows they can't own one decent pot among them."

Pressed by my father's silence, or maybe simply needing to share her burden with another human being, Mrs. Leibowitz had admitted finally that she'd been to consult a Gypsy woman about her Hava. "A soothsayer, of all things. Did you ever?" Freyde asked again.

"Never," I assured Freyde, and asked if the soothsayer had anything to tell the poor woman.

"Useless babble," Freyde said, but excitement animated her usual drone. "Worse than useless," she continued, and then, lowering her voice again, she revealed that the soothsayer had in fact had a vision, which she related to Mrs. Leibowitz, a vision of Hava returning to her home.

"Then she's alive still?" Mrs. Leibowitz asked. "I knew it! All this time I knew it. Does a mother not feel the beating of her daughter's heart even if time and distance separate them? But tell me, where is she and when will I see her?"

But the soothsayer's face was somber. "She's alive, Mrs., but all is not well."

"Oooyyy," Mrs. Leibowitz's wail went up at once. "I knew it. All this time I knew it, but still I dared to hope. Oy, my poor Hava."

"Her poor, sweet little Havele, whom she was happy to force into a marriage with that fish merchant," commented Sara, who had joined us and was already rolling her eyes at Freyde's story. Freyde ignored the interruption.

"Not well?" Mrs. Leibowitz asked the soothsayer. "What, not well? She's not coming home to die, is she? Oh, no, don't tell me."

But of course she wanted to know and she had paid her kopecks.

"She's coming home for a death, but not her own," the woman said in such an ominous tone that Mrs. Leibowitz ran from her presence as if she had just recognized the Angel of Death in disguise.

"It wasn't the Angel of Death she was running from, but something far worse," Sara said.

"What?" Freyde and I asked in unison.

"The truth," Sara pronounced. "The plain truth. Which is that Hava Leibowitz ran away from her mother and all her mother's plans for her. And that she won't be back except to put the woman in the ground. That's the truth of the matter."

Freyde didn't argue. "The woman's a witch and always has been."

"They wanted her for my uncle Beryl," said Rivka, who had just joined us. "But he wouldn't have her because she was a witch even then. So she can run all she wants, but where will it get her? There are things your legs can't save you from. Believe me, I know."

Mrs. Leibowitz was still trying to hurry when my father saw her by the side of the road, but the weight of what she was trying to escape, as well as her own respectable girth, made sustained hurrying difficult.

"Do you think Hava might come back, then?" I asked Freyde. "And did the soothsayer say where she has been all this while?"

"What?" Freyde droned. "Is Tsila's stepdaughter so enlightened and well educated now that she puts her faith in the babble of an old Gypsy soothsayer?" The other women laughed, and a familiar shame returned to me, more painful for the pleasure I'd been taking from its brief absence.

Sara was disappointed in me. I could feel her censure as we walked away from Freyde's stall. She didn't take my hand as she usually did when we walked in the evening, didn't speak at all until we were well clear of the marketplace and on the path to the river.

"I never thought the day would come when Freyde and I would see eye to eye on something," she said.

"What?" I asked.

I had a choice, Sara said. I could drown in superstition, turning for the rest of my life to soothsayers, rabbis, and the like for answers, or I could join the other young people who were emerging, finally, from the haze of ignorance that had enslaved us for so long.

She told me then about a wedding that had taken place just the night before in Kalinkovich. It was a traditional wedding, with the bride circling the groom seven times and the seven blessings recited. But at the end of the last blessing, the young couples' friends from work had surrounded the canopy, and a young man had climbed on a chair to address the crowd. "What have we just witnessed here?" the young man asked. "Jumbled mutterings by a cleric in a greasy caftan!" A wave of shock passed through the crowd. "Is this what will unite the couple standing here before us? No!" the orator shouted. "It is love that will unite them. Love and loyalty to each other and to the proletariat, which, when it comes to power, will do away forever with all such ceremonies. Down with musty ceremonies!" The young people began to shout. "Down with clerics in their greasy caftans! Long live the Bund of Poland, Russia, and Lithuania!"

"This really happened?" I asked.

"Of course," Sara assured me, grinning widely. The leader of her study circle, Malka, had been one of the young people in attendance. "The bride's mother fainted, Malka told me. From shame. Would you not have loved to have been there?"

I nodded.

"So start coming to the study circle, then."

My continuing absence from the study circle was becoming a wider and harder wedge between Sara and me, but it met in the evening, the very time of day when Tsila was most uncomfortable and disturbed by premonitions about her pregnancy. My father was out in the evenings, attending the learning at the *shul* or at meetings of the town's self-defense group, and when Tsila was alone in the darkening house she sank into gloom. The only thing that seemed to soothe her, at that time of day, was the sound of my voice reading the Psalms, so I would read to her for minutes or hours, depending on the night, until I had lulled her into sleep. Only then did I feel free to leave. But by then the study circle was finished for the night, so it was to the river that I went, to cool myself in its waters.

Sara often met me at the river, and she told me what Malka had taught that evening. It was usually history or economics, and as I listened, trying to catch Sara's excitement, I knew in my heart that I was not the serious girl she had mistaken me for. As Sara talked, her words knocked against my ears, but it was the scent of the river that entered me, the coolness of the water against my skin. I was a dreamer, and I feared Sara was beginning to suspect as much.

"If you'd come to Malka's you'd already have known all you want about Hava. And it would be the truth you would know, not the half-baked foolishness of a soothsayer."

My mind snapped to attention as it never did during Sara's discourses on history and economics.

"You have news about Hava?" I asked.

"Hava lives in Gomel and works at the glassworks there," Sara said.

"Gomel?" I asked, vaguely disappointed. Gomel was so close. I had imagined her in America or Palestine or dead in a ditch, but never in a factory in the next city over. "How do you know?" I asked.

"Malka's from there. Her family lives in New America."

"New America?" I asked, my mind filling with visions of broad avenues and modern houses.

"Don't get so excited," Sara said with a smile. "I think the name's meant in jest. From what Malka tells us, conditions in that part of town are even worse than they are here, though I don't see how anything could be worse than the mental backwardness we have to endure in this pit of ignorance. Anyway, a few years ago a girl moved into the cellar apartment of her family's building. A young woman with no family, completely destitute . . ."

"Hava?" I asked.

Sara nodded. "Malka helped her find a job at the factory, saving her from I can't even tell you what kind of work." Sara looked at me meaningfully. "Now she not only has a job, but she's opened her heart to other girls like herself running from the backwardness she escaped from, to ensure they don't suffer as she did. A bed she can't offer them, of course. She herself can only afford a corner large enough for her own bed—she shares the room with six other girls. But tea she never fails to offer, no matter what the hour. And a warm heart."

"You learned this at your study circle?" I asked.

Sara nodded. "But I can't say any more," she said. "What happens in the group is secret. I shouldn't even have said what I did."

NO ONE BLAMED AARON LEV FOR THE ECONOMIC MIS-fortune into which we fell that summer. Have we sunk so low, people asked, that now a man is fired for taking a moment out of the workday to address his Creator? For that's what Aaron Lev was doing the day he encountered Mrs. Leibowitz. He had turned off the main road from Kalinkovich and onto a secondary road. It was hardly a road, more of a track, one wagon's width across, cutting through an area of thick forest and leading to nowhere but a few desolate villages. So narrow was the track that the tops of trees met overhead, forming a canopy, a thick green canopy through which the sun penetrated only in dapples and shafts. And why had he done this? Why had he taken such a detour when he was being paid for the speed with which he transported goods, as well as the care? "To recite the *Minchah* service," Tsila said tersely. For it was there, apparently, under that canopy of greenery, in the shafts of late afternoon light that he felt—more strongly than in any other place or at any other time—the presence of the Creator.

No one blamed Noam either. Times are not so easy, people said, that Noam should be expected to pay a coachman who cuts long detours out of his workday. Especially *this* coachman, they added with knowing looks all around.

I didn't ignore the comments and innuendos that Noam's firing of my father had created—I have never been one who could dismiss as nothing the opinions of others—but neither did I fall into despair. I had hope that summer, hope that the comments would soon cease, that my family's luck would soon change, that the opinions about my father and Tsila would soon be forever altered. The source of my hope was the new life that was taking form in Tsila's womb.

Tsila's condition, while not the best, was not deteriorating either, and as she safely passed through the sixth and then the seventh month of pregnancy I began to feel that all was turning out well. Such is the power of new life. I began to imagine the child that was forming inside her and all the changes his birth would bring. For it would be a boy, I decided. That's what I wanted. A brother to love and take care of, a brother to prove that our household was like other households, and Tsila and Aaron Lev a couple like any other; a brother to forever shut the mouths of those who deemed Tsila too sour, and Aaron Lev too weak and our household too cursed to take part in the miracle of creation that is the legacy of every living being.

It was life I turned my hopes to—this is what I'm telling you now—the life forming in Tsila's womb in which I placed all my faith and dreams for the future. Remember that, if not my name.

THE WEEKS PASSED, WARM AND RAINY AND SWEET WITH the smells of ripening. The sorrows of Tishah-b'Av were behind us and just ahead were the weddings and festivities of Shabbes Nachamu, the Sabbath of Comfort, when we turn our thoughts from the destruction of Jerusalem to our hopes of deliverance and redemption.

On the Wednesday of that week I came home later than usual. It was evening already; the lamp should have been lit, Tsila should have been getting supper in the slow dreamlike way she had begun to move that summer, as if the air around her had thickened to water. Instead, a dark silence greeted me. I remained in the doorway for a moment, thinking I was alone.

"Close the door," I heard at length from the darkness. Tsila's voice, though it was so dull it was barely recognizable. I saw her then, as my eyes grew used to the darkness, her slumping form on the bench, leaning against the wall. I went to her, taking her hand as I crouched beside her.

"What is it?" I asked. Her hand was cold and limp in mine.

She turned to me—there was a sickening sweetness to her breath—and looked as if she had not understood the question I had put to her.

"Are you ill?" I asked, the beginning of fear in my chest.

"No," she said dully, turning her head away from me to stare straight ahead.

My father wasn't home yet, but he would be soon. She wanted me to light the lamp, prepare supper. Cold borscht, she thought, sliced cucumbers. The day had been warm, had it not? I started to do as she'd told me, but she just sat there unmoving. I brought her a glass of water. She took it in her hand but didn't drink it. "Drink," I told her.

"For what?"

"You'll feel better. It's very warm in here." It was stifling, the heat of the day trapped within the four walls of our home.

Tsila didn't answer, nor did she drink.

I dropped to the floor beside her, looking to her face for direction, but she had no direction to give me. I tried to meet her eye but her gaze was fastened on the wall ahead. I lay a hand on her arm. Her skin was warm. She didn't move away, so I removed the glass from her hand and stayed crouched beside her, stroking her arm softly, daring at length to place my head on her abdomen, the hard domed surface beneath which I heard nothing but the quick beating of Tsila's heart, the shallow intake and outflow of her breathing.

I don't know how long it was before my father came home. I didn't hear him approach but was aware at some point of the door opening, another's breath as he stood there looking into the darkness.

"Get Dvoire," he said as soon as he saw what was before him. It was a command so unlike my father's usual way of speaking, so harsh in its decisiveness, that I felt as if startled from a deep slumber.

He was beside Tsila before I had even risen to my feet, taking her face in his hands, lifting her chin gently until her eyes met his. She didn't look away. Then he was behind her on the bench, his chest supporting her back, his arms . . . two, four, six pairs of arms it seemed he had, so completely did he engulf her in his embrace. Only her hair escaped, spilling over the length of his arms, and her gaze, her fading, vacant gaze.

> *Comfort Ye, Comfort Ye, My people,*
> *Bid Jerusalem take heart,*
> *And proclaim unto her*
> *That her time of service is accomplished.*
> *Her guilt is paid off;*
> *She hath received of the Lord's hand*
> *Double for her sins.*

Shabbes Nachamu offered no comfort. The women's section fell silent as I entered the *shul*. Word had reached the town of the scene Dvoire had come upon when I brought her back to our house: no baby or any sign of one coming, Tsila with a vacancy in her eyes, and Aaron Lev engulfing her as if to trap her fleeing soul in his embrace.

"Out!" Dvoire commanded, as she always did when a husband had not already fled the situation. She was used to obedience—I was already at the stove heating water as she had commanded—but Aaron Lev looked at Dvoire and only tightened his hold on his wife. "Out!" Dvoire said again, one hand on her hip, the other pointing to the door, but Aaron Lev refused to untangle himself. He looked at Dvoire strangely, then shielded Tsila's eyes from Dvoire's with his open hand.

He had been a young child when his parents were taken, Tsila had told me, no more than two or three. His father had gone in the night while he slept, but his mother was still alive as he crouched beside her the next day, applying cloths to her face. The cloths were no longer cool or wet, and his mother's requests for such comforts had ceased, but still he applied them. His mother's eyes were closed, her cheeks sinking as life seeped from her flesh.

That was a summer day as hot and still as this one. The light had moved from the one window in the room to the other, then faded as Aaron Lev crouched beside his mother. No one had been by the house that day—it was a time of epidemic—and he was frightened as well as hungry, thirsty, lonely. As daylight fled the room, though, a visitor finally came. He didn't knock or announce himself in the usual manner but slipped unseen into the shadows, only his voice alerting Aaron Lev to his presence, the voice of an old man, deep and gentle. "Leave her now, Arele," the voice entreated. "Let her rest."

Aaron turned to the sound of that voice, and the eyes that met his calmed his fear. They were the same eyes that gazed upon him now: patient eyes full of wisdom and compassion, eyes entirely out of place in Dvoire's face. As a child of three he had removed his hands from his mother's face, turned from her, just for an instant, to meet those eyes, and in that instant they had shifted to his mother and she had slipped from him forever. Now he made no such mistake. He shielded Tsila's gaze with his hand, and with his own gaze fastened hard on Dvoire, he met her command with his own.

"Out!" he said, his voice so harsh that Dvoire started and retreated a step. Still, she didn't flee. She was a confident woman, if not skilled. She was used to fear and pain and had dealt with more than a few difficult husbands. She prided herself on knowing when to be strict and when to cajole and comfort. "Aaron Lev," she purred now, her voice a roll of velvet. But Aaron Lev was not fooled.

"Out!" he said again, and a violence rose in his eyes, a violence unlike any Dvoire had encountered in a husband awaiting the birth of a child. Afraid both to face it and to turn her back to it, Dvoire backed out of the house, then hurried into town, her tongue laden with tales of strangeness and bewitching in the house of Aaron Lev on the hill.

Sing, O heavens and be joyful, O earth
And break forth into singing, O mountains;
For the Lord hath comforted his people,
And hath compassion upon his afflicted.

"How is Tsila?" Lipsa whispered to me. She alone of all the women in *shul* had shifted on the bench to make a place for me.

"Not so good," I answered.

Tsila had been alone in the house when she'd felt the pain in her back. She had thought at first she was mistaken. It was too early, all wrong, this ever tightening band of pain. She mistook the baby for a clot of blood at first, a clot as large as one of the river rats that roamed the bank at night. Then she saw the perfect head, the tiny hand clenched against its fate. She tore off a strip of the cobalt brocade, wrapped him in it, and turned him into the ground at the edge of our yard.

It's no surprise, I heard whispered all around the women's section of the *shul. There's a sourness in that woman, is there not?* they whispered, even as they extended their hands to me in comfort. *And a weakness in the man. Yes, a weakness.*

"Tell Tsila I'll come to see her later," Lipsa said, patting my hand as she had always done to reassure me.

SARA WAS WAITING FOR ME OUTSIDE *SHUL.* AS SHE walked me home she urged me to ignore the talk about my family, chiding me for heeding every bit of gossip that assaulted my ears.

I listened to Sara's words halfheartedly. There was such an aching pressure in my chest: grief about my baby brother, dead, my own hopes buried with him in the corner of our yard, while all the love and longing that I'd felt for him lived within me still, and shame as well that ours was not a home that could sustain new life.

"Why do you listen to all the gossiping *yentas* when there's obviously not a grain of truth in anything they say?" Sara asked me.

"Even in the most wicked gossip there is usually a grain of truth," I responded, thinking that if my father was not actually bewitched, as people were saying, he was certainly strange in his behavior. He had not left Tsila's side since he had chased Dvoire from the house, insisting on feeding Tsila every spoonful of food she could swallow and performing other, more personal tasks that would more properly have been left to me or her mother.

"What truth?" Sara asked. "One has your mother cavorting with the teamster Noam, excuse my vulgarity, and another with the capitalist Entelman. What grain of truth can you possibly find in such—"

"My mother?" I asked. "Mr. Entelman?"

While Sara immediately regretted having opened her mouth, I would not allow her to shut it again until she had told me all she had heard.

"There's nothing to tell," she insisted. "Stupidities about your mother, Mr. Entelman, his music room, I don't know."

"What stupidities?" I persisted.

"Lies," Sara said. "Baseness. Don't look at me that way."

"What way?" I asked.

"Don't hang on to gossip as if your truth can be found in it," Sara said.

I said nothing.

" 'The mouths of the foolish pour out foolishness,' " Sara quoted, the first and only time I ever heard words of Torah pass her lips.

When I continued to say nothing, she asked if I thought mine was the only family whose good name had been besmirched in the mud that passed for human discourse in our town. "Do you think it was easy for me when my mother started her *heder*?"

I remembered, then, the comments I had overheard when word first spread that Hodel the widow had taken it upon herself to educate the girls of the town. *Old maids. That's what she'll produce. Dried-up spinsters full of nothing but letters.*

"Better she should have remained a charity case like all the other widows. That the *yentas* would have approved of," Sara said, a bitterness creeping into her voice. *Oh, thank you, Mrs. Chayvitz, for your kindness to a poor widow and her children,* Sara wheedled, extending her hand for alms as a beggar would. "Yes, that would have been more acceptable. Then Zelda Chayvitz and her cronies could have collected a few more *mitzvahs* for themselves by giving charity compassionately to the poor widow Hodel."

Sara strode ahead, her pace quickening as her anger mounted, then she stopped in her tracks. "I know the truth about your mother," she said to me. "I know the truth behind all the gossip and I can tell you what it is."

I waited, hardly daring to breathe.

"Your mother turned her back on the good women of this town. She turned her back on the so-called help they offered and the plans they made for her, thereby cheating them of the precious *mitzvahs* they're forever trying to amass for themselves. Even when her own plans failed and she had to follow theirs, she kept her back to them, and for that they'll forever take their revenge. That's the truth behind the talk you bother yourself over." And with that pronouncement Sara resumed walking.

I fell into step beside her, disappointment heavy within me. I admired the neatness of Sara's explanation, the certainty of her conviction, but try as I might to impose it on my own mind, unruly thoughts escaped its net.

"It wasn't just the women of this town that my mother turned her back on," I said to Sara, a shame I hadn't anticipated rising hot within me. The unnaturalness of my mother's final act—that's what I wanted to speak of. Her turning from life, newly born and her own. Could it not be that the endless talk about her was simply an attempt to find the story, the one story, that might finally explain the inexplicable? But I said none of that, for shame choked my voice, shame that I—my mere existence—had not only been insufficient to root her in this life but had proved the ultimate provocation for the unfathomable within her. Sara took my hand, and we walked in silence for a while.

"It isn't a person's origins or pedigree that determine her worth," Sara said quietly. "It's the actions one takes or fails to take in one's life. Come to Malka's study group," she urged me. "You'll find your truth there."

CHAPTER NINE

*I*T WASN'T SARA'S URGINGS, THOUGH, THAT FINALLY led me to Malka's study circle, not a sudden interest in "my truth," as Sara called it, or in action, or in meeting young people who didn't care about a person's pedigree. It was grief, a grief that in that early stage was still simple in its demands of me: to find what comfort I could by immersing myself in the same world Sara had inhabited.

The last time I saw her was four evenings before her death. She was leaving the next day for Gomel. "On private business," she said, her face bursting with pride and self-importance. "I absolutely can't breathe a word about it to anyone." Though for me she would make an exception.

A new pamphlet had recently been printed in Mozyr. Illegally, of course. Was it Gozhansky's *A Letter to Agitators*? Dikshtein's *Who Lives by What*? I can't even remember, but Sara had been elected to carry copies of it to Gomel for distribution there. She would go alone, disguised in a schoolgirl's uniform, with her hair in braids and a book satchel slung over her shoulder. But instead of books of arithmetic and grammar, the satchel would be filled with the pamphlets.

"You're going alone?" I asked, feeling envy and apprehension in equal parts.

"Absolutely," she answered with a confidence that sparked yet more envy in me. "I'm the youngest in the group, the least likely to arouse suspicion."

"How will you know what to do once you get there?" I asked.

"I have instructions," she said.

"Someone will meet you?"

"I can't say."

"Hava Leibowitz?" I persisted.

"I can't say another word."

She had already fabricated several lies to cover her absence. One for her mother and one for her employer, Mrs. Gold. "A lot of revolutionary work involves creating lies that are believable," she informed me, and certainly she had mastered that aspect of her calling.

"So do you have to rush home?" she asked me then.

"Not tonight," I said with a pang of misgiving. A few weeks had passed since Tsila had lost her baby, and in those weeks I had made a habit of returning home directly after leaving Mrs. Entelman's, forgoing my early evening walks with Sara.

With the approach of cooler weather, Aaron Lev was working as a shoemaker again and had to resume his excursions to neighboring villages, excursions that sometimes kept him away several nights at a time. While Tsila had recovered sufficiently by then to recommence her dressmaking and household duties, her sharpness had not yet returned to her, and without it she was unarmed against the gloom that descended on her every evening just before nightfall. I could feel it hovering around her the moment I entered our home, a gloom so heavy that I feared it would suffocate her if its full weight came to rest on her heart. I therefore tried to be home before nightfall, sensing my company provided distraction and some comfort.

"Tsila's not alone tonight," I said. "Her mother's visiting."

"Shall we go for a walk, then?" Sara asked, linking her arm through mine.

We walked toward the swamp. I wanted to show her the cranes, to show her that I too had my secrets.

There were always cranes in the marshes during the warm months. They arrived in early spring soon after the ice broke on the river and could be seen throughout the spring and summer walking around, singly or in pairs, searching for food with their long beaks. In the fall they converged on a field that I knew, thousands of them from all over the swamp, where they chattered and murmured and called to each other before flying off for the winter. Usually it happened later in the autumn, but that year the weather had turned early and the cranes began to gather in preparation for their journey.

"Should we be going here?" Sara asked nervously as I led her across the footbridge that led to the swamp. The sun was beginning to sink and a gray mist rose up from the marshes.

"It's okay," I assured her. There was comfort in the thick, rank air closing in around us, my baby brother's soul among the vapors we inhaled. I took Sara's hand as I led her into the mist.

We walked along the paths that were so familiar to me, Sara's grip tight on my hand, and it wasn't long before we heard the noise.

"What's that?" Sara asked, stopping in her tracks.

"Listen," I said, putting my finger to my lips to stop any sound that might scare them into flight.

We walked a bit further, and there before us was the field with its crowd of chattering cranes.

Sara watched, a look of wonder on her face. "What on earth are they discussing?" she whispered to me.

I shrugged my shoulders. Who could know?

"How long will they be here?"

"A few weeks. A month."

"And then?"

"And then . . ." I spread my arms wide and flung them skyward. "They'll take off, all in one motion."

"For Africa?" she asked.

"That's right," I said with the same self-assurance I had seen Sara display earlier that evening, although I really had no idea where the cranes flew to when they left us.

THE POGROM IN GOMEL BEGAN AS SUCH THINGS OFTEN do: over a trifle. In this case, it was the price of a barrel of herring. The woman selling the herring, a Jew, wanted six rubles for the barrel. Her customer, a Christian, offered one ruble fifty. A fight ensued, Jews fighting Christians, Christians fighting Jews.

That was Friday, Sara's first day in the city. By that evening the agitation against the Jews had begun, venomous words calculated to stoke any embers of hatred that smoldered in the hearts of the Christian townspeople. Effective words: on Saturday the first riots began. The speeches continued, words like streams of kerosene poured onto the fires of hatred. On Sunday, more riots.

This time the Jews were armed, prepared to defend themselves. Was it not helplessness that had encouraged the rioting crowd to slaughter in Kishenev, in the way that a weak and cowering dog incites the pack to rip it apart? This is what the Jews of Gomel asked themselves as they heard the rising fury of the rioting crowd. There would be no repeat of Kishenev in Gomel, they decided, no women dragged naked through the streets by their hair, no babies held by their feet as hoodlums bashed their heads against the pavement. Not in Gomel. The Bund had organized a defense of the city, dividing it into districts, each with its own squadron of armed protectors.

On Monday, though, when the defenders of the Jewish section of town went to block the marauding crowd from entering their streets, they, in turn, were blocked by soldiers. The rioters swarmed the streets, shattering, plundering, beating . . . but the soldiers stood on guard for the attackers, beating and arresting any Jews trying to come to the aid of their own.

By the end, hundreds of Jewish homes and businesses had been destroyed, scores of Jews lay injured, and several were dead. Sara was among the dead.

Arise and go now to the city of slaughter;
Into its courtyards wend thy way;

The young man on my left began the reading of Bialik's poem. It was the first meeting of the study circle since Sara's death. Dissatisfied with the religious mumblings at the funeral, they had decided to honor Sara's memory in a way that they felt would be truer to her life and in keeping with her wishes: with a reading and discussion of Bialik's "City of Slaughter."

Behold on tree, on stone, on fence, on mural clay,
The spattered blood and dried brains of the dead.

I had heard the poem before. Sara had read it to me on one of the hot summer nights when we had met to cool ourselves in the river long after everyone else had gone to bed. Sara hadn't swum that night but had remained on the bank, reading to me as I treaded water a few feet away. It was a still night but not peaceful. The words Sara recited disturbed the air. When I quieted my own movements I could feel the uneasy bodies of everyone else in the town tossing sleeplessly in their beds.

"Kishenev did not just happen," Sara told me when she finished reading. "It was planned by the government, stage-managed from its earliest stirrings, to vent anger and frustration that could be turned against the government, to misdirect its expression. And it wasn't the first time."

I remembered Tsila telling me how the government had incited a wave of pogroms and expulsions twenty years earlier, following the assassination of Alexander II.

"Not the first time. No," Sara agreed with herself. "But something's going to change now."

The perfumes will be wafted from the acacia bud
And half its blossoms will be feathers,
Whose smell is the smell of blood!

The air had been thick with feathers, Sara had told me. For miles around, feathers had fallen like snow in the warm spring air carpeting the streets, blanketing the faces of the dead. Feathers from the shredded mattresses of Jewish homes, from the pillows that had once cushioned sleeping heads.

And, spiting thee, strange incense they will bring—
Banish thy loathing—all the beauty of the spring,

I had expected a small group of young women, maybe ten or so, arranged in a circle so that no one was ahead or behind anyone else, not even Malka. That was how Sara had described it. But for this occasion, this memorial to their fallen comrade, the room was crammed full of young people of both sexes, every space on the benches filled and more standing against the back walls and in the spaces between the benches.

Upon the mound lie two, and both are headless—
A Jew and his hound.
The self-same axe struck both, and both were flung
Upon the self-same heap where swine seek dung;

The poem was passed from person to person, each reading a line or two before passing it on to his neighbor. Such variety in tone and timbre . . . some of those present could barely read, but no one rushed them. They took the time they needed to sound each word, and the one or two who couldn't read at all still held the text in their own hands while a neighbor read their lines.

Descend then, to the cellars of the town,
There where the virginal daughters of thy folk were fouled,

There was a gentleness to the voice that read those lines, a tenderness that caressed the violence of the lines. I looked up and saw the boy I had encountered in the swamp a few years earlier, the boy who had rendered a single note of sadness out of one of the reeds I had collected for Tsila. The sadness he had evoked that day had since come to fruition, the only thing, it seemed, that had come to fruition since I had last seen him. He was a young man now, and even in that room crowded with like-minded young people, something in his voice reached more deeply into me than the others. I strained to get a better look at him but could see only his profile—sharp and gaunt, his skin sallow in the dim light of the room.

> *How did their menfolk bear it, how did they bear this yoke?*
> *They crawled forth from their holes, they fled to the house of the Lord,*
> *They offered thanks to Him, the sweet benedictory word.*

As the poem passed from person to person, the atmosphere of sadness that had filled the room began to give way to a building anger, an anger that seemed as directed at the victims of the slaughter as at the perpetrators.

> *The Cohanim sallied forth, to the Rabbi's house they flitted:*
> *Tell me, O Rabbi, tell, is my own wife permitted?*

The poem, it seemed to me, scorned those who had died, for their own helpless martyrdom, and scorned too those who had survived, for their cowardice. Was this not a sacrilege, I wondered, a dishonor to the dead and living alike?

> *Come, now, and I will bring thee to their lairs,*
> *The privies, jakes and pigpens where the heirs*
> *Of Hasmoneans lay, with trembling knees,*
> *Concealed and cowering,—the sons of the Maccabees!*

The poem was moving ever closer to me, would soon be in my own hands, my own voice expected to ring out in the silence of the room. Apprehension hardened to a knot in my stomach. I thought of Sara's mother at the cemetery, a figure as twisted in grief as the most gnarled of the junipers in the swamp.

Brief-weary and forespent, a dark Shekinah
Runs to each nook and cannot find its rest;
Wishes to weep, but weeping does not come;
Would roar; is dumb.

I thought of the cranes on their field in the swamp. The weather had been mild all week and they seemed in no hurry to bring an end to their gathering. That is where I wanted to be, alone with the cranes in their last moments of communion with each other, alone with the memories of the last moments I had spent with Sara. But the poem was handed to me, a few sheets of flimsy paper, gray and grubby from all the sets of hands it had already passed through. The words were barely legible, between the poor quality of the paper and the dim light of the room. Was this a fitting tribute to my friend? And yet, as I held those sheets of well-worn paper in my hands and my eyes passed over the words printed upon them, a surge of energy flowed into me, as if with these few sheets of paper came the combined vigor of all the hands that had touched it before mine, and all the eyes that had beheld these words before mine had. My voice, when I started to read, surprised me with its strength.

Its head beneath its wing, its wing outspread
Over the shadows of the martyr'd dead,
Its tears in dimness and in silence shed.

A pair of hands received the poem I passed to them, but though the poem left my grasp, the energy it had carried with it did not ebb from me. I listened with heightened awareness to the reading, noticed even more clearly than before the faces and voices of those around me.

It is a preacher mounts the pulpit now.
He opens his mouth, he stutters, stammers. Hark
The empty verses from his speaking flow.

It was Breina, the youngest daughter of the rabbi of the new *shul*, who read those lines. A few weeks earlier her sister Hadassah had married the son of the Slutsk Rav, and now, Freyde had told me, a quick match was being sought for Breina. Freyde didn't know why. "It's not like she's an old maid, at sixteen. What's the rush? Are they afraid her beauty won't keep another year?" I understood from the anger in Breina's voice as she read that it wasn't her beauty her parents feared wouldn't keep.

> *The old attend his doctrine, and they nod.*
> *The young ones hearken to his speech; they yawn.*
> *The mark of death is on their brows; their God*
> *Has utterly forsaken every one.*

Breina continued reading, longer than others before her had, but no one reached for the poem until she had read as much as she wanted. The poem passed then to a woman sitting in the dimness of a corner of the room.

> What is thy business here, O son of man?
> Rise, to the desert flee!
> The cup of affliction thither bear with thee!

Her voice was deep, forceful yet not forced. I glanced up and saw that it was Hava Leibowitz, returned to our town, as the soothsayer had predicted, for a death not her own. I remembered her as a clumsy girl, an ungainly presence stooping beside her mother, always the more notice-able for her attempts to make herself smaller, but the woman she had be-come bore little resemblance to the girl she had been. There was still a bulk to her physical presence, but it seemed proportional now to the size of the personality that dwelled within. Dressed austerely in high-necked dress and pince-nez, her hair pulled into a tight bun from which no strand escaped—there was a severity to this Hava's physical presence, and an authority to her voice that forced other eyes in the room—not just mine—to seek her out. Why had she returned to this place, I wondered, a place she had once fled. To honor Sara, I told myself, but Tsila's voice echoed in my head. *Like Lot's wife,* Tsila had said about Hava the morn-ing after she fled. *She never could resist a disaster, that one.*

The poem passed finally to Malka, who finished the reading and then calmly informed us that the discussion planned for after the read-ing would have to be postponed on account of a report that the police had received word of this meeting and might, at any moment, launch a raid. We were to leave at once, in absolute silence, and disperse imme-diately. And with that, the room emptied so quickly that by the time I stepped alone into the cool night air there was no sign that the evening's proceedings had been anything other than a dream.

Siberia, November 1911

Bitter Heshvan begins with this new moon. Bitter, for it is the only moon that brings us no holidays. In every other month we have been given something to celebrate: a feast, a fast, an occasion to exalt, to remember. But in Heshvan there is only the passage of days, and what dreary days they are. Here at Maltzev, the cold has returned, imparting its own sort of bitterness, but in the Polyseh too, there was always a sadness to this month. The sky, so glorious for the festivals of Tishri, would darken and lower itself over the flat landscape. The rains would begin, the roads turn to mud. Leaves lost their color and hung lifelessly, waiting to fall. Fields lay naked and half flooded. There is no beauty to Heshvan, I thought as a girl. The eye turns inward, awaiting the bright frosts of Kislev. And yet, the beauty must be found. So Tsila instructed me the Heshvan following the loss of her child. Otherwise our blessing of each new day, our thanks to the Creator, will be uttered with a falseness of feeling.

I have a particular bitterness this Heshvan. The letters from Bayla, so regular for so long, have stopped.

The last letter came in the spring. There were the usual inquiries about my health, the usual reassurances about you, your sweetness and intelligence, and about how when the time was right—*the minute the time is right, and that's a solemn vow*—all would be revealed to you about who your mother really is. And then three paragraphs that filled me with sadness, a story meant to provide a moment of amusement.

"Last night the Zalmans entertained a special guest for dinner," Bayla wrote. "The new partner that has recently joined Yehuda in business. Sam Eisenberg is his name. Not a bad-looking man, though self-satisfied. I didn't like the look he gave me when he walked in: coolly appraising, as if I am yet another piece of merchandise he might easily acquire. And his conversation! As he and Yehuda sat at the table waiting to be served, he talked of nothing but profits—of which there seems to be no shortage in his life. Can you imagine such a bore? Or do I mean a boor? I promptly spilled the soup on him. Not on purpose, but what difference? There it was, Shendel's famous chicken soup all over Sam Eisenberg's lap. And scalding hot it was too.

"I was mortified, of course, and immediately chased hot with cold— a whole pitcher of cold water, I threw into his lap—then I fell to my knees as I tried to clean him up, but really what I felt—once I realized he wasn't seriously injured—was satisfaction. I shouldn't have—the man was quite scalded, and I could have lost my job right there, and where would that have left me? But I felt strangely satisfied to have caused some pain to this man who, just moments earlier, had looked me over with a superior air.

"My satisfaction was short-lived, however, for do you know what he said? As Shendel tried to pry me off of him, all apology to him and anger to me, he put a restraining arm on Shendel's and told her to let me be, for when in his life had he ever encountered a woman who could cause such pain and such pleasure all in the same moment? That is what he said, the boor. At dinner. In mixed company. Can you imagine such nerve?"

I could imagine it all too clearly. The scene rose up vividly in my mind the moment Bayla described it. Sam Eisenberg, successful and handsome, but more hungry than satisfied, despite Bayla's mistaken first impression. Ravenous, in fact—he is a man of huge appetites. It's his first dinner at the home of his new partner. The talk is of business, of profits—present and future. Of expansion. He's talking, for his tongue is smooth, but his mind is on the woman coming through the door from the kitchen, carrying a large, steaming tray. She is tall and very pale, with wavy red hair hanging down to her waist. She gives the appearance of calm, placidity even, as she carries in the tray, but two spots of color burn in her cheeks, as if great feelings roil inside her, surfacing there, in those two burning spots. And where else, Sam wonders. Where else on that long, white body might her passion surface? That is his thought as he sees the tray begin to tilt. Yes, he sees it happening. He watches the tray tilt slightly, sees the bowls as they begin to slide, but like so many of us who see our fate before us, he is powerless to stop it.

He will marry Bayla, this I knew as I read the story she sent to amuse me. He will bestow his name on her, his fortune. He will welcome her into the life he has made in this new country, she and the child she has brought with her from the old. He will embrace the child as well as the woman, adopt the child as his own, for that's the sort of man he is, this Sam Eisenberg. Generous as he is ravenous. And Bayla won't refuse him. Why would she, a woman who has never felt the unreserved love of a man? So she can continue to serve Shendel when she might instead sit as a guest at her table? So she can raise a child not her own in poverty, ever waiting for the mother who will not come to claim her? No. Bayla is neither stupid nor stubborn. She will marry Sam Eisenberg, if she hasn't already, and allow him to adopt my daughter as his own. You, my lovely.

CHAPTER TEN

1903

"THE BEAUTY OF LIFE IS NOT ALWAYS OBVIOUS," TSILA said to me that dreary Heshvan after the summer of deaths. "But it must be found. That is our task here. To find the beauty of His work and make it manifest."

On a dull afternoon of that month I entered the music room of the Entelman household. I had finished work early that day—Mrs. Entelman was tired, more tired than usual, and wanted only to be left alone in her darkened room. She had received a letter from Shendel that day, an event that at one time would have brought her pleasure but now seemed only to deepen her exhaustion. The mail had arrived after breakfast, but she had not read the letter then. She had placed it on her night table, where it had sat, unopened, throughout the morning.

"Honeysuckle," she muttered at one point as she sniffed the envelope beside her. "A cloying fragrance, don't you agree? It has always given me a headache."

It was the change in weather that was giving her a headache, I suggested. A wind had risen with the dawn—if you could call such grayness dawn. A cold wind, from the north.

"Maybe you're right. Would you be a dear and bring me a compress. Not too cold—you know how I like it."

And so she lay all morning, neither speaking nor moving. And so I had to sit as well—Mrs. Entelman didn't like activity around her when suffering one of her headaches. She refused lunch, swallowing only two spoonfuls of consommé before pushing away the tray, but she did at least remove the compress from her eyes and sit up in her bed. And after I took away the tray she reached for the letter beside her.

She read without comment or expression, letting each scented page flutter to the floor beside her as she finished with it. I stooped to pick up the scattered pages.

"Put it all in the fire," she said, and when I stared at her in confusion, she said, "Go on now, don't just stand there like a statue—did I not ask you to do something for me? And this too," she said, holding out the sweet-smelling envelope with two fingers. "If she is no longer able to bring herself to obey the commandment of honoring her parents, she can at least have to her credit the *mitzvah* of providing her old mother with some warmth. Come on, now. I can't hold this all day."

Mrs. Entelman watched me as I fed her daughter's letter to the fire, then she sighed deeply, settled back into her pillows, and put the compress back on her eyes. "To think I should end up in this way," she said. "As if I never had a daughter, and she no mother."

"You still have a daughter," I commented, as I remained by the fireplace and watched Shendel's letter curl and blacken, then turn to ash.

Mrs. Entelman didn't answer but she smiled. "Your mother also used to answer back," she said from behind her compress. "She was cheeky, high in spirits. Or so it seemed." Mrs. Entelman was quiet for a few moments, then added, "Your mother was happy when she worked here. Don't mind what you hear."

"I've heard nothing," I said quickly.

"And don't start lying to me now," she said. "Lying is a sin, as you've surely been taught." She removed the compress and opened her eyes to see a blush rise to my face. "But at least your lies will never break your mother's heart. You can be thankful that your circumstances have saved you from that sin, at least."

In what way has Shendel broken your heart, I might have asked then, for does not compassion light the way to the beauty in others? But such was the bitterness of my own suffering that Heshvan that it blinded me to the suffering before me. I felt only disdain for Mrs. Entelman, impatience that she should carry on in such a way—lying in splendor, burning letters from her daughter—while Tsila and the widow Hodel worked their fingers to the bone as their own children rotted in the earth.

"Can I do anything else for you?" I asked Mrs. Entelman. There was a coldness to my voice.

"Just bring me my tea, put it on my night table, and leave me for the day."

I did as she asked, arranging her tea and lemon within her reach, quietly shutting the door to her bedroom, then descending the narrow back staircase to the kitchen. But instead of proceeding straight ahead and out through the kitchen door, I turned at the foot of the stairway toward the high, grand foyer of the main entrance of the house, then down the hallway that led to the music room.

I did not know beforehand that I was going to do such a thing, did not even know why, exactly, I was heading for that room. I had never been there before—I had no business in that part of the house—but as I walked along the hall, I remembered Sara's voice as she tried to deny the rumors she had heard. *Baseness,* she had said. *Stupidities about your mother, Mr. Entelman, his music room. I don't know.*

The door to the music room was shut. In a normal state of mind I would have turned around then. I would have realized that I could be fired for sneaking around the house in such a way. I would have been afraid of whom I might encounter behind that closed, heavy door. Whom I might disturb. But there was a pressure inside me that day. An anger. It had pushed aside fear and shame and emboldened me.

The room was huge, with high ceilings and tall windows and floors of polished wood. The floors were covered with rugs—Persian rugs in shades of blue and rose. The sofa was deep rose in color and velvet to the touch. The armchair was the same. I settled myself in the armchair and wondered if my mother had once sat there before me.

Minutes passed. The gray of the afternoon pressed up against the window but could not enter the rosy room. The chair in which I sat was soft; it swallowed me deeply. Rain began to fall, a cold Heshvan rain, but the room was warm and plush. Too warm, in fact. All that velvet, perhaps. A layer of dust lay on the piano. Not a thick layer, but dust nonetheless. Enough to show that the room was little used. Yet in the vase on the piano was a sprig of white blossoms. Fresh blossoms.

I extricated myself from the armchair and walked over to the piano, certain that I must be mistaken, but I wasn't mistaken. The blossoms in the vase on the piano were real. Almond blossoms. In Heshvan. I touched one lightly with the tip of my finger, then removed the sprig from the vase and held its sweet fragrance to my nose.

"Beautiful, aren't they?" a voice inquired. It was a man's voice, deep and sonorous, and I swung around to face it.

I had known he would come. From the moment I had entered the room I had known. I just had to wait, and then I would face him. For what purpose, I wasn't sure yet. Just to face him. Eye to eye. But as I stood there with the sprig of almond blossoms in my hand, it was not his eyes I faced but the floor—a swirl of blue and rose.

"They're from my greenhouse," he said.

The blossoms, he meant.

"I haven't seen you before. Are you new here?"

I saw his legs advance across the room. His shoes were of fine leather and well made. There was a fineness to the stitches, a care that had been taken. It was Aaron Lev's work—I recognized the precision— and a feeling of comfort filled me. Then I felt his hand on my chin, my gaze being lifted to meet his.

His eyes were my own. I saw it right away. I had thought, always, that my eyes were my mother's, but they were not. They were his. And as I stared into the same eyes that had met mine in the mirror every morning and evening of my life, I knew without a doubt and without a care to the how or why of the thing that the man I faced at that moment was my father.

Did he recognize me as well? He said nothing.

"I'm sorry to have disturbed you," I told him. There was a calmness within me. And an anger, cooling after a lifetime of hot shame. "I'm in your wife's employ and have no business in this part of your house."

He released my face, and I walked quickly and silently from the room.

CHAPTER ELEVEN

1904

AARON LEV MADE HIS WAY SLOWLY HOME IN THE WANING
light of the winter afternoon. I watched him as he walked. His day had
been a success, I would later hear him tell Tsila. The whole week, in
fact. But there was no hint of that in his shuffling gait. He looked to me
the same as always—a man who had departed early the previous Sunday
for a neighboring village, shoemaking materials in hand, who was now
returning home on a Thursday afternoon with a pocket only slightly
heavier with coins than it had been when he set out.

The weather had been fine all week. Bright, cold days, giving way
to clear, starry nights, the kind of weather he had always loved best.
That morning the snow had sparkled so brightly in the bold sunlight
that to behold the day directly actually hurt one's eyes. A mere hint, he
would tell Tsila, of the blinding brilliance of the Divine presence. Would
that He might begin dropping such hints with more frequency. Only as
he had started for home had the sky darkened and snow begun to fall.
It was a fine snow, and dry. And now, as evening fell, his path was cushioned underfoot, and the dark pines that crowded the narrow road bent
a bit under their soft burden.

It had been a difficult autumn. Tsila had recovered from her illness
only to be afflicted by a savage restlessness. She seemed unable any
longer to find any place of repose. Nothing she saw refreshed her, noth-

ing she did provided satisfaction. She worked incessantly to no purpose, sewing a seam only to tear it out in frustration, dyeing a yard of cloth only to bemoan the dullness of the new hue. In the fields around her she saw only dreary sameness, in the forests and marshes dampness and shadow. Even her dreams provided no escape. She tossed unhappily through the night, rising unrested in the darkness before dawn. And while she didn't throw off the hand Aaron Lev offered in comfort, neither did she quiet beneath it.

"I still dream of fish," I heard her confess to him in a whisper one night. "Swimming fish, all night long. They torment me."

"It will pass," Aaron Lev told her. "Everything passes, and this will too." But when, and at what cost? As he trudged home at the end of another week he bent ever lower under the burden of his life.

I watched this man—my father, and yet not—and thought back to that night in Heshvan when I had arrived home late and drenched to the bone.

"Where were you?" Tsila had asked, falling on me. "Out so late on a night such as this! I thought something had happened to you."

"I'm sorry," I had apologized. Then I had announced that from that day on I would no longer be working for the Entelmans.

"What?" Tsila cried. "What did you do?"

"I didn't do anything. I've just decided I will no longer work there. I'll be seeking other employment, starting tomorrow."

"What other employment?" Tsila had asked. Her sharpness, though eroded, was not completely gone.

"I'll find something. I'll work at a factory if necessary."

"What happened?" Tsila had asked.

"Nothing happened."

"Then you will return there."

"I will not return there."

"You will not leave her employ to work at a factory for half the wages and twice the hours. Not while you're living under my roof, you won't."

"I'll work for Mrs. Gold, then. She hasn't found anyone to replace Sara."

"She won't pay you half of what you've been getting. Mrs. Entelman has been very generous with you. And she has not exactly over-worked you."

To this I had drawn myself up in great indignation and said: "I spit on her charity." And the very next day I presented myself to Mrs. Gold and accepted far more difficult working conditions for half the wages I had been receiving.

Never once had I offered Aaron Lev any sort of explanation, though I well knew what sort of hardship the reduction in my wages presented for the household. Had he wondered what had caused such strange be-havior? Did he wonder about me at all? Just what was he thinking as he made his way home at the end of the week? He looked so weary, so very old. He offered no hint that the fine winter weather earlier that day might have gladdened him, no hint that enough hope still lived within him to sustain him for another day. I watched him with a mix of pity, anger, and tenderness until he disappeared into the darkness.

"IT WAS *HIM*, WASN'T IT?" TSILA HAD ASKED ME ON THE night that I had announced I was quitting the Entelmans. I had gone to bed soon after my announcement, too exhausted by the day's events to eat any supper, too tired, even, for a cup of tea. I was exhausted but not able to sleep. I lay in my bed listening to the rain against the roof, the crackling of the fire, Tsila's sighs as she struggled with a dress that should have been finished and delivered already, Aaron Lev's sugges-tion that she put it away for the night and see if it didn't look better in the morning. I heard Aaron Lev leave for the evening meeting he at-tended. Then, as soon as the door shut behind him, Tsila was by my bed. "It was him, wasn't it? Mr. Entelman. What did he do to you?"

"Nothing," I said.

"Don't tell me nothing, when you come home in such a state."

I sat up in bed and looked at her. She wasn't my mother, had never tried to be, but she loved me, I realized.

"He did nothing," I repeated. "I ran into him in the hall. I met his eyes. That's all that happened. Nothing."

Tsila pulled a chair over and sat down beside me, as she did whenever I was ill.

"What was said between you?"

"Nothing," I said. "A man such as that feels no need to speak to his own daughter who is working as a maid in his house."

Tsila raised her eyebrows, but only slightly. "You are not his daughter," she said calmly, as if unsurprised that I should assert that I was. And in her lack of surprise, I found confirmation of what I already knew.

"I'm not Aaron Lev's," I said.

"Oh, but you are."

"No. I know the truth. I saw it today." And when Tsila didn't contradict me right away, I continued. "That's why Aaron Lev didn't send for me. That's why I spent six years at Lipsa's."

"You spent those years at Lipsa's because the circumstances weren't right for him to keep you. He was away often for his work—how could he care for you? A young child needs a woman's hand."

"I'm not his," I said, a feeling of despondency washing over me now. All afternoon and evening I had felt a calmness, the calmness that comes from finally seeing what has always been visible. Now, though, I began to feel the loss that knowledge entailed.

"He was married to your mother when you were conceived, married to her when you were born. You're a child of that marriage. The only living child. He sent for you the moment the circumstances were right."

"I'm not his," I said again, remembering how once, after hearing me read a passage aloud, he had looked at me in wonder for a moment, then said to Tsila that each generation stands on the shoulders of its parents. "In that way every generation can stand a little taller and see a little further than the one before," he had explained with pride, yes, pride in his voice. It was his shoulders I stood on, I understood, his and Tsila's shoulders that were imprinted on my feet. I knew the fine edge of Tsila's, the gentle slope of Aaron Lev's. I had found my balance—precarious, yes, but not so much that I couldn't spring a little. So on what would I stand now, I wondered. On the sucking mud of the swamp? "I know the truth," I said.

"No," Tsila countered. "You think you know the truth, but you don't. You saw something in that man's face, a certain similarity of features, perhaps, and from this you draw your great truth. 'I'm not his,' you keep saying about your father who raised you, as if saying such a thing, out loud in his home, doesn't constitute disrespect enough for an entire lifetime."

"I don't intend disrespect," I said feebly.

"Then what do you intend?" There was anger in her now. "To ruin our lives as well as your own? To humiliate your father in his own home? To declare yourself a bastard so that you can be damned unto the tenth generation. Is this what you intend?"

"Of course not," I said, angry myself now. "I'm just trying to speak the truth for once."

"Well, *I'm not his* is not the truth."

"Then what is?"

Tsila hesitated, but just for an instant. "You were not his, but now you are."

I WAS ALONE, HIDDEN IN A THICK STAND OF PINES, AS I watched Aaron Lev and waited for Malka. Malka had wanted a quiet place for our meeting, a place where we could converse without any danger of being overheard. I had suggested a spot in the swamp, a knoll that I knew by the broken-down shack where Tsila had first taken me, but Malka preferred the forest on the south end of town.

The air was mild, milder than the clear coldness of previous evenings, but with the falling snow had come a dampness that chilled me as I waited. Malka was late, and we had made no plan about how long I should wait for her. Everything about our arrangements had been vague, even the purpose of the meeting itself. She had called me aside as I left the study circle a few nights before and said she had something to discuss with me. Could I meet her at the appointed place and time and not tell another living soul? There had been tension in her face, fear or excitement, I couldn't tell.

At first her lateness did not diminish the sense of anticipation I felt as I waited. I was not a longtime member of the study circle, so to be singled out by Malka for a private meeting was an unexpected honor. She must have seen something special in me, I reasoned. A trustworthiness, perhaps. A sense of loyalty. *Vanity of vanities,* I know now, but at the time I only wanted to be noticed for some quality uniquely my own. Sara had singled me out for her affections because of qualities I did not even know I possessed until she saw them in me. Serious, she called me, intelligent. And such is the power of friendship that once she saw them I did too, and I strove to develop them further. I could remember the sweetness of feeling remarkable, and I longed for the person I had been in her presence as much as I longed for a glimpse of her face, her sidelong glance, the flare of her nostrils and rise in her voice as she warmed to her outrage about some injustice or other. To think, then, that Malka might have seen something special in me filled me with a sense of possibility that I hadn't felt in long months. If it was trustworthiness she had seen, then I would prove myself trustworthy; if loyalty, then I'd be as loyal as Ruth.

Time passed, though, and there was still no sign of Malka. It wasn't like her to be careless about time, not like her to be vague about anything. As evening came on and I continued to wait, I felt the first prickles of fear.

I remembered the first meeting of the study circle I'd attended after the memorial for Sara. We had met on a Shabbes afternoon, in the forest, since it was becoming too difficult to find a place in town where our secrecy could be assured. There were fourteen girls at that meeting, more than Sara had described, and Malka had welcomed the newcomers and suggested that we start by going around the circle and introducing ourselves. Not just by name, she added, but by the circumstances and conditions of our lives. In this way, Malka explained, we would enter into the development of our class consciousness.

I had been afraid to start, since some of the girls there were the very ones whose stares and whispers had made my life such a torment. But as they took their turns and spoke in quiet voices about the hardships in their own lives, I began to feel the lifting of a curtain that had always hung between us. I had not understood until then that Mirel too felt shame at the treatment she received when delivering laundry to the wealthier households in town, or that beneath Breina's aloofness was fear that a marriage might be forced upon her, revulsion at the prospects chosen so far by her parents.

When it was my turn to speak I wasn't sure how I'd begin. I felt my heart beat fast and I feared my voice would tremble and the others would smirk and then turn to each other with knowing nods and glances.

"My mother walked into the river on the day of my birth," I heard myself say, and then my voice gave way.

There was a silence that seemed interminable as the group waited for me to continue, but no one whispered or snickered.

"Do you have anything else you want to add?" Malka asked finally, her tone as matter-of-fact as if I had revealed nothing more than that my father's employer often cheated him on his wages.

I had planned to describe how I had come to live with Tsila and Aaron Lev, and the current circumstances of our lives, but I shook my head, not trusting my voice.

"Your mother did not take her own life," Malka said firmly.

But she had, and I knew it, and so did everyone else sitting there.

"Your mother's life was taken from her. She was murdered. Do you understand what I'm saying?"

I shook my head, too shocked by her words—by the violence of the word *murder*—to answer.

"It was the humiliations your mother had to bear that made her life unendurable, the injustices of our current social and economic system."

And yet, hadn't others borne injustice and survived? Surely Malka knew that. Didn't others bear injustice and still rise to meet each day? Wasn't the taking of a life—one's own life, another's—the ultimate sin against God, who created us, the ultimate sin against creation itself?

"We will honor your mother's memory," Malka said.

A memory enshrouded in whispers, rumors, and shame. There was nothing to honor, I found myself thinking, but then, wasn't that also a sin? Wasn't the honoring of one's parents a commandment as essential as the injunction against the taking of a life?

"We'll expose the conditions that caused your mother's death," Malka said. "And free our world forever from such injustice."

NIGHT HAD FALLEN AS I WAITED FOR MALKA, BUT I DARED not light my lantern. I began stamping my feet and clapping my hands to ward off the chill that was settling on me. I didn't know how long I had been waiting. What seemed like hours could have been only minutes, but it was possible that it was, in fact, hours that had elapsed since I had seen Aaron Lev trudging home. I decided to recite the Psalms in order to calm myself and mark the passing time.

Happy is the man that hath not walked in the counsel of the wicked, I began. *Nor stood in the way of sinners, / Nor sat in the seat of the scornful.* I recited slowly, my voice a whisper. *Why are the nations in an uproar? And why do the peoples mutter in vain?*

The first five Psalms were short, no more than a few verses each. Ten minutes could not possibly have passed. I decided to continue. Five more. Maybe ten. And then, if Malka had still not arrived, I would have to assume a complication had arisen and I would return to town.

O Lord, do not punish me in anger, do not chastise me in fury. Have mercy on me, Lord, for I languish; heal me, for my bones shake with terror.

A stranger had come through town that day, Freyde had told me when I stopped by there after leaving Mrs. Gold's. A Jew, Freyde said, but one who spoke a language she had never heard before. Strange sounds, though not unpleasant—he said it was Spanish. It seemed to roll mostly from the forward half of his tongue, as if the throat, too busy with breathing, had no part to play in speech. "It would suit you well," Freyde added, a reference to my scarred throat, which she had never actually seen, hidden as it was by my clothing, but which she and some of the other women in town seemed unable to let fade from their imaginations.

In the Lord I take refuge; / How can you say to me, / Take to the hills like a bird!

Freyde's references to my scar disturbed me. She had been referring to it more often, as she anticipated the problems it would cause when the time came to find me a match. "With everything else you have going against you, to be marked as well for an early death . . ."

Her comment was a cruelty, nothing else, and recognizing it as such, I told her I wasn't interested in her nonsense.

She raised her eyebrows, as surprised by my boldness as I was.

"I suppose you've become too high-minded for the likes of me," she responded.

When before had I ever spoken to Freyde in such a way? Never. And I knew the reason I had now was my attendance at Malka's study group.

"You can imagine yourself as too high-minded for the ground you are forced to walk," Freyde continued. "But none of your fancy notions can change the fact that a husband must be found for you, and it won't be easy with the handprint of death at your throat."

Fret not thyself because of evildoers, I whispered intently, trying to push such morbid thoughts from my mind. It was all nonsense, I knew. The mischief of a mind still enslaved by superstition. Nothing more. *Neither be thou envious against them that work unrighteousness,* I whispered. I was at the Thirty-seventh Psalm already, and still no Malka. Then I heard an answering: *For they shall soon wither like the grass. And fade as the green herb.*

I recognized the voice. How could I not? It was the boy I had met in the swamp, the young man whose voice at the memorial meeting for Sara had touched me no less deeply than it had the first time I encountered him and thought he was my own dead brother. Could it have been my thoughts of my own death just a few moments before that had summoned him now? The thought chilled me. And though I knew such a thought was backward and superstitious, my hand moved instinctively to my throat.

Trust in the Lord, and do good, he continued. *Dwell in the land and trust faithfulness.*

He lit his lantern, its light glowing softly between us. I had not seen him since the meeting following Sara's death. Now he stood before me, his belongings tied in a cloth bundle at the end of the stick he held over his shoulder.

"Who are you?" I asked.

"Wolf," he answered.

"I'm Miriam."

"I know."

"You know? How do you know?"

To that he simply shrugged his shoulders.

"And where is Malka?" I asked.

"That I don't know."

"She was supposed to meet me here at least an hour ago. I've been waiting, as you can see, but . . ."

"Your arrangements with Malka should remain strictly between you and her," he said, and though his voice remained gentle, there was a harshness to his reprimand. "You don't know who I am. Perhaps I'm an informer for the Okhrana."

"So what if you are?" I asked quickly, ashamed at my indiscretion. "Are friends no longer allowed to meet for a walk in the forest on a winter night? Are girlish secrets now a matter of interest to the Okhrana?"

I looked at him closely, a young man of slight build, his cap pulled low on his head, his features soft in the light of his lantern.

"And where are you heading on such a night?" I asked him.

"For a walk. Just like you."

"An evening stroll?" I asked. "With all your worldly possessions hanging from your shoulder? Or am I being too nosy now? After all, for all you know I could be an informer for the Okhrana."

"That's no joking matter," he said then, his voice low and grave. "Malka's been arrested."

"Impossible," I said, fear rising in my chest.

Wolf tied his lantern and his bundle to separate limbs of a tree and felt around his pockets for a cigarette.

"Why would you say such a thing?" I asked.

Wolf lit his cigarette, inhaled deeply, then handed it to me. I handed it back to him unsmoked.

"I need your help," he said. I waited. He smoked his cigarette with rapid, sharp intakes, then extinguished it, grinding it into the snow with his foot. He untied his bundle from the tree, pulled out of it a package wrapped in cotton cloth, and handed it to me. It was a small package but heavy for its size. "I need you to hide this," he said. "I'm not sure for how long."

"What is it?" I asked. I started to unwrap the cloth right before his eyes.

"Please don't," he implored me. "The less you know about this, the safer you'll be."

"It's ignorance that endangers, not knowledge," I responded.

"As a rule, yes," Wolf agreed. "But . . ."

"Either you trust me or you don't," I said, and held his package out to him to take it back. He didn't take it from me.

"It's dynamite," he said.

"Dynamite?" I had expected words: pamphlets, propaganda.

"Only seven pounds, but powerful."

"And you want me to take this . . . this agent of destruction, into my home, where we have only recently mourned a death . . ."

"It's an agent of creation," he said.

"Dynamite?" I asked, incredulous now.

"Destruction births creation," he said softly.

I admit I felt a certain thrill when he said that, a thrill too that I should be chosen for such a task, entrusted with such a secret. Had he heard about me from Malka, I wondered. Had I been mentioned as someone particularly trustworthy and able?

"Are you with the Bund?" I asked him.

"I was," he said. "But not anymore."

There was frustration with the Bund that winter following the pogroms in Kishenev and Gomel. What was the good of building a Jewish proletariat, some were asking, when our fellow non-Jewish proletarians saw us as more evil than the tsarist oppressor? And where was the wisdom in building a workers' movement slowly and methodically through study circles, strikes, and demonstrations when Cossacks and other agents of the Tsar were galloping into crowds of such strikers and demonstrators, beating and trampling everyone in their path? "How can we wait for the proletariat to develop its strength when all around us men, women, and children are being felled like trees?" Breina had asked angrily at our last meeting. "Not even like trees, for what tree is tortured before feeling the blade of the axe?"

I waited for Wolf to make his argument now, to convince me of the merits of his dynamite.

"I've had word I'm to be arrested," he said. "There have been other arrests, rumors of more coming. I'm leaving the country immediately, temporarily, until . . ."

"But why me?" I asked him, feeling the weight of the dynamite in my arms. "Surely there are others you know better than me, others you can trust?"

"Quite honestly, there aren't. Not right now. There's obviously an informer at work. I thought I'd be arrested as I headed out of town. I was waiting for the sound of footsteps chasing after me as I crossed the bridge out of town, as I slipped into the forest. Then I heard a voice, a woman's voice, reciting the Psalms. It couldn't be, I told myself. Why would anyone be standing in the middle of the forest on a winter's night, in total darkness, no less, reciting the Psalms? It was a dream, I thought. There was an instant when I even wondered if it was my own death coming for me. Silly, I know." He smiled wanly. "I was afraid," he admitted. "And then I realized it was you."

"Do you remember our first meeting?" I asked him. I don't know why; there was so much else of a practical nature I should have tried to extract from him.

"In the swamp?" he asked me, and nodded.

I remembered the grayness of his skin at that first meeting, the yellow of his eyes, and the initial shock I had felt, the repugnance that had given way to the recognition of my own life in another.

"I thought at first you were my brother."

"I *am* your brother."

"My dead brother . . ."

He put a finger to my lips, and something opened inside me. "Do what I ask," he implored me. "Even if you're not sure why. It will lead to good, I promise."

Such were the words Lipsa had used when she first instructed me on following the commandments of the Torah. I was a young child then, no more than three or four years of age. Each commandment has its purpose, she explained, each its place on the path. Ours was not to understand but to follow the path. "And where does the path lead?" I asked, for even a child of three knows each path in the forest has its unique destination. "To faith," Lipsa answered.

"Someone will contact you. I promise," Wolf said again.

And with that he disappeared into the forest.

Siberia, December 1911

A moment from my childhood; it rose to mind this morning. A peaceful moment, early in my first summer with Tsila and Aaron Lev. I had recovered from my illness, and I was in the yard with Aaron Lev, who was building the chair that was to be mine. It started to rain, a fine summer rain, and we took shelter under the overhang of the roof. We watched the falling rain in silence for a while, and then he said to me, "It doesn't matter to a drop of water where it lands."

It was the first he had spoken to me directly, and I experienced a feeling of comfort, a sensation, in that moment, of being held, weightless, in the embrace of his voice.

"It's the way of all water to flow downward to the sea," he said as we watched the drops of water pool, then slide down the incline toward the road.

They could join this rivulet or that, I understood him

to mean, this stream or the other. One might seem nicer than the next, one swifter, but such differences were only momentary, insignificant, for no matter where they fell, they would find their way downward, ever downward to the sea.

As I recalled that moment, I experienced again the comfort of it, the sense I had had of being carried swiftly and effortlessly by the flow of life itself. Comfort passed quickly from me, though, for all around me was ice—we are encased in ice this time of year. All around me were drops of water frozen in time and suspended in their voyage to the sea.

I felt my mind turning, a shift to discomfort, a panic, mild still but rising. I felt myself encased in ice, entrapped within a single frozen drop of rain. I stood up and paced the length of our room to clear my mind of the image, but I couldn't. With each passing moment the ice was thickening around me, layer upon layer, forming an ever more impenetrable shell. The colors of life beyond still filtered through, but not the shape. Soon the colors would be gone as well.

"Are you all right?" Natasha's voice.

"The ice," I said.

Natasha rose from the table and approached me. "What ice?" she asked.

"On the walls. All around us."

"The ice will melt," she told me, her voice a deliberate calmness. "It forms every winter, and every springtime it melts."

"And finds its way to the sea?"

"That's right," she said, her voice still calm, but alarm clearly visible on her face.

"But for us it's different," I told Natasha. "Human beings are not like drops of water. It is not in our nature to flow effortlessly to our fate."

I felt her arms embrace me, the warmth of her wasted body.

It is only through our own actions that we can place ourselves on the proper path, I remembered Lipsa telling me.

And every act we undertook was significant in that it either furthered us along our proper path or diverted us from our intended fate.

"We can lose our own fate," I told Natasha.

That's why the Almighty gave the Torah to us and not to drops of water, Lipsa taught me. *To guide us to our proper path. The Torah lights our way.*

I buried my face in Natasha's neck and covered my ears.

"Talk to me," she said.

This is your fate, I heard Tsila's voice as my heart pounded in my ears.

"Talk to me," Natasha said again.

Listen to its strength. Do you think it's so easily diverted? I raised my head and looked into Natasha's face.

"It's nothing," I told her. "Double agents." That's what we call our turning thoughts.

1904

IT IS NO SIMPLE MATTER TO HIDE A PACKAGE OF EXPLO-
sives in quarters as close as the ones I shared with Tsila and Aaron Lev.
Even transporting it home was not without its complications. The package was about the size of an average tractate of the Talmud—*Baba
Matzia*, perhaps—but heavier. I tucked it under my coat and began to
think about where I might hope to conceal such a secret from Tsila's ob-
servant eye.

That was not all that occupied my thoughts as I walked back
through the forest toward town. The news of Malka's arrest had
shocked me, despite all I knew about the dangers of our meetings.
Would she be sent to prison now, I wondered, to desolate Siberia? And
would we, the other members of the group, also be arrested? Was that,
then, what she'd hoped to talk to me about, the growing danger of arrest, the ever tightening net? I thought again of that first meeting when
she'd told me how I could honor the memory of my mother. Who else
in our pious village had ever offered me guidance on how to observe
that most basic of commandments? I shuddered now to think of her
alone and at the mercy of her jailers.

And who was Wolf, I wondered. Was it really just coincidence that
he'd encountered me in the forest? He'd said he was no longer with the
Bund but had told me nothing more. And I, as if in a spell, had asked

him nothing of use. He had frightened me with his dynamite, his talk of informers, his *destruction births creation*. And who was to say he wasn't the very informer he was warning me about? But he had thrilled me too, I couldn't deny it. And I could still feel the pressure of his finger on my mouth, the opening inside myself. *It will lead to good,* he'd promised as I'd surrendered to my trust.

I felt the weight of the explosives that I carried, the danger of my action, and it frightened me but excited me also. Whose hands had these explosives passed through before finding their way into mine? And to whom and to what would they lead me?

I approached the town from the south, through the wealthier section. The streets were quiet—they always were here—the spacious homes peaceful in the falling snow. The Entelmans' home also looked peaceful, its gables and steep roof blanketed in snow, its lit windows glowing softly, promising comfort and warmth. But I knew there was another life beneath the one that was obviously visible. I stood by the front gate and imagined I knew exactly the life of that house: Ghitel and one of the younger maids sitting at the kitchen table polishing silver, Mrs. Entelman lying alone in her room, heavy-headed from her valerian but not asleep, Mr. Entelman standing by the piano in the music room, inhaling the scent of the fresh almond blossoms that he could procure with one easy snap of his fingers, no matter what the season of the year.

I could practically see Ghitel at the table in the kitchen—so well did I know the workings of that household—each piece of polished silver adding to the growing pile on her right, the unpolished in a diminishing pile on her left. What was Ghitel discussing with her young helper tonight, I wondered. She had always gossiped with me about maids who had worked there before. Had I now become one of the topics of her conversations? That strange girl who left for no good reason to go work for that stingy Mrs. Gold?

My eyes shifted to the upstairs window, Mrs. Entelman's room—still lit—where I had spent so many hours. Pleasant hours, I had to admit, especially when compared to my present job at Mrs. Gold's, where I spent my days climbing up and down ladders searching the crammed shelves for the goods customers wanted. My days at Mrs.

Entelman's seemed dreamlike, in contrast. While Mrs. Entelman had a streak of cruelty, it was not as wide as some, nor was she without a compensating kindness. Rare was the day when she hadn't invited me to pour myself a cup of tea as she drank her own. *I spit on her charity*, I said softly to remind myself of why I had left there, but as I stood by that gate, cold in the falling snow, I craved for a moment the warmth, the conversation, and the hot cup of tea I knew would await me had I never stormed out of that house. Gone, suddenly, was the sense of excitement I had felt only moments before. I was tired now, and cold, and it frightened me to feel the hardness of the package wedged under my coat.

The light went out in Mrs. Entelman's room. She would toss sleeplessly now for hours—or so she would report to the girl who showed up with her tea in the morning. And what else would she talk about to the girl who had replaced me? Why had she hired me in the first place, I wondered. Was it cruelty or kindness or some other instinct entirely? Surely she had known who I was.

And what about Mr. Entelman, I dared to wonder for the first time since I had last left his house. Had he recognized who stood before him that afternoon? My eyes were shaped like his, it was true, but perhaps he had looked into them, seen all I had beheld in my life, and recognized nothing of his own. Had he been kind to my mother, I wondered, and then my mind veered away from him and back to the more comfortable kitchen, where Ghitel still sat polishing and gossiping. I could hear Ghitel's complaints about her daughter, who, now that she was finally pregnant, suddenly thought herself too delicate to get out of bed first in the morning and start the fire—*She makes her husband do it, did you ever?*—but the remembered rhythms of Ghitel's gossip didn't soothe me.

My beginnings were there, I felt, in that warmly lit house I could never again enter. My future was not unlike the dynamite tucked beneath my coat—a hard compactness, the strength of whose unexploded power I could not even begin to guess at. And my fate—would it not be determined from some meeting of the two?

"Your fate is here," Tsila had told me once, placing my hand on my heart. I felt the wildness of its beat as I stood at the Entelmans' gate and despaired.

I EXPECTED THE TOWN TO BE ASLEEP. SO MUCH HAD happened that I thought it must be close to midnight. But it was still early in the evening and people were out in the streets in the lower part of town. It was Thursday night; stores were open late to enable every-one to buy what they needed for Shabbes. People finishing up the day's business scurried about with heads bent and shoulders hunched against the snow. "Good evening," I greeted everyone I passed with as casual a tone as I could manage, trying all the while to look like it was the falling snow that made me clutch my coat so tightly. As I ducked into the alley that ran behind Lipsa's, a noisy group of boys returning home from *heder* almost pushed me into the wall. "Watch it," I told them, clutching my precious package to my abdomen. "Sorry, sorry," a few of them muttered, followed moments later by a snowball whizzing by my head. "Miriam," I heard someone call me. It was Benny, Simple Sorel's oldest brother. I had been hired by his mother a few weeks earlier to draft a letter to the Governor of our *gubernia*, making a case for Benny's exemption from the military service. "He's too clumsy," his mother had instructed me to write. "He's too stupid. Tell them he can't remember the beginning of a sentence by the time he gets to the end of it. Tell them he came out of me backward and hasn't known up from down since."

It had proved useless to point out that each year the Governor received a thousand such letters about the clumsiness and stupidity of the Jews, and that each year he ignored them. His mother had insisted I write it, and then, as the weeks passed and her Benny remained unin-ducted, she became convinced that my letter had saved him.

Benny was under no such illusion—he knew the draft officers just hadn't yet reached the swamps of the Polyseh for that year's crop of re-cruits—but he had developed a liking for me as I sat in his mother's house writing insulting things about him.

"Wait up," he called after me now as I hurried to get home with seven pounds of explosives under my coat. I waited. "What's that witch done to you now?" he asked. "Did she make you stand outside all day to catch customers? You look like a snowman."

Mrs. Gold, he meant. It had become Benny's habit to drop in on me at work, supposedly to make a purchase. He would ask for several items before making up his mind, observe how Mrs. Gold ordered me around, then wait for me after work to offer his indignation on my behalf and call her a witch. At first I hadn't minded. There was something pleasant about his attention. I soon realized, however, that the items he asked for were always those on the highest shelves, and it began to annoy me that Benny's motive, apart from winning my favor with his sympathy, was to look up my skirt as I climbed up and down the ladder.

"I see they haven't drafted you yet," I answered his greeting.

"Thanks to you," he said, beginning to brush the evening's accumulation of snow from my coat. "I'm on my way to Kugelmass's. Would you like to come?"

Tsvi Kugelmass, the son of the grocer, had recently taken it into his head that it was the Yiddish language that was the source of many of our troubles, the Yiddish language that symbolized the oppression we had suffered and the degradation we had sunk to during our long exile in hostile lands. If the Jews of Russia would begin speaking Hebrew instead of Yiddish, Tsvi and his friends reasoned, we would begin to regain our dignity and throw off the yoke of our oppression. With this in mind, Tsvi had begun holding soirées where young people of both sexes stayed up until all hours conversing together in Hebrew.

I wasn't interested in Kugelmass's soirées. No one from that group had ever extended me a cordial greeting—in Hebrew or in Yiddish— and they were all planning to move to the Holy Land, where, from what I had heard, they would likely perish from malaria.

"I'm tired," I said to Benny.

"She keeps you too late. You should tell her you'll go on strike." He smiled at his own joke.

"I'm not coming from work," I said. "She let me out early because I wasn't feeling well."

"Is that why you're walking like an old woman?" Benny asked me. Hunched, he meant. Over the package of dynamite that I held against my belly.

"Yes," I lied. "I have terrible cramps."

"Then I'd better walk you home."

"The soirée at Kugelmass's," I reminded him.

"Oh, they'll still be there when I get back," he said, falling into step beside me.

He was a decent person, I thought, as we walked together through the back alleys of town. And he made a decent living as a shingle maker. He was the kind of man, I realized, who could be suggested as a match for me, his simpleminded sister enough of a mark against his value to put him in the running for one whose mother had disappeared into the river. And there would be no good reason for me to refuse him.

I felt the dynamite slip a bit under my coat and I shifted it a little. "Your offer to walk me home is very kind," I told him, "but a kinder thing would be to stop in on Ida and see if she has enough wood for tonight." We were just passing the widow Ida's, and though I knew she had enough wood—it was I who checked on her every few days; I had ever since I'd delivered the news about her Moishe—I also knew Benny would not refuse my suggestion. He was decent.

I WAS WELL AWARE THAT TSILA MIGHT FIND THE DYNA-mite hidden in our home—our quarters weren't large, as I have mentioned, and I couldn't hide it outside for fear of how dampness might affect it. That she would find it the very next day, however, was unexpected. I had decided, after much consideration, to wrap it in the cobalt brocade. That, I thought, would afford at least a few weeks of safety. The half-finished dress lay at the bottom of Tsila's pile of fabrics, where she had placed it, carefully folded, the morning after she had wrapped her dead child in one piece of the skirt. I thought the very sight of it reminded her of her deepest grief and disappointment. I did not realize it was for that reason that she pulled it out of the pile every day to stare long and hard at it.

I arrived home from work well before dark the next afternoon. It was Friday; every store in town closed early to prepare for Shabbes. Aaron Lev had come home already and departed for the bathhouse. Our house was spotless, the table covered with a white cloth and set. Tsila was sitting in her chair with the cobalt brocade on her lap. "What is this?" she asked me, as she pulled back the material of the bodice to reveal what lay enfolded within.

"Dynamite," I said simply. I had never lied to her and did not begin then.

"Dynamite," she repeated. I waited for her anger, but she said nothing more. She refolded the material carefully around the dynamite, placed it gently on the floor beside her sewing machine, and covered it exactly as I had, with the rest of her fabrics. She told me then to clean myself up and get changed for Shabbes.

WHEN AARON LEV CAME HOME FROM *SHUL* THAT FRIDAY night, he brought with him a guest. There were always a few out-of-towners in *shul* on Friday nights, travelers on their way to here or there who, of course, had to stay put once Shabbes descended, and it was customary to invite them home for a proper meal.

Tsila and I heard the approaching footsteps. We had not exchanged a word since she had returned the dynamite to its hiding place. She had lit the candles at the appointed time and opened the *siddur* to chant the Song of Songs, as we did every Friday night. I had opened my *siddur* and joined her.

This was usually my favorite time of the week, this hour of dusk after the lighting of the candles when Tsila and I read the Song of Songs together. The reading was an expression of our love for the Sabbath Bride, Tsila had explained to me once, and as we read it in the darkening Friday evenings, I could always feel the presence of the Sabbath entering the room. As we read it that evening, though, the awaited feeling of peace eluded me.

Tsila was furious, I thought, and how could she not be? *With this you have thanked me,* she would say to me soon. *With this you have ex-pressed your gratitude for my years of devotion and care.* I had accepted seven pounds of dynamite from a terrorist and hidden it in the heart of her home. I couldn't explain why; there was no excuse. I braced myself for what would soon be unleashed.

Like a lily among thorns, Tsila read aloud. *So is my beloved among the maidens.*

She was calm as she read, her anger not yet in her voice. I glanced at her face, but it too appeared calm. *My beloved is a cluster of myrrh,* she continued reading, as she had every Friday night since she had first taken me into her home. *My beloved called to me and said: Rise my love, my friend, and come away.*

I joined her in the reading, willing a calmness into my voice to match her own. We finished just as we heard my father's approach.

"Your father is here," she said, meeting my gaze. Her eyes at that moment were steady and clear. Gone now was the dullness that had clouded them in the first weeks following the baby's death, the furtive glancing away that had followed as restlessness took her over. As we heard my father's footsteps, she held my gaze as she hadn't done in many months.

Aaron Lev paused at the door to stomp his feet and clear them of snow. "Good Shabbes," he said as he opened the door.

"Good Shabbes," Tsila answered.

"I've brought a guest."

"So I see. Good Shabbes," Tsila greeted the guest, and we assem-bled around the table to sing "Shalom Aleichem."

The guest's name escapes me now but he was a peddler of string.

"String?" Tsila repeated. "And what else?"

"Nothing else," our guest answered. He hunched over the soup I had placed before him, slurping it noisily into his mouth.

"And from that you support a family?" Tsila asked.

"We manage," he answered. He lifted his face from his bowl long enough for Tsila to pour another ladleful in, then continued his slurping.

"You're from around here?" Tsila asked.

"Not far," the guest answered.

In that way the dinner continued, attempts at conversation gradually dropping off as our guest hungrily consumed everything we put before him.

"A little more chicken?" Tsila asked him, returning her own portion to the serving dish so that he could eat it.

When Aaron Lev was finished eating, he pushed his plate away and began humming a Shabbes *niggun*. Our guest continued eating, but eventually he too was finished and joined Aaron Lev's singing. They continued like this until Tsila brought tea and a plate of dried fruit. The guest drank three glasses of tea and finished all the fruit on the plate. When he and Aaron Lev had finished the grace after meals, he thanked us and left.

"The poor man," Aaron Lev said as soon as the door closed. It was clear from his tone that he was already thanking the Almighty for the blessings of his own life, which, compared to those of our departed guest, seemed many and generous.

"Poor man," Tsila agreed. "But do you think you're somehow above such a wretch?"

"Not above," Aaron Lev said quietly. "Just more fortunate."

"Today you're more fortunate, but tomorrow? The day after?"

"No one knows what the future will bring."

"Nothing good," Tsila said.

"We don't know . . ."

"We do know," Tsila said. "We may not know if you'll turn into a starving peddler, like our honored guest, wandering from village to village with nothing to offer but a ball of string. We may not know if we'll die this year from starvation or next year from a pogrom. But we do know that prosperity, comfort, a decent life—that none of these things will come to us. Never. Not if we stay here. There is no life for us here." She looked at me.

It was this she had come to, then.

"We're leaving," she said to Aaron Lev.

Aaron Lev didn't answer right away. He closed his eyes as he often did when difficult words loomed between him and Tsila, but then he smiled. It was a peaceful smile, as if a pleasantness had just filled him, a remembered fragrance, perhaps: apricots in a bowl on a table where he once sat, warm in summer sunlight, between his mother on one side and his father on the other. His eyes still closed, he inhaled deeply through nostrils thickened by years of leather and death, smiling still, as if he smelled only the sweetness of those apricots, felt only the warmth of that memory spreading inside him as easily as any spilled substance will spread when newly released from a vessel that has contained it. "We're leaving," he agreed when he opened his eyes.

Just one week earlier, after evening prayers, as he and the other men in the *shul* had huddled around the stove, reluctant to venture back out into the winter night, Hayyim Frumkin had pulled out of his pocket the most recent letter from his brother Shmulik who had departed for the Holy Land three years earlier. "This winter went easier than the last," Shmulik had written. "The rains, thank God, were plentiful, and now, as I raise my eyes to the window, I can see the buds of the almond trees swollen with new life, ready to burst into blossom." As Hayyim read those words, all eyes of the group had shifted to the window of the room in which they were gathered, a window so thickly frosted that they could not see through it to the cold darkness beyond. "We have a proper four-sided house now," the letter went on, "more reliable water. And relations with our Arab neighbors have improved since the incident I related in my last letter."

"We'll go there," Aaron Lev told us now. "To the Holy Land."

We could leave within the year, he reasoned, after the hardest frost had passed but before the spring melt, when the entrapping mud might slow us. We would go by rail to Odessa, and from there by boat, arriving in the Holy Land in the first heat of summer.

"And exchange one desert for another?" Tsila asked.

"We'll make the desert bloom," Aaron Lev answered, as some of the younger men in town had been saying—albeit more persuasively.

"Stop with the preaching."

"If Shmulik Frumkin has managed there, anyone can," Aaron Lev countered. Shmulik the Goat is what everyone called the younger Frumkin after he clambered onto the roof of his *heder* one afternoon to escape his *melamed*'s rod and then refused to come down. Neither bright nor diligent in his studies, he had seemed destined for a life of unredeemed ignorance. Yet now he tended vineyards in the Holy Land, pulled green onions out of the earth all winter long, and had new potatoes by Pesach. "We'll go to Petakh Tikva," Aaron Lev announced. "Doesn't your mother have a cousin there?"

"He died," Tsila answered.

"We'll go anyway," Aaron Lev said. "We'll grow grapes like Shmulik Frumkin does. Never mind grapes. We'll grow apricots, a whole orchard of them."

Tsila looked at Aaron Lev for a few moments, as if she were giving his idea serious consideration, then she spoke. "We're going to Argentina."

"Argentina?"

"A man stopped by the house this week," Tsila explained. "Was it just yesterday? Yes, it must have been. He was on his way out of town, heading toward Mozyr by way of the swamp. He stopped to ask if he was following the right road. It was cold, the snow was coming. I offered him a glass of tea, which he accepted."

"A Jew?" Aaron Lev asked.

"A Jew," Tsila answered, "but the Yiddish that he spoke was unusual. There was a strange rhythm to it. A lilt. Speak to me in your own language, I told him, then I closed my eyes to listen."

"You closed your eyes while a strange man was drinking tea in your house?" Aaron Lev asked.

" 'What is this language that flies out of your mouth like music?' I asked him. 'Spanish,' he told me.

"Spanish," Tsila repeated, allowing the sound of it to linger on her tongue.

"Spanish?" Aaron Lev asked.

"He's from Argentina. He works for the Baron de Hirsch."

"And from this you deduced that we too should go live . . ."

"There was a beauty to the language," Tsila told him.

It was the dynamite, I knew.

"Español," Tsila said, the smooth slide of it warming her mouth in a way—may God forgive her—that the Holy Tongue obviously did not.

"Argentina?" Aaron Lev asked again.

"It's as warm as the Holy Land, but the soil is deep and fertile."

It was the dynamite, without a doubt. This is what I thought at the time. She should have been angry. She should have been fearful, for she well understood the danger of the situation. But she was neither of these. There was a composure to her, a clarity, as if when she had discovered what it was she held in her lap, wrapped in the very same fabric in which she had enwrapped her own dead child—a fabric she had once thought would dress a bride, her own sister—a calm had descended on her. A sudden calm, unexpected and unforeseen after what seemed, in contrast, a lifetime of agitation. And in that calm a truth revealed itself in the way that an object submerged in murky waters is suddenly visible once the storm passes. "There is nothing for us here but death," she said to Aaron Lev. "We still have time to make a life."

"A life, yes," Aaron Lev agreed. "But Argentina?"

"People say the Baron's colonies there are holding their own." She meant the agricultural colonies in Argentina that had been founded for landless Russian Jews by the Baron de Hirsch. "And I've heard the Christians there don't hate the Jews."

"There were problems with drought," Aaron Lev responded. "Or was it locusts? Locusts, I think. But that was a few years back," he allowed. "Conditions may have improved."

"You can grow your apricots there," Tsila said. "We could leave in the summer."

Late in the summer, Tsila decided, to allow her enough time to earn the money for our passage. That she would be able to earn our passage by then was not in question. Already she brought a focus to her discussion with Aaron Lev, a concentration that when applied to her work would win back double the customers she had lost during her long months of pregnancy and illness.

And the dynamite? It remained where I had hidden it, unseen but not unfelt, its destructive potential manifesting itself as a silence between me and Tsila, a dense, compact silence that blocked the flow of life that had always passed between us. We said less and less to each other—how could I explain having brought such danger to our home, our lives? And in the constant presence of such an act, what else was there to talk about? I began to see the dynamite—my act of accepting it—as an island that had risen out of the river that had once been my life with Tsila, an obstacle forcing a divergence of two currents that had once flowed as one.

Only once did she ask me about it. "Who gave it to you?" she asked, looking up from her work late one evening.

"A boy," I answered. "I don't know his name." The first lie now lay between us.

"A boy," she repeated. "Whose name you don't know."

I waited for her anger, her cutting sarcasm, her outraged disbelief, but nothing came. Nothing. That is what I had placed between us, an absence of substance as deadly as any explosive.

"A boy whose name she doesn't know," Tsila repeated. To herself, not to me. She returned her focus to her work.

A FEW WEEKS LATER, ON A PARTICULARLY COLD AFTER-noon, a young woman, well dressed in a lambswool coat and hat, en-tered Mrs. Gold's store.

"Can I help you?" Mrs. Gold demanded, before the girl had even fully entered.

"Yes. Good afternoon," the girl said softly, pulling aside her scarf to reveal more of her long, bony face.

"Good afternoon," Mrs. Gold answered.

"I'm wondering . . . my brother and I are just passing through on our way . . ."

I waited with curiosity to hear why she and her brother would have pulled off the main road to stop in such an out-of-the-way place.

"My brother has fallen ill," the girl said. "He's running a high fever, so we're stopping the night here. I'm wondering if you have ice compresses."

Ice there was plenty of outside, and all she needed to do was wrap some in a piece of cloth, which is what I would have suggested had Mrs. Gold not already pulled out the more expensive of her two compresses and begun her instructions on the most efficacious way of applying it.

"I know it's not too much further to Mozyr," the girl was saying. "But with his fever so high and the temperature outside already so cold, and dropping, it seems—"

"Never mind Mozyr," Mrs. Gold interrupted. "Markowitz has rooms above the tavern, very warm, my own father-in-law stayed in them once. This was a few years ago now, of course, but what's a few years to a room? It's mortals like us who bear the ravages of time. Is your brother taking quinine?"

"I don't think—"

"Miriam! Bring me some tablets of quinine."

I moved the ladder to the pharmaceutical supplies.

"I think just some soap, maybe. If you have it."

"Of course we have it."

I moved the ladder to the hygiene supplies.

"And also . . ." The whole time the girl spoke, her voice was so low that one had to strain to hear it. And her skin had an unhealthy pallor, as if her blood had long ceased to rush beneath its surface. "Some writing paper. It doesn't have to be the highest quality."

"Poor quality you can get at Zirl's on the other side of the market. Here we carry only the best," Mrs. Gold informed her. "Over there," Mrs. Gold directed me. "The top shelf. How many times do you have to be told something before you remember?" She smiled apologetically at her customer.

"I'd like to write a letter to my parents to inform them . . ."

"You'll need ink, then. Miriam!"

"Yes, ink," the girl said.

"Postage I can't help you with, though," Mrs. Gold said.

The door to the store opened again and Benny entered.

"You again!" Mrs. Gold greeted him.

Benny had been coming to Mrs. Gold's store ever more frequently—almost daily—since discovering my family's plan to move to Argentina. "Argentina!" he had repeated when I first told him. He was walking me home after work one night. We were just passing the widow Ida's. It was a clear night, and cold. Our lanterns cast a shifting light onto the snow. Benny fell silent as we began to climb the hill to my house.

"It's warm there," I told him. "They speak Spanish."

He remained silent—unusual for Benny, who liked to fill any silence with joking and banter.

"Tsila says the Christians there don't hate the Jews," I elaborated.

Still no answer from Benny.

"We'll grow apricots," I said.

"And do you want to go?" Benny asked finally. "Do you want to go to this Argentina and grow apricots?"

"I don't know," I had to admit. My life had certainly become lonelier and more difficult since the night I'd met Wolf in the forest. A few days after Malka's arrest Breina and another girl had also been arrested. The study circle had temporarily suspended its meetings, but even if it hadn't, I couldn't have attended. Tsila insisted now that I come home immediately after work, to sit night after night with no company but her silence. And on Shabbes, the one day I didn't have to work, I wasn't allowed to go anywhere except *shul.* There were many days when I thought anything at all would be better than the life I was living, yet when I tried to imagine what awaited me in Argentina, nothing rose to mind.

Benny stopped walking and turned to face me. "You don't have to go, you know."

"Of course I do," I said lightly. There was something in his tone that made me want to skip to the end of this conversation. "What am I supposed to do when Tsila and Aaron Lev leave? Move in with the witch?"

"You don't have to go," Benny repeated, ignoring my feeble attempt at humor. There was something ghastly about his face—his square chin, his broad nostrils—lit from below by his lantern. I raised my own lantern to make his face more recognizably Benny's.

"I know why you're going, why they're taking you away from here," he said.

Now my body tightened to an animal's caution. Was it the dynamite Benny was referring to? It had to be. But how could Benny know of it? Was it possible that Benny had been sent to retrieve it from me?

"I know what they say about you," he told me.

I waited.

"That you'll never find a bridegroom," he said.

"I won't?"

Benny took a deep breath. "I don't believe in any of that nonsense. That's all it is. Nonsense."

"What's nonsense?" I asked, scarcely breathing.

"You know," he said, unwilling to say it. But then he did. Say it. "Declaring someone a bastard. And unto the tenth generation, no less. It's utter nonsense, nothing more." Benny was declaring himself modern, as well as decent. "To me, you're who you are. I don't care about your parentage."

I said nothing, of course. One needs air to speak, and Benny's words had emptied me like a punch to my deepest gut. Here was something that had never reached my ears before, despite the whispers that had assaulted me all my life. Here was my secret, my great discovery about myself, revealed to be as widely shared as the filthy copper kopecks that passed through every hand in town. And here I had been imagining how I might refuse Benny if he were proposed as a possible match for me, flattering myself that he might be too dull for my liking, imagining that I could pick and choose from among prospective bridegrooms.

"You don't have to run to Argentina," Benny said. "There's a new world dawning, even here. Not right here, of course. We'd have to go to Odessa or somewhere to find a rabbi willing to marry us. And God help us both if my mother gets wind of it first. But I'll marry you, Miriam. You don't have to go to Argentina to find a man willing to marry you."

BENNY STAMPED HIS FEET AS HE ENTERED MRS. GOLD'S and pulled off his mitts to warm his face with his hands. "Good afternoon," he said to all and no one in particular. I had not spoken to him since turning wordlessly from his proposal to me.

"Good afternoon," said the young woman in the lambskin coat, catching Benny's eyes with a boldness that seemed to me a bit unseemly.

"I need some kerosene," Benny said. "Oh, and some goose fat, so I don't get frostbite on my way home." He positioned himself beside my ladder as I climbed for the goose fat.

"But also . . . ," the girl continued to Mrs. Gold, "he has these peculiar boils developing on his face."

"Who?" Benny asked me.

I ignored him, the mere sight of him a renewed humiliation.

"Not boils, exactly, more like pustules. I'm wondering if there's a pharmacy where I can get something for that."

"A pharmacy? In this backwater?" Benny asked, laughing. "You'll have to go to Mozyr for that, sister."

I climbed down the ladder and added up his purchases.

"You don't need a pharmacy to treat boils," Mrs. Gold said.

"Pustules, really."

"Pustules, boils, carbuncles—it doesn't matter what you call them. I have something that will help. Guaranteed."

"Powdered cobwebs," Benny muttered.

"Have you not paid yet?" Mrs. Gold asked.

"I've paid."

"So what are you still doing here? Do you want me to have you arrested for loitering?"

"Good afternoon," Benny said, taking his leave.

"I have something that will help your brother, but I have to mix it up," Mrs. Gold said. "You'll have to wait."

"Mmmm. I don't really want to leave him sitting in the coach. He'll catch his death."

"God forbid."

"Can your girl deliver it to me later?"

"It won't be until the end of the day," Mrs. Gold answered.

"That's all right," said the girl with a little smile, the first she had managed since entering the store. She was dour when she wasn't being bold with young men she had just met. "I'll pay extra, of course."

"Of course," Mrs. Gold said.

MARKOWITZ'S TAVERN WAS A DARK-WALLED ROOM WITH a clay floor and a low beamed ceiling kept aloft by thick wooden posts. Windowless and partly subterranean, it might easily have been used as a root cellar, but Markowitz had filled it instead with long tables, rough benches, a stove, and a counter from behind which he, his wife, and daughters served vodka, whiskey, brandy, and simple meals. On that evening, as on any winter evening, the tables closest to the stove at the center of the room were filled. At one, Kugelmass and his friends carried on a lively debate in Hebrew. The other tables were filled with peasants from neighboring villages stopping for a drink on the way home from the market. At the table closest to the stove Noam and some of the other coachmen warmed themselves on whiskey after their day on the road. Noam used one of the supporting posts as a backrest, leaning against it as he watched me make my way across the tavern. I went straight to the counter to ask Dina, the younger of the Markowitz daughters, to direct me to my customer's room.

"I can direct you," she answered, "but since when have you started visiting young men in their bedrooms?" She spoke loudly enough for all in the room to hear, obviously amused by this unexpected opportunity for entertainment.

"It's not the young man I'm visiting, but his sister," I responded, my voice quavering with anger and shame. "I have medicine to deliver." I held up the bottle of medicine as proof.

"So deliver it," Dina said, indicating a table by the far wall, where, now that my eyes had grown accustomed to the smoky dimness, I could see a lone female figure seated.

I made my way over to her table. She was eating a supper of herring, black bread, salted cucumbers, and tea.

"It isn't really cobwebs, is it?" she asked as I handed her the bottle.

"It may have some cobweb in it," I allowed, "but it's very effective."

"I've heard the same said about exorcisms," she said. She put some herring on a piece of bread and handed it to me. "Doesn't your employer give you time off to eat during the day?" she asked as she watched how quickly the herring disappeared down my throat.

"Usually," I answered, though that particular day had been so busy that neither Mrs. Gold nor I had had a moment's break.

"You're entitled to a lunch hour every day, you know," the girl said.

I glanced nervously around to see who might be listening, who might report us to the town's Russian officials.

The girl smiled at my nervous glances and handed me another piece of bread and herring. "I have regards for you from your friend Wolf," she said.

The herring, so delicious an instant before, was now a hard lump in my chest.

"Perhaps now you can understand why I'm less than enthusiastic about your employer's magic cobweb potions," she said. "I'm looking for more effective medicine for the illness that afflicts us all."

She spoke in a normal conversational tone that blended unnoticed into the noise of the room. My voice, when I answered, matched hers. "I have what you need," I answered, and as I did I felt an immediate quickening of my blood and a sharpening of my senses. "I can deliver it to you here tomorrow," I said.

The girl smiled. "It's my hope that my brother and I will leave here early tomorrow morning. Perhaps you can meet my coach on the road toward the bridge?"

I assured her I could, and we arranged a time.

"Thank you for your help," she said. Behind my back I heard Dina's laughter, familiar and unfriendly. "Wolf said you'd not let us down."

The thought that Wolf had spoken about me, and spoken highly, filled me with a pride that lifted me from the discomfort I felt at the sound of Dina's laughter.

"I would like to help you some more," I said.

She looked at me without speaking. Dina's laughter continued behind me, joined now by some of the men at the teamsters' table.

In front of me, the young woman nodded. "Then perhaps you will," she said without smiling. "My name is Dora," she informed me, extending her hand.

"And I'm Miriam."

*S*he was a woman in love with death. That's what
you'll likely hear about Dora. If you hear anything at all.
*She was a woman in love with death. No man could hope
to compete.*

Dora's specialty within the Combat Battalion of the
Socialist Revolutionary Party was the chemistry of explosives. It was she who loaded the bombs for many of the
party's "daring blows." But it was not the nature of her
specialty, rather the single-mindedness of it that led some
of her comrades to their opinions about her.

"There is only one sort of explosion that interests
Dora," I heard your father say of her once. It was a joke, of
course, and a crude one at that, but so persuasive is your
father with words, and so influential now within his new
party, that I fear his assessment of Dora will stand when all
others have fallen silent.

She studied obstetrics before she joined the party.

Does that sound like a woman in love with death? She was in Lydia's class—our Lydia here—and dropped out only because she could no longer, in good conscience, continue to deliver babies into misery and injustice. "Does a physician's duty not extend to healing society?" she asked Lydia, a question that, in time, led Lydia along the same path as Dora. "When this country is restored to health by revolution, it will be my great joy to deliver new life into it."

Blowpipe bombs were her forte. It was her handiwork that felled the Grand Duke Sergius Alexandrovich—Governor General of Moscow and brother-in-law of the Tsar. She was arrested soon after and went mad within months of her incarceration in the Fortress of Peter and Paul. News of her death in a lunatic asylum reached us in the winter of 1908. We still don't know how she died.

CHAPTER THIRTEEN

I LEFT MY HOME LATE IN THE WINTER OF 1904. IT was just after Purim, the exact time of year that I had first gone to live with Tsila and Aaron Lev. The older Mrs. Frumkin, Shmulik the Goat's mother, was making a trip to Kiev with her daughter Zivia. There was a free clinic there, a surgical clinic, and they were hoping something could be done about the tumor that protruded ever larger from the base of Mrs. Frumkin's spine. Since the river was not yet navigable, the Frumkins were taking the longer, more expensive route: by coach to Kalinkovich, where they would transfer to a train. And I, on Tsila's decision, was traveling with them.

A week earlier a proposed match for Tsila's younger sister, Taube, had been broken by the prospective bridegroom's family in the final stages of negotiation. It had been a good match, an excellent family—the young man in question was from a merchant family in Kiev—and the Hero and Rosa had been visibly elated that a wedding for Taube was finally imminent.

Taube, at twenty-four, should have been long married already, and certainly there had been no shortage of men suggested for her over the years. She was fussy, though, her tastes and expectations far exceeding both her beauty and the value of her dowry; and her parents were lenient—misguided, many called them. They were loathe to force their daughters into marriages.

The most recent proposal, brought by an aging but still tireless Chippa, had seemed at first too good to be true. Here was a man, finally, whose wealth and place of residence matched Taube's inflated aspirations, and whose shortcomings—four children from a deceased first wife—were not ones of character or health. The usual inquiries into background and family revealed no unpleasant surprises, and the bride and groom soon met and declared themselves agreeable to the match. It seemed, at last, that Taube was to be settled into a normal life. Plans were made for a wedding before Pesach; fittings for her trousseau began. But then a fatal complication arose.

"I could have lived in Kiev," Taube wailed as I opened the door to our house one evening after work. She was seated on the floor by Tsila's chair, her head in her older sister's lap.

"Who would want to live in such a city, anyway?" Tsila asked, stroking her sister's long, pale hair. "A city where an honest Jew is forbidden to reside—who needs such a city? *Feh!*"

It was Kiev's residency laws that Tsila was referring to, the constant round-ups and evictions, the near impossibility for a Jew from the poorer classes to obtain a permit to legally reside there.

"*I* wanted to live there," Taube wailed.

"It will all work out, I'm sure," Tsila clucked. "His family is probably just angling for an increase in your dowry."

"It will not work out," Taube said, raising her tear-streaked face from Tsila's lap. "It's over. And I'm ruined."

"Hush now. You're hardly ruined," Tsila said, impatience beginning to tighten her voice.

"I'm ruined," Taube repeated. "And all because of Bayla."

"Bayla?" Tsila snapped. "What does Bayla have to do with this?"

It seemed the prospective bridegroom's uncle had decided, at the last minute, to conduct further inquiries into Taube's family. What had taken him so long, Taube didn't know. He certainly hadn't had to dig very deep to unearth Bayla. She was living practically under their noses, right there in Kiev.

"Kiev?" Tsila asked. "With *him*?"

"How should I know? With a bunch of nihilists, apparently." A fresh burst of weeping convulsed Taube's face. She tried to throw herself back into Tsila's lap, but Tsila wouldn't have her.

"Nihilists?" Tsila asked. "I really don't think so, Taube."

"Yes, nihilists. I'm absolutely certain of it. That's exactly the word Herschel's father used when he broke the engagement."

"How did the uncle find her?"

"What do you mean, how? He dug a bit, and like a mole she emerged to the light. He said she looks ill—deathly pale, like a ghost—and is completely ill-mannered. She didn't even invite him in, the uncle of her future brother-in-law. She just stood in the doorway of her house, looking ghastly, neglecting to offer the uncle so much as a glass of tea. Can you imagine? So that was that. I can't very well blame the uncle for his report—or the family for their decision. Who would want to be associated through marriage with such . . ." Taube's mouth twisted unbecomingly now. "Such scum," she said, at which point Tsila slapped her once across the face.

"I'm going to Kiev," Tsila had announced immediately upon awakening the morning after Taube's visit. It was still dark out, but we were all up, preparing to start our day. Aaron Lev was standing by the stove, waiting for the kettle to boil. He took a lemon from the basket that hung by the dish rack, rolled it between his two hands, then cut it and divided it among three glasses.

"Bayla needs me," Tsila said. "She came to me in my dream."

Aaron Lev nodded. He poured hot water into the three glasses, then handed one to Tsila and one to me. "Did she say what she needs you for?" he asked.

"Not in so many words," Tsila said.

Aaron Lev nodded again and drank his hot lemon-water. "If she needs you so much she could have sent you a letter," he said. Ten months had now passed without a word from Bayla.

"She's too ashamed to write me," Tsila said. "He still hasn't married her. She's ashamed to admit I was right."

"How do you know he hasn't married her?"

"A sister knows these things. He's abandoned her and now she's afraid to face those who knew all along that it would end this way. It's shame that's keeping her in Kiev now, not her great revolutionary convictions. Bayla's no revolutionary."

"She *was* showing inclinations that way before she left," Aaron Lev reminded Tsila.

"Only because of *him,*" Tsila said. "Inclinations of various sorts she's always had, depending on whom she was trying to please or befriend. But inclinations don't harden into convictions with Bayla. Her nature is too tender. She's like putty that never sets, ready to be reshaped by every pair of hands that hold her."

Aaron Lev raised one eyebrow but said nothing. Tsila cradled her hot drink in her hands and held its heat to her forehead as she thought about her sister. "She should come to Argentina with us. She can start fresh there, make a new life." She looked up at Aaron Lev.

"You're going to travel all the way to Kiev just to invite her to join us in Argentina?" Aaron Lev asked. "It's such a busy time for you," he said, glancing at the pile of fabrics in Tsila's work area. Tsila followed his glance. It would be at least two weeks until she had worked her way through her backlog of orders. And by then there would be more, as Pesach and Easter approached.

"Mrs. Frumkin and her daughter are leaving for Kiev in a week," Aaron Lev said. "Can't you send a letter to Bayla with them?"

"There's enough talk about Bayla already without sending that Zivia in to see for herself. The mouth on that woman!"

"Tsila, Tsila," Aaron Lev entreated. "What makes you think Bayla would even want—"

"I'll go," I said.

"You?" Tsila turned on me. "You expect me to trust you on such a journey when I can't even let you out of my sight for an evening without you bringing God knows what into our home?"

I had not known until then that she had told Aaron Lev about the dynamite.

"Maybe she'd be better to be away from here for a while," Aaron Lev suggested as if I were no longer in the room. "She can travel with the Frumkins, stay with them in Kiev. They're decent people—I went to *heder* with Shmulik. They'll look out for her."

"Mrs. Frumkin's an idiot. And that Zivia's no brighter."

"It doesn't take genius to get to Kiev and back. It might do her some good. And they'll only be gone a week or so. Two weeks at most."

Tsila didn't answer, but neither did she argue. Aaron Lev began pulling on his overclothes, preparing to leave for the day.

"If I trust you with this, will you act with the maturity and responsibility we expect?" Tsila asked, turning to me. It was the first time she had turned her full attention to me in weeks.

So welcome was the return of her interest, the possibility of regaining her trust, that I resolved on the spot to do her bidding successfully in Kiev, to convince Bayla to join us in Argentina, to restore to Tsila not only her sister whom she had all but given up as lost forever but myself as well.

THE DAY OF MY DEPARTURE WAS AS CHEERLESS AS THE one ten years earlier when Lipsa had led me by the hand up the very road that Noam's coach was now taking me down. My future was no more discernible to me than it had been then—I could not even see the shape of the following day—but as I settled myself on the hard bench of Noam's coach, arranging sheepskins around myself for warmth, it was hope and excitement that filled me.

Noam's was not the only coach heading into Kalinkovich that day. The coaches were now traveling in caravan formation due to an increase in attacks by bandits along the way. Noam's was in the lead and the Frumkins and I were his only passengers.

No one spoke. What was there to speak about? The driving was treacherous; our eyes scanned the thick forest through which we were traveling, wary of who might emerge at any time. It was a gray, misty day. The pines crowding the road seemed black in a light that failed to illuminate the green of their boughs. Mrs. Frumkin moaned every time the runners on the coach hit a rut, a constant occurrence, since the ice was softening, rendering the road a washboard. I wondered if she might die before she made it as far, even, as Kalinkovich. And then I wondered if I would be forced to turn around if she died or if I might be allowed to continue on my own to Kiev. I settled into a huddle beneath the sheepskins and asked the Almighty's help in subduing my selfish thoughts.

I HAD BEEN LOOKING FORWARD TO THE TRAIN JOURNEY from the moment the plans for my trip were first formulated, but the scene inside the third-class car headed for Gomel was disappointingly familiar. Here were rows of seats as hard as those of Noam's coach, the usual winter smells of wet sheepskin, onions, and herring. My fellow passengers were not the exotic mix of strangers I had imagined, but the same peasants and Jews I could see on any market day. We found seats near the stove at the end of the car, and Mrs. Frumkin's daughter sipped tea.

As the conductors readied the train for departure, vendors crowded the platform selling cigarettes, cabbage pies, seeds, and other snacks. A bell rang once, then twice. Passengers rushed around the platform directing porters, collecting wayward children. The third bell rang, followed by the engine whistle, and then, almost indiscernibly, the train started rolling slowly forward.

A steady drizzle had begun to fall. For hours we passed through nothing but the same forest and mist-enshrouded swamp that I had seen every day of my life until then, yet there was newness in the very motion of the train itself, a strangeness in doing nothing but peering out a window at unfolding landscape. Here and there were villages, all the same with their huddled houses, gray in the drizzle, and their flat fields, mostly mud and stubble with a few ragged patches of snow still clinging to them.

The station in Gomel was like the one in Kalinkovich, except more so. Here were the same beggars, the same priests with their long hair and robes. The Kalinkovich station had featured several posters of little yellow-skinned monkeys with slits for eyes running in all directions from the huge, white fist of a Russian soldier. This was for the Russo-Japanese war, which had begun only three months before. In Gomel, the posters showed instead a large Cossack hat from under which a swarm of spiderlike Japanese tried to escape, and the caption, "Catch them by the hatful!"

The waiting room was larger than the one in Kalinkovich, but seating was just as scarce. All the benches were filled, and entire families, many of them emigrants, sprawled on the floor, surrounded by their trunks and baskets. The emigrants were Jews, mostly, leaving Russia in ever growing numbers as a new wave of pogroms spread across the country and a more ravenous draft was instituted for the war with Japan. The room had only one stove to heat it, but the air was stuffy and close. A well-dressed gentile woman in a long fur coat covered her nose delicately as she wound her way through the crowd. Mrs. Frumkin's hand went to her heart soon after we entered from the platform, and she declared that she could go no further.

"It's not much farther, Mamma," her daughter Zivia reassured her. The train to Kiev was, in fact, in the station. The first warning bell had already rung. "Come," Zivia urged her mother. But Mrs. Frumkin remained where she was, fanning her face and declaring herself faint.

"A little water," Zivia murmured, and a woman seated on a trunk nearby called for water. "Quick," she yelled. "A woman's sick."

"I can't go on," Mrs. Frumkin moaned.

"What did she say?" someone asked the woman on the trunk.

"She's dying," someone answered.

"Make room," someone else yelled, clearing one of the benches. "A woman's dying."

"She's not dying," Zivia said. "She's ill. I'm taking her to the clinic in Kiev for treatment."

A disapproving murmur rippled through the crowd that had now gathered around us. The woman was obviously dying, and the daughter was uncaring, cold. "Give the poor woman some air," someone said. "Some water." Mrs. Frumkin sank onto the bench while the group argued about the best course of further action.

Anxiety filled me, the first I had felt since leaving my home. My legs were suddenly heavy, my arms weak, my head so light it felt like it was floating away. Instead of traveling to Kiev and finding Bayla, I would be stranded in Gomel, attending to Mrs. Frumkin. Or worse: accompanying her and her daughter home on the next westbound train, which, according to the assembled group, would be there within one to three hours. Meanwhile, the second warning of the Kiev-bound train sounded—two clangs of the stationmaster's bell.

People around me started moving, surging past me toward the platform. Among them was another mother-daughter pair with a porter. The mother looked as sickly as Mrs. Frumkin, but it was she who seemed to be guiding her daughter, whose face wore a dazed expression, and whose eyes blinked rapidly as if she had recently emerged from total darkness into a light that disturbed her. They were coming straight toward me, and though I could have stepped out of their way, out of the path of that stream of passengers, I didn't.

"Kiev?" the porter asked me, looking at my ticket. He instructed me to follow them, which I did, past the blue cars of first class, the tan cars of second, arriving finally at the third-class cars just as the final warning rang out. I looked back as I stepped onto the train, half expecting the Frumkins to be hurrying after me, but they were nowhere in sight.

It was night by then, and I was exhausted. The mother of the pair—Mrs. Kaminsky, she introduced herself—insisted I sit with them and pushed me into the seat by the window.

"Are you sure you or your daughter don't want the window?" I asked, my relief about being on the train far outweighing any second thoughts about what I had just done.

"It's too cold for me. And my daughter is nervous when she's hemmed in."

The daughter looked nervous even sitting on the aisle. Her face glistened with sweat and her eyelids continued to flutter rapidly in what I now realized was a tic. As soon as the train began to move, however, her eyelids closed, her mouth fell open, and she began to snore softly.

I closed my eyes as well and felt myself sinking almost immediately into welcome sleep.

"Have you ever felt such hard seats?" Mrs. Kaminsky asked me.

I shook my head no without opening my eyes. Mrs. Kaminsky shifted in her seat.

"Here. Eat this," she said, poking me in the ribs until I opened my eyes.

"I'm not hungry," I told her.

"I'm a sick woman," she said as she began to eat the roll I had refused. "Sick with worry about my daughter. That's why we're going to Kiev."

I didn't respond.

"There's a *rebbe* there, Rav Shpira. You've heard of him, perhaps? It's said he can heal anybody, though between you and me, I worry she's beyond help." She glanced at her daughter, out of whose open mouth flowed a fine stream of spittle. "And you?" Mrs. Kaminsky asked. "What takes you on such a journey all alone. You have living parents?"

"Yes," I said, recognizing for the first time since bolting from the Frumkins just what I had done and how angry Tsila would be when she heard. I explained that my aunt was about to be married in Kiev but had been ill. I didn't know what made me tell such a story except that it was easier than the truth.

"Already she's sick? Even before the wedding?" Mrs. Kaminsky took a bite of her roll and settled in for a description of Bayla's symptoms, but when I was unable to provide any she looked at me through narrowed eyes as if appraising me anew. "And your parents sent *you* to care for her?"

"There was no one else who could go," I mumbled.

"I see," Mrs. Kaminsky said in a tone that made me wonder what it was that had suddenly come clear to her, but she asked nothing further, and after a while I felt my eyes closing again.

The rhythm of the train was soothing to me, and I soon pushed out all thoughts of Tsila's anger and my own irresponsibility, musing instead about Mrs. Kaminsky and her miracle-working *rebbe*. Mrs. Kaminsky's attempt to find a cure for her daughter from such a charlatan reminded me of Lipsa's scheme to trick my luck when I was a baby. *Futility,* I thought. *Backwardness.* And yet, as I drifted toward sleep, the clicking of the wheels on the track measuring the growing distance between my present and my past, I had the distinct sensation of having tricked my luck at last, of having slipped free of it in that moment that I slipped away from the Frumkins. I fell asleep to the image of my rotten luck running haplessly around the Gomel station, asking everyone if they'd seen a girl like me, trying—too late now—to find me once again.

I don't know how long I'd been sleeping when I felt Mrs. Kaminsky's finger in my ribs again and the odor of hard-boiled eggs permeating my nostrils.

"Eat," she said, pushing an egg at me when she saw my eyes open a slit.

"I can't," I protested.

"You're too thin," she insisted. "Everyone will think you're sickly like your aunt, and then you'll never find a husband."

I remembered the humiliating marriage proposal I had already received from Benny and closed my eyes again. I counted the clicks of the train over the tracks, each click taking me farther from ever having to see the likes of Benny, Dina Markowitz, Freyde . . . I fell into a deep sleep then that took me into Kiev.

IT WAS SUNNY IN KIEV. COUNTLESS GOLD CUPOLAS glinted from the wooded hillside of the city as we crossed the bridge over the Dnieper. I had left my home in late winter, but here it was spring. The trees were not yet in leaf, but buds were swollen on their limbs, and beneath us sparkled the vast Dnieper, blue in the morning light and free of ice.

The Dnieper was in flood, of course, ravaging the poorer low-lying parts of town, further polluting the already filthy water supply of the city, but I didn't know this. I saw only the vastness of its waters, the beauty of the cliffs that rose from its shores, the sun-touched domes and rooftops that peeked out from the hillside, beckoning me to enter the city.

"You'll come to us if you have a problem," Mrs. Kaminsky said as we parted, giving me the address of the relatives where she and her daughter were staying.

I thanked Mrs. Kaminsky and tucked away her address, relieved to be free of her, her nervous daughter, and her hard-boiled eggs. I emerged alone from the station into the pale spring light and understood how far I had traveled in the night. Nowhere were the half-starved oxen that roamed the streets of our town, the patroling geese, the ribbons of mud we called roads, the rough gray wagons and nags that were our only transport besides our own legs, the coachmen in their long sheepskin coats and mud-splattered boots. The road outside the station was wide and paved in yellow stone. The cabmen in the lineup sat high and upright on their boxes, immaculate in blue cloaks tied with brightly colored sashes. Their caps, also blue, sat high and upright on their heads; their gleaming boots were spotless. Even their horses seemed more refined than those from my town. Sleek and well fed, they were proud in their elaborate harness, tossing their heads imperiously, steam flowing from their nostrils.

"Can you take me to Zchiliansky Street?" I asked a cabman, showing him the paper on which Taube had written Bayla's address. He was fair and broad faced, with a thick neck and a yellow mustache that he had waxed to fine points on either end. He studied the paper carefully, twirling his mustache as he did, then he looked at me. "Twenty-five kopecks," he said, his Russian as accented with Ukrainian as mine was with Yiddish.

"First time in Kiev?" he asked me, and I felt immediately the shabbiness of my appearance, this despite the new dress of fine linen I wore beneath my coat and the new boots I had found by my bedside the morning of my departure.

"First time," I admitted, ignoring Mrs. Kaminsky's warnings about Kievans who lay in wait to take advantage of bumpkins like me.

"Then I'll take you the scenic route. No extra charge." And he offered his arm to help me into his cab.

Fineness, I thought, as we joined the stream of cabs leaving the station for the city, and *fineness,* I thought again, as I looked at the sights all around me. The streets we drove along were wide and paved with a yellow stone that matched perfectly the yellow stone of the buildings we passed. All the streets were lined with trees, leafless now but still gracious in size and in span. I noticed a large brick building the color of blood. "The university," the driver announced; then, not long after, we turned onto a wide boulevard thronged with people where the buildings—three to five stories, most of them—had shops on the street level with huge plate glass windows in which merchandise was displayed. "The Krestchatik," the driver called out.

Many promenading the Krestchatik were elegant and finely dressed, yet many were not. I saw two women in spring coats trimmed with fur strolling arm in arm, peering into shop windows. They ignored the man in boots of bark selling shoelaces from a tray, the legless woman calling from the curb about the high quality of the gingerbread she was selling.

Down the center of the boulevard rolled a horseless tram, powered, seemingly, by a life force within itself. It was electric, I knew—I was no illiterate bumpkin, no peasant from Cockroachville of the sort I would later see mocked in the Kievan newspapers. I had read of this tram—it was the first in the empire—and seen a depiction of it in a book from Hodel's lending library. Still, to know of something is not to experience it, and my heart beat with sheer joy at the wonders unfolding before me.

Here was a city draped gracefully across its hilly landscape, nestling into its ravines, crowning its peaks with gilded domes and crosses. At each turn the driver made, a new vista opened up. "The Podol," he called out, indicating with his hand the flat district beneath us that extended toward the river. "Pechersk," he announced, gesturing vaguely to a neighborhood perched on a wooded ridge above us. The sky above the ridge was high and blue. The air sweeping in from the steppe smelled clean, fresh. This, at long last, was fineness, I thought, as we passed an elaborately gilded gate, leading to what, I couldn't imagine.

We rode away from the center of town then, to a residential area. Here the streets were narrower, quieter, the houses built of wood, some covered with rough plaster. "Zchiliansky Street," the driver announced as he made another turn, then came to a stop. He helped me out of the cab and, as promised, collected not a kopeck more than the twenty-five we had agreed on at the station.

A young, harried-looking woman answered the door at Bayla's apartment. Thick strands of dark hair fell across her face from the knot she had arranged earlier in the day. Two pale, dark-eyed children clung to her legs. She scowled upon seeing me, and her scowl only deepened when I asked if Bayla was home. She didn't know any Bayla, she told me, not even glancing at the scrap of paper I had thrust in her face, the piece of paper on which Taube had carefully written the address. The previous tenants had moved out. "Gone," the woman said, with a slice of her hand. She didn't know where, and the landlord was away. If he was here he wouldn't want to be bothered, she added. She didn't want to be bothered either; that much was clear. She didn't bid me good day before shutting the door in my face.

I was not discouraged by the woman's rudeness. I had encountered rudeness far more personal from the very first moments of my life. Nor was I frightened to be alone in a city where I knew not a soul. Here was life, I thought, as the city pulsed around me. Here, my fate, I felt certain. The bright throb of the city matched perfectly the beat of my own heart. Bayla was here somewhere; I would find her. But first I needed a place to stay for the night. I walked to the nearest busy street and hailed another cab. The cabman's coat, while still blue, was not as immaculate as the first. Nor was his horse as sleek or well fed. I told him the Kaminsky address, negotiating a fee of twenty kopecks, as if hiring a cab in Kiev was no stranger to me than bartering for a dozen eggs at the market, and he took me away from the wide boulevards that had so entranced me to the dark narrow lanes of the Jewish quarter.

Mrs. Kaminsky and her daughter were having a snack of tea and hard-boiled eggs when I arrived at their relative's apartment. It was in the low-lying Ploskaya, a neighborhood of steep-roofed one-story wooden houses, much like the ones in the town I was from but more crowded together. The Kaminskys' house was near the river, but not so near that their street was flooded. The stench of sewage from the flood, however, permeated the dingy kitchen in which they were seated.

"Your aunt was not there to greet you," Mrs. Kaminsky said when she saw me, no note of surprise in her face or her tone. She had not liked the sounds of this aunt of mine, it was obvious, had doubted from the start the reliability of a woman who could not keep her health long enough to reach the marriage canopy.

"She's moved," I said.

"Moved?"

"Gone," I said, slicing my hand through the air as the woman at the apartment had.

"And you don't know where?"

At this Mrs. Kaminsky glanced at her cousin whose apartment it was. There were two rooms besides the cramped, brown-walled kitchen in which we were seated—ample space, certainly, for the family of eight that normally occupied it. But now there was Mrs. Kaminsky and her daughter as well. The cousin nodded at Mrs. Kaminsky, who then turned back to me.

"So you'll stay here, then," she said. "It's settled."

Her daughter's eyelashes fluttered even more rapidly than I had seen them yet as she placed a glass of tea and a hard-boiled egg on the table before me.

In the darkness that night, though, there was no flutter to the daughter. Her voice was smooth as satin as we lay on the narrow kitchen benches that were our beds for the night. Her name was Tsirel, and she was twenty-four years old. Her eyelids had always fluttered, she told me. This was not the problem for which she was seeking help from Rav Shpira. Her fluttering eyelids were not, in fact, a problem at all. They were merely the outward expression of the extreme sensitivity of her soul, a soul that could not bear an unobstructed view of this world's injustice.

"This is what my husband explained to me the night we were betrothed," Tsirel confided.

"You're married?" I asked. This made no sense. Why the urgency to see the *Rebbe* then, if a husband for her had already been found?

"I *was* married," Tsirel corrected me.

She was nineteen when the match was arranged. The prospective bridegroom had been forewarned about the strange movements of her eyelids, but he was not deterred. "We'll become acquainted without seeing each other," he declared, and so they had, conversing with each other from behind a sheet that was extended between them. By the time he actually saw her he had come to love the softness of the voice that spoke from behind the sheet, the kindness and goodness that he perceived within her.

The wedding took place the week before Chanukah. The weather was dismal, but still hundreds came; the bridegroom was the son of the famous Rav Frisch.

"On that day I knew the full measure of happiness this world can offer," Tsirel told me. "And then, the full measure of its sadness."

"What happened?" I asked.

"He died," Tsirel said. "But not from disease or any kind of violence. He was taken from me by sweetness and succulence."

A demon, I thought. Lilith.

"He choked on a piece of chicken," Tsirel said.

"Chicken?"

"At our wedding meal."

I shifted uncomfortably on my bench. I had heard of the tragedy, of course. It was so legendary that I hadn't realized it had happened in my lifetime. The young man who died was considered a saint: good in every way and brilliant as a scholar. For such a life to meet such an end. And on such an occasion. Suspicion fell as suspicions do. On the bride.

"I'm cursed," Tsirel said. "No man will ever have me for his bride again. I was obviously previously promised to someone else who didn't release me."

"But to whom?" I asked.

"If I only knew that . . ." Tsirel sighed deeply. "That's why I'm here."

"To find out who you belong to?"

"To remove any claims on me. To remove the curse."

She was silent then. I listened to the unfamiliar sounds of the house around me, the breathing of an entire family of strangers in the next room.

"I've been cursed all my life as well," I told Tsirel after a while.

"You have?" she asked. There was no joy in her voice, no satisfaction in another sharing her misfortune. Her bridegroom had been right about her; she was a good and gentle soul. She said nothing more for a while, then I felt her warm breath on my face as she crouched beside me in the dark, the light pressure of her hand on my shoulder.

"You'll come with me to see the *Rebbe*," she said.

"Your *rebbe* can't help me," I told her. Mine was not a simple case of haunting or a claim from beyond. There were the circumstances of my birth, first of all, which no one in my town would ever forget. There was the fact that I was a *mamzer*, a bastard, a legal status from which no rabbi could release me. "My situation's not the same as yours," I said, and as I said it, I felt a lightness I was unaccustomed to when thinking about my origins. It was a sensation not unlike what I had felt on the train when, drifting into sleep, I had felt myself freed from the clutches of my luck.

"He can help you," Tsirel said again. "He's been known to work miracles."

I didn't answer.

Tsirel remained crouched by my side a while longer, then with a slight squeeze of my shoulder released me.

I didn't rest that night for the disorientation that I felt. It wasn't the strangeness of the bench on which I lay, or the sounds so different from those that I was used to. It was my own body that felt new and strange to me, a sudden lightness I hadn't felt before. I would drift into sleep only to feel a sensation of buoyancy, as if the air in the room was too thin to hold me down. Uncluttered air, that's what it was, air that lacked the whispers and rumors and unnamed presences that had always weighed so heavily upon me. It wasn't uninhabited, of course; no air is. But it was inhabited by strangers, utter strangers whose presence I couldn't feel, whose weight fell elsewhere, on shoulders not my own.

And it wasn't just the air of that particular house. All day long I had breathed the air of strangers. A thin, light air—the air of indifference—I had moved freely through it. No one knew me in Kiev, no one cared who I was, where I came from. It could be dangerous, I supposed, to be so alone, but I felt no danger, only joy.

CHAPTER FOURTEEN

*B*Y THE END OF MY FIFTH DAY IN KIEV I STILL HAD not found Bayla. I had spent my time in the city inquiring after her at every pharmacy I could find, certain each time I saw the symbol of an apothecary that this would be the one where she was working. As the shrugs of the shoulders and shakes of the heads mounted, however, doubts began to nag at me. Who said Bayla was even working at a pharmacy, I wondered now as I made my way back to the Kaminsky apartment. And if she was, who said I would be able to find her? Kiev was a big city, was it not? It could be weeks before I had tracked down every pharmacy. Maybe months. And meanwhile I had already overstayed my welcome at the Kaminskys.

It was late in the afternoon when I turned onto the Krestchatik, crowded with shoppers and browsers. The weather had shifted during the day, the sky darkening so that now it loomed low and black over the boulevard, the golden domes of the city unnaturally bright against it. The wind had stiffened, sweeping sand and bits of garbage down the sidewalk. The streetlights had not come on yet, but the store windows were brightly lit, garish almost, in the eerie light of the approaching storm. I noticed a pharmacy up ahead that I had not yet stopped at, but paused first in front of a confectioner's window to admire the pyramids of sugared plums, cherries, and pears. Someone jostled me from behind, an old woman with a basket of rolls. I wasn't hungry, but farther up the sidewalk I saw a policeman sauntering toward us. With no permit for an extended stay in the city, I didn't want to attract his notice, so I negotiated with the old woman until he had passed.

"*Barin*," a cigarette vendor called out to the well-dressed man just ahead of me. "Buy a pack of Doves. Ten for five kopecks." The vendor was tall and well built, with a tray of cigarettes hanging off his neck and a tattered cap on his thick black curls.

"Leib," I said, for it was him.

He looked at me in confusion. We had never met, after all. I had seen him once in the swamp when he had walked past with Golda, and another time at the demonstration by the bridge when Sara had told me who he was.

"I'm Miriam," I told him. "Bayla's niece."

"Ah, yes, Miriam," he said without a moment's hesitation. He smiled and took my hand as if it were the most natural thing in the world that he should encounter me in the Krestchatik in this way. "And what brings you to Kiev? Come, shall we walk?"

Did I wonder why Leib, a teacher by training, was working now as a street peddler in Kiev? No, I did not. The sight of him in that role was no stranger to me at the time than anything else I had encountered those first few days in Kiev. I fell into step beside him and told him that I had come to Kiev to find Bayla.

"Has something happened in her family?" Leib asked, his handsome face a study of concern. Tsila was wrong about him, I decided at that moment. He obviously loved Bayla and had probably married her as promised.

"No, no, everything's all right. It's just . . ." I could hardly tell him Tsila's worries that he'd abandoned Bayla. "We're moving to Argentina, and Tsila wanted Bayla to know."

"Argentina." Leib exhaled a low whistle. "That's a long way." He stopped walking and tipped his hat at a newspaper vendor a few feet away. The newspaper vendor nodded and we turned back in the direction in which we had come. "What happened to St. Petersburg?"

"St. Petersburg?" I asked.

"Yes. Bayla tells me that her sister always dreamed of being a dress-maker in the capital."

"I don't think so," I said, though I remembered the fashion maga-zines from St. Petersburg that Tsila used to receive twice a year when I first went to live with her, magazines that she later declared wasted in a town such as ours. "I don't think my stepmother was ever one to waste her dreams on a city where Jews are prohibited to reside."

"Or to dare to dream of changing that wrong," Leib said. He smiled warmly, his dark eyes meeting mine.

"I wouldn't know," I mumbled, suddenly flustered. I felt a flush fill my cheeks as he looked at me that way. There was such intensity to his gaze that I felt, for that moment, that there must be something within myself—an attractiveness of feature, perhaps, or a charming mannerism—that justified such attention.

"So you haven't yet told me what brings you to Kiev all alone. You are alone?"

I confirmed I was alone and felt the courage of that from his atten-tive gaze. I confessed the reason I had come and the change within my-self I had felt my very first day there, reading from his expression how admirable and extraordinary he found me. "And now that I've found you perhaps I can stay in Kiev a few days longer before returning home. If you and Bayla wouldn't mind, of course . . ."

Something in my words broke the spell. Leib didn't frown or ex-press any displeasure, but his gaze shifted, his attention wandered. Away from my extraordinariness to some other thought or concern. He told me he had to get back to work now, but that he would meet me in a while in a café a few doors down. He gave me some money and told me to buy myself something while I waited.

I had not, until then, ever entered an eating establishment that was not run by Jews, never eaten any food that was not strictly kosher. Even the roll I had bought earlier from the old woman had not passed my lips. This was how I lived, how I had always lived. By habit or by faith, I didn't know. Was I aware of the chasm that was opening between my future and my past as I entered the café Leib had directed me to, a chasm that widened with every step I took? I think now that I must have been, for I remember so clearly the lurch in my gut as I stepped through the door of the café. But then I remember too the pleasure of that sensation, the promises it seemed to hold within it.

It was a splendid café, large and cavernous, with marble tables and gilded mirrors on the walls, and filled at that time of day with the hum of conversation and the clinking of spoons against saucers. A haze of tobacco thickened the air and mixed with the aromas of coffee and perfume rising from each table, the light scent of orange peel. Between the tables glided waiters dressed in black with starched white cloths hanging from their forearms. They held their silver trays high in the air, their upper bodies not moving as they glided around the room, except to bow slightly when they delivered their orders.

I seated myself at a three-legged marble table near the door. On one side of it sat a group of sailors, on the other, three ladies having tea. The ladies glanced at me, then bent their heads so close to each other that the feathers on their hats met and bobbed as one with each whispered tidbit of gossip.

A waiter approached and stood by my table without looking at me. Momentary panic rose within me. He had discovered who I was; his disdain was palpable. I feared that as soon as I opened my mouth all conversation in the room would cease, all the clinking spoons would fall silent, the haze would clear, and all eyes would turn to the table by the door where the waiter, white cloth hanging like a flag on his forearm, would extend that forearm . . .

"Coffee, please," I said.

The waiter did not move, did not respond in any way, did not appear, in fact, to have heard me. I glanced wildly about. The feathers at the next table continued to bob. On the other side of me, laughter burst like gunshot. I spun around. The sailors were leaning back, relaxed, laughing, their half-eaten dishes of ice cream strewn about the table before them.

The waiter was still standing beside me. I looked at him, but his eyes were fixed at a point somewhere above my head.

"And some ice cream," I said.

"Vanilla or pistachio?"

"Pistachio. Please."

He nodded and glided away.

I glanced at the sailors again. Their black uniforms emblazoned with vivid gold insignias reminded me of the gold-edged dress for Lena Chayvitz that Tsila had been struggling with before I left. On the sailors' caps were narrow ribbons with the name of their ship: *Azimuth.* One of the sailors met my glance and smiled broadly, revealing strong yellow teeth. I quickly looked away.

The coffee, when it arrived, was unlike anything I had ever tasted. Thick and dark, it was bitter on my tongue yet infused with an underlying sweetness. I drank it slowly, savoring its richness, a feeling of warmth and well-being spreading through me.

Customers entered and exited, some lingering by the door to wait for friends or to scan the room for the table they wanted. Though I was half turned from the door, I could sense the comings and goings, I could hear the rain when it started, pounding against the street outside. I tasted a spoonful of ice cream, but its creamy sweetness, while pleasant enough, didn't entice me. I took another sip of coffee, enjoying the dark bitterness coating my tongue.

The downpour had ended by the time I finally left the café, but the city still dripped all around me. Leib had not kept his appointment with me. Probably he had never meant to. And I, in my weakness, had failed to obtain any information about Bayla's whereabouts while I still had the chance. A flush filled my cheeks as it had earlier when I had stood talking to him on the street, but it was shame I felt now, shame that the pleasure I had taken in his gaze could have so distracted me from my purpose.

Still, I was not entirely discouraged. If anything, I felt a strengthening of my resolve. If Leib could break his promise to meet me at a café, mere moments after making it, who knew what promises he had made to Bayla and then broken? Tsila had been right to worry about her sister, right to send me to find Bayla, and find her I would. Of that I felt certain.

The air of the city was cool and fresh after the rain, and my step felt quick, my body light. I began composing a letter to Tsila and Aaron Lev as I walked, the second letter since my arrival in Kiev. In the first I had assured them of my safe arrival, and of my intention to return home immediately after contacting Bayla. Now I informed them of my failure to find Bayla at the address we'd been given, my search of the pharmacies around town, my odd encounter with Leib. *I'll stay until I find her,* I composed, though how I would manage this I hadn't quite figured out yet. I had no permit to remain in the city, no prospect for employment, no place to live. I'll find a job, I thought, a proper place to live. Had I not managed to stay here for five days already without problems or mishaps? *It won't be for long,* I promised Tsila and Aaron Lev. *I have every confidence I'll find Bayla.*

But here I hesitated. How to explain the confidence I felt when, actually, I was no closer to finding Bayla than I'd been at any point since my arrival in Kiev, when my encounter with Leib had left me, in fact, with the impression—vague but undeniable—that Bayla might not wish to be found. *Every confidence,* I repeated, but when I searched for words to explain that confidence, my mind filled only with the feeling of the air against my skin, the buoyancy of my body as I walked, the shine of Leib's curls beneath his tattered cap.

"YOU CAN'T STAY HERE," THE YOUNGER MRS. KAMINSKY greeted me when I arrived back at her apartment that evening. Tsirel and her mother had already departed the city. They had met with Rav Shpira, not once but three times, and were returning to their home now with his full assurance that all claims to Tsirel had been removed and she could proceed with a new match. I had expected my hostess to cool toward me after their departure—had felt her cooling already the evening before as Tsirel and her mother packed their belongings—and I was fully prepared now to find lodgings on my own, but the idea of having to do it so soon unnerved me more than a little.

"What do you need, money for your train fare home?" Mrs. Kaminsky asked me, misinterpreting my look of dismay. She grabbed her purse and began to rummage through it.

"I don't need money," I said. The ruble notes that Tsila had given me were still in the lining of my coat, where she had hidden them. "If I could just stay with you a few more nights . . ."

My hostess jutted out her lower lip and exhaled sharply, blowing away from her eyes a clump of hair that had escaped her kerchief.

"Just until I find my aunt." My newfound confidence seemed to be evaporating into the very air of the city that had given it rise.

"This isn't a hostel for runaways."

"I'm not a runaway," I said.

"Then go home to your parents, where you properly belong."

"My parents have already left for Argentina," I said. The lie was automatic and unplanned, as if my tongue alone retained the necessary will to stay in Kiev. "Just one more night," I pleaded.

Mrs. Kaminsky sighed deeply. "Mrs. Plotkin at number seven rents beds. Four rubles a month if she hasn't raised it. Have you found a job yet?"

I shook my head.

"A residence permit?"

I didn't answer. Mrs. Kaminsky sighed again. "I hear Shamsky's is looking for girls."

"SHE CALLS HERSELF *MRS*. PLOTKIN, BUT THERE'S never been a Mr., as far as anyone knows," said Hinda, the smaller of two girls about my age who came over to meet me as I drew water in the courtyard of Mrs. Plotkin's a few mornings later. "Not that she let that get in the way of her having a family. I've heard that each of her four brats has a different father."

"Oh, hush, Hinda," said the other, a tall skinny girl with too much hair and too little face and small round glasses that kept sliding off her nose. "I'm Masha," she introduced herself. "And this is my sister, Hinda. We live at number nine. In the cellar."

"So how much is she charging you?" Hinda asked. She was the younger of the two and could have been pretty, with her smooth black hair and eyes bright as onyx, but her temperament was bad; I could see that straight off. It had narrowed her eyes to glittering slits and twisted her smile to a smirk.

"Five rubles," I said.

"Five?" the two of them repeated in unison.

"For what, a bed in her kitchen?" Hinda asked.

"It's right beside the oven," I pointed out.

"That's a sin," Masha said.

"I'm lucky she rented it to me at all."

When I had first knocked at Mrs. Plotkin's door, she had only opened it a crack, demanding to know what I wanted before allowing me entry.

"I heard you have a bed to rent," I told her.

"Who said?" she asked.

"Mrs. Kaminsky at number eleven."

"Well, Mrs. Kaminsky at number eleven should mind her own business," Mrs. Plotkin responded, but she opened the door a crack wider so I could see her face, deeply wrinkled and sunken around a toothless mouth. "You have your permit?" she asked.

I told her I didn't.

"And Mrs. Kaminsky sent you here?" Not a wisp of hair escaped her kerchief, and her eyebrows were hairless ridges.

"I have enough money to cover a month's rent."

"How do you know what I charge for a month's rent? Wait, let me guess . . . Mrs. Kaminsky at number eleven told you."

I nodded, and Mrs. Plotkin smiled then, a tired smile, as if we had just shared a joke about the state of the world. "So?" she asked. "What's the rent?"

"Four rubles," I said.

"That's for girls who have residence permits. For those who don't . . . to tell you the truth, eight rubles wouldn't be enough."

"Four and a half," I offered.

"It's not worth my trouble."

"All right, then," I said, beginning to walk away.

"Seven," she called after me.

"I can find an entire room for that."

"Six, and that's final."

"Five, and I'll pay you up front today."

"Of course you'll pay me up front. Do I look like a lending bank to you? But for such a reduced rent, you'll do some chores for me as well."

She had shown me to my bed then. It was a cot, behind the stove in the kitchen. This I didn't mind, for I had been dreading the dark damp of a basement. No sooner had I put down my bag, though, when Mrs. Plotkin began listing all the chores I would perform to make up for the reduction in rent, beginning with lighting the stove and drawing the day's water first thing in the morning.

"Is there something wrong with this water?" I asked Hinda and Masha. The water in the courtyard's cistern had a peculiar brownish red tinge to it.

They both stared at me for a moment. "How long did you say you've been in Kiev?" Hinda asked.

"I didn't."

Hinda smirked while Masha explained that the water was drawn directly from the Dnieper and unfiltered. It was that way in all the poorer neighborhoods, and some of the richer ones as well. It was at its worst this time of year, when the spring flooding drew the sewage of an entire winter into the river all at once. "There's already cholera breaking out and it's not even Pesach yet. But tell me," she said, "have you found employment?"

I admitted I hadn't.

"Do you have residence papers?"

"No," I said, and she told me, as Mrs. Kaminsky had, that Shamsky's was looking for girls.

"What's Shamsky's?" I asked.

"What's *Shamsky's*?!" Hinda's smirk had progressed to a sneer.

Masha informed me that the Shamsky family ran a large sugar plant and they were known to turn a blind eye to the missing paperwork of new migrants. "It makes for more loyal employees, if you know what I mean."

"They can pay lower without worrying about a strike," Hinda explained. "It's a far walk from here, though. We're lucky where we work. It's just fifteen minutes."

They worked in a confectionary factory in the Podol, she explained, work that was not unlike what I would be doing if I found employment at Shamsky's. "We wrap candy, you'll wrap sugar," she said.

"All day?" I asked, swallowing hard.

"From seven until seven, with an hour off for lunch. It's not hard, but the pay's low until you get the hang of it. It was only thirteen kopecks a pood last year, but I hear they're up to fourteen kopecks now."

"I made eleven rubles last month," Hinda bragged.

"But you can't expect to make near that at the beginning," Masha said. "No one does."

"Especially not at Shamsky's," Hinda snickered.

"You'll catch on quickly enough, though," Masha assured me.

I smiled at them both, trying to keep my discouragement to myself as I realized what it would take to support myself in Kiev while I looked for Bayla.

"You'll move in with us at the end of the month," Masha was saying. "Three and a half rubles for a bed, and the group of us share a pot of soup at night, which saves even more."

I kept smiling, stiffly I'm sure, as I imagined waking up in a seeping basement every morning to Masha's advice and Hinda's smirk. I could only hope that my wages would stretch enough to cover the rent at Mrs. Plotkin's, the merits of those accommodations were all the clearer for having encountered the alternative. Mrs. Plotkin was brusque but not unfriendly now that we had agreed upon the rent. She didn't ask where I had come from or why I was here. And when I had sat down with her four boys the night before to teach them the *aleph-bes,* she had smiled to herself as she stood by the stove, later placing a bowl of soup before me, though that was not included in the rent.

THE SPRING PROCEEDED SLOWLY AT FIRST, THE FLOOD-waters ebbing gradually as the poplars and chestnuts put out their first tiny leaves. Then a week of heat, and the greenery thickened into a canopy overhead through which the sunlight dappled the sidewalks and boulevards. Maybugs flew through open windows, nightingales sang in the night, and the warm breeze carried the fragrance of lilacs that blossomed purple and white against the red cliffs of the city.

I woke up very early each morning and drew the day's water before heading out across the city for Shamsky's. Yes, I was working at the Shamsky's refinery, walking an hour across the city to wrap sugar twelve hours a day, then walking back an hour in the evening. The work was tiring but not complicated. The only part of the workday I truly dreaded was right at the end when the security guards would pat us down to check that we had not stolen sugar from the owners. Every afternoon as my arms and shoulders tired and my legs began to cramp, the dread would build inside me. And every evening the anger, as the guards' hands groped me in places no one else had ever touched. The shame.

Still, I was not unhappy with the work. It wasn't long before I was earning close to two and a half rubles a week, and this brought me both pleasure and pride. The thought that I carried my own earnings in my pocket pleased me, as did the freedom of deciding how to spend them—buying a bag of sunflower seeds on my way home, or stopping at a confectionary for a candied plum, or saving for a new hat or dress if I chose to—and not having to report any of my decisions to anyone.

I had no friends at work but could have had I wished. One girl in particular sought to draw me in. Tonya was her name, a girl with upswept auburn hair whose fierce profile and piercing eyes resembled a hawk's. She often invited me to join the group that gathered in the canteen during lunchtime and met for various activities after work hours as well. I was not cold to Tonya's overtures—I appreciated such friendliness—and sometimes I joined her group during lunch. My evenings, however, I chose to spend alone, searching for Bayla.

I walked through the city most evenings after work, from the neighborhood near the sugar plant where workers' plywood hovels spilled over hillsides and the ravine bottoms were rotten with garbage, to the wide boulevards of Lypky, with its lime trees and grand mansions, where the Shamsky family had its residence. And at every pharmacy I saw along the way, I stopped in to inquire after Bayla. Wherever I walked there were dangers, I knew, dangers that Mrs. Plotkin warned me about whenever I returned from my solitary wanderings. In the Lypky I would be arrested for loitering, she was sure. Near the ravines I would be raped and left to die. This had happened just the year before to another girl, also new from the *shtetl*. That girl had been older than I was but just as foolish, Mrs. Plotkin said, walking about alone all the time. Did I want to end up dead in a ditch, Mrs. Plotkin wondered.

THE SPRING PROGRESSED. MORNINGS WERE FRESH AND mild, the evenings filled with light. People poured out onto the streets in the lengthening evenings: strutting sailors on leave from their ships, gazing young couples escaping airless apartments, gentlemen with their ladies on their arms. Smartly dressed factory girls sashayed by with smug smiles. They had quick retorts for the young men who begged for their kisses as they passed, but they barely wasted a glance at their duller cousins from the countryside who stood kerchiefed and barefoot on every street corner with their flowers for sale in pails of water, their slices of gingerbread, their jugs of cold milk that they promised was fresh. I watched but was careful not to be watched, alert always for police or other officials who might stop me and ask for my papers.

I bought my refreshments from the vendors on the streets. The woman selling buns who had jostled me the day I met Leib worked a long stretch of sidewalk on the Krestchatik. Her buns were so stale that they had to be soaked in milk to be eaten, but they were five kopecks cheaper a dozen than anyone else's. On Fundkleyev Street, near the François Café, was a vendor whose hot cheesecakes were loaded with raisins. To get to her, though, I had to endure the beggar stationed beside her who muttered so loudly about the filth of the Jews that his venom entered me every time I had to pass him, poisoning me with momentary shame and doubts about my own cleanliness. "Don't mind him," the vendor would tell me as she handed me my cheesecake, but one day she dropped the coins I had given her into his wooden bowl.

Every week I received a letter from Tsila ordering me home at once, and every week I sent a letter back assuring her and Aaron Lev that I was safe at Mrs. Plotkin's, that my search for Bayla was progressing well, that the wages I was earning would help with my passage to Argentina. Did I recognize my own deceit in those letters I sent so faithfully? How could I not? How could I continue to pretend it was my search for Bayla that was keeping me in Kiev? But how could I turn away from the longing that filled me those first few weeks in Kiev, a longing for a new life— my own life—that seemed to be reaching for me at last?

One evening I stopped in at the café where I had waited for Leib. I had received a letter from Tsila earlier that day. I was to return home immediately, she told me once again. I ordered a cup of rich and bitter coffee—so much more enticing than the tea I drank at home—and wrote back to Tsila that I would return home very soon. Then I read the newspaper—full of news, as always, of disease in the city and disaster in the war with Japan. And trouble in the Polyseh, I read that evening in the *Kievskaya Mysl'*, a paper less liberal than others in the city. The scoundrel Andrey Gon and his company of bandits were still at large in the swamp, the article reported. An entire detachment of dragoons and forest guards had failed to capture him. He emerged with regularity to conduct his shameful raids on isolated estates, only to disappear into the bog and quicksand where no arm of the law could reach. And this was just one example of the disreputable denizens of that lawless region, the article continued. Bandits and beggars had long made their home there—this was nothing new—but now it was known to foster encampments of revolutionary terrorists as well. The entire swamp should be drained, the writer declared. Worse than merely useless land, it had now become a festering boil whose poisonous elements threatened the very life of the regime.

A festering boil? Poisonous elements? An exaggeration; still, I remembered the vapors that wafted from the swamp, the stunted land-scape shrouded in mist, and as I put down the paper I had a sensation of cold damp brushing up against my skin. It was fleeting but real, the first I had felt it since my arrival in Kiev: a familiar clamminess—my past? my destiny?—close at hand. I gulped down the last of my coffee, left a pile of coins on the table, and hurried out into the warmth of the evening.

The street was thronged with people, the air warm and thick, though darkness had fallen by now. I threaded my way through the crowd, ignoring the glares I received as I wedged my way between peo-ple, the admonishments to watch where I was going. My skin was warm and moist with sweat as it pressed against the warm, moist skin of strangers. The clamminess I had felt earlier was nothing now. A mem-ory. A fear.

At the other end of the Krestchatik a crowd gathered around an organ-grinder. It was the one with the red-and-green parrot whose spe-cialty was "The Waves of the Danube." He played other songs too, of course—"Oh the Box Is Full to Bursting," "Yearning for the Fatherland"—but it was "The Waves of the Danube" that always drew his largest crowds. I drew closer, expecting to hear the familiar waltz and to join the rhythmic swaying of the crowd. The crowd was strangely still, though, as I approached, and what I heard was not a waltz but a piercing sadness, a longing so deep it had the radiance of joy. "Bitter Parting," the organ-grinder was playing, and I closed my eyes to listen, while all around me the crowd grew larger and larger—passersby stop-ping, caught, perhaps, as I had been by the sound of their own longing, suddenly easier to bear for the beauty that the organ-grinder had found in it.

When he finished "Bitter Parting" there was a momentary hush, then he asked, as he always did, if anyone cared to try a lucky dip. "Only five kopecks," he offered, and I felt my head nodding yes. I had tried the lucky dip before, allowing his parrot to pick out a colored slip of paper with a prediction printed on it. Each time before, the prediction had been obscure—*Beware the orange cat at dusk,* for example—as if the parrot had mistakenly pulled out a truth meant for someone else, but that evening he chose one that was meant for me alone. *Dark eyes will bring you good luck,* the prediction promised, and relief flooded me. "What does it say?" I heard people asking around me. A man beside me looked over my shoulder and read the prediction out loud. An approving murmur passed through the crowd, and as the organ played the first notes of "The Waves of the Danube," I was filled with hope about my future.

THE OUTBREAK OF CHOLERA DID NOT SUBSIDE WITH THE ebbing of the floodwaters but persisted, spreading as the weather warmed. As more cases were reported in our neighborhood, Mrs. Plotkin took it into her head that all the water that I drew in the morning should be boiled before I left for work. This was onerous to me, not only for the extra time it took out of my morning, and the heat it generated in the already overheated kitchen, but also for the earnings it took out of my pocket. The additional wood needed to boil our water was a cost Mrs. Plotkin insisted I share.

"What?!" Masha shrieked when she heard this latest outrage. She and Hinda were also being careful with their water, of course, drinking only tea or hot water, but to have to boil the water that was used for washing, and to then be required to share the cost of this eccentricity . . . "You'll move in with us," Masha insisted. "What do you need with that hag?"

I heard Masha's indignation but my mind was elsewhere. A letter had arrived from Tsila, informing me that if I did not return home immediately she would come to Kiev herself to retrieve me. I could no longer pretend to Tsila or myself that I was going to find Bayla in my haphazard wanderings through the city, and in the absence of that purpose I knew I did not have the will to defy Tsila outright, face to face, in Kiev. I bought a train ticket for the following week and wrote Tsila of my plans.

As the cholera worsened, agitation about it increased. In the newspapers, on the streets, during breaks at work, that was what everyone discussed. The corruption of the city council was to blame, many said.

How else to explain the continuing filthiness of the city's water when the problem could so easily be corrected by the simple installation of filters?

A girl at work fell ill—Olga was her name—and a collection was taken up on her behalf.

"How's this going to help?" asked Tonya, fastening her piercing gaze on each of us in turn. We were in the canteen having lunch, the group of us who lived too far to go home for the midday meal.

"What do you mean *how*?" asked Anna, who was taking up the collection. "It will buy food, medication, help with the rent . . ."

"That's not what I mean," Tonya said. "I'm asking what good are isolated acts of charity? It's like running around hell trying to put out brushfires."

Anna turned a dull face to Tonya. "Are you suggesting we shouldn't help Olga?"

"You know that's not what I'm suggesting." Tonya dropped a few kopecks into the box. "I'm simply posing a question. What are we doing about the larger problem?"

Now, Tonya was a popular girl, admired for her quick laugh and for her quick hands that never failed to wrap close to four poods of sugar a day. At that moment, however, all of the girls shifted uncomfortably around her. A few cast glances at the guards, the security guards who patted us down each evening, watched over us throughout the day, and eavesdropped on our every conversation.

"What larger problem?" Anna asked.

"Oh, forget it. Just forget it," Tonya said. She had a quick temper to match her quick laugh and quick hands.

"The water supply," I said quietly. "That's the larger problem that no one seems able to address."

"Willing to address," Tonya corrected. "They're able to but not willing. But that's just a symptom. Just one small symptom of the corrupting greed of capitalism."

"The installation of filters shouldn't be such a complicated matter," I said. I had read all about it in the *Kievskaya Gazeta* just the evening before.

"But it might cost some money," Tonya said, excitement or anger flushing her face. "It might cause a few kopecks to slip through the greasy fingers of certain city councilmen."

"I, for one, have no interest in this discussion," Anna said loudly. Too loudly. It was obvious she was speaking for the benefit of the security guard.

"Oh, relax, Anna, will you?" Tonya said. "No one's going to arrest you before you get home to your Grishka tonight. I promise you. But tell us," she said, leaning over to run her hand over Anna's stomach. "Has he given you a present yet?"

Everyone laughed then, except Anna, whose cheeks filled with color.

IT WAS THE FOLLOWING DAY THAT TONYA INVITED ME TO join her for a night of theater, an invitation I accepted. I'd enjoyed my exchange with her in the canteen, and she obviously felt the same. I looked forward to the evening ahead.

She was waiting for me outside the factory gate after work and threaded her arm through mine as we walked toward the center of town.

"It was such a relief when you spoke up yesterday," she told me. "I feel sometimes that I'm the only one around who sees things as they are."

"It's lonely," I agreed, remembering the pleasure I'd taken in the sharpness of her arguments, enjoying the warmth of her arm on mine after so many weeks on my own.

"Infuriating," Tonya corrected. "It's not their stupidity. I don't mind stupidity. It's cowardice I can't abide."

She talked for some time about the cowardice of girls like Anna, and I noted the education in her speech. I had noticed it before and asked now how she came to be working at the sugar factory.

"I'm an agitator," she admitted without a moment's hesitation. "A failed agitator," she added with the quick laugh that made her so popular at work. "What needs changing in Russia is so obvious that it doesn't even bear saying—or so I think—and yet I say it, and say it again, and still I receive only dull stares in response."

"You're too impatient," I replied, remembering the kindness of Malka's responses to everyone in our study circle and the gentleness of her corrections. Tonya was quiet for a few minutes, and, concerned that I had offended her, I started to apologize.

"Do you think I don't already know that I'm not cut out for agitation?" she interrupted sharply. She was quiet for a few minutes more, kicking at loose paving stones as we walked. "Do you think you're the first to tell me I'm impatient?"

"I'm sorry," I said. "I didn't mean to . . ."

"If you're going to speak your mind, then don't undo it by apologizing. I can't abide people who don't stand behind what they say," she told me, and I held my tongue to avoid angering her further.

"And what's so great about patience, anyway?" she asked. "Has it done our long-suffering countrymen any good?"

The peasants, she meant. Not the Jews. And yet she referred to them as "our" countrymen. It occurred to me she might not even know I was Jewish.

"Has patience ever brought land and food to those who need it?" she asked me. "Of course not. How could waiting like a dumb ox ever bring about change?"

I worried I had ruined the atmosphere of the evening, but in the very next breath her expression and tone changed. Her face relaxed, her brow unfurrowed. "But enough about that. What about you? How did you come to work at the factory? You're not from around Kiev. I can tell from your accent."

"I'm a runaway," I said.

"Really?"

"No. Not really," I told her, but in the instant that I formed that word—*runaway*—I saw my luck dashing around the station in Gomel in those first moments after it realized I'd escaped. The idea of it made me smile.

"What's so funny?" Tonya asked.

"Nothing," I said, and told her how I had hurried away from the

Frumkins in Gomel, traveled to Kiev on my own, and stayed here all these weeks without permission.

This is how you thank those who love you, I heard Tsila rage as I told Tonya what I had done, Tsila's hurt and anger not diminished in the least by the distance it had traveled to reach me. *This is how you love them in return. In that you're no different from your mother.* I fell silent as the truth of my actions confronted me.

"We need more people like you," Tonya said. "People who create their own permission instead of waiting endlessly for it to be granted. Patience and compliance are overrated virtues, don't you think?"

There was such charm to the smile Tonya turned on me at that moment that I didn't mention the return ticket home I had already bought, on Tsila's orders.

"What do you come from?" Tonya asked.

"The Polyseh. I just told you."

"I mean your background." She focused her sharp gold eyes on my face, and I felt dark and oily under their scrutiny.

"I'm Jewish," I said quickly, well aware that her interest in me might end with those words.

"I don't mean that," she said crossly. "Such distinctions are irrelevant among comrades. I mean your class background. What does your father do?"

"He's a shoemaker," I said.

"Ah," she responded, her face softening. "A shoemaker." She laid her hand on top of my arm. "Then there's probably much *you* can teach *me.*"

I *dreamed of you* again last night. I felt the weight of you, your life. I heard your cry and rose to it, but as I reached the surface of my consciousness I knew it wasn't you. Maria, perhaps. She's been crying out more often in her sleep. Or maybe it was Vera, though her moans no longer carry any hint of the lusty life I'd heard. I was still asleep but knew that I had lost you once again.

I hovered at the edge of wakefulness, trying to regain you, trying to sink back deep within myself, back to deepest sleep, the only place where you and I can meet, but dread had taken hold of me by then. It filled me with a weight so unlike your own. It dragged me from sleep as surely as the guards who held me back when they first tore you from my arms.

When I opened my eyes our cell was bathed in light, the cold pale wash of the Siberian moon. I thought I wouldn't sleep, so heavy was the dread I felt, yet when I closed my eyes you came to me again, a girl of six now, slight and dark with long black hair to the middle of your back. You turned toward me. The contours of your face were your father's but shadowed with experiences all your own. Your eyes were dark like mine and bright with the life I've lost you to.

CHAPTER FIFTEEN

1904

I DID NOT EXPECT THE SOLOVITSKY THEATER IN KIEV TO be anything like the hall at the new *shul* where we held our Purim entertainments, of course, but neither was I prepared for the opulence that greeted me, the heavy floral scent in the entry hall, the corridors lined with mirrors framed in gold, the rows of seats upholstered in sky-blue velvet.

We sat in the very highest balcony, from where you could hardly see the stage. The play that night was called *Madame Sans-Gêne,* and long before the end of the first act I wondered why Tonya had chosen it. It was not that I didn't enjoy myself. Just to watch the ladies in the boxes below me with their bared white shoulders and mother-of-pearl opera glasses was entertainment enough, and the dresses were so exquisite that I regretted Tsila not having the opportunity to see them.

But the play was dull, the only excitement coming at the close of the first act, when Tonya whispered, "Get ready," and handed me a stack of leaflets: "Citizens! Demand Your Right to Clean Water!" As soon as the curtain fell, she dropped a handful of the leaflets over the railing. They drifted like flakes of snow toward the bejeweled heads below us. "Quick," she commanded me as she dropped some more. I followed her lead and let mine go as well. I watched a hundred sheets of paper fluttering down, but I didn't see them land. Tonya had already grabbed my hand and pulled me down the many stairs and out the side door to the street.

"Act normal," she whispered, bending her head to mine and giggling, as if she had just confided the name of the man that she loved. Thus we walked, like two giggling schoolgirls, but we were not far from the theater when we heard calls of "Halt," and we started to run.

I felt a tight grip close around one arm, then the other, a wrenching backward of both my arms, an imposed immobility. My mind froze, racing neither forward to fear nor backward to regret, merely recording, without thought or emotion, the unfolding assaults on my senses. I saw the blue serge of the gendarme who restrained me, the glances and stares of passersby. I heard a voice, familiar and yet not, pleading on my behalf. "Let her go," I heard as if from a great distance. "Let her go, I beg you. She is entirely innocent."

I looked down as my feet started moving beneath me. They were my own feet, familiar in the boots that Aaron Lev had made for me, yet moving as if by the will of another. They were my own brown leather boots, new this year and stitched with Aaron Lev's fine, careful hand, but scuffed now and dusty compared to the shiny boots they walked between. Such a gloss those other boots had. Such a high black shine. Like the beetles I used to watch in our garden at home: huge, black, and glistening. And my own feet, two dull brown grubs trapped between them.

The cobblestones were uneven and I stumbled. My arms wrenched backward, upward, sending a jolt of pain through my back. I tried to walk carefully but couldn't. I could no longer feel the feet that stepped beneath me. I could no longer feel the arms by which I was propelled relentlessly forward. There was only pain, hot and radiant, spreading throughout my upper back.

The cobblestones gave way, at length, to flatness, the flat gray stone of stairs leading upward, the rougher stone of a corridor. More stairs, down this time. The light was dim, the air musty and damp. A clanging of metal against metal, a door opening, and I was flung into darkness.

"Pigs," I heard muttered beside me. It was Tonya. "Are you all right?" Her voice rose, disembodied, out of utter darkness. I closed my eyes to more quickly acclimatize, but when I opened them again I could see no more than before. We'd been thrown into the bowels of the earth, foul and dark. There was no light, no escape. Panic rose in me. "Are you all right?" I heard again, more urgently than before. "I can't see," I said, panic cracking my voice.

There was laughter then, not Tonya's. I bolted upright to a sitting position. "Who's there?" I demanded, my heart beating wildly. I felt a warmth on my arm, a living warmth. I shrieked.

"It's only me," Tonya said, her voice quiet, gentle.

"Who laughed?" I asked, to more laughter.

"Better settle your friend down, little auntie, or she'll scare herself to death," someone said. A woman's voice.

"Close your eyes," Tonya whispered.

"I did already."

"Never mind her eyes. Get yourselves off the floor," someone said, and as she did, I became aware of the damp beneath me, the sliminess of it. I bolted to my feet, producing another round of laughter. "Relax, little auntie. It's only shit."

I sniffed my hands and arms, but the smell of excrement was so strong all around me that I couldn't determine its source.

"There's a cot here," someone said. I was beginning to make out shapes now. A hand took mine and led me a few steps. I felt the edge of the cot against me and lowered myself onto it. Tonya joined me.

"You're shivering," she said as she lay down beside me.

The surface beneath us was hard and lumpy, but dry. Tonya put her arms around me. Her body was warm against mine. Within minutes there were snores all around us. "They won't keep you long," Tonya whispered. "You just have to get through tonight."

"How do you know?"

"I know them," she said.

"I don't have papers."

"It doesn't matter," she assured me. "They'll evict you from the city. That's all they'll do."

"You're sure?" I asked.

"Absolutely."

"And you?"

"They can't harm me," she said. "Not really."

I SLEPT—I DON'T KNOW HOW—AND WHEN I WOKE I WAS on a narrow straw cot in a cell. Light, still dim, leaked through a narrow window high above us, illuminating the faces of the eight other women who shared the cell, women who looked no different from any of the vendors or shopgirls I often saw on my nightly walks along the Krestchatik. Tonya was already up, sitting on the edge of our cot.

"Caught working without your ticket?" one of the older women asked.

"What ticket?" I asked, producing the heartiest round of laughter yet.

"We're politicals," Tonya said sternly, to which one of the younger women took a few prancing steps, curtsied, and said, "Well, excuse us. We're just here for trying to earn a living."

The floor, I was relieved to see, was only dirt, turned to muck in places from the moisture of the ground. There were two buckets, both filled with excrement, but we would all be taken to the latrine later in the morning, one of the women informed us. "Once a day, whether you need to or not."

"What if I have to go again?" I asked.

"This isn't the Rossiya Hotel."

"I couldn't tell," I responded, and for the first time the laughter wasn't mocking in tone.

WHEN THE GUARD CAME TO BRING US OUR TEA AND bread Tonya asked when we would be charged. The guard ignored her. She asked again when he came to take us, handcuffed and in pairs, to the latrine, and again he ignored her.

Some of the other women were released that morning, and late in the afternoon, two guards came for me.

"You see?" Tonya said, embracing me. "I told you."

The guards positioned themselves on either side of me to march me up the staircase, down a long corridor, through a courtyard, up more stairs into another section of the building, and down another corridor. We had left the holding jail now and entered the prison itself. As we walked, I heard a rhythmic banging against the wooden doors that we passed and voices raised in song.

"What's that?" I asked, but the guards stared ahead as if they heard nothing.

The song was for me, I soon realized. The other prisoners were watching my progress through the keyholes of their cells, banging against their doors, shouting greetings as I passed and raising their voices in song. And while my fear didn't leave me, not at all, the attention was momentarily warming.

We climbed another set of stairs, entering a corridor where the silence was broken only by the sound of our own footsteps proceeding down its stony length, and stopped finally at a room where an official was seated at a desk, reading a document. He didn't look up at our arrival but continued reading, twirling his mustache as he did. For some time I stood in the doorway flanked by my two guards, who did nothing to draw his attention. At length he glanced up as if he had just noticed our presence.

Not fat, but full. Oozing fullness and satiation. Those were the words that filled my mind when I first met the eyes of the Colonel Gendarme who would question me. Out of a recess in my mind rose Bayla's description of a prospective bridegroom Chippa had once brought to her, for such was the man who faced me that day. Such was the man in whose hands my future now lay.

"Sit, please," he invited me. His tone was polite. "You may leave us," he said to the guards.

There was no air in the room—the one window was covered by a dark, heavy drape—and when the door first shut behind the guards, a

momentary terror rose in me that I was to be entombed, now and forever, with that oozing Colonel.

He returned his attention to the document for a few moments, then
looked back at me.

"May I see your residence permit?" he asked. A reasonable request
in a reasonable tone. I froze in dread to hear it.

"Did you hear me?" he asked.

"I did."

"And?"

"It's at my house," I said.

"Don't lie. You really don't want to be lying to me, I can promise
you that." He smiled. "You see, we've been to your house. Your dear
Mrs. Plotkin's."

Fear gripped me at a deeper level now. How did he know where I
lived?

"You're surprised, I can see."

I said nothing.

"Do you think I don't know who you are? Who your friend is?"

"Tonya?" I asked.

"*Tonya*," he spat, as if the name had a particularly unpleasant feel on
his tongue. "Do you think we're unaware of the vermin that scuttle before our eyes?"

There had to be an informer at work. Anna, perhaps. A security
guard.

"I know you're illegal here in Kiev. I know also that this is your first
offense." He smiled again. "I don't want to keep you any more than you
want to stay here, I assure you." Then he pushed a document over to my
side of the desk, the document he had been studying so carefully when
I first entered the room. "Can you read?" he asked, as my eyes slid over
the text.

"I don't know anything about this," I said. I understood I was
meant to confirm the document that attested to my having witnessed
Tonya participating in all manner of activities designed to bring down
the government.

"I don't understand," he responded. "First you ask for release, then when I show you how to achieve it, you refuse." He rose from his chair behind the desk and walked over to the window, where he pulled back a corner of the drape to survey the darkening day outside. He stood for a long while in that meditative pose, so long that it seemed he had forgotten my presence.

"Tonya and I have only started to become friends. That was our first outing together. You must know that," I said, but when he turned to me I could see a change had come over him. He walked over to me, half stood, half sat against the edge of his desk, and surveyed me coldly. He leaned forward, his face so close now that I could see the pores on his cheeks, feel his breath on my face as he spoke.

"If you're such an innocent as you claim, then why did all your cohorts sing to you as you walked by on your way here?" he asked. "And such a song! Such an uproar! I could hear it from here."

"I don't know," I said, and he slapped me across my face, first with the front of his hand, then with the back.

A terrible rage rose in me then. Terrible because it obliterated everything else within me. Pain, fear, confusion—all was incinerated in the flash of that rage. I remember little of what followed. Certainly I don't remember spitting in his face, but there was my spit, streaked with the blood of my split lip, sliding down his white, full face.

There was an instant, but just an instant, where I could see surprise in his face. It was gone as he reached into his pocket for a handkerchief. He cleaned his face carefully, leaving no trace of my spit, then, just as carefully, refolded his handkerchief and replaced it in his pocket. Then he slapped me with a force that slammed my head against the hard back of the chair.

THE CELL THE GUARDS TOOK ME TO WAS NOT THE ONE I had just left. They led me down a corridor of the prison, past a series of wooden doors, opened one, unlocked my handcuffs, and pushed me in. The push was hard enough that, again, I was flung to the floor. I heard the door shut behind me, the closing thud, the scrape of a key turning in a lock, and then silence. Immediately I felt cold. A damp, evil cold. The floor of this cell was stone, cold and damp against me. I lay there a while, unable to move. The fear, the pain in my head, the awareness that things had turned against me. I knew I should move. I knew I should raise myself from that surface, but I couldn't. I remained where they had flung me, half sitting, half lying—I don't know how long. Was it an hour? Ten minutes? Half the night? A trembling seized me, a trembling so terrible I could not stand up, but I had to, I knew. The stone of the floor was drawing my heat, sucking the warmth from the very core of me. If I stayed where I was, by morning it would have my life. "Stand," I commanded myself, and I did, finally, and began pacing the confines of the cell.

It was a small cell, nine steps by six steps. Against one wall was a cot. Against another, a small table. Aside from that there was a stool, a bucket, a high barred window through which, at that hour of the evening, I could see only darkness. The door was thick wood with a keyhole through which I could see the long corridor we had passed, lined with wooden doors and lit now with lamps.

I ran my fingers along the walls. They were like the floors: cold stone and seeping. Weeping, I thought, but the tears were cold. The tears of the Angel of Death. The tears of my dead brother who had tormented me in my mother's womb and wouldn't rest as long as I had in me the breath of life that had been denied him. I remembered the cold damp I had felt brushing against me in the café a few weeks earlier. I had run outside then to escape its touch, to surround myself with the moist warmth of living flesh, but there was no running now. Death had caught me once again and surrounded me.

I could hear his breathing, raspy and harsh. My heart pounded heavily in my chest. "I know you," I told him, struggling to keep my voice strong and steady. I ran my hand along the clammy skin of the cell, then brought my fingers to my face—so hot considering the trembling in me—and cooled it with his moisture. "I know you," I told him again. "You're the same weakling that you always were."

His breathing continued, labored, shallow. I continued my pacing as if unconcerned. "I know you," I said again, hoping to scare him away with the strength of my voice. "You're nothing before me." I paced some more, the length and width of the cell, then I bent to look out the keyhole and found the light blocked. A guard was peering in. I screamed.

"Calm yourself, little sister," he said, as the women had the night before. He was an old man; I could hear it in his voice.

I asked him for water, and the sound of my own voice making that simple request calmed me some. He told me I couldn't have any until morning.

"But I must have some." My mouth was parched, my thirst unendurable. "I have to drink," I told him, the edge of terror rising again in my voice.

"Calm yourself," he said, but harshly now, and there was an authority in his harshness that pierced the haze of my panic. I resumed my pacing but my mind raced to more earthly fears. Where was Tonya now, and what would they do to her? And what about Mrs. Plotkin? What had she thought when the police had come to her home? What had they told her? What had they done to her and her boys? Had they accused her of harboring a criminal in her home? And was that what I was now, a criminal? Of what sort? What crime would I be charged with? Public mischief? Treason against the Tsar? Would I be held for a week? A month? Ten years? Would I be shackled in a dungeon? Sent to Siberia? And what about Tsila and Aaron Lev? Would they ever know what became of me? Would they even care? Would they wash their hands of me because of my betrayal of their affection and care?

I felt a hand on my back, a cool clammy hand raising the hairs along my spine as it brushed lightly toward my neck. "You're nothing before me," I whispered again with all the intent of a prayer.

I was afraid to lie down, afraid to shut my eyes in that place, but knew that I must. The cot was fastened in place, impossible to move from those cool, seeping walls. I lay down anyway and shut my eyes. I forced my body to stillness, but my mind continued racing. They cannot hold me, I told myself, but I knew that they could. Was this my fate, then, I wondered, to lie in this cage with only my dead brother for company? Was this the place that my yearnings and desires had always been destined to lead me?

In the morning my brother was gone. I opened my eyes to a gray stone cell, a pale light, and not long after that a guard entered my cell with bread and tea. I asked him how long I would be held and he shrugged his shoulders before leaving. I sat on the stool by the desk, waiting—for what, I wasn't sure. The panic of the night before had subsided. In its place, a deep weariness. Through the window of my cell, now that it was morning, I could see an expanse of sky. On that day it was white.

I sat all morning on my stool, but no one came except the guard bringing me bread, soup, and tea. The afternoon I spent on my bed: a straw mattress atop an iron bracket, with rough sheets and a gray blanket. It was quiet in my cell; I could hear only the footsteps of the guards in the corridor and the tapping of rodents in the pipes. I knew from this quiet that my window must open onto an inner courtyard, a realization that made escape seem impossible. I moved the stool to the wall below the window, but I could not see out until I had pulled the table over as well and stood on the stool atop the table. The scene outside was as I had imagined: a small courtyard around which two prisoners listlessly walked. I worried briefly about what punishment I might suffer if discovered while atop my viewing tower, but no one came to my cell until evening, when the third meal of the day, bread and tea, was brought to me.

"Have you any idea when I might be released?" I asked the guard who brought my supper, but again I received no answer.

Days passed and no charge was laid against me. A week. Two weeks. I was not charged, nor was I released, nor was I returned to the Colonel Gendarme for questioning. Was this to be my punishment, then, I began to wonder, was this the colonel's payment for that gob of spit on his face? Would I languish here forever now, uncharged, untried, and forgotten? I had no human contact. The questions I asked the guards yielded nothing more than a shrug, a vacant stare. I had no letters, no visitors. The old guard who had watched me through the keyhole the first night never reappeared. Even my dead brother seemed to have forgotten my existence. Sleep was the only relief to my days, sleep and that brief instant upon awakening, before awareness resettled heavily upon me.

At the end of my second week, the guard who brought my lunch announced that I would now be allowed books and paper. A privilege, I knew, but there was no one to bring these things to me, no one outside who knew where I existed, if I continued to exist at all, and so it only plunged me deeper into despair.

SPRING TURNED TO SUMMER. I WATCHED THE CHANGING sky outside my window and waited for warmth and fragrance to penetrate the stone walls of my cell. The air in my cell, however, remained musty and damp. And heavy. So very heavy. Its dampness seeped into my body, weighing me down, so that the simple act of rising in the morning soon became an ordeal requiring a strength I didn't think I possessed. The swallows came, as they always do, flying freely through the open bars of my windows, and then they went.

One long afternoon as I lay on my bed wrapped in my blanket it occurred to me that the tapping I was hearing was too unvarying to be rodents. I reached out a hand and tapped on the pipe that connected my cot to the wall. I immediately received a response in kind. I tapped again—twice this time—and the same thing happened. I sat up now, startled. A series of taps followed. I listened carefully with surging excitement to the pattern that emerged. It was an alphabet, I realized, and by the end of that afternoon I had learned a new alphabet that, like any alphabet, was a key to an entire new world whose gates now lay open before me.

The name of the prisoner resident beneath me was Larissa Semyonovna Petrova. Like me, she was a political, though she had been charged already with sedition against the government and conspiracy with the intent to kill. She was joyously awaiting trial.

"They moved me miles from my home in an attempt to break me through isolation," she tapped. "But of course I am never alone here. It was there, in my previous existence, that I was alone."

"Where's your home?" I tapped back.

"Here."

"But before here?"

"I was without a home before I entered these walls that house so many of my brothers and sisters."

I put the question another way. "Where do your parents reside?"

"I have no parents. I am a child of the revolutionary ideals that birthed me."

She was arrested for her attempt on the life of the Governor of Tula—the Butcher of Tula, she called him. "The butcher who gave the orders to shoot into unarmed crowds, to burn villages to the ground, to rape and pillage at will." There was a long pause, and then, "We have heard about your innocence," Larissa tapped. "Your daring."

"You have?"

"Oh, yes," came Larissa's response.

Word of my spit had apparently spread throughout the prison, and in the telling been transformed into a symbol of innocent strength prevailing in the face of depravity.

"We are honored to have you among us," Larissa tapped.

And so began an exchange that greatly changed my experience in prison. Hours that had dragged endlessly were filled now with tapped conversations. Larissa told me of her life on her father's estate—her life before birth, as she called it—and asked me detailed questions about my own. She described her vision of a world where all would be clothed and fed and free of the degradations that currently worked their poison at every level of society.

"Change is coming," she promised. "And there's nothing they can do to stop it. They think they're extinguishing us here, our spirit, but the opposite is true. They're gestating revolution in their prisons."

I couldn't agree that my own spirit wasn't being extinguished. I thought of the long days I had spent unable to lift myself from my cot, the panic I had felt my first night alone in my cell when I'd sensed death seeping from the walls that enclosed me. I told Larissa about it, and she said I was not unique in my reactions. "Many of us have felt what you've described. How can we not feel the presence of death, imprisoned as we are in the heart of their evil?" she asked. "But it is precisely from the heart of decay that new life springs forth. It's a law of nature, operative in the social order as well . . ."

She continued tapping, but I was still thinking about my first night in my cell, the terror I'd felt.

"As full of peril as the womb," Larissa was saying. "But as full of promise too. We'll deliver ourselves from this and be reborn, each of us. Transformed. Mark my words."

My mind traveled far from Larissa's talk of gestating revolution to my own gestation, the thirst my mother had felt during her pregnancy with me, her unearthly thirst, a longing for death as my own life took form within her. And yet, had I not managed to survive that ordeal? Had I not sensed death seeping from the walls of my mother's womb and still escaped into life? There was some comfort for me in that thought.

SOME AFTERNOONS LARISSA AND I DIDN'T TALK ABOUT ourselves or the coming revolution. She would tap poetry—Pushkin, mostly—into my cell. "It's not really decadent," she assured me. I hadn't imagined that it was. For two afternoons running I lay with my eyes closed as the lines of *Eugene Onegin* spilled into my cell.

We had practical communications too, of course. Larissa understood the workings of the prison and how to obtain information from outside. She knew the names and affiliations of all the political prisoners around us. She knew who had been most recently arrested and who was about to be released.

"Have you heard anything about Tonya?" I asked her.

"Released," she told me. "To her great shame." And to my almost unendurable envy.

She told me one day that a relative of mine had come to visit and been turned away.

"Who?" I asked.

"That I don't know. But you must be vocal in demanding your rights, relentless in your demands, refusing food and water if necessary. They will respond to nothing less."

I could no more imagine refusing food and water than refusing the air I drew into my lungs. While Larissa seemed to draw her strength from the ideas and aspirations that she shared with me, what little strength I possessed seemed rooted in the realm of the physical. "I think I could refuse food for a month and at the end of it I would be hungry, but still without any rights," I told her.

There was a momentary silence, then, "Perhaps, but you would also be possessed of a strength you didn't previously know as your own."

"Perhaps," I agreed.

I ate my breakfast the next morning, however, and soon after, a guard appeared at my cell. "This arrived for you," he said, handing me a stack of paper and a pen and ink. He couldn't tell me who had brought it, not even if it was a man or a woman.

"Be careful," Larissa warned me. "What appears as a privilege is usually a trap. They do nothing for good. Everything you write will be read and used against you."

I thanked her but could not resist the pen. It was a quill, but not like any I had admired in the stores of Kiev. The feather was neither brilliant in color nor majestic in shape, but small and black—the impenetrable black of a crow—and ugly to my eye. How, then, to explain the sensation I had when I took it in my hand? I held that pen and felt as my own the strength of the wing from which it had been taken. I dipped it in ink and began to write. *I am cold,* I wrote. Simple words—how to explain the joy I felt in their expression, the sudden certainty of my own existence that filled me as the words took form under my hand? *It is the summer of my seventeenth year, and I am always cold.* The quill nestled in the fold of my fingers as if hand and pen were one instrument, moving across the paper as a bird that glides through air.

LARISSA'S TRIAL APPROACHED. "I AM TO BE READY AT the first light of morning," she tapped to me one evening. "Rejoice for me." She was certain she would be sentenced to death, and as the moment approached she awaited this judgment in what can only be described as a state of exultancy. "The ultimate beauty of a revolutionary's life is the sacrifice of that life for humanity," she quoted to me that evening.

This, then, was what she had meant with all her talk of rebirth. This was to be her transformation.

"Are you not afraid?" I asked.

"Is a leaf afraid when it surrenders itself to nourish the next year's growth?"

"Leaves aren't sentient," I tapped back.

"More's the pity that they don't know the beauty of their sacrifice."

But later, much later that night, long after we should have all been asleep, I heard a light tapping. "Miriam," she tapped.

"I'm awake," I tapped back.

"There are moments when I'm afraid."

I WAS UP BEFORE FIRST LIGHT THE NEXT MORNING BUT heard no movement in the cell beneath me. I tapped lightly on the pipe by my bed, then with more force, but of course there was nothing. They had already taken her. The guard arrived with my breakfast but I couldn't eat it.

I sat on my cot, then on my stool, then paced the narrow width and length of my cell. Before noon I heard a tap in the pipe. Impossible, I knew, but she was back, alive, her trial unaccountably postponed. "I feel the hand of my father in this," she tapped. "I feel the weight of my so-called privilege in this postponement."

And with those very words I felt a great lifting inside my chest.

"I fear that in the name of that privilege—a privilege that I detest, that I loathe, that I renounce with every fiber of my being—I'm to be denied the only privilege I have ever sought: that of dying for the cause."

"Was your father there?" I asked.

"Of course."

They had taken her in leg irons through the dark streets to a military officers headquarters, where she had been led into a small side room and told to wait. She had waited for hours without food or drink. "I welcomed those rigors," she told me. Then her father had entered the room.

"He was in full military regalia. It offended my eye to see him. I turned away from him in utter repugnance, but he misunderstood. 'Don't be ashamed before me,' he told me, as if it was *I* who should feel shame for my life. He took my face into his hands so that I was forced to look into the eyes of the man who gave me physical life but is not my father. 'Be thankful that the wounds you inflicted were not mortal. Mercy may still be granted,' he said, and a great vileness rose in me.

"I told him, of course, that my hatred of the autocracy was so great I could not accept its mercy, and he told me that Mercy didn't ask for permission before doing her bidding. He was hurt, I could see—I know this man since my birth, after all, and could see the wound I was inflicting—and I felt pity for him despite—or because—of the despicable nature of his life. He turned from me then and left the room, but a guard came in soon after to tell me the trial was postponed, and I knew my father had worked his influence."

I was not merely happy at Larissa's news. I was euphoric, wildly elated that she was back in her cell and alive. I wept from relief, happy for once that she could not see me as we conversed. I could not pretend to share her disappointment at the extension of her life, but neither could I admit to her the full extent of the joy it brought me. "As beautiful as your death would be, it is far better that you should live to partake in the victory that is surely coming," was what I tapped to her.

A SONG WENT UP ONE MORNING IN JULY, THE SAME SONG I had heard the first morning I was marched through the corridor to questioning. I recognized it now as the "Marseillaise" and assumed, at first, that a new political prisoner was being welcomed. But there was an excitement to the singing, a bright tension, an air of celebration that surpassed anything I had heard so far. I climbed to my window and saw banners of red cloth unfurled from almost every window around the courtyard.

"Rejoice, little sister," Larissa tapped on my wall. "Von Plehve is killed at last."

I knew Von Plehve, knew of him at least. As Minister of the Interior he had been hated across Russia for the repressiveness of his order, his utter disregard for human life. And Jews held a special grudge against him, for it was he who was said to have sanctioned the pogrom in Kishenev, he who was said to have declared his support for the struggle of the Christian populace against its enemies.

"Down with the autocracy!" a cry rose up from the other side of the courtyard. "Long live the revolution!" someone on our side answered. "Long live the Socialist Revolutionary Party!"

I waited for the suppression by the guards that would surely follow such a commotion, the heavy footsteps, the shouts, the clanging of locks and doors, but there was no response from the prison authorities—none I could hear. The singing continued undisturbed, the shouting, until late in the morning when it gradually subsided, then faded away. When the guard brought my bread and soup at lunch there was no indication from him or from me that anything but a usual morning had just passed.

I asked Larissa that afternoon about the banners of red cloth that had been hung from the windows around the courtyard during the morning's celebration. I had seen them before, but not in such profusion. During my daily exercise period, lengths of red cloth were often unfurled, then hastily withdrawn, from various windows around the courtyard.

"They are meant as a signal of solidarity," Larissa explained. "A signal that you are not alone in these stone walls. We know how alone you often feel," she tapped. "We watch you through our windows as you walk around the courtyard. We see the sadness in the stoop of your shoulders. I hear it traveling through your fingertips in the messages you send to me. But you are not alone. We want you to know that you are not alone."

A feeling of warmth spread through me then, not unlike what I had felt during my first march to questioning. I asked Larissa how such cloth was obtained.

"To tell you that might endanger you," she tapped back, but when new sheets were issued to me the following week, a piece of red cotton was folded within them. I too began unfurling red cloth when Larissa alerted me that a political was exercising in the yard, and in that action felt a weakening of the stone walls that enclosed me.

SUMMER TURNED TO FALL. MY SEVENTEENTH BIRTHDAY came and went. "I'm to be tried tomorrow," Larissa tapped to me one afternoon, and a fear welled so large within me that I couldn't respond.

It was a clear evening, the first chill of autumn in the air. Rosh Hashanah was approaching and the beginning of the Days of Awe. In every Jewish village and town, Jews would soon be streaming to the synagogue. Along every grand boulevard and from every back alley and lane: women in their finest dresses, men in their flowing caftans. "A good Yonteff," they would be greeting each other. "May you be inscribed and sealed for a good year."

As I stood on my viewing tower the night before Larissa's trial, watching the sky out my window, I imagined Tsila and Aaron Lev making their way down the hill into town. They always walked together to the synagogue on the eve of Rosh Hashanah. Tsila's dress would be severe—as befitting the somberness of the holiday—but well cut. Her hair would be swept under a large, brimmed hat, her head barely turning left or right as she returned the greetings of her neighbors. Her sojourn in that town in the swamp was almost finished. If all had progressed as planned they would be leaving for Argentina immediately after Sukkos. Just a few more weeks and they would be gone from Russia forever. Would I be in their thoughts as they addressed the King of Kings on this year's day of judgment and remembrance? Would they enter a plea on my behalf? A despairing loneliness filled me.

I awoke before first light as I had on the morning of Larissa's previous, postponed trial, and as before, there was no response to my tap. I refused breakfast as I had before and spent the morning pacing my cell, waiting for the news that mercy had been granted, that she was to be transported, alive, to Siberia.

The tap came late in the afternoon. "Rejoice for me, my sister," she said, and my grief was a physical weight that pushed all breath from my lungs.

The hanging would take place at night, Larissa told me. "They do their work in darkness, but our hopes and ideals bring light even to that." It would be before the next dawn, in the courtyard right outside my window. There would be singing, she said, voices raised from within and without the prison. "You'll sing too, my little sister. It will be a beautiful death."

It was not, of course, beautiful. It was her life that had been beautiful, her thoughts and dreams that she tapped out to me in the precious hours of our friendship, her hopes for a better world, her generosity. Her death, when it came, was ugly. I heard its approach as I lay sleepless that night. I heard the hammering in the darkness as the scaffold was built, then a moan, a terrible moan that swept the prison like a wind bringing pain and destruction. Was it her moan? I don't know. I had never heard her voice to recognize it.

She had planned to make a statement. This she had told me. She had planned to assert her disdain for a regime that murdered its young but could never silence their cause. "Take my life," she had planned to say. "You can never silence the ideals that fueled it." As the moan died away, though, and I waited for her voice, there was only silence, a dark deadly silence into which she soon fell.

I listened to her die. Even as a rhythmic beating of hands and feet was taken up throughout the prison, I listened for her life and kept it company in its struggle. I could not possibly have heard her last gasp. This I know. The uproar in the prison was so great by then that it drowned out even the cawing of crows that always heralded dawn. But I heard her death—one lone sigh—through the uproar. I felt her last breath as it traveled upward, a soft breeze on my skin, warm with all she had been, and then nothing.

There was singing, as she'd promised. With the first light of dawn, singing from within and without the prison. "Farewell, my sister," the voices sang. "Honorably you passed on." And there were speeches. From prison windows, from the streets beyond. Some were close enough that I could make out their words, some were just a drone of meaningless sounds. I didn't join the singing or strain to hear the speeches. I stayed curled on my cot, curled around the cold hard knot at my core.

A week later, on a cool autumn morning during the fifth month of my imprisonment, two guards entered my cell after breakfast. I didn't ask if I was to be charged at last. I no longer cared.

"Gather your belongings," they told me.

I took my pen and the sheets of paper on which, until Larissa's death, I had recorded daily the physical fact of my existence. They took me through the courtyard to the prison anteroom, where in exchange for my canvas prison gown I was given the brown linen dress that Tsila had sewn for me and the boots that Aaron Lev had made for my big trip to Kiev.

"Well, go on, then," the prison master said to me. "You're free to leave."

I took my belongings without another word, signed the release that I had received them, and exited from the prison onto the street. I was once again a free subject in the realm of His Imperial Highness, Tsar Nicholas II.

Siberia, February 1912

Tsila's letters are full of light. I open them and the fullness of her life escapes the envelope, filling my gray mind with color.

"It is summer," she writes, just as the ice of our winter hardens around us to such a thickness that I fear this will be the year that we are permanently sealed from the rest of the world. "The heat in this city is heavy but not oppressive. As I sit at my table writing to you I feel a light breeze drifting in through the open window."

Here too a window is open. The wind blew it out and they haven't replaced it yet. Cold howls at the opening but quiets once it finds its way inside. It is not a living cold that shifts and changes but a bitter stillness, a stagnancy that presses upon us hour after hour, day after day, month after month. It is immutable, despite the efforts of our valiant stove, the heat of our twelve bodies. We are nothing against this cold.

"And music. It too wafts through my window."

There is always music in the city where they now live, a music not unlike ours in its longing, Tsila says, but filled with a dark heat. "Like the thickest of summer nights in the swamp," she writes.

I close my eyes to remember those nights, the air so saturated it could no longer hold its own moisture, a beating life suspended in its heavy heat. I hear that beat, that heat, its insistence. It wafts through the open windows of a warm apartment.

"Your father is not yet home," Tsila writes. Home is their apartment above Tsila's dress shop in Buenos Aires, the city Tsila insisted they move to from the Baron's colony, a city where the fineness of Tsila's work is apparently not wasted. "He works late these summer evenings, but is without the weariness that I long thought would sink him into an early grave."

Aaron Lev has opened a fruit stand in the market there. He spends his days arranging and rearranging pyramids of fruit. The apricots have been particularly sweet this year, Tsila reports, but the grapes are late and, for some reason, lacking in sugar.

She doesn't inquire how I am. She never does. "I trust you're well," is what she says. "You have never lacked for strength."

"Your father and I are also strong now, stronger with each passing day. It's the feeling of freedom that we awaken to every morning, the sunlight, the fineness of this city. All this nourishes us and the child that will be born, God willing, before Pesach."

Heat fills me then. An intense rush of heat. I feel it burst in my sore, cough-racked chest, then radiate to the furthest reaches of my stiffened body. I bask in it as I once basked in the sunlight that pooled on my brightly colored quilt in the early hours of the morning. And as it ebbs from me, I still feel its effects in the loosening of my limbs, a light tingling in my shoulders and chest.

"Meanwhile, we await your arrival with growing impatience," she writes, as she does in all of her letters. As if it is willfulness that keeps me here, sheer laziness that stops me from escaping and making my way to Argentina. That she expects me to escape is clear. It's the very least I can do, her impatience implies, given the trouble she took to raise me. *I did not raise you to waste yourself in this way,* I hear beneath her words. *I did not raise you to rot in Siberia.*

That my sentence is life does not impress Tsila. We all receive a life sentence at the moment of our birth, she has written me repeatedly. It is a sin to break under the weight of it.

CHAPTER SIXTEEN

1 9 0 4

"SO THEY'VE RELEASED YOU," MRS. PLOTKIN SAID AS she eyed me through the crack of her front door.

"This morning," I answered. I had not really expected her to let me in, had hoped only that she would return my clothes and suitcase and the few other belongings that I possessed at the time of my arrest.

"I've already rented out your bed," she informed me.

"Yes, of course. I was only hoping . . ."

"You've had a lot of callers," she said, opening the door a little wider.

"I'm sorry," I murmured. "I was just . . ."

"Well, come in, come in, don't just stand there giving all the neighbors something to talk about."

I followed her to the kitchen, where she poured me a glass of tea and broke off a generous chunk of sugar, half of which she kept for herself, gumming it in her toothless mouth. I drank the tea quickly and noisily, sucking it through the sugar. Mrs. Plotkin watched me drink and when I was finished, she poured me a second glass and handed me another chunk of sugar, which I dissolved into the tea until it was a sweet and sticky syrup.

"Did they injure you?" she asked. Her eyes were pinpricks on my face.

"No," I said.

She nodded then, relaxed her gaze. "They came here the night you disappeared. That's how I knew where you were. From the way they tore the place apart I thought maybe you had committed a crime, but then I remembered how they are. It's been many years since they've paid me a visit, but some things you remember, no?"

"I'm sorry," I said again.

"What did you do?"

"I distributed pamphlets."

"What sorts of pamphlets?"

"About the water, telling citizens to demand their right to clean drinking water."

Mrs. Plotkin nodded, her lips working between her gums.

"I'm very sorry to have brought such trouble to your house," I said.

"The police were no more trouble than any pack of dogs tearing through my house and shitting where they please. Your mother's visit, though—that caused me grief."

"My mother?"

"She came to fetch you home, only to find out you'd been arrested. Nice, I thought. Very nice to find out in that way that this is the sort of girl I had taken in under my roof. A girl who ran away from home and lied to her parents."

I felt the heat rising in my face.

"And to think I've wasted tears mourning that I never had a daughter."

"What did you tell her?"

"What could I tell her? That her daughter led me to believe that she had no parents who cared? That her daughter preferred to live with strangers than with her own flesh and blood? Do I look like someone who takes pleasure from being cruel to others? I told her you were always polite and tidy and were obviously well brought up, that you paid your rent on time and were pleasant in your demeanor, and that you were teaching my boys to read. I managed to get a little smile from her with that, but just a little one, because she was clearly sick at heart from worrying over you. Still, a mother's love doesn't die just from being cast off in that way, so she went immediately to the prison, where, of course, they told her nothing and denied her a meeting with you. She left some things for you there. A pen, paper, some books, I think, food."

"I only received the pen and paper."

"And were lucky in that. She spent two nights here, in your bed." Mrs. Plotkin leaned closer to examine my face. "You don't look a thing like her."

"No. That's right."

"No resemblance whatsoever."

"None," I agreed.

"Not in feature. Not in coloring."

"Not in temperament either," I replied.

Mrs. Plotkin sighed and rose from the table. She went into the alcove where she slept and returned with two envelopes. "She left a letter for you should you turn up here after your release. And a second letter arrived, by post, just this week."

I took both letters and brought them instinctively to my face, but there was nothing of Tsila in their smell. Both letters were sealed. The first had been hand delivered by Tsila, the second had foreign stamps on it.

"You'll have missed your chance to sail for Argentina by now."

"I have?"

"It's too late in the season, I would think. You'll have to wait until spring."

This hadn't occurred to me before. It might have had I spent any time imagining what I would do once I was released from prison, but I had not. Since Larissa's death I had lain on my bed, day after day, with no thoughts I could remember, just a sensation of coldness, an awareness of the gray chill of the prison permeating me ever deeper, taking me over, transforming me into one of the stones that surrounded me.

"Maybe you should read your mother's letters," Mrs. Plotkin suggested, but I couldn't right then. With the realization that Tsila and Aaron Lev had already left for Argentina came a sudden rush of feeling, sickening after weeks of stillness. Nausea rose within me, tears welled in my eyes.

"What will I do?" I asked Mrs. Plotkin. I had no papers, no money, no place to stay for the night. "I have nothing. No one."

Mrs. Plotkin raised the bald ridges above her eyes where her eyebrows should have been. "What about your comrades?" she asked.

"My comrades? What are you talking about? I have no comrades. I'm alone in the world."

Mrs. Plotkin looked no more sympathetic. "Enough with the melodrama," she said. "What about your so-called aunt?"

"My aunt?"

"So she introduced herself."

Was it possible, I wondered. "Pale with long red hair?"

"Pale, yes. I couldn't tell you about her hair, since it was covered like a proper housewife. Not that she fooled me with that getup. Not for a minute. She came by just a few weeks ago and gave me an address to give to you, right here in Kiev. I asked if she had just moved here, and she said no, she had been here for a while already. As if I was born yesterday. Do you think I was born yesterday?" she asked me. "Do you think if you had such a proper married aunt living in Kiev you would have been paying rent to a stranger?"

"I suppose not," I said.

"You *suppose* not," Mrs. Plotkin muttered. "She was insistent that I give you her address if and when you should turn up." Mrs. Plotkin handed me a slip of paper on which an address was written in Bayla's hand. "She's lucky I am who I am, this aunt of yours, but her luck won't hold if she remains careless. Handing out her address like that to strangers. In her line of work."

"She's a pharmacist," I said.

"And I'm a sorcerer," Mrs. Plotkin replied. She refilled my glass with tea and took another piece of sugar between her gums. She watched me read the slip of paper Bayla had left for me and when I had finished she said, "I could have turned her in."

"For what?" I asked.

"Don't insult me," she said. "Do you think you're smarter than I am? Do you think I'd still be alive if I couldn't recognize who was standing on my own doorstep?"

"I'm sorry," I said.

"Enough with the apologies. You don't fool me. None of you do.

Now get out of here before word gets out that I'm harboring the likes of you."

Mrs. Plotkin remained seated as I rose to leave.

"And good luck to you," she said before the door shut behind me.

Mrs. Plotkin had been wrong about Bayla's carelessness. The address Bayla had left for me was not her own but that of a landlord who owned several buildings in the neighborhood. He asked for my papers, and I, fearing rearrest, quickly apologized for taking his time and started backing away. "Wait," he said. "Perhaps I can help you." I was afraid but remembered that it was Bayla who had directed me to him, an address written in Bayla's recognizable hand. He asked my name, and I told him, fear heavy in my chest. He said that for four rubles he could direct me to a bed that he rented to new migrants who lacked their proper papers. I remembered the ten rubles that Tsila had sewn into the lining of my coat before I left home. "Go around the back," he instructed me as he folded my money into his palm. "It's down the stairs in the laneway."

I found the apartment—four stairs leading down to a low doorway. I knocked, and it was Bayla who answered. "At last," she said, enfolding me in her embrace. She ushered me in, leading me through a darkness more tunnel than hallway. The entire apartment seemed more like a burrow than a human habitation, but the kitchen was warmly lit, and for the second time that afternoon I was seated at a worn wooden table with a steaming glass of tea before me. We drank our tea in silence, our eyes meeting often. She placed her hand lightly atop my own.

"I've been so worried. From the moment I heard you were in Kiev. I don't know what possessed Tsila to send you after me."

"Worry," I said.

Bayla smiled and shook her head. "And then to hear of your arrest . . ." She squeezed my hand.

"Tsila and Aaron Lev have left already for Argentina," I said.

"Yes, I know. I was in touch with Tsila after your arrest."

So the purpose for my trip to Kiev had been accomplished: Bayla had finally gotten in touch with Tsila. And all I had to do was get myself arrested and held for several months.

"I've been so proud of you," Bayla said. "So very proud. To hear of your defiance during questioning . . ." She stroked my cheek.

"How did you hear about that?"

"They're as infiltrated by us as we are by them," she said with a slight smile.

"And have you heard anything about Tonya?"

"Only that she was released. And long before you were."

"Did you know that on the night of our arrest she invited me to join her for a night of theater, but never mentioned her plans for our part of the performance?"

Bayla raised her eyebrows. "That I didn't know."

I waited for her outrage about Tonya's recklessness and deceit.

"Well, you certainly received a crash course on the injustice of the regime," Bayla said. "The arbitrariness of what passes for rule of law . . . and your own strength," Bayla went on quickly. "Your own courage. I'm so very proud of you." She cupped my chin in her hand and kissed my forehead. "But enough talk. You must be hungry."

I wasn't, though I had consumed nothing but tea and sugar that day.

"You should eat anyway," she said, and as she rose to get me some food I remembered the letters.

"Tsila's letters," I said, reaching into the pocket of my coat to pull them out. These were the first letters I had ever received and I opened them with clumsy, trembling fingers. "Should I read them aloud?"

"Only if you wish."

"My dear Miriam," I read aloud. "I came to bring you home, only to be told by your landlady that you'd been arrested. For what, I still don't know, nor can anyone tell me how long you'll be held. Everyone I speak to has a different opinion, a different experience to relate. The amount of time they'll hold you seems to depend to some degree on the charge, but not entirely, and, of course, since you've not yet been charged with any crime—so far as anyone knows—there's no telling when they'll let you go. Your landlady says it's better when there's no charge, since her husband was charged right away and then sent to

Siberia, where he died. A great comfort she is—I was up half the night. And meanwhile, our passage to Argentina has been booked for the end of the summer, and we can only pray, your father and I, that you will be free by then."

"To think she's still praying, given all that she knows," Bayla said, placing a plate of bread and cheese before me.

"Be strong," Tsila commanded me in parting. The letter was dated the twenty-fifth of Iyar, 5664, early in the summer, just weeks after my arrest.

The second letter was dated the first of October, 1904. "A new calendar for a new life," she began. "We postponed our passage once, then a second time, but we were afraid to push it off any further, for fear of running into the winter. It will be of no comfort to you, of course, that our hearts were heavy as we slipped away from the land, but no purpose was being served by our waiting. This way, at least, we will have made a start by the time you arrive.

"The journey over was unpleasant but by no means unbearable. The weather was fine, except for one stormy patch, so we were fortunate in that—and upon landing at the island of Cuba, along the way, our ship was thronged by boats of peddlers selling varieties of fruit so sweet and flowing in juices that they seemed of a different species altogether from what our Reizel has been selling to us all these years. While I wished you were there eating them with us, I trusted at that moment the correctness of our decision. All our lives we tried to squeeze what little sweetness we could out of our situations, but there's no sweetness in Russia, and if there were, it would never flow to us."

"We will make it flow to us," Bayla said. "A sweetness the likes of which she doesn't dare imagine."

"Our arrival in Argentina was uneventful—officials here bear no resemblance to those we suffered in Russia."

"For now," Bayla said. "Capitalism is still new there, don't forget."

"Are they all capitalists there?"

"They're certainly not socialists."

"We had no time to form an impression of Buenos Aires," the letter continued, "as we were quickly whisked away to the colony that will be our home. The name of the colony is Clara, named after the Baroness herself, and it is the largest of the Jewish colonies in the Entre Rios province. Within it are nineteen villages. Ours is called Ida. On first impression, it is not what I expected, I won't pretend that it is—a scattering of villages across an empty plain—but we have a good roof over our heads, and the earth beneath our feet is solid and firm, unlike that in the swamp, which never could support the weight of the lives we tried to build upon it."

"She's always had a way with words," Bayla said, a touch of wistfulness in her voice.

"The spring planting was under way when we arrived. The seasons are reversed here, don't forget, and much warmer. Wheat is the major crop, though we'll grow flax, hay, barley, and rye as well. Aaron Lev is used to hard physical labor, of course, but many of the other men of the colony seem never to have bent their bodies over anything other than a tractate of Talmud. Yields, we have already heard, are not what they should be. It's the water, they say. The lack of it. We are to be as cursed here by its scarcity as we were in the swamp by its excess. It hides so deep in the ground that our well had to be dug to a depth of thirty meters, and it has barely rained since our arrival. A drought—very unusual for here, apparently. And yet—how can I say this to you?—in that very curse lies the beauty of this place. There is a density of color to a sky undiluted by moisture, a clarity to the landscape such as I've never seen before. It's as if the waterlogged air in the swamp obstructed my vision as surely as tears in my eyes that never dried—though I would never say that aloud, of course, not with all the worry about the drought."

"I should hope not," Bayla muttered. "Talk about decadent."

"There is little I say aloud," the letter continued. "Not because our fellow colonists are any worse company than the neighbors we bid farewell to back in Russia. They are not. But neither are they better. The men sigh a lot but seem, as a whole, more happily disposed to this new life than the women, who waste a good part of each day weeping for that great glory of an existence we left behind. It's a difficult life here, I won't deny it, but I sense an excellence to this new country, to an earth undrenched with blood, to the Argentinians who have been so welcoming and seem—even though they are Christians—to be free of the hatred that plagued us in Russia."

"Give them time," Bayla said, which surprised me.

"Why should they come to hate us there?" I asked.

"Capitalism creates hatred. That's its nature. It divides people from each other by creating conditions whereby one group survives at the expense of the other. It takes the human heart—which is wholly innocent, despite what the priests and rabbis might have us believe—and perverts it into an instrument of hatred."

The letter continued with a brief description of the house Tsila and Aaron Lev occupied—made entirely of brick—the garden she had planted. "Be strong," she concluded. "We await your arrival."

"Will you go?" Bayla asked.

How can I convey the fear that overtook me then, the dread of embarking alone on such a voyage when I was so tired, so cold, so unable to imagine what might await me at the other end.

"In the spring," I said, reluctant to tell Bayla of my sudden fear when, just moments earlier, she had been so proud of my courage.

"Are you sure?" she asked, looking at me closely.

"Of course I'm sure. Why wouldn't I be sure?" I was so tired at that moment, I could think of nothing I wanted except sleep.

"I'm relieved to hear you say that, I must confess," Bayla said. Her face was flushed, and I was moved and reassured that my decision to stay the winter meant so much to her. "Tsila left the money for your passage with me . . ."

"Tsila left me money?" I felt a lift inside me. A warmth. They hadn't simply disappeared, leaving nothing but regretful thoughts behind. They'd left me money so I could join them.

"But I'm afraid I've spent it."

"You've what?"

"I didn't expect you to be released quite so soon."

"You spent the money Tsila left for my passage?"

"I'll make it back for you long before spring. I promise. I absolutely promise."

"You spent the money Tsila left for me?" I asked again in disbelief.

"I'm sorry," Bayla said, without any obvious regret.

Would I have left that fall? I've often wondered. If I'd had the money Tsila had left me—a promise of something waiting for me on the other side—would I have suddenly been less afraid of the journey across the ocean?

"I'm truly sorry," Bayla said again some time later. I had not touched the food she had put before me, and we had not exchanged a word since her confession.

"I'm tired," I said.

"Would you like me to show you to your bed?"

I followed Bayla to a cot in a small room off the kitchen and fell immediately into a long, dreamless sleep.

WHEN I AWOKE IT WAS EVENING AND THE ROOM WAS dim, save for the far corner where one weak lamp was lit. Bayla was sitting on the foot of my bed.

"I was supposed to leave Kiev for a few months," she said when she saw my open eyes. "But now I won't."

I was heavy with sleep and the room seemed to be moving under the flickering light of the lamp.

"Where were you supposed to be going?"

"I can't tell you."

"You can go," I said, more angry now than exhausted.

"No. I'm not leaving you here alone."

"Go," I said. It was disgust that I felt. She hardly even seemed like Bayla anymore. This woman I once knew so well made stiff pronouncements about decadence and the human heart but didn't care that Tonya had misled and endangered me. This new Bayla no longer knew enough not to rob her own niece. And yet, even in my anger I couldn't deny my own relief that she was not going to leave me there for the winter. I started to cough and sat up to clear my lungs.

"You were coughing in your sleep," Bayla said.

"I'm always cold."

She reached over to feel my forehead, first with her hand, then her lips. "I don't think you have a fever," she murmured, then, "you can't stay here after tonight, I'm afraid . . ."

"I can't?"

"But I know of a vacancy. It's not safe for you to stay with me right now. I can't tell you why, so please don't ask me."

"Is it Leib?"

"Leib? What does Leib have to do . . . ?"

"Did he abandon you here? Is that what you're ashamed for me to see . . . ?"

"I'm not ashamed."

". . . that you're living alone here, abandoned . . ."

"Miriam, Miriam," she said softly, shaking her head. "Just when I think that maybe you've grown up, maybe you've grown beyond the petty, narrow concerns of the *shtetl* . . ."

"What, then?" I asked.

She was still shaking her head, but she was smiling too, a little sadly, a little fondly. "I'm going to tell you something now. I'm going to tell you because I owe you this truth. If you're going to continue to associate with me, I want you to know exactly who you're associating with."

So perhaps she did have some misgivings about Tonya's prank, after all.

"I want you to know that I no longer confine myself to making speeches. I believe that the evil we're fighting in Russia requires weaponry more powerful than speech now."

"Like what?" I asked.

"Don't pretend to be more naive than you are. It wasn't an easy decision, believe me, but they make a mockery of peaceful protest, riding into crowds the way they do, beating and trampling anyone in their path. They throw sixteen-year-old girls into prison for months on end, and for what? For daring to distribute pamphlets. They murder their own young because they can't control . . ."

Something nudged at me then, a feeling of dread unattached to any thought.

"I know what you're thinking," she said. "I see it in your face.

You're thinking, 'What could be more powerful than speech,' right? 'What could be more powerful than words? It was with the letters of the alphabet, after all, that the Almighty created heaven and earth.' Do you think I don't know what Tsila taught you? Do you think I didn't learn the same things from my own mother?"

I hadn't been thinking any of that at all. I had been trying to identify what it was that was filling me with dread.

"But the great Almighty is nowhere in evidence," Bayla continued, "And, meanwhile, innocents are being murdered as speeches are being made."

My mind filled then with a body swinging from a scaffold, a woman's body in a dress of cobalt brocade.

"It's not that I no longer believe in agitation and education. They're still central components of our work. But they're not enough, Miriam, and never will be."

I could see the body swinging slowly, as if rocked by a gentle breeze.

"I didn't want to have to shock you like this today, your first day out."

Bayla placed her hand over mine to comfort me, but it was Bayla who was the innocent here, I thought, thinking she could shock me with her allusions to violence, after all I'd experienced in prison.

"I hope you can understand now why I may have seemed a bit distant today, why I don't want you taking the risk of staying with me, or even associating closely with me until you've had the chance to think about what I've told you and can make an informed decision. Your own decision.

"I don't like to criticize a comrade," she added. "But what Tonya did was unconscionable."

I nodded, mollified by that acknowledgment. "Where's the apartment you were telling me about?"

"It's not far. Just a few streets over."

"And who lives there?"

"Three girls not much older than you. Zelda is a *feldsher* who devotes herself to caring for the poorest and sickest in the city. She was a medical student at Kiev University but dropped out because of her ideals. She goes into the poorest neighborhoods every day, at great risk to her own health and safety. Esther and Nina both work in textiles and are active in the movement. They're all nice girls. You'll be all right there, I promise."

She reached across me to the bureau by the bed and opened a drawer.

"What about Leib?" I asked.

"What about him?"

The drawer was full of passports, scores of blue, internal passports. She pulled one out.

"Has he been living here with you?"

"He has. But he's left Kiev already."

"And you were supposed to join him?"

"I was. Do you have a pen?"

I gave her the quill that Tsila had brought me during my imprisonment.

"Won't he be mad?"

"It's not like that between us. Complications arise. It's the nature of our work. We both understand this."

"I ran into him my first week here, you know."

"He told me." She dipped the quill in the ink. "What would you like your new name to be?"

"You can make me a passport just like that?"

She smiled.

"What did Leib tell you about our meeting?"

"Just that he ran into you."

"That's all?" I asked, disappointed.

"Enough with Leib," she scolded. "Tell me your new name."

"What's wrong with my old one?"

"Miriam's fine but you need to change your last name. It's for your own security."

I thought about it for a while.

"So?" she prodded. "What will it be?"

"Entelman," I said, and she looked up sharply. "No," she said. "I don't think that's a good name for you."

"Why not?" I asked.

"I don't think you should bring honor to that name."

"If I'm going to join the movement I'm going to do it in the name of Entelman."

"*Join the movement.* Listen to you. You don't know what you're doing. You're a few hours out of prison and can barely keep your eyes open."

"Miriam Entelman," I repeated, and though Bayla shook her head, she wrote it down then as I had directed. From another drawer she pulled out a stamp, which she used with a bureaucrat's flourish. "There," she said, handing me my passport. "Welcome to Kiev."

CHAPTER SEVENTEEN

*T*HE COLD CAME EARLY THAT YEAR. BY NOVEMBER we
were in the full frost of winter. Mornings were bitter when we rose in
darkness to light the stove.

Our apartment consisted of one room in the basement of a house.
There were four beds in it, a stove, and a table around which we gathered to eat and hold discussions. The room was cramped but tidy—
each of us made our bed neatly every morning and swept around and
beneath it—and although we lived below ground, there were two high
windows at street level through which natural light streamed in during
the first hour of the day. We shared one armoire for our clothes and kept
the rest of our belongings in trunks under our beds. Nina and Esther
had lamps that lent some light to the room, and Zelda had erected a long
shelf on the wall between the windows on which we kept our books and
a photograph of Zelda's departed parents.

We cooked and cleaned as a group, in that way keeping down our
expenses. We shared bread and tea in the morning before leaving for
work, and bread and soup and more tea in the evenings after returning
home. After our evening meal we gathered with other young people,
men as well as women, to discuss the coming revolution.

I was working at a ribbon factory in the Podol that autumn—a workshop, really, located in the back room of the owner's house. My flatmate

Nina also worked there and it was she who had found me the job. The wages were lower than what I had earned wrapping sugar, and I found the work punishing in its stillness. For eleven hours I had to sit on a stool, only the small muscles of my fingers and eyes allowed their full range of movement. At lunchtime I stamped my feet and swung my arms around me, hoping, in this way, to encourage the movement of my blood. All day I longed to feel my blood rushing its warmth to my furthest reaches, but this never happened until the end of the workday, when Nina and I hurried arm in arm through the dark, icy streets.

I tried those first weeks after my release from prison not to let my thoughts drift backward, but memories rose out of me with a power of their own: images of Tsila's hands, the slope of Aaron Lev's shoulders, Sara's face. A tapping sound at work would startle me, swing me around to its source: just a girl at the table behind me adjusting the dowel on which she wound her ribbons. Moments of terror or bitter sadness floated free of any other content, like clouds of darkness settling heavily upon me. It was only as I rushed through the streets with Nina after work that I began to feel a lightening of my mood, a relief that persisted as I gathered with others to discuss problems and issues not exclusively my own.

We gathered at different locations every night to avoid raids by the police. We would come singly or in pairs, staggered in our arrivals so as not to attract unwanted attention. The doorways we knocked on never looked any different from all the ones we had passed on our way, and I always had a moment of fear that a door would open one night only to reveal the Colonel Gendarme who had questioned me in prison, and nothing behind him but a cold, bare room. This never happened, of course. The rooms I stepped into each evening were warm with all the young people gathered there, and filled with smoke and laughter and voices raised in argument and discussion.

There was hope in the air that autumn. The public's response to Von Plehve's assassination had exposed the weakness of the autocracy, and not just to youth like us. It seemed like there was nowhere in the empire that Von Plehve's passing had been mourned. Instead, people had celebrated openly, taking their joy to the streets in some cities and praising the Socialist Revolutionary Party, whose Combat Battalion had carried out the assassination. The money that now poured into the coffers of the various revolutionary parties was said to be coming from all segments of society, and it was widely believed that the longer the Tsar held firm against meaningful reform, the greater would be the blow that felled him. As we met each evening to discuss the relative merits of strikes and demonstrations versus terrorist attacks, of incremental reform versus revolution, we didn't imagine—none of us did—that the despotism could last much longer. The pressure that was building seemed unstoppable.

The dam of autocracy will crumble under the force of a cleansing tide. That was a phrase we used often, a phrase that inspired me at the time.

BAYLA STAYED IN KIEV, AS PROMISED, BUT HAD TO MOVE from her apartment.

"So Leib *was* mad," I said, to which she laughed and tousled my hair.

"You seem to think Leib and I are just another bourgeois couple. Do you think I made him mad, so now he's sending me home to Mother?"

Not to mother, perhaps, but packing, definitely. As I sat at her table she was piling her belongings into baskets.

"I don't take my orders from Leib," she said. "We're comrades. Equals. We were meeting—I can't tell you where—to work together on an operation. When my plans changed he found someone equally competent to replace me. And Leib wasn't *mad*, as you keep expecting. His only interest is in the outcome of the operation, not who participates in it."

"Then why are you moving?"

"For my own work," she said.

"You can't do it from here?"

"No, actually, I can't."

I watched her pack for a few more minutes. "Are you ever going to speak honestly with me again?" I asked her.

She looked up, surprised, then colored a little. "I *am* speaking honestly with you."

"No, you're not. You're talking in code about your various unnamed operations and mysterious *work*. Do you think I'm a child?" I asked. "A fool?"

She looked at me for a few minutes, then came and sat with me at the table.

"What do you want to know?"

"What you're doing. Why."

She nodded. "There's a lot I can't tell you, you understand." I waited.

"I started with speeches," she said. "Agitation. Education. I was with the Bund. I joined them soon after taking my job in Mozyr. And it wasn't Leib who drew me in, contrary to popular opinion."

"Tsila's opinion. And I'd hardly call her popular."

"True enough," Bayla conceded, and smiled. "In any case, I was drawn to the Bund by my own conscience, my own values. It was the Bund who helped people who were being exploited at work, whose pay had been withheld, who were fired for no reason. I didn't face these problems personally, and if I had I could have stood up for myself. I'm educated and have a sense of my own worth. My mother saw to that, despite the wretchedness of her own life."

Rosa's life, wretched? This I hadn't heard. Rosa with her enlightened attitudes, which she always found the opportunity to express? Rosa with her good china and silver that she'd brought with her from Mlnsk?

"I felt I had something to offer, a way to be useful, after a life that could only be described as utterly useless. When I think of the time I wasted sitting around waiting to be married, running to Tsila's with gossip . . ."

A longing filled me as I imagined Bayla and Tsila sitting at our table as they used to, laughing about Chippa's latest proposal, but Bayla shook her head as if to clear it of those memories.

"Suddenly, after a lifetime of drifting, I had a purpose. I could read Russian—most of the workers, if they could read at all, only read Hebrew and Yiddish. And more than that, I had an inner conviction that life could be different. Finer. From my mother again, though her vision of what constitutes fineness is very different from my own."

I remembered Tsila talking to me about fineness, the wistfulness in her voice, my own sadness that whatever it was she longed for was not to be found in the life that I knew.

"I began by educating workers."

"You ran a study circle?"

"I attended one first, and then I started one. I taught reading, history, economics. I led discussions about justice, respect for all humanity . . . but I felt restless. Because of the slowness of the work, the snail's pace at which workers were learning, while injustice, meanwhile, proceeded at a full gallop. The members of my study circle painstakingly grasped the difference between A and B while their children died of preventable diseases and their cousins were massacred in Kishenev.

"I started agitating beyond my study circle, but my restlessness continued. I felt I wasn't being effective, wasn't making the best use of my own strengths and skills." She paused now before proceeding. "I have talented hands, you know."

"You do?"

"Why the surprise? Aren't my father and Tsila similarly endowed?"

"Your father and Tsila, yes."

"But the talent skipped me, right? That's what you think. That's what everyone has always thought. Kind, simple Bayla . . ."

"It did always seem . . ."

"The talent didn't skip me," she said sharply. "It was just buried in the circumstances of my life. Yes, buried," she repeated, as if I had contradicted her. "For it certainly isn't with a needle that my hands come to life. Or in the kitchen, God knows—my cooking's barely palatable. But with chemicals. I have an affinity with chemicals. I discovered this at the pharmacy in Mozyr."

"An affinity?"

"They speak to me, whispering their secrets, and my hands can decipher their murmurings."

"You hear chemicals whispering to you?"

Her color rose. "It's an unusual talent, I know. And it might easily have remained unrevealed throughout my lifetime, creating nothing but that unexplained sense of waste within myself that I had until I left for Mozyr, that vague sense of unease that buried talents often produce. But I was fated to be born in this country, at this time in history . . ."

I continued to stare at her.

"I make bombs," she told me. "Of the highest possible caliber." Her face filled with pride. "I can transform the impurest of Russian materials into bombs of Macedonian quality. And if you don't mind me bragging a little, my temperament is such that I remain calm under the most trying of circumstances, loading and unloading explosives as if measuring flour into a bowl." She smiled at me.

A thrill ran through me at that moment, the same fear-tinged excitement as when I had accepted the dynamite from Wolf.

"Does Tsila know?" I asked her.

"*Tsila?* Are you crazy? Why on earth . . . ?" Bayla looked at me closely. "I shouldn't have told you," she said. "You act so mature sometimes that it's easy for me to forget what a child you still are, your mind running always to what Tsila might think."

I regretted the question, of course. I didn't know what had possessed me to ask it. Bayla's smile as she spoke, perhaps, the pride in her face. It had reminded me of Tsila's face when she stepped back from a dress she'd been making to admire the beauty of her work. Except that what Bayla was now creating . . . *I feel I should be sewing a shroud out of this brocade,* I remembered Tsila saying that afternoon that she and Bayla had argued, and the thrill that had fluttered through me just a moment earlier turned heavily to dread.

"What if you get caught?" I asked.

"I knew I shouldn't have told you." Bayla was quiet for a few minutes, her expression distant. I tried to think of something to say, but the dread I felt was so heavy in my chest that I knew it would creep into my voice if I spoke. We sat in silence for some time, then, "Tsila does know. I told her when she came to Kiev."

"You *told* her?"

"God knows I shouldn't have, but she made me so angry, ordering me to come to Argentina after your release, telling me I'd find a life there. A husband, she meant. As if I have no life. As if I have no will or ideals. As if I have nothing except my supposed shame about my supposed abandonment by Leib."

"It wasn't my proudest moment." She smiled ruefully. "When I think that I betrayed my comrades' code of behavior and self-discipline to try to prove to Tsila that there's more to me than she thought." Bayla shrugged and shook her head.

"What did she say?" I asked.

"Nothing worth repeating, believe me. She only sees the danger of my work, not the possibilities."

I told Bayla about Tsila's reaction to the dynamite I'd brought home, her conviction that there was only death awaiting us in Russia.

"She called me an agent of death," Bayla said, blushing deeply. "She couldn't even bring herself to imagine the new life I'm trying to bring forth."

THAT NOVEMBER TYPHUS BROKE OUT IN THE CITY. That's how it seemed to go in Kiev: cholera in the warmer months, typhus in the cold. In the summer it was the water that caused illness; in the winter, the crowded conditions: too many unwashed bodies exchanging lice in airless rooms.

"Have you heard the latest?" Nina asked at one of our evening gatherings. "Councilman Zalevsky has decided a plague barracks should be set up outside city limits for the *teeming migratory masses*. Can you believe it? This is how they mean to deal with the housing shortage and the outbreak of disease. A plague barracks!"

"Who are the *teeming migratory masses*?" Esther asked, which brought a round of laughter.

"Us, my dear," someone answered.

"Most of the working population of Kiev."

"They want us to work for them by day—make their clothes, produce their sugar, create their profits, serve their food—and then clear out of the city by night so that their so-called better class of citizen won't have to breathe air sullied by our presence," Nina said. "That's their thinking now, but they have another thought coming, don't they?"

There was agreement all around, and plans were made for pamphlets to be printed and distributed at everyone's place of work.

"YOU HAVE TALENT," ESTHER SAID TO ME THAT NIGHT. Nina and Zelda were already asleep, and Esther and I were at the table by the stove, Esther with a glass of tea and I with the pen Tsila had brought to me in prison and a sheet of paper. I had seen a coat in a store window on my way to work that morning. It was a warm-looking coat, and lovely in its lines, but it was the color that had drawn my eye, a blue entirely out of place in the gray of that autumn, a vivid blue full of light, like that of the quilt with which Tsila had welcomed me into her home. As I sketched the coat in black ink, Esther watched admiringly.

"What color is it?" she asked.

"Blue," I said, though that didn't begin to describe what shimmered in my mind.

"I've been thinking of having a dress made," Esther confided. "Can I show you?"

She took the pen from me, and on a new sheet of paper she drew a dress she had seen in a magazine.

"What do you think?" she asked when she had finished. "It's also blue. Like your coat."

"It's very smart," I said.

"The collar's lace. The cuffs as well."

"And the dress?"

"Cashmere wool."

I raised my eyebrows.

"I know I can't afford it, but I just can't help daydreaming about how nice it would be. I look pretty in blue—my mother always told me. Because of my eyes."

"There's too much skirt," I said, looking at the sketch. Esther was a big girl and at risk of looking like a lake in that dress if something wasn't done to break up the expanse of blue skirt. I took the pen back and drew in a trim of ribbon. Then I lowered the waistline a bit. "Satin ribbon for the trim," I said. "I cut some just this week."

Esther took the drawing, studied it, then smiled broadly. "You have definite talent."

"I know a thing or two about dressmaking," I admitted.

"You won't tell the others about this, will you?"

"There's no crime in wanting a dress."

"They already think I'm shallow."

"No, they don't," I assured her.

"I almost died of embarrassment when I asked that stupid question tonight about the teeming migratory masses."

"It's not stupid to ask questions. And everyone knows how committed you are," I said, to which she burst into tears.

"I'm not interested in pamphlets."

"That's all right," I said, not certain why a disinterest in pamphlets would cause her to weep.

"What good are pamphlets when most of those affected can't even read them?"

"Those who can read them explain them to those who can't."

She continued crying, her shoulders heaving with each new sob.

"I didn't join the movement to distribute pamphlets," she said. "If I'm going to be arrested and bring shame onto my family I want it to be for something valuable. Not pamphlets, for God's sake."

"It's really all right, Esther," I said. "No one's going to think the worse of you if you decide not to distribute pamphlets."

She continued sobbing, and as I looked on helplessly I wondered if she was unbalanced.

"You really don't have to have anything to do with pamphlets," I said as gently as I could.

"I can't even read them," she whispered.

"You can't?" I whispered back.

She shook her head without meeting my eyes. And so we began, that night, with the first letter of the Russian alphabet.

IT WAS THE FOLLOWING SUNDAY THAT WE WENT TO THE ravine. Esther had asked around at work for a seamstress who might be able to make her the dress she wanted for a price she could afford. It was the material, of course, the widths of blue cashmere that would prove the most costly, but apparently there was a woman named Magda living in one of the ravines who could obtain any material in any color, and for half the price that one would pay elsewhere. Esther was going to find this Magda and she wanted me to accompany her.

"Don't be crazy," I told her. "How do you expect to find this one woman named Magda among the masses of people who live in the ravines?"

"I have specific directions," Esther answered.

It was recklessness to venture into the ravine—at the height of a typhus outbreak, no less—to pursue a rumor of a woman selling fabrics. Fabrics that were obviously stolen. It was pure recklessness, not to mention a waste of time and energy that might otherwise be spent in a productive manner. And yet . . . no, I told myself. The very idea of devoting half a day to the sole purpose of procuring blue cashmere for a dress . . . worse than reckless, it was decadent. How, then, to explain the appeal of the proposition, the lifting of my spirits when I woke up Sunday morning and remembered that this was the morning for our ill-conceived outing, the giddiness I felt as we walked hand in hand toward the ravine with no objective other than finding the exact shade of blue cashmere that would most complement Esther's sparkling eyes?

It was a dreary morning. The sky was leaden, the trees sheathed in ice, their uppermost branches disappearing into the mist. As we approached the ravine I began to feel nervous. "You know the ravines are dangerous," I said to Esther.

"No kidding." she said.

Our flatmate Zelda had been entering the ravines for weeks now to attend the ill and dying. I suddenly felt ashamed that I had never offered to accompany Zelda to help with her work, while the mere mention of a search for blue cashmere was enough to lure me. I said this to Esther and she nodded. "I'll die of embarrassment, for certain, if Zelda finds out. Nina, I don't mind so much. But Zelda . . . she's so serious."

"Ardent," I said.

"Stern."

"Totally committed."

"Boring," Esther pronounced, with a slight smile.

"You think so?"

"She never laughs."

"Maybe she doesn't see anything funny in people's suffering."

"Do you think she'll laugh more after the revolution?"

"Hard to say," I had to admit.

The fog thickened as we descended into the ravine and was acrid now with smoke. Shacks like packing crates crowded the hillside, their arrangement haphazard. Some were built of wood and scraps of metal, others of bales of straw with sacking hung for a door. Their sources of heat were outside—squat clay ovens from which smoke billowed from broken pipe, and fires, open fires around which people huddled to keep warm.

"I think it's just a bit farther on," Esther said, turning sharply between two hovels.

At one fire I saw the organ grinder who had played "Bitter Parting" the previous spring. He was roasting a small piece of meat, and with him were three boys. His sons, perhaps. Or not—the shaping hand of hunger was stronger on their skull-like faces than any family influence might once have been. They stared at the fire, riveted by the roasting meat. A river rat, I thought, from the shape of it, though it could have been a squirrel.

"Do you think a parrot could survive a winter here?" I asked Esther.

"A parrot?" she released a peal of high, clear laughter, then she smacked me playfully. "What do you care about parrots?"

I told her then about the prediction that the parrot had picked out for me just weeks before my arrest. He was a beautiful parrot, I told her. Red and green, with stripes of blue across his wings. *Dark eyes will bring you good luck,* he had promised, filling me with hope for my future.

"I had the same prediction," Esther told me, squeezing my hand, "but from a different parrot."

THE DWELLING WE STOPPED AT WAS BETTER THAN MOST, with walls made of boards and a roof of tin, but the doorway was covered only with sacking. "Hello," Esther called, but there was no answer. "Hello," she called again. "I'm looking for Magda."

An old woman pulled aside the sacking. "Are you Magda?" Esther asked. The woman didn't answer but stared at Esther through eyes so cloudy that I wondered if she was blind. "We're looking for fabric," Esther said.

"What kind?"

"Blue cashmere wool."

The woman turned back into her dwelling without a word but didn't pull the sacking closed. I could see a young child sitting on the dirt floor near the entrance. He had a pot between his legs and a small hill of stones beside him that he was piling systematically into the pot. The back section of the dwelling was covered with what looked like rags, layers of rags, upon which lay a figure that I couldn't make out clearly in the dimness. From her moans I knew she was a woman. The moans increased as the other woman rooted through the rags until finally she pulled something out and returned to us.

"This," she said, showing Esther a sample square of cashmere wool in a rich shade of blue.

It was a beautiful fabric and the price she named was so low that it surprised me when Esther started haggling. The price came down a bit, but not much. "How much do you need?" she asked. Esther told her and the woman narrowed her eyes, patted Esther all over, then increased the quantity by a yard. "I'll have it for you next week," she promised. "And you?" she asked, turning to me.

"Tell her about the blue of your coat," Esther prodded, so I did, and once again the woman disappeared into her dwelling. But when she returned she did not have what I was seeking.

"It's lighter," I told her, looking at the sample she had brought. "Darker," I said, as she pulled out another sample. "More luminous," I said, shaking my head to the third. "Richer."

"What you're looking for doesn't exist," she told me finally.

"But it does," I insisted.

"In here, maybe," she said, pointing to my head, "but not in this world."

I described the location of the store where I had seen it.

"If there was such a color, do you think I wouldn't have it?"

"It's there," I insisted, and she promised that if it was really in the window, as I claimed, she would obtain the fabric for me, and for a price I would not believe was of this world.

"Come back next week," she told me, as she had told Esther.

THE NEXT SUNDAY ESTHER WAS ILL. ZELDA ASSURED HER that the fever and headache she had wasn't serious, but she could not raise herself from her bed.

"Please go get my fabric," she begged me, pressing her rubles into my hand.

"We'll go together next week," I promised her. A meeting was going to be held that day in our apartment and I wanted to attend it. Councilman Zalefsky's plan for a plague barracks had ignited such anger throughout the city that a demonstration was being planned for the very next week. It was going to be huge, Nina said. Fierce. "Like nothing we've seen yet," she promised, her eyes shining as she imagined it. I wanted to help plan it.

"I can't wait for next week," Esther said, her eyes filling with tears. "By next week, who knows? I could well be dead."

"God forbid," I said quickly. "Why would you say that? Zelda already told you it's nothing serious."

"What does Zelda know? Has she been inside my head to see why it pounds so?"

"I want to be here for the meeting."

"You can still make the meeting. How long will it take you to go to the ravine? An hour. Two hours. You go, you buy the material, you come back. The meeting doesn't start till noon."

"I'm not even sure I can remember how to find the right place."

"Please," Esther said. "If I'm going to die, at least let me have obtained one thing I wanted in life. Just one thing. It's not so much to ask for. One thing, in my entire life. A few widths of blue cashmere wool. I'm begging you now."

She looked at me then, her blue eyes shimmering with tears.

THERE WAS NO ANSWER TO MY CALL WHEN I ARRIVED AT Magda's dwelling, nor was there smoke billowing out of her oven. I called again, without expecting an answer, but this time a voice called back, "Go away."

I identified myself and, again, there was no answer. I reminded her that she had told me to come on that day, but she still refused to answer, so I turned to leave, and as I did I saw Wolf. He was sitting by a fire in front of a wooden shack no more than twenty strides from where I stood. Had he been there the previous week as well? I couldn't know, but as I approached him his face was so serene I felt he had been awaiting my arrival for some time.

"Hello," I said.

"Hello."

"What are you doing here?" I asked him.

"Having my breakfast. Would you like some?"

He had a samovar boiling, a tarnished silver samovar as elegant as any I had ever seen. He poured me a glass of tea and handed me a piece of bread.

"Where did you get that samovar?" I asked.

"From my mother, may she rest in peace."

"You shouldn't have it sitting out like that."

"Why not?"

"It's dangerous," I said, sweeping my hand to encompass the tumbles of hovels around us. "Everyone can see it."

"And why shouldn't they? It's beautiful, is it not?"

"People have been killed for less."

"People are being killed as we speak. Meanwhile your tea is getting cold. Why don't you drink it?"

I drank the tea as he suggested. It was strong and warming.

"What are you doing here?" I asked him again.

"The same could be asked of you. Bothering a woman whose daughter died this week."

"Magda's daughter died?"

"In childbirth. The baby was in the wrong position."

"The poor woman," I said, remembering the moaning I had heard from atop Magda's pile of rags.

We sat in silence for a few moments.

"Her suffering was terrible," Wolf said at length. "Her screams went on for two days, with no one but her mother attending. Not that anyone could have helped. He was very badly stuck, impossible to dislodge."

"Did no one offer to help?"

"They're not well liked. Magda's a thief and doesn't restrict herself to the belongings of strangers."

"Still . . ."

Wolf shrugged. "I kept the boy here with me through it all. He would have been better somewhere else, though, somewhere where he couldn't hear her screams."

I looked at Wolf closely as we sat across from each other drinking tea. He was terribly thin—his face formed more of hollows than of flesh—and his skin was the color of bone. His teeth, though, continued to blacken in his mouth—a sign of life, Tsila had once told me, for it's the teeth of the dead that are always strong. And his dark eyes were glimmers of light in his face.

"Why are you here?" I asked again. "I thought you'd left Russia." For had he not been on his way to the border, under threat of arrest, that night I had met him in the forest and accepted his dynamite into my possession?

"I did leave. And then I returned."

"But why?"

"It's a long story," he said. "And not one I particularly feel like telling right now."

We finished our tea in silence. I thought maybe I should leave; he obviously didn't want to talk. But then, he didn't seem to mind my presence. And I felt oddly comfortable sitting there with him. I remembered our first meeting in the swamp, a comfort the same as I was feeling now.

"Are you from Mozyr?" I asked him.

"Kalinkovich."

"And are your parents still there?"

"My mother's dead. And I never had a father."

"I'm sorry," I said.

"Not nearly as sorry as my aunt who had to raise me," he smiled. "I shouldn't blame her, I suppose—she took me in, after all—but she couldn't bear the sight of me."

"Why not?" I asked.

"She looked at me and saw only her own shame, the shame her sister had brought to the family by bearing me. She despised me, and her children did too. There was no one in that house who looked at me and saw anything other than their own shame and hatred. You can understand, perhaps, why I spent a lot of time alone in the swamp." He met my eyes. "It was the only place I felt at home."

"I also felt at home there," I told him.

"You were gathering reeds that first time we met. I surprised you, frightened you—I could see it in your face. But you didn't look away."

I remembered that one note he had played on the reed he took from me, that sound of pure sorrow.

He poured some more tea and we sat again in silence. It was a comfortable silence; there was a spaciousness to it, and after a little while I began to have the sensation of myself expanding within that spaciousness. The sensation was physical, my muscles relaxing, tension draining. And as we continued to sit like that I felt my mind expanding too, opening to images and colors I hadn't seen for months: green meadows of early spring rolling to a blue horizon, flashes of orange fish in the river, the honey of Tsila's hair as she released it down her back each evening. I closed my eyes, at ease despite the squalor that surrounded us, and felt myself floating on the colors that unreeled in my mind.

When I opened my eyes again the gray of the ravine assaulted me. Wolf was looking at me and I was embarrassed to have sat there as I had, eyes closed, imagining myself floating, expanding . . . "I'm sorry," I said.

"For what?" he asked. "You're tired."

"I am," I agreed. "Ever since my time in prison."

"You were in prison? What happened? Not the dynamite . . ."

"No, no," I said.

"If I could tell you how much I regret—"

"It wasn't the dynamite," I repeated. Though wasn't my acceptance of the dynamite the first step I had taken away from Tsila and Aaron Lev, my first step along the path that led to my eventual imprisonment? I remembered the weight of it in my arms, the life I thought might be contained in its unexploded power. "It's a long story, and not one I particularly feel like telling right now."

He smiled.

I had been longer than expected already, and the meeting at our apartment would soon begin.

"I need to go now," I told him.

"Good-bye, then," he said, holding my eyes as I rose to leave.

THE BELLS OF ST. ANDREW'S CHURCH WERE PEALING AS I rushed down Andreev slope toward the Podol. It was later than I had thought. Two o'clock already. Was it possible I had sat that long with Wolf?

By the time I reached Alexander Street I was running. I cut into an alley that formed a shortcut to our street, and there a man blocked my way. "Don't go home," he said to me in a low and urgent whisper. I recognized him as a resident of one of the neighboring apartments. "There's been a raid," he said.

I didn't want to believe him, yet as I proceeded past him I felt the first weight of fear in my chest. My pace slowed and my limbs grew heavier. I turned onto my street and walked toward my house. There were no police on the street, and the entrance to our apartment looked the same as always, the door shut, offering no hint of what lay within. I descended the stairs to our door and tried it. It was unlocked. I opened it and understood why Mrs. Plotkin had referred to the police who had come to her place as a pack of dogs.

The table and four beds had been turned upside down, the contents of the armoire strewn on the floor. Our books were also on the floor, some of them torn at the bindings. The frame that had held the photo of Zelda's parents was shattered, the photo itself ripped to shreds. Our trunks had been opened and emptied, the contents piled on the floor. Our crockery was all smashed to pieces, as was every glass in the house. I saw the pen that Tsila had left for me when I was in prison. It was lying among shards of broken glass. I picked it up and slipped it into the pocket of my coat, then I left the apartment, shutting the door behind me.

I WENT DIRECTLY TO BAYLA'S NEW APARTMENT, BUT SHE wasn't home, and suddenly I became fearful that she too had been taken, and that the Okhrana were still there, behind the door, waiting, just waiting, knowing I would turn up. It was panic, nothing more, but I so terrified myself with the thought that I ran into the street and kept running. I was aware I was drawing glances but was unable to stop. I turned into a side street, the sort of back lane every female resident of the city knew to avoid, and forced myself to stop running, though to do so went against all my instincts. I walked then with no sense of where I was going, aware only of the waning light of day. It was not until I saw

Wolf looking up at me with confusion that I realized where I had come. I became aware of myself, the shaking of my body.

"There's been a raid," I managed to tell him.

"You'll stay with me," he said immediately, and took me into his dwelling. I stood in the doorway until he lit a lamp. He had made a home for himself out of that shack in the ravine. A red-and-black carpet was thrown over the dirt floor. He had set up a chair in one corner; a crate beside it was filled with books. Beside the chair was a cot, which he led me to. He pulled back the blankets and told me to lie down. Then he covered me.

He pulled the chair closer to the cot and sat down beside me.

"They won't be held long," he told me. The new Minister of the Interior had instituted a series of reforms since Von Plehve's assassination, an easing of the restrictions on free speech and association, a strengthening of the rule of law. "They'll be released within a few weeks. A month at most."

"Can you promise me that?"

"No, I can't," he admitted.

"And when they're released, then what?"

"I can't answer that either," he said.

There was a fury to my shaking, to the clattering of my teeth. "I'm cold," I told him. "Always cold."

"It's fear," he said.

"It's death," I told him.

He tucked the blankets closer around me.

"I have a hard knot of coldness inside me. Ever since my imprisonment."

He laid the flat of his hand on the center of my chest.

"Here?" he asked.

"Deeper," I said. I felt the firm pressure of his hand through the thickness of the blankets. "It has always been near me, but until now, outside me. In my moments of weakness he has always tried to embrace me."

"Shhh," Wolf said, pressing harder.

"He never leaves me alone," I said. "I've felt his touch while drinking coffee in a crowded café, while walking alone on a hot summer night. My whole life he has stalked me, always close, waiting for his opening. And now he's inside me."

"It's grief," he told me.

"I shared my mother's womb with him."

"With grief?"

"With death."

He loosened the blankets and slipped in beside me.

"He lured my mother, but that wasn't enough. Nothing is ever enough for him. He's never satiated."

"Shhh," Wolf said again.

"I thought you were him the first time I saw you," I whispered.

"Death?" he asked, a slight quaver in his voice.

"My dead brother come to retrieve me."

And maybe he was, I thought. Was it not he who had handed me the dynamite that night in the forest, an agent of death that he promised would lead to good?

He pulled the pin from my hair to release it, then he held my head against the quiet, steady beating of his heart. I felt his lips resting against the top of my forehead, the first tears sliding down my face.

I don't know how long he held me like that, or how long I wept. I felt the wetness of his shirt from my tears, the taste of salt in my mouth, the exhaustion of my body from weeping, and still he held me. An hour, half the night, I don't know—I cried until I had no more strength for it, and when I was finally still, Wolf slipped out from under the blankets to moisten a cloth for my face. He washed my face, then lay the cloth against my eyes. I felt the heaviness of my exhaustion but did not surrender to sleep until I felt the full length of his body warm against mine again, the smooth skin of his neck against my cheek and the rhythm of his heart pulsing beneath my lips.

A *bird blew* into our cell today. A strange event. It's winter here; the wind is high and the earth lies hidden under snow. The bird was a crow, obviously lost, and very close to death. It blew through our open window and landed—stunned and stunning us—right in the middle of our table. A dream, I might have thought, had my cell-mates not shared the same vision. It lay motionless and we looked on in silence, no one daring to say what she thought.

I would like to tell you that it lived, that we warmed its frozen body, filled its starving mouth, and released it to the sky, but it didn't. It died right there on our table, before twelve shocked sets of eyes.

Was this an omen, then? Perhaps, but today I saw it as a crow—unfortunate, yes, and dead, but nothing other. Still, it brought to mind—perhaps because of the way it fell from the sky—something Tsila told me once, a legend that when the temple was destroyed the letters of the Holy Scrolls flew into the sky. Tsila didn't tell me what the letters did up there, or if they sprouted wings, but I imagined that they did sprout wings and then turned into birds. I would watch the birds that wheeled and dove in the marshes and fields around me and know that they were the scattered letters of the Holy Scrolls, the secret of creation, forming and reforming in the sky, and we just had to lift our eyes to see it.

CHAPTER EIGHTEEN

1904

AT FIRST I HARDLY VENTURED FROM WOLF'S BED. I slept most of the day while he sat outside in the cold of that early winter, serving tea from the samovar that had once been his mother's. He was not often alone. I would hear him talking by the fire, the low tones of his voice soothing me back into a sleep that I could not quite rise out of. His guests were varied—I would hear the gruff voices of men, the laughter of women, the quick chatter of children who would not live to see another winter. From the thickness of sleep I would hear his discussions with the water porters, his advice to the sick, his suggestions to the group that had formed to defend against the hooligans that ruled the ravine by night. One day I heard the unmistakable voice of the organ-grinder. I wanted to ask him to sing a song for me, but I could not pull myself from my stuporous sleep.

Some days Wolf would try to coax me to join him at the fire, but I was too tired, too afraid of what might happen if I showed my face outside. I can't say what it was I feared, exactly, but the weight of it was heavy in my chest. It was fear, not death, I told myself, though sometimes my cough made me wonder. Other days Wolf would leave to go into the city to get food, medicine for some of the residents, other supplies. I stayed in his bed, waiting for his return.

"THERE WAS A PLACE IN THE SWAMP WHERE I USED TO find food," Wolf told me one day. It was a cold morning and very damp. I had just started going outside—it must have been December, or maybe late November—and though I was sitting close to the fire, I could not warm the stiffness out of my joints or the ache from my muscles. "Loaves of bread, baskets of eggs, fruit in season—I assumed it was peasant women who came to leave their food, for reasons nobody could remember anymore. But then, on Pesach, I saw that there was matzah." He handed me a glass of hot tea.

"I know the place," I said. "A fallen-down old cabin by a channel shallow enough in springtime to reach only midway up the thighs of a woman."

He smiled. "And so you do know exactly the place."

"I went with Tsila once. It was a long time ago, soon after I first went to live with her and my father. We left bread, some fruit."

"For whom? Did she say?"

" *'You never know who is hungry,'* is all that she told me. I didn't know others left food there as well."

"I tried not to eat what I found, but I was so often hungry."

"Why would you try not to eat it?"

"I knew it was meant for someone else."

"For anyone who was hungry, surely. It was *tzedakah,* after all."

"It was for a boy that once lived in your town."

"A boy?"

"He couldn't speak. He couldn't utter a sound. An idiot, people thought. Worse than a simpleton, for what simpleton can't manage to produce a few sounds? His family was ashamed of him. The townspeople ignored him. The townschildren teased him mercilessly . . . and then one night there was a fire. And while everyone else who lived in the house managed to escape—all the other children from all the other families—the boy didn't. He wasn't in his bed when his father went to rouse him, but then neither was he outside with the other children. And at that point it was too late to go back into the house for him—though some fathers would have. Already beams of fire were falling inside. The boy was gone, left to burn in the fire."

I had heard a similar story before, but in another village, not ours. A boy who couldn't speak. Worse than a simpleton, as Wolf had said, except that he could communicate with birds. He couldn't utter a word of Torah, but geese would follow in a line behind him, and migrating birds would stop to rest on his shoulders. He was teased by the others in the village, and his own parents were said to be ashamed of him. And then one day there was a flood, and though everyone claimed afterward that they had tried to save him, he was, in fact, the only one who drowned. It was a tragedy, and a terrible shame on that village, which suffered all manner of afflictions forever after. I told this to Wolf, and he smiled, "I'm sure the variations are endless."

"So none of it's true."

"To the contrary," Wolf said. "The boy's soul mingled with the smoke of the fire that had claimed him. It hovered over the town and neighboring swamp, cursing those who had tormented him in life, causing troubles from barrenness to ill temper . . ."

"There was certainly no shortage of ill temper in our town."

". . . to marital discord to hemorrhoids."

"Hemorrhoids? I don't think so." Though I did remember old Rakhmiel Schneider hobbling past our house once, in obvious discomfort, heading into the swamp with a basket of eggs and bread. "Where did you hear such a story?"

"I tried not to eat the food, as I told you, but I was less and less welcome at my aunt's, and I was hungry, always hungry. One day when I arrived there I found apples, Antonov apples, my very favorite kind. I waited for a long time, trying to resist them, but after a while I couldn't. I emerged from the shadows, and as I did someone shrieked. It was a girl, a few years older than I.

" 'Don't be afraid,' I told her. 'I'm alone.'

" 'And obviously hungry,' she responded, affecting a calmness that she obviously didn't feel. When she handed me the bread she had brought I could see she was trembling. 'Eat,' she told me, trying to look me in the eye but failing. Then, in a whisper so soft I wasn't sure I had heard her correctly, 'We're so sorry about how we treated you.'

"I took the bread, but it tasted sour to me. I was as lonely as I was hungry, after all. Lonelier. I craved human warmth more than bread, and to see how frightened that girl was in my presence . . . I know I'm no beauty to look at, but still . . . I felt repulsive, less than human." He paused. "So unlike my first encounter with you."

I remembered how the shock that I too had felt when first seeing him had given way to comfort when I forced myself to meet his gaze and recognized the life beneath his ravaged features.

"But then," he continued, "just a few months later, I encountered that same girl again. This time it was at one of the gatherings of Bundists that used to take place every Shabbes afternoon in the forest on the other side of your town."

"They still take place, as far as I know," I told him.

"She was there, and much changed from the trembling thing I had seen in the swamp. She recognized me right away and came over, full of apologies for her behavior that day. Her imagination had been over-worked, she explained, poisoned by the superstitions that had enslaved her at the time but that she had now shed, she assured me. 'To think I believed it was enough to leave some scraps of *tzedakah*. That that would somehow remedy the conditions that caused his death. And to think that in so doing I ended up treating you as we once treated him. As an outcast, someone to be feared.'

"On and on she went until I finally asked her what she was talking about. That's when she told me about the boy. *Murdered by the callousness of a system that assigns lesser value to some lives than to others,* said my new comrade, who then went on to vow that we would smash the structures that led to such devaluing of human life."

Wolf paused. "Comforting words at the time, since I had spent my whole life on the receiving end of such callousness." He smiled. "I joined the Bund soon after, though I think I knew even then which structure I personally believed most responsible for the devaluing of human life."

"And what structure is that?" I asked, knowing already that he wouldn't say capitalism, or even the autocracy.

"The very one that, turned a certain way, most values life in all its forms. The human heart," he said. "And where will we be if we smash it?"

I WAS ALWAYS COLD DURING THE DAYS, BUT AT NIGHT I was not. We would lie together in the warmth of his bed, bits of conversation floating up from us like fragments of dreams, like the colors that had unreeled from my mind into the silence of our first meeting in the ravine. Most often, though, we wouldn't speak. The steady beat of his heart against mine would soothe me into sleep and reassure me on awakening. I began, in time, to feel a stirring in my chest, a wakefulness by day, a restlessness. The movement of my life within my veins again.

ONE MORNING AS I WAS SITTING BY THE FIRE WITH WOLF, three men came by to discuss a rumor they had heard. A raid was being planned on the ravine, it seemed, a sweep to clear the city of its criminal element. Shelters would be razed, people driven out. As the men discussed possible responses, I noticed Magda come out of her shack and bend over her stove.

I had seen Magda often since coming to live in the ravine—her shack was only steps away—but we had not yet exchanged greetings. I thought she didn't remember me. We had met only once, after all, and perhaps her grief about her daughter's death had clouded her memory of the days preceding it. On this particular morning, although she was standing close by, I was only half aware of her presence. I was listening to the discussion around our fire, wondering what I would do if I heard the sound of horses' hooves thundering into the ravine. I only turned my full attention to her when she strode over to our fire, waving the wooden spoon in her hand.

"What are you staring at?" she demanded of me.

"Nothing," I said.

"Am I nothing, then?" she shouted. "Do I look like nothing to you?"

Some of the men started laughing and making comments of a lewd nature.

"Keep your eyes to yourself," Magda warned me, waving her spoon close to my face.

I apologized, for she frightened me a little: the look in her eyes—it was hatred—and the waving spoon, more weapon than utensil at that moment.

"And your friend owes me money," she told me. "Does she think she can send me chasing after her fabrics and not pay me?"

"My friend's been arrested."

"That's not my problem."

"Then go collect your money," I snapped. "I'm sure you know where the jail is."

I regretted that comment and the men's laughter that accompanied it, not because of tenderness for Magda's feelings but for reasons of caution, an awareness that to have an enemy as my neighbor was folly. Magda glared at me and strode back to her shack, and a few moments later I followed her.

She was stirring a kasha gruel for her grandson, the smell of which made my mouth water. She didn't look up from her task. I still had the money Esther had given me, though I had not thought about it until then. I reached into my coat pocket, retrieved the silver coins, and held them out to Magda. At this she looked up.

"Stir this," she told me. "And make sure to keep scraping the bottom."

She went into her hut and returned a moment later with the cashmere that Esther had ordered. My breath caught at the sight: the blue of a summer sky, there in front of me, in Magda's swollen hands.

I took off my glove to run a finger lightly over it, half afraid it might dissolve, that it was just my own longing I was seeing.

"It won't bite you," Magda said. "Take it already. You're burning my kasha."

I took it from her and held it gingerly to my cheek—too cold to feel its softness—then my lips.

"I can get you anything," she said. "Even the material for that coat you wanted."

"You saw it?" I asked, remembering the coat, the promise of that vivid blue.

Magda nodded. "It will cost you."

WHEN I WENT BACK TO MY OWN FIRE, THE OTHER MEN were gone.

"What's that?" Wolf asked me.

"Cashmere wool," I told him.

"I see that, but how did you get it?"

"I bought it. It's Esther's," I explained.

"You bought cashmere wool? With what?"

"With money. What do you think?"

"You have money?"

"From Esther," I said. "And a few rubles left from Tsila."

He nodded and said nothing more, and a few minutes later he left the ravine on his errands.

I spent that day as I spent all the others: tidying our shack, then lying, wrapped in blankets, waiting for Wolf's return, but I felt uneasy. It wasn't just the darkness of his shack, which, so comforting at first, had begun by then to feel oppressive. It was something beyond my own growing restlessness. There had been a look on Wolf's face when I told him I had money, something I hadn't seen in his expression before. Hurt, I thought, but not only. Anger.

I unwrapped the blankets and emerged from the hut. It had been a bright day and the last rays of afternoon sun still lingered high on the hillside. Most of the ravine, though, was already in shadow. As I looked at the tumbles of hovels, the fires that burned, the restless, constant surge of movement, I saw Wolf from a distance. I recognized his walk, a quick flitting motion. He moved like a shadow. I watched him approach.

He sat himself right beside me so we looked out together down the smoky length of the ravine.

"What did you do in town?" I asked him.

"What I always do. I got us some food, kerosene, an ointment for that girl who split her knee."

"And how did you pay for it?" I asked him.

"Since when do you care?"

It was only then that I felt ashamed, only then aware of the physical demands of life, which had not ceased just because I had ceased being able to meet them. I had not only not given any thought to the matter but I had gone and bought a luxury fabric with money Wolf hadn't even known I possessed, money that could have been put to our survival.

"I'm sorry," I said, and reached into the lining of my coat, where I still had the last of the rubles Tsila had hidden there. I pulled them out, and he didn't refuse them.

It was getting dark by then. We moved inside. Wolf lit the lamp. "Hungry?" he asked.

"A little." I was ravenous, having eaten nothing but bread since the morning.

"I brought you a surprise," he said with a smile that transformed his face into a boy's. He reached into his pocket. "Close your eyes."

I did, and when I opened them again he was holding out his hand to me. In his open palm were two eggs.

"They're beautiful," I said, running my finger lightly over their perfect shells.

"They're duck eggs."

"I know."

"Shall I fry them up?"

I nodded, but as I ate I felt little enjoyment, despite my earlier hunger.

"Have you been stealing everything you bring back?" I whispered later as we huddled together in bed.

"What do you think?" he answered, sending through me a new

wave of shame that he'd been risking arrest every day while I lay in his bed wrapped in blankets, that until then I had not opened my eyes to how he was keeping us alive. I was up and dressed before first light, ready to join the stream of residents who left the ravine every day to work, or look for it.

AS DIFFICULT AS CONDITIONS WERE IN THE RAVINE, I found it worse to leave it. The same streets that had so delighted me just half a year before seemed cold now and mined with a deadly indifference. Not one face flickered recognition of my own. Eyes I met shifted away. Where once I'd felt a freedom in being so unknown, a sense of possibility, now I only felt a danger. My smiles of greeting were not returned. I began to wonder what I looked like, how I smelled. I quickened my pace in response to my growing fear, and instead of going to the ribbon factory to ask about work, I turned into Bayla's street.

"Oh my God," she said when she saw me. She led me into a set of rooms as dark and cramped as the ones she'd lived in before. "I've been frantic with worry. No one's known where you were. Your flatmates and some of the others have already been released, and still no word from you. I was afraid . . . where have you been?" she asked.

"In a ravine."

"A ravine? Are you serious?"

I told her about going to the ravine for Esther's fabric, about seeing a friend there, returning to him after the raid.

"A friend? What friend?"

"His name is Wolf."

"Wolf? You're staying with a man named Wolf in a ravine? Are you crazy?"

"I know him from home," I said, and Bayla's scowl deepened. "It's not what you think."

Bayla was eyeing me closely now. "We'll get to what I think in a little while. In the meantime, you need a bath."

"I do?"

She nodded, and I was mortified. I had been scrupulous about washing myself that morning despite the difficulty of procuring and heating water in our hut.

"Hey," she said, softening as she saw my expression. "It's only dirt." I nodded, looking miserably at the floor. Bayla tugged lightly on my braid. "Come on now," she said.

I CANNOT DESCRIBE TO YOU THE PLEASURE OF STEPPING into the bath that Bayla prepared for me in the middle of that tiny kitchen, the warmth that slowly engulfed me. I could not remember ever having been so warm, so comfortably drowsy. I steeped in it for a long while, my eyes closed, while Bayla sat beside me.

"Wolf was right," I murmured sleepily at one point.

"Mmm?" Bayla responded, pouring a pitcher of warm water over my shoulders and neck.

"He told me everyone would be released."

"Just who is this Wolf, anyway?" Bayla asked. "His last name isn't Slatkin, by any chance, is it?"

"Zonnenberg," I said. "Who's Wolf Slatkin?"

"Oh, just an unfortunate who worked with us briefly. Wolf was his code name, actually. I suppose Slatkin was too, come to think of it." She dipped the pitcher into the bath again and poured more water over me. "You should wash your hair. It smells like smoke. Then I'll have to check you for lice, I'm afraid."

"Did you ever hear a story about a boy from our village who died needlessly in a fire?" I asked her.

"What do you mean by needlessly?"

"No one cared enough about his life to save it. Because he was some sort of imbecile."

"I know a hundred stories like that. A thousand. Why do you think I joined the movement? Dunk now."

"But did you know there was a place in the swamp where people used to leave offerings to him?"

"I think I remember a *bubbe meise* like that. There were so many *bubbe meises* growing up it's hard to keep them all straight." She started soaping my hair. "Is that one of the things Lipsa told you when you were little? No, wait, let me guess. She took you there once and left an offering so that your luck would change for the better."

"It was Tsila who took me."

"What?"

I dunked and rinsed the soap from my hair.

"I don't believe it," Bayla said when I reemerged from the water.

"She wanted a baby."

"I know, but . . ." She rose to get another kettleful of hot water from the stove. "I guess it's no sillier than the appeals to God that she was always making."

"Praying, you mean?"

"Mmm," Bayla said. She started pouring warm water over my shoulders and I closed my eyes again.

"I know of a vacancy just two streets over," Bayla said as I was drying myself.

"I'm fine where I am for now," I said, and Bayla's eyes widened. "It's money I need, not a place to stay. I came in to tell you I'm okay and to start looking for a job."

"Do you have any idea how dangerous the ravines are?"

"I feel safer there," I said.

"Safer??" she repeated, but how could I explain the ease I felt with Wolf, the dissolving of the cold knot in my chest when he pressed the warmth of his palm against it? "You'll catch your death there," she said.

"God forbid. It's brought me luck, if anything. Had I not been there on the day of the raid . . . ," I began, but then I remembered what Bayla had said earlier about my flatmates being released. "Everyone's been freed now?" I asked. "Zelda, Esther, Nina?"

Bayla nodded. "Within weeks of their arrest. It's the reforms."

It was as Wolf had said the night of the raid. The reforms instituted following Von Plehve's assassination, the easing of restrictions on free association and speech, an adherence, in certain cases, to the rule of law.

"It shows the effectiveness of terror," Bayla said as we sat down again at the table.

"How so?"

"Think it through for yourself."

I did think about it then, how one assassination had managed to accomplish overnight what countless strikes and demonstrations had failed to bring about. I said this to Bayla.

"Exactly," she responded, but her mind was already elsewhere. "I'm worried about you."

"You don't have to worry."

"Just who is this Wolf?"

"I told you already. A boy I knew from home."

"What boy from home? There were no Zonnenbergs."

"I met him in the swamp."

"In the swamp?"

"Yes, that's right."

"And then again in the ravine?"

I nodded. And before that in the forest, at night, I thought.

Bayla was looking at me closely now. "Just what is he doing in the ravine?"

"Living," I said.

"And on what, exactly? How does he support himself?" she asked.

"He steals."

"I see." She nodded. "And you? Do you steal as well?" she asked, and then her face flamed with color as she remembered, perhaps, that she also stole, and from me, her own niece. She looked at me a moment longer, then reached for her purse. "I have some money I can give you, to tide you over until you find a job." She reached across the table, took my hand, and filled it with silver rubles. "I owe you," she said.

Siberia, May 1912

When I went out to the courtyard today I stood in the area that will be our garden this summer. It's early spring and we've had three days of sun. Our garden is in a corner of the courtyard that's protected from the worst of the winds by two of the walls that enclose us. The walls reflect the sun inward, creating an effect not unlike that of a greenhouse. I stood quietly and felt, for the first time in months, the warmth of the sun on my back. For one moment I was nothing but warmth. I had no thoughts, no hopes, no memories—just a fleeting sensation of warmth. It was happiness.

Then Natasha came out with the bag of potatoes we'd saved through the winter for planting. She was a beautiful woman once, and even now her eyes are clear and blue in a face delicate as porcelain. She reached into the bag and her mind shattered. I saw it happen. Nothing moved in her face, but at the back of her eyes there was a sudden shadow, a dark mass of matter: the pile of rubble that a moment before had been her mind.

She pulled a potato out of the bag and held it out to me. I took it from her and it collapsed into mush from the slight pressure of my fingers. She pulled out another potato as rotten as the first.

"It's all right," I told her. "We'll compost these. Masha has another bag somewhere, I'm almost certain."

She pulled out a third potato and crushed it in her hand. Slime seeped out from between her fingers and still she kept pulling more rot from the bag that should have held next year's seed.

She took one of my hands then and placed it on the side of her head. She placed my other hand on the other side of her head.

"Press," she said. My hands were dripping with slime.

"Stop it," I said, dropping my hands.

"Press," she said again, repositioning my hands on either side of her head.

I pressed lightly; her skull seemed soft.

"My head is filled with maggots," she said to me. "While the rest of you dream of life, escape—who knows what else?—they crawl over my brain, devouring it. If you press harder they'll stream from my eyes and nostrils."

I dropped my hands, at a loss for what to say, how to comfort. I couldn't shake the sensation I had had of her skull beginning to give way under the pressure of my touch.

"Soon there'll be nothing left of me but seething maggots," she said. "Compost. And for what?"

"For this," I said. I scooped a handful of warm spring earth from the garden and pressed it into her hand.

CHAPTER NINETEEN

1905

IT WAS A COLD EVENING IN EARLY JANUARY WHEN I arrived at Bayla's apartment again. She embraced me when she opened the door. "You've heard, then," she said.

"Heard what?"

"About the massacre."

"What massacre?"

"What massacre? Where have you been?"

"In the ravine."

"Yes, of course." But her mind wasn't on me or my whereabouts. "There was a massacre yesterday," she told me. "In St. Petersburg. Thousands of peaceful demonstrators who had come to supplicate from the Tsar. I can't believe you haven't heard."

"Tell me," I said.

"I'll read you the petition they brought to him, their cherished Tsar." She disappeared into a back room and returned a moment later with a piece of paper, from which she read:

SIRE

We, the workers and inhabitants of St. Petersburg, of various estates, our wives, our children, and our aged, helpless parents, come to THEE, O SIRE, to seek justice and protection. We are impoverished; we are oppressed, overburdened with excessive toil, contemptuously treated . . . We are suffocating in despotism and lawlessness. O SIRE we have no strength left, and our endurance is at an end. We have reached that frightful moment when death is better than the prolongation of unbearable sufferings . . .

Bayla looked up from the paper. She was exhausted, her eyes rimmed in pink, but her face, though drawn, was flushed with emotion.

"They came from all over the city, peaceful in their intentions, women and children at the front, dressed in their Sunday best, and giving the sign of the cross to the soldiers that they passed. Red flags had been banned so as not to inflame the forces of reaction. They carried only a portrait of the Tsar with a large white banner proclaiming, 'Soldiers do not shoot at the people.'

"Masses of soldiers lined the route, barring the way to the Winter Palace. The marchers continued peacefully. They moved as one, forward, toward the wall of infantry that blocked their way, but as they approached the Narva Gates the first squadron of cavalry charged. Some of the marchers fled but most continued. Then, the first shots. Warning shots at first—two warning salvos were fired into the air, but then . . ." Bayla brought her hands to her face and dropped her head.

"They shot into the crowd?"

"At close range," she said. "And the firing continued even as the people fled in panic. They were mown down by gunfire, trampled by the pursuing horses. Cossacks swooped down from their horses, slashing people with their sabers, cutting them open, letting loose with bloodcurdling cries of exhilaration as they did so.

"But, still, the people didn't give up. Finding one way blocked, they took another, up the Nevsky Prospekt, pressing on to the Palace Square. Tens upon thousands of marchers. They arrived at the palace, where many believed they would be met with refreshments to celebrate their peaceful presentation of their just and worthy cause—they're like children; I hate to have to say it—only to be met by cannons and cavalry.

The crowd pressed forward, jeering now. The soldiers used whips at first to fend off the marchers, then they took up firing positions. The marchers dropped to their knees. Men, women, and children. The men removed their caps. They crossed themselves, on their knees. Then a bugle sounded and the soldiers fired. Into the crowd that knelt before them. The front lines fell, then the people behind. Young children, who had climbed trees for safety or a better view, fell from their perches like birds caught in a hunt."

"Yesterday?" I asked. "This happened yesterday?"

It had been a beautiful day, sunny and bright. I had sat outside our shack feeling the winter sun on my face.

"There were riots all night after the carnage, windows smashed, policemen beaten, soldiers encircled by furious crowds, barricades built in the workers' districts . . . a spontaneous outburst of revolutionary violence such as we've not seen until now."

BAYLA AND I WERE ALONE IN THE APARTMENT WHEN I first came, but Leib arrived soon after, his cap and coat dusted with snow, his face flushed with cold and excitement. "What's this?" he asked when he saw me sitting at the table.

"I believe you two have already met," Bayla said.

"Last spring. On the Krestchatik," I told him.

"Yes, I remember." He approached the table, took my hand, and raised it to his lips. His mustache was frosted from the cold outside, but his lips were warm when they pressed against my skin. Then he took Bayla's hand and did the same. Finally he pulled up a chair and joined us.

"What news, Leib?" Bayla asked, addressing him in Russian.

"The revolution has begun," Leib announced, also in Russian. "The violence is spreading like wildfire in the wake of the news of the massacre. Riots, lootings, beatings . . ." Leib removed his wet cap and placed it on the table. *Boorish* crossed my mind as he did so, despite the import of the news he was bringing. He looked at Bayla with a long and steady gaze. His eyes were dark and serious, his lashes long as a girl's. "The swell has finally broken, and it won't be turned back now."

"Is the violence . . . organized?" Bayla asked.

"Not yet. The people are too angry, their betrayal too raw. But it will be organized. Soon. Very soon."

Bayla nodded.

"We're to continue with our work as we've been doing. We can't afford to let our excitement distract us. Our blows must be relentless, battering at them from all sides, all quarters."

"Are you to return to Moscow, then?"

He flashed her a look I couldn't interpret, then he looked at me. "How did she find out where we're living?" he asked Bayla.

"Oh, stop it, Leib. She's more trustworthy than half our so-called comrades, and you know it."

"Why are you here?" he asked me, switching back into Yiddish.

"I was hoping to stay the night with Bayla."

I had spent the entire day in town, looking fruitlessly for work. By the time the last door shut in my face it was too late to walk alone back into the ravine.

"You can't stay here," he told me.

"I have no other place."

"Why can't you go home?"

"It's too late in the evening. I'm living in a ravine."

"A ravine? That's unusual." He was curious now, and I enjoyed the sharpening of his attention. "And what took you to Kiev's infamous ravines?"

"A piece of blue fabric," I said.

He looked at me closely, and a slow smile opened his face. He leaned back in his chair, which suddenly seemed too small for him. As he stretched out his long legs, melting snow slid off his boots into a small puddle on the floor.

"And did you find your blue fabric?"

"Not the one I was looking for."

"Well, what did you find, then?"

I showed him the blue cashmere that I had brought with me that day. I had hoped Bayla might know Esther's whereabouts so I could give it to her.

Leib leaned forward to look. Then he ran his finger along the fabric as gently as I had when I first saw it. "Beautiful," he said. "There's something about it that reminds me of *The Blue Bird.* Have you seen it?"

"She's been living in a ravine, Leib," Bayla said, a tightness in her voice.

"Of course. I'm sorry." He shook his head. "It's a play I had the opportunity to see in Moscow. It's about . . . well, a blue bird, obviously." He smiled again. "Which is a fabulous and fantastic creature that everyone covets. It's kept in a cage, supposedly for its own protection. But really it's because of the greed of people who can only take pleasure in its beauty if they own it exclusively and control it. At the end of the play, though, it escapes and flies free."

The plot sounded as dull as *Madame Sans-Gêne.*

"It's all in the staging, of course," he said, as if reading my thoughts. "And it's symbolic, the bird representing the human spirit, which is imprisoned now . . . but I don't have to explain that to you. You're obviously an intelligent girl.

"But tell me," he said, looking closely at my face now. "How do you find conditions in the ravine?"

"Cold," I said.

He nodded. "When I first went into one and saw how it was, I realized what unmined veins of humanity the ravines are. Wretched now, yes, but richer in potential than any seams of ore that a miner might empty for profit."

I thought of the hillside across from our shack. It was so thick with humanity that it seemed to be heaving, like a carcass alive with maggots that seethe on its surface. I said this to Leib and he nodded again, still looking at me, and began stroking his mustache.

"Can you just imagine the power of the blast when it finally ignites?" he asked me.

"Leave her be now, Leib," Bayla said. "Can't you see she's exhausted?

"There's no harm in you spending the night here," she said to me. "I don't want you out walking alone tonight."

IT WAS LATE THE FOLLOWING AFTERNOON BEFORE I arrived back in the ravine. I had had another day of failure looking for a job, and as I descended into the smoke and soot of the ravine I felt a sense of defeat and growing anxiety.

Wolf was sitting on a crate outside our shack. He smiled at my approach.

"I was at Bayla's," I said.

"That's what I hoped."

"Have you heard what's going on?" I asked him. The massacre in Petersburg, I meant. The spreading outrage.

He nodded.

"I could hear a demonstration a few streets over on my walk back here," I told him.

"A demonstration or a riot?" he asked.

"I don't know." I'd heard shouting, breaking glass, and had hurried nervously along.

Wolf pulled up another crate for me to sit on and began peeling an orange.

"An orange!" I said. "What's the occasion?"

"I sold the samovar."

I looked at him.

"We don't know what's coming," he said.

He handed me a segment of orange, and as it burst in my mouth I thought I'd never tasted anything so sweet. He handed me another and I ate it slowly, trying to make it last, peeling the membrane off it before eating the pulp.

"The revolution has started," I told him.

"So they say," he responded, and I felt a surge of impatience.

We went to bed early that night, but I couldn't sleep. I was on edge, alert to every sound outside our shack, uncomfortable in the narrowness of our bed, restless. Hours passed, it seemed. Wolf was so still beside me that I thought he was asleep, but then, his voice:

"There was a feeling of illness in me as I waited for Von Plehve to approach," he said.

I waited for him to continue, but he didn't. There was shouting in the distance. Men's voices raised and angry. It was a sound no different from any I'd been hearing since arriving in the ravine two months earlier, but with the knowledge of the massacre and escalating violence each shout now sounded like a threat. My body tensed as I heard footsteps approaching, and though they ran past our shack without slowing, my tension remained.

It was a long while before Wolf spoke again, so long that I thought perhaps I had momentarily dropped into sleep after all and dreamed his words, but then he continued. It had been late in the previous winter, he told me, that a small group of the Combat Battalion of the Socialist Revolutionary Party had gathered in St. Petersburg for the first attempt on Von Plehve. That's where he had gone, directly from Geneva, just one month after giving me the dynamite, the seven pounds of dynamite that would be used for the primary bomb in that operation. They had arrived in the capital in February, and disguised as cab drivers and peddlers, they had then taken up positions in the streets around the Fontanka to observe their target's comings and goings.

"That's how we prepared for assassination," he said. "We disguised ourselves as vendors and the like and observed our target for as long as it took to learn his habits and routines."

I remembered running into Leib disguised as a tobacco vendor on the Krestchatik the previous April, and I wondered now what sort of scheme I might have inadvertently interrupted.

"By the middle of March we knew with absolute confidence what route Von Plehve would take on what day, and where we could strike to minimize the danger to others. On the eighteenth of March we were in our positions. Our main striker was disguised as a cab driver in a lineup of cabs on the Fontanka. I was stationed on a bridge above the Fontanka. It was my job to alert our main striker, with a tip of my hat, to the first sign of Von Plehve's approach."

"Were you scared?" I asked.

"Yes," he said. "Scared, and something else as well. Von Plehve was a murderer, I knew, responsible for the deaths of countless innocent people, but as I stood there, awaiting his approach, I did not feel in myself the justice that would soon be ours. To steel myself to the task ahead I imagined the lineups of corpses after the Kishenev massacre, each inert body a mother or a father, a daughter or a son. I imagined the bodies, and the lives that had been destroyed by each of those deaths. Bile rose in my throat, but I did not feel the restorative power of the act I was about to commit. I tried to, but I simply could not.

"Minutes passed, and with each one we were closer to the act. My heart beat faster and heavier in my chest, each beat ominous in sound. I imagined scores of policemen descending upon us from all sides, each beat of my heart the heavy fall of a boot. I imagined the impact of the bomb on living flesh, the thud of imploding bone and sinew. I could no longer concentrate on my task, the beat of my heart distracting me, planting dreadful images in my mind.

"I ran," he said. "I abandoned my comrades. I left my duties knowing that I was dooming the operation to failure. I walked quickly from the Fontanka and caught the tram to the outskirts of the city, to a workers' suburb, where I knew I could pass several hours without drawing attention to myself. I was in an agitated state, as you can imagine, sweating heavily despite the chill of the day, breathless and faint.

"I wandered the narrow streets and laneways of the area, scarcely aware of my surroundings. I found myself suddenly in a cluttered shop that sold housewares. I don't know what drew me in there. The quiet, perhaps—the noise of the street was unbearable in my state of turmoil. I stood in the quiet dimness of the shop for a few moments trying to calm myself and steady my breathing. I looked up at a shelf crammed full with crockery and pots. It was the sort of crockery my mother had used every day.

"I had been in a terrible state of agitation until then. Agitation and panic, and also shame, deep shame about my cowardice. But in the dimness of that shop, surrounded by the housewares of my childhood, a relief filled me, a relief almost indescribable in its pleasure. That I was still alive; it was that simple. That I could feel the unpleasantness of my life—the shame and the panic of that moment—and the pleasure of it too, the pleasure of the relief that was filling me. That I had not taken a life that wasn't mine to take."

He paused again, and I waited for him to continue.

"I left Petersburg that evening. On my own, of course. My comrades would have forgiven me a moment of cowardice—we were all inexperienced—but my betrayal ran deeper than cowardice. I had realized in St. Petersburg that I love life more than justice."

We lay together for a long time in silence after he had finished speaking.

"I think there are places where such choices don't have to be made," I said finally. "Between life and justice. Places where the two co-exist. Maybe after the revolution this will be one of them."

"Utopias," he said. "They don't exist."

"America," I said. "Argentina." Just mouthing those words had a particular sweetness that night.

"To remain alive is to accept injustice. That's the fact that can't be changed."

In the long silence that followed, the shouting started up again. Usually by now Magda would have thrust her head outside the curtain of her doorway to yell at the drunks to quiet down. That night, though, she didn't. The noise continued, ominous and threatening.

"There's no life for us here," I told Wolf, and waited. Did I hope he would close his eyes then and dream of apricots, as Aaron Lev had done when Tsila said the same to him?

"This is my life," he answered. "There is no other."

IN THE WEEK FOLLOWING BLOODY SUNDAY—AS THE massacre in St. Petersburg was now being called—the level of protest and revolutionary violence increased steadily. Major demonstrations continued in cities across the empire, more and more university students went out on strike, and the unrest was said to be spreading to the countryside. I continued to look for work, without any luck, arriving at Bayla's one afternoon, discouraged and looking for hot tea and company. Leib answered the door.

"You again," he said, but not unkindly.

"I'm sorry to bother you. I know I shouldn't just be dropping in . . ."

"I don't mind the bother," he said, a smile beginning. "Bayla's out, but make yourself at home."

As I went into the kitchen to make myself tea he disappeared into the bedroom. When he reemerged sometime later his hands were behind his back.

"I have something for you," he said, then he held out a tiny blue bird carved out of wood. "I saw it in the market and it reminded me of you."

"You bought this for me?"

I held it in the palm of my hand. It fit perfectly. And it was so finely carved—each feather defined, each ridge of muscle slightly raised. The tiny claws were rough and sharp against the pads of my fingers.

"Do you like it?" he asked.

"Very much," I said, and then he kissed me.

Had the kiss been hard or rough I might have recoiled, pushed him off, but it was soft, his mustache like the brush of a feather against my lips, my face, my neck.

"Don't be frightened," he whispered, continuing to brush me lightly with his mouth as his hands began undressing me.

It was very fast after that, but I can't pretend I felt no pleasure. He continued whispering to me, a stream of hushed endearments as soothing as the sound of rushing water. And there was heat in his hands. As they moved over the surfaces of my body, my blood surged beneath them, rising to the surface of my skin to meet his touch. He would not have entered me had I pushed him away. That I believe to this day. But I didn't push him away, and the shock of pain I felt at first had a sharpness of feeling that wasn't entirely unpleasant.

When it was over he was as gentle as he had been at the start. He drew his fingers softly over my features, along the long bridge of my nose, the soft skin of my eyelids, the ridge of my lips, the broad sweep of my cheek, as if encoding my face in the memory of his hands, his touch in the memory of my skin. And I watched in wonder as he washed our mingled fluids from my thighs. The blood of my body, the white liquid of his, red and white, as Tsila had once explained. Your life, though I didn't recognize you yet.

"YOU SHOULDN'T BE RESENTFUL ABOUT DORA," LEIB said to Bayla that night at dinner, as she filled his bowl with soup.

"More bread?" Bayla asked, turning to me, the rising spots of color in her checks the only sign that she had heard Leib's words.

I shook my head. I couldn't eat a bite.

"Are you feeling all right?" she asked me, pressing her hand to my forehead to see if I was feverish. "You feel a little warm," she said. "And you're flushed."

"I'm fine," I said, forcing myself to swallow a spoonful of soup.

Leib had already finished his serving and was holding out his bowl for more.

What have we done? I had asked him when we were dressed again and drinking the tea I had started to prepare on my arrival. "We've made love," he told me, then, seeing my expression, "It's nothing to be ashamed of. There's no purer act in the world."

But what about Bayla, I had thought, then asked aloud. What would we tell her? Leib smiled, and then he softly traced the outline of my mouth with his finger. It was exactly what Tsila had done years before when I first spoke after my illness. *Your mouth is lovely,* she had said, her prayer that the words from my mouth would always merit the gift of speech. "We each have our own separate relationship with Bayla," Leib told me. "And we'll each tell her what our separate consciences dictate."

"IT'S NOT I WHO DECIDED SHE SHOULD JOIN ME," LEIB declared now to Bayla, helping himself to more bread.

Dora, I thought through my haze of shame and confusion. They were still talking about Dora. I forced my mind to the conversation.

"Who decided, then?" Bayla asked.

"The Frenchman himself. And only because you decided to withdraw."

"Why are you still following directives from Geneva?" she asked.

"What do you mean *I*? We all are. You included, dare I remind you?"

"Why should we follow a leadership that has not yet returned to Russia given what's going on here?"

"They don't feel the time is ripe yet. Disorder is not revolution. You know that. The masses still need to be prepared for armed conflict before the revolution can possibly take hold."

I could not believe at first that Leib would be able to have such a conversation after what had happened between us just hours before. And yet I found myself drawn into it, grateful for the distraction this subject offered. I took a bite of bread.

"So they'll stage-manage the preparations while sitting in Geneva?" Bayla asked.

"Are you questioning the party leadership now?"

Bayla began to eat her soup. After three swallows, though, she put her spoon down again.

"Why Dora?" she asked.

Leib looked at Bayla as if genuinely surprised by the question. "Why on earth not?"

Bayla looked at Leib with no expression.

"You certainly can't think I would have had anything to do with it."

Bayla said nothing but continued to stare at Leib.

"There's nothing personal in any of this."

"So you say tonight."

"Bayla, Bayla," Leib chided her, switching into Yiddish now; they'd been speaking in Russian until then. "The personal doesn't exist for Dora. You know that as well as I do."

"It's not Dora's motives I'm questioning."

Leib looked at Bayla without anger or warmth. "Petty jealousies only divide us," he said quietly.

"DORA?" I ASKED BAYLA AS WE WASHED UP THE DISHES. I had thought I would never be able to face her again, but what had happened between me and Leib that afternoon seemed so unreal, so impossible that it seemed almost like a bubble—separate and contained—in the flow of familiarity between me and Bayla.

"It doesn't matter," Bayla said, the spots of color still flaming in her cheeks.

"But Dora?" I asked again. "The Dora I met last winter?"

Bayla didn't answer. She plunged her hands into the sudsy water in the sink and pulled out a bowl for rinsing.

"She's not even pretty."

"Shallowness doesn't become you," Bayla said.

"Have you seen my cap?" Leib called from the other room. He was packing for his departure for Moscow.

"It's in here," Bayla called.

Leib came into the kitchen and picked his cap off the chair.

"And don't forget your fur-lined gloves." She handed me a dish to dry.

"Where are they?"

"On the desk in the bedroom. Where you left them."

He came up to Bayla and embraced her from behind. She held herself stiffly at first, not bothering to remove her hands from the basin of dishwater, as if his embrace was a momentary annoyance that was keeping her from getting on with the task at hand, but when he kissed her neck she softened a little and her head bent back toward his. He whispered something in her ear and they both laughed, then he kissed her once on the top of her head before releasing her and returning to his packing.

"He doesn't love me, you know," she said as soon as he had left the room.

"Of course he does," I responded quickly, but his behavior confused me. I didn't doubt the genuineness of what had passed between us that afternoon, but neither did I doubt what I had just seen before me.

"Only if you consider the feeling one has for an old pair of shoes to be love," Bayla said.

"It doesn't look that way to me," I said, not sure what to make of the display of marital affection I had just seen.

"*You?* What do you know of these things? You're just a girl."

"No, I'm not," I said with some vehemence, but Bayla didn't notice. Her mind was still on Leib.

"There's always been someone else. Did you know that?" she asked.

She knew, I thought at that moment. She had to know. But then, I thought, How could she?

"Right from the beginning," Bayla continued. "Though I didn't know it then. I'm not supposed to care," she said, and it was only then that she looked me straight in the face. "It's my own lack of purity that makes me care."

"Lack of purity?" I could barely speak.

"Oh, yes," she said. "Pure love isn't possessive in nature. Didn't you know that? The very fact that I feel possessive reveals an impurity in my love for Leib, an underlying confusion of love with private ownership."

"It does?"

"Mmm," she said. She rinsed the last bowl and handed it to me to dry.

"I don't understand," I said.

"Of course you don't. My sister didn't raise you to understand nonsense."

Siberia, June 1912

For a month I've been unable to add a word to these pages. It's not illness that's kept me away but despair. I had hoped, when I started, to create for you what my own mother denied me. An understanding of who I was, how I lived, how you came to be. A voice from the silence of death. But as I've put my pen to paper, day by day, week by week, I see only the gaps in what I've written, the distortions, the falseness of trying to impose one version of truth on a life.

Here, for example, are several versions of one moment, each one as true and as false as the next: your father was faithless, but I was taken with him anyway. I had no love for your father but took pleasure in his touch. I was a girl and your father violated my innocence. I took pride in luring your father from Bayla.

For too long I've felt only the failure of my task, the unlockable mystery of a single human heart. Today, though,

I awakened with a feeling of excitement. It had come to me, at last, how to reach you. But as I fed the first few pages to the flames, Lydia rushed across the room to stop me. "Your life is in those pages," she said. "I can't let you destroy it. I won't."

I wasn't destroying it, of course, but releasing it. And already, as the first letters flew into the air, I felt a corresponding lightening of my own spirit.

But Lydia begged me, and I relented, after extracting from her a solemn oath that at the moment of my death she'll burn every page. And then, at last, the letters that I've written will be unfastened from the static order I've imposed on them, free to form and reform all the truths of who I was, I am. And then you'll understand. If you'll just remember to raise your eyes to look.

CHAPTER TWENTY

1905

THE RAID ON THE RAVINE TOOK PLACE THE THIRD WEEK of January. I returned from the city late one afternoon and all that remained was rubble. The dwellings people had constructed for themselves had been razed, but already their components—the wood and straw that had formed walls, the scraps of tin roofing—were being carried away for reconstruction somewhere else. There was an antlike quality to the stream of people leaving the ravine with bales of straw and sheets of metal slung across their backs. Wolf was nowhere to be seen.

Two men were picking through the wood that had once formed the walls of our shelter. There was no sign of any of Wolf's belongings—not a book or blanket or piece of kitchenware in sight—but then I saw the quill pen Tsila had brought me when I was in prison. It was lying in the mud, mistaken, perhaps for the worthless feather of a crow. I slipped it into the pocket of my coat and left the ravine.

Leib had already departed for Moscow by then. I would not see him again. I stayed with Bayla after the raid, and in the last week of January we vacated her apartment for another.

"OUR NEW QUARTERS WILL BE A LITTLE GRANDER THAN what you're used to," Bayla had warned me with a slight smile. As we passed through an ornate gate in the Lypky, the "Palace District" of Kiev, and walked up a tree-lined avenue to what truly appeared to be a palace, I thought a terrible mistake had been made. It had to be a miscommunication of some sort, a trap that would lead—in mere moments, I was certain—to our arrest. What other business could Bayla and I possibly have in a mansion such as this?

But there was no mistake. We were greeted by a servant who led us into the house in silence. We followed him down a long vaulted hallway to a drawing room whose pale, cool beauty made the Entelmans' music room seem, in contrast, a kaleidoscopic stall in a bazaar. Here the walls were covered in pale gray silk, and the ceiling was the airiest of blues. Across the ceiling drifted two large birds, though even they were muted in color, as if the artist had painted the scarlet of their plumage, then applied a coat of powder so as not to excite the senses of anyone whose eyes happened to drift upward toward their flight. The room was empty except for a dark-haired woman about Bayla's age who was seated behind a desk when we entered.

"You've arrived," she said, rising to greet us. Her dress was gray silk but darker than the walls, and it rustled slightly as she walked toward us. Her eyes—also gray—were clear and calm as they grazed me. She kissed Bayla once on each cheek, then extended her hand to me. "I'm Nastya," she said.

"I'm Miriam," I responded, and as I took her hand I felt the energy that coiled within her.

She was Nastasia Alexandrovna Borisov, daughter of Brigadier General Alexander Borisov, who was away that winter, on duty in the Far East, where the disastrous war with Japan continued to rage. Nastya's mother was dead and in her father's absence Nastya had established his home as a safe house for the Socialist Revolutionary Party, a place where pamphlets could be stored, meetings held, messages exchanged. In that winter of the failed revolution the General's house had also come to be used as a transfer point for arms that were being smuggled into Russia, and with Bayla's arrival, a lab for bomb making was set up.

It was risky, of course, to establish a lab in a house with so many comings and goings, but Nastya was utterly confident in the security of the venture. "This house has always sheltered clandestine activities," she said. "But only decadent ones before now." She raised an eyebrow archly and I felt a heat creep into my cheeks. "I don't think you can quite imagine the size of this place," Nastya continued. "The privacy it affords. If you time your entries and exits properly and use only the door that I show you, no one will even know you've taken up residence here."

"But what about the servants?" Bayla asked.

"They'll never be the wiser," Nastya promised.

Her dress was exquisite in the simplicity of its lines and I marveled at my own shallowness to be admiring such details at such a time.

"There's an entire apartment on the second floor that's sitting empty," Nastya said. "We used to use it for guests, family members who came to spend the winter, but now . . ."

Who could know what emotion she experienced in that momentary pause as she thought about the change in her family's situation? Was it her mother's death that came to mind? Her father's absence? Her own betrayal of them that surfaced briefly in that slight knitting of her eyebrows, the almost imperceptible twitch of her lips?

"Its windows are draped now, its furnishings covered. The servants never enter it. It's perfect," she assured us. "There's probably no place more perfect, in fact. Who would ever suspect that the main explosives lab for southern Russia would lie in the bosom of the household of a Brigadier General?"

There was an impishness to Nastya's smile then, a mirth so infectious that as she led us up the stairway and through the dark cavernous halls to our quarters I felt less an atmosphere of revolutionary purpose than the excitement of embarking on an adventure.

"She thrives on risk," Bayla said as soon as we were left on our own. "In case you hadn't noticed. She's extremely brave, of course, but she takes too much pleasure in her own fear. It's not that she isn't committed to the cause. She is. Utterly committed. But her attraction to danger, the delight she takes in the ironies she's setting up in this house . . . it could at some point become a danger to us."

I HAD INTENDED TO WORK WHEN I MOVED IN WITH Bayla—I'd found a job, finally, as a folder at a printer's—but she assured me that I didn't have to. "You're ill," she said, and that was true. My cough had gotten worse again, and I was often feverish at night.

I hung the bird Leib had given me by the window near my bed. It was the first thing I saw in the morning, the last thing at night. "That's beautiful," Bayla said when she first saw it. "It's like the bird Leib was telling us about."

Told *me*, I thought, not *us*. Then a wave of shame so strong I thought I might drown in it. Bayla had already paid me back almost all of the money for my passage and had given me a place to live, but my trespass against her remained unacknowledged and unconfessed, and could never be repaid. Or so I thought at the time.

BAYLA ROSE EARLY EACH MORNING AND LEFT OUR BEDroom for her lab. She didn't return to our room until late in the evening. She told me to rest, but I found the days long. I was restless, uneasy, plagued by fears and doubts that could no longer be contained beneath the surface. The revolution had begun; that's what I kept hearing. Already hundreds of thousands of workers were on strike across the empire. But in our quiet room in that second-floor apartment there was a stillness disturbed only by the troubled ruminations of my mind.

I left our room one morning and went down to Nastya's quarters. I told her I wanted to help with whatever they were doing. She smiled and said she needed someone to help her with her errands.

"Your errands?" I asked, surprised and insulted that she would treat me as her servant.

The shopping basket Nastya gave me was of standard size, and she showed me then how pamphlets could be hidden under a layer of vegetables, eggs, and meat. And at first it was just that. Pamphlets. But weapons were being smuggled into Russia in great numbers that winter, and soon there were occasions when my pickups and deliveries consisted of guns, dynamite, and other munitions. It was Nastya who prepared and went over my "shopping list" at the beginning of each day, and Nastya who coordinated my deliveries. It was Nastya also who taught me how to shoot one of the Browning revolvers that I had just transported from another safe house.

It was dangerous work, of course, and there were times I felt that danger keenly—a clenching spasm in my gut at the sight of policemen sauntering my way, a heavy dread as I waited to see who might open a door at which I had knocked. But as the days and weeks passed without incident, what I began to feel most was exhaustion, a gray layer of it settling heavily on me, smothering any spark of color or light. I woke up tired after nights of dreamless sleep, and as I made my way through the dark early morning streets of the city the weariness was sometimes so heavy upon me that I thought I would not get through to the end of the day.

IN FEBRUARY WE HEARD OF THE SUCCESS OF LEIB AND Dora's operation. The Grand Duke Sergius Alexandrovich, Governor General of Moscow and brother-in-law to the Tsar, was dead, assassinated by a bomb thrown at his carriage. So severe had the blast been that his head was torn off and shattered, his body mutilated. Only one hand remained intact for purposes of identification.

"Her bombs are always effective," Nastya said, referring to Dora's handiwork. "She's the only one whose skill can be compared to yours."

Bayla nodded but said nothing.

"He was a vile man, impervious to the suffering he caused. Listen," Nastya said. We listened, as she had directed, and at first heard only the crackling of the fire in the stove, the ticking of the clock, the soft intake and outflow of our own breathing, but then I heard a slight rustling of branches outside, a gentle wind brushing against the house. "The earth itself is sighing in relief for having been freed from the burden of bearing him."

"Please, Nastya," Bayla sighed. "You sound like the old *bubbies* from my village."

"I'm honored to be compared to the salt of the earth."

"You'd be less honored if you knew them," Bayla said, smiling a little.

"So you *haven't* forgotten how to smile," Nastya commented, and Bayla cast her eyes away.

"It's horrible about the coachman," Bayla said. The Grand Duke's coachman, Andrei Rudinkin, had been severely, possibly mortally wounded by the blast. As had the primary striker, Kaliakev, who had been arrested on the spot.

"Horrible, yes," Nastya responded. "But unavoidable. Only blood can change the color of history."

Gorky's words, those, and Bayla nodded her agreement, but her own face at that moment appeared bloodless.

THE WEARINESS I FELT UPON WAKING PERSISTED. THERE were days now when I was so tired that as I went about my errands I felt as if I were trying to walk while submerged under water.

"You're ill," Bayla said when I told her about my exhaustion. "You shouldn't be doing what you're doing. I've already spoken to Nastya about it."

"You have?" I asked, annoyed to be treated as a child.

I continued my activities, but as the weeks wore on and my weariness began to be accompanied by nausea I realized it wasn't illness I was feeling. There was a power to that nausea, an insistence that I recognized at once: the force of a new life pulling on my own.

"I need to find Wolf," I announced to Bayla one evening as we prepared for bed. For that's what I'd decided. That's where I would go when Bayla turned me out. People were beginning to drift back into the ravine by then. He would let me stay. I could sleep in the warmth of his bed until spring.

Bayla looked at me sharply, then sat down on my bed and waited for me to go on.

"It's not right for me to be here any longer . . ." My voice trailed off.

For a while Bayla said nothing. Then she took my hand. "I have the same instinct," she said. "I wasn't going to tell you. I thought it was bad luck to say it aloud. I thought it was just my own fear, superstition . . ."

I looked at her, uncomprehending.

"For days now I've had a bad feeling, a crawling at the back of my neck."

As she said that I felt the skin on my own neck start to prickle, a familiar clamminess.

"It's time to leave," she said. "It's not safe here anymore. I know another house . . ."

I couldn't speak. I just nodded.

"Not a word to anyone," she said, her finger on her lips. "I don't know who can and can't be trusted. We'll leave first thing tomorrow."

She rose from my bed and went to the lamp to extinguish it.

"I'm pregnant," I told her.

She paused, then turned to face me. Her face was a darker shade of red than I had ever seen in her, but her voice was calm when she asked me how I knew.

"I just know," I said, and told her about the nausea.

"It might be illness."

"I've missed two periods."

"A lot of us miss periods. It happens with the fear of the work. Nausea as well. Do you think I don't often feel nauseated?"

"And my exhaustion," I reminded her.

"It's fear," she said. "We all experience it."

She was quiet for a few minutes and then she asked, "Have you been . . . intimate with Wolf?"

"With Leib," I said. It seemed she stared at me for an eternity before she slapped my face.

IT WAS HER JEALOUSY THAT MADE HER SLAP ME. THIS she told me later, in a letter. And her own regret. It was at that moment, she told me, that she realized the extent of the lie she'd been living, the devastation it had wrought, how far-reaching. It was at that moment she knew what she wanted but had turned away from. A husband who loved her. A baby. Creation, not destruction.

"And so I hit you," she wrote. "Please forgive me."

That night, though, there were just accusations, words flung in anger, resentment. She accused me of betrayal, of cheapness, of other, worse things. "Is this how you reward my sister's care for you? By crawling into the marital bed of your own aunt? By behaving like a whore, like a pig who can't even think through the implications of her own body's greed?"

If I had known where Wolf was that night, perhaps I would have left. But I didn't. I had nowhere to go, it was winter, and my instinct for life was stronger than my shame. I turned away from Bayla's anger and waited for the morning. Bayla rose first. It was just after five when she sighed deeply, then got out of bed. I heard her because I hadn't been asleep. She lit the lamp and the stove and put water on to boil. I got out of bed. Neither of us said good morning, but we were excessively polite as we handed each other cups, utensils, tea.

"Have more sugar. You need it," Bayla said, her voice constricted from the excesses of the night before.

"Thank you," I said, heaping more sugar into my glass, though the very sight of it made me want to vomit.

"I couldn't believe what you told me last night . . . And to think I worried about the men you might meet in that ravine, when it was my own husband, in my own home . . ." She met my eye. "You'll come with me to the other safe house."

I shook my head. "I'll be all right in the ravine."

"You don't even know for certain that this Wolf is there."

"He's there," I said.

"I have a bad feeling."

"Now you sound like Tsila."

She shrugged. "At least let me tell you where I'm going, how to find me if you need to." Which she did. And then she left.

I HEARD THE COMMOTION BEFORE THEY REACHED ME— the heavy footsteps on the stairs, Nastya's cries of indignation. It sounded like an entire squadron running through the house, and though I don't remember reaching for the revolver, it was in my hand when they crashed through the door.

It was the noise of them, I thought later, the smashing noise that I wanted to silence. My own fear rising like bile that I wanted to still. It was my own death that I wanted to mow down as it crashed through the door to claim me. It was the moment itself that I wanted to obliterate. I raised the revolver in my hand and pulled the trigger as Nastya had taught me. A crack like glass breaking. One of the gendarme's hands went to his chest and his face registered concern. Consternation. That was all. There was no blood, no spreading stain. I don't even know if I knew yet what I had done as I watched him fall, felt myself falling, being felled. I had no sensation of pain as my head hit the floor.

The *hat you survived* was a miracle. I feared I had lost
you. That was all I feared when I first came back to consciousness, when I surfaced to the pain that was my consciousness. I had been dragged from the house by my hair,
Nastya told me. "He wound your braid around his hand,"
she whispered, holding my head in her lap. "He yanked
you with a force that lifted your body from the ground."

"Who?" I wanted to ask, but I couldn't. My mouth
was too dry, my lips caked with blood.

"One of the officers," Nastya said, as if she had
reached into my mind and heard my confusion. "He
pulled you through the house that way, and down all
the stairs."

It was this that saved me. This that saved you too. Had
he dragged me by my feet, my head bouncing against the
marble of the General's front stairway, we would have been
dead before we hit the bottom stair.

Nastya held my head but didn't stroke it. The throbbing was so painful that I couldn't have endured her caress. My hand went down between my legs.

"They didn't violate you," she whispered. "I've been with you the entire time."

But it wasn't my own violation that concerned me. It was your life. I felt between my legs and there was no wetness. I knew you had survived.

I HAVE NEVER FELT REMORSE FOR THE LIFE I TOOK. NOT when I realized what I'd done, not when they brought me to trial, not in the long months and years that have followed. I've tried to, many times, but cannot. There's an area of numbness in me, a void. Its size and shape matches the heart of the man that I killed. It's a wilderness, an emptiness, an utter absence of compassion.

Nor do I regret my moment with your father, the heat in his touch, the taste of his mouth, the wonder I experienced as I carried you to life. I won't deny the hurt I brought to Bayla, the betrayal that she felt, but what I gave her in the end was far more precious than anything I ever took.

While I feel no shame about the revolutionary activities in which I partook, I feel no glory either. The events of 1905 are well known: the rising tide of revolution, the glorious victory of the Manifesto of Freedom and its promises, the betrayal that followed, the pogroms, the reprisals. *I will break all of you like dogs while you get your freedom,* a police officer in Zhitomir told the citizens of that town. And in that instance he was as good as his word. *Attack the Jews,* Officer Pirozhkov urged his fellow Kievans, and they did. For days.

It was blood, all blood. The country flowed in blood. And when it was over nothing had changed.

BAYLA WAS ARRESTED ON THE TREE-LINED AVENUE
THAT led to the entrance of the Borisov mansion. She had come back
to get me just hours after leaving. I never saw her in prison—she was
held in another cell—and she was released in the amnesty of October
1905, as were the other members of the Combat Battalion who had
been arrested in the betrayals of that March and whose crimes were not
capital. The betrayer, it came out later, was the Frenchman himself.
The commander of the Socialist Revolutionaries' Combat Battalion
and mastermind of all its most successful operations, including and especially the Von Plehve assassination, its greatest victory. He turned
everyone in. His entire battalion. Why? We don't know. Who can know
the human heart?

I DIDN'T BETRAY BAYLA AT MY TRIAL, AND IN THIS ALONE
I feel some pride. She would not have been pardoned had the true
nature of her role—her great skill—been revealed. They thought all
that was mine, and what difference to me, really? My crime was already
capital.

Bayla left for Montreal soon after her release, for the life she'd realized she wanted when I told her of my pregnancy with you. But not before saving you. Not before making the necessary inquiries and taking
the necessary actions—at great risk to herself—to pull you from almost
certain death. She's your mother now.

It was Shendel and Yehuda who sent the money for your passage,
Shendel and Yehuda who provided Bayla with work. Amends, perhaps,
for the disastrous match with his cousin Leib that Yehuda had once
helped arrange. And why Montreal instead of Argentina? Why the appeal to Shendel and not to her own sister? That Bayla has never told
me. Pride, I suspect, an unwillingness to face Tsila's satisfaction that
she'd been right. Though maybe she'll tell you differently.

NASTYA ESCAPED. DORA WENT MAD WITHIN MONTHS OF her arrest and died not long after in an asylum. Your father eluded capture altogether, making his way to Geneva, where I hear he's joined the Mensheviks. And Wolf? I don't know, but I dream of him sometimes, moving like a shadow through the wreckage.

It was early in the summer that I first felt you move. The countryside was on fire, manors burning to the ground, torched by the very hands that had always tended them. Smoke wafted through our open window; the sky was lit at night. You turned inside me, and I felt a joy and fear at once. I had been sentenced by then and thought I would hang at your birth.

I was still with Nastya and the other women who poured into our crowded cell as the revolution progressed. The prisons were so crowded that year that even the punishment cells held no less than two or three prisoners at a time. "She'll save your life," Nastya said as she felt you move under her hand. "They won't hang a pregnant woman, and the new order will come to life before your child does. Your life will be spared." And it was, in the amnesties of that October.

There was no new order, though, just the briefest of lulls in the old. You were born in the week of the pogroms; the screams of the dead pierced our dreams. You flew out of me like a bird. I named you Hayya.

THERE'S A DREAM I HAVE THAT STARTED WHEN THEY took you from my arms. I'm in the streets of Kiev, the winter streets, making my way home at the end of the day. But I'm not weary in my dream, nor am I cold. I'm walking home through snowy streets, the light is fading. It's twilight. I see the colored lights of a skating rink up ahead and hear the sounds of a brass band playing. They're playing "Bitter Parting," and I stop by the side of the rink to listen. The music is poignant but it doesn't make me sad.

The rink is filled with skaters, men and women, boys and girls. The young men skate solo, some go backward, not bothering to look over their shoulders as they circle the rink. Others skate in pistol fashion, with one leg bent and the other stretched out straight. The girls skate in groups, chatting and giggling as they circle. They are all in long coats, their hands tucked into muffs. They call to a friend, "Come, come," they call, but they never call her by name.

I look beside me and there in the gathering darkness is a young girl. She's wearing the blue coat I saw in the window in Kiev. It's a blue more lovely than any I have ever seen. She has a black fur hat and and a black fur muff, and the braid that hangs down her back is as dark as mine. She steps away from me onto the ice to join her friends. Is it you, I wonder, or me? You, I think. Or maybe both.

Night falls, but the blue of her coat is so filled with light that it glows as she circles the rink. It's the only thing I see as everything else in the dream fades into the darkness: a swatch of blue light circling in my mind. I awaken with a feeling of peace that lingers for a moment before dissolving.

All the characters in this novel are fictional and any resemblance to actual living or historical people is purely coincidental, with the following exceptions: the character of Dora is based on Dora Brilliant, who was an explosives expert with the Socialist Revolutionary Party. The "Frenchman" refers to Evno F. Azeff, chief of the Socialist Revolutionary's Combat Battalion, mastermind of many of its plots and informing all the while to the Okhrana. Grigor Gershuni was the head of the Combat Battalion until he was betrayed by Azeff and arrested in 1903. The character of Nastya is based on the Izmailovich sisters, daughters of a Brigadier General who was on duty in the Far East in 1904–1905. Their home, in their father's absence, became the headquarters of the Socialist Revolutionary Party in Minsk. (Katerina Izmailovich was killed following her attempted assassination of Admiral G. P. Chukhnin. Alexandra Izmailovich received a commuted death sentence for her attempted assassination of Governor Kurlov of Minsk, and was imprisoned at Maltzev.) Quotes by Larissa Petrova at her trial are a combination of quotes by Maria Spiridonova, the Izmailovich sisters, Katerina Breshkovskaya, and Vera Figner.

ACKNOWLEDGMENTS

Your Mouth Is Lovely is a work of fiction, but it is set in a particular time and place that I have tried to portray as accurately as possible. I read many personal memoirs and historical works during the course of researching and writing this book. The following were particularly helpful:

Simon Solomon's *My Jewish Roots* (Jewish Publication Society of America, 1956) provided vivid descriptions of the Pripet marshes, as well as some of the details about local Jewish customs and beliefs and accounts of Bundist and other radical activities in the Kalinkovich region that appear in this novel. Michael Hamm's *Kiev, A Portrait 1800–1917* (Princeton University Press, 1993), and Konstantin Pavstovsky's *Story of a Life* (Harvill Press, 1966) provided me with many details and images of life in Kiev and its ravines in 1904–1905. It was in Martha Maxwell's *Narodniki Women* (Pergamon Press, 1990) that I learned about the daily life of the Socialist Revolutionary women who were imprisoned at Maltzev between 1906 and 1912. Maxwell's book was also an invaluable source of information about the mind-sets and activities of the women who turned to terror during that time.

For the events of January 9, 1905, Bloody Sunday, I turned to Orlando Figes's *A People's Tragedy: The Russian Revolution, 1891–1924* (Penguin Books, 1998). The translation of the petition to the Tsar on page 321 is from Walter Sablinsky's *The Road to Bloody Sunday* and is used by permission of Princeton University Press. I found detailed descriptions of the assassinations of Von Plehve and Grand Duke Sergius Alexandrovich in Boris Savinkov's *Memoirs of a Terrorist* (Albert and Charles Boni, 1931. Translated by Joseph Shaplen).

The title of this book is from the Song of Songs 4:3. I learned about the prayer by the same name, recited by Lipsa on page 35, in *A Book of Jewish Women's Prayers,* compiled by Norman Tarnor (Jason Aronson, Inc., 1995).

The Hasidic tale on page 127 is from *Jewish Folktales,* selected and retold by Pinhas Sadeh, translated by Hillel Halkin (Anchor Books, 1989), and is used by permission of Doubleday.

Other books I'd like to single out include: Zvi Gitelman's *A Century of Ambivalence* (Indiana University Press, 2000); Richard Stite's *The Women's Liberation Movement in Russia: Feminism, Nihilism and Bolshevism, 1860–1930* (Princeton University Press, 1978); Ezra Mendelssohn's *Class Struggle in the Pale* (Cambridge University Press, 1970); *The Merit of Our Mothers* (compiled by Tracy Guren Klirs, Hebrew Union College Press, 1993); Barbara Alpern Engel's *Between the Fields and the City* (Cambridge University Press, 1996); Naomi Shepherd's *A Price Below Rubies* (Harvard University Press, 1993); Marie Sukloff's *The Life Story of a Russian Exile* (The Century Company, 1915); *The Russian Worker: Life and Labor Under the Tsarist Regime,* edited by Victoria E. Bonnell (University of California Press, 1983); I. Steinberg's *Spiridonova* (Methuen and Company, 1935); *The Jewish Encyclopedia,* edited by Isidore Singer (Funk and Wagnalls, 1901); Alberto Gerchunoff's *Jewish Gauchos of the Pampas* (Abelard Schuman, 1955); Hirsz Abramowicz's *Profiles of a Lost World: Memoirs of East European Jewish Life Before WW2* (Wayne State University Press in cooperation with the YIVO Institute for Jewish Research, 1999); *The Shtetl Book,* by David G. Roskies and Diane K. Roskies (Ktav Publishing House, 1975); *Born One Year Before the Turn of the Century* (an oral history by Minnie Fisher, Community Documentation Workshop, 1976); Yaffa Eliach's *There Once Was a World* (Little, Brown and Company, 1998).

The Bialik poem, "City of Slaughter," was translated by A. M. Klein, and is used by permission of the University of Toronto Press.

I want to thank Robert Daum, Barbara Alpern Engel, Allan Nadler, and Michael Silberstein for generously sharing their expertise and answering questions I had about historical facts and points of Jewish custom, observance, and history. A special thanks to Barbara Engel for being such an inspiring teacher. It was in her seminar on nineteenth-century Russian social history in the winter of 1986 that some of the seeds of this novel were sown.

The following people read part or all of early drafts of this novel and offered helpful observations and criticisms: Nancy Pollak, Aletha Worrall, Dianne Richler, Martin Richler, Diane Comet Richler, Anita Braha, Susan Ouriou, Shira Rosan, Bonnie Burnard, Michelle Comet, Tova Hartman Halbertal, Barbara Engel, Camilla Jenkins, Helen Mintz, Jay Schneiders. Special thanks to Barbara Kuhne, Golda Och, Vicki Trerise, Lydia Kwa, Carmen Rodriguez, and Janet Richler Ostro.

Thanks to my agent, Dean Cooke, and my editors, Julia Serebrinsky and Iris Tupholme, for their insightful questions and suggestions, their enthusiasm, and their encouragement.

Thanks to the Canada Council for the Arts and the B.C. Arts Council for their financial support in the writing of this book.

An excerpt of this book appeared in *Prairie Fire* in autumn 1999 and in the *Journey Prize Anthology*, 2000.

Thanks to Frank Murducco and sons of the Calabria Cafe in Vancouver, B.C., where most of this novel was written.

And finally, thanks to Vicki Trerise, the eye of the storm.

NANCY RICHLER's first novel, *Throwaway Angels*, was shortlisted for
the Arthur Ellis First Novel Award. *Your Mouth is Lovely* won the
2003 Canadian Jewish Book Award for Fiction. Her short
stories have been published in *Room of One's Own*,
Fireweed, *Fiddlehead*, *Prairie Fire*, *The New
Quarterly*, and *The Journey Prize
Anthology*. Nancy Richler
lives in Vancouver.